C000186256

Ming's Kingdom

MING'S KINGDOM

Nicol Williamson

HUTCHINSON
LONDON

The right of Nicol Williamson to be identified as the
Author of this work has been asserted by Nicol Williamson
in accordance with the Copyright, Designs and Patents Act 1988

1 3 5 7 9 10 8 6 4 2

This edition first published in 1996 by Hutchinson

Random House (UK) Limited
20 Vauxhall Bridge Road, London SW1V 2SA

Random House Australia (Pty) Limited
20 Alfred Street, Milsons Point, Sydney,
New South Wales 2061, Australia

Random House New Zealand Limited
18 Poland Road, Glenfield, Auckland 10, New Zealand

Random House South Africa (Pty) Limited
PO Box 337, Bergvlei, 2012 South Africa

A CiP record for this book is available from the British Library

Papers used by Random House UK Limited are natural,
recyclable products made from wood grown in sustainable forests.
The manufacturing processes conform to the environmental
regulations of the country of origin.

ISBN 0 09 179222 3

Typeset in Bembo by Deltatype Ltd, Ellesmere Port, Cheshire
Printed and bound in Great Britain by Mackays of Chatham plc,
Chatham, Kent

For my son, Luke, and
to the memory of Hugh, my
father, and Tom Reader

1

'DO I LOVE YOU? Oh my, do I, baby 'deed I do . . .'
Singing quietly, he took his seat on the MGM
Grand. His movie was done with, and he had bade
farewell to Baalburg where they image-fucked and worshipped
gold and where Jehovah had no name.

Soaring up and away, he saw the receding sheds of human
sacrifice where the bullshit flourished thick and slab, sheds of the
Baalburg merchants in the valley of lost angels. He closed his eyes
and breathed the vaguely perfumed aeroplane air.

> *At their day's end the legion epitaph*
> *So many, many names engraved thereon*
> *And writ with Napier's bones upon their graph,*
> Mene mene tekel upharsin.

So eastwards. On to Gotham sped Rick Neilsen, finally to marry.
Adrienne Louise Rader, his love, the girl from Bluebell Road in
the old Mid-west. Grasping a glass of post-takeoff champagne, he
watched it fizz – each beaded bubble winking at the brim
conjuring a thought of her. He settled back, humming, 'And do I
want you, oh my, do I, baby, 'deed I do.'

She was a fledgling actress, a stunning honey blonde with mud-
green eyes, globe breasts, tight flat belly over slate grey pubes and
smooth as marble solid little bottom. Her body was compact and
muscular; the skin a polished olive. Though her build made her a
fatal inch and a half too short, in high heels with a swell of perfect
chevroned calves, she was a dream walking; a hunky-dory little
vision. But above the powerful jaw with its sharp white teeth and
the so straight nose, it was the tight-in-the-corner wanton eyes that
drew you in; long lashed under soft brown brows; the eyes of a

Mongol Horde princess. She had the pure, innocent sexuality that young sprint swim girls have, firm and milky, poised, waiting for the race. Her square shoulders and beautifully rounded arms ended at a pair of small, unpretty hands, thick around the knuckles. This was how Zeus, reluctantly, had let her go at last into the mortal world, leaving his mark upon her. Rick had loved those hands, clasping on long walks their imperfection. Holding her, you could feel the physical power within her, plangent almost, like the low and throaty timbre of her voice when they were alone, before she would kiss him, her lips opening with a small wet smack, like an infant waiting for its spoon-fed pulp or a seal receiving fish. Tall and rangy himself, he had never been drawn to willowy girls with legs up to their armpits. He preferred the hard, athletic, quick and sporty type.

They had met in New York, while he was doing a play. Captivated by her eyes, her voice and, very soon, all else, he'd fallen utterly in love. Rick had been staying at the apartment of a hair crimper at the time, a funny looking manikin sporting a suspicious-looking thatch that put you in mind of auburn shredded wheat. Standing five foot three in Mickey Mouse boots, Follicous was an alarming name-dropper (he could not pronounce the final 'I' in follicles), who ached to swing with the barons and earls and stitch himself into worldwide high society. Fat chance. None the less, it was at Folly's suggestion that Rick took Adrienne, for the first time, to the Stone Resort, where snug in the pocket of a snowscaped valley they had played backgammon by a roaring fire and she'd pushed the twin beds close so they could lie even closer. 'King,' she had dubbed his cock. 'Sweet King.'

Their love-making had been thrilling and adventurous. On the morning of their departure he had led her to the squat oak table in the centre of the vast high room, where he'd sculpted her almost, hands caressing her marble-girl beauty as she'd knelt before him with a magic grace, open and eager. For close on twenty minutes she took the whole stiff length of him without a murmur, just a series of little gasps while he marvelled at her capacity. 'Like throwing a frank down Route 66', he had thought and, even as he was loving her, hearing echoing lines of Beckett: 'The thud, thud, thud of the old plunger, pestling the unalterable.'

After, she stood giggling at him over by the door, flushed and knowing. When he asked what she was laughing about, she replied, 'Oh, I was just wondering.'

'What?'

'How I'm going to get through the rest of my life without that table.' And she burst into brilliant laughter.

Later, hearing his own booming laugh from the bathroom, she came running to the door. Combing his hair in the mirror, he had remembered an old schoolboy ditty, altering the words to describe her sexual compass:

> *When I saunter down to the beach for a swim,*
> *The men all remark on the size of my quim.*
> *I'll bet you a dollar it's like a horse's collar*
> *'Cos I've stretched it in McBurneys' gym.*

'And what are *you* laughing at?' she teased, a coquette at the bathroom door.

'Nothing.'

'Come on. What?'

'Nothing.'

There was a sweat on him, a glow, as she came to him, running her hands up over his shoulders, drawing out his crooked smile. She stood, head on one side, her eyes two wanton sparklers. 'You naughty boy,' she chided throatily. 'You naughty, salty dog, you.' Her mouth smacking open for the seal kiss.

She was the fourth of five children born to a German-American family. No other blood and no room for outsiders. She, however, in opting for Rick, had chosen to go outside, a choice that was to have deep and far-reaching consequences. Firstly, in the shape of Mickey, her brother, older by some eighteen months ('He's a dancer,' Adrienne had confided to Rick), who, bumming around New York and getting wind of the relationship, put in a sudden, unbargained-for appearance, inviting himself to dinner most evenings Rick and she were together, to possessively compete for her attention.

3

In those early days, Rick could seldom find peace from him. Most evenings that Rick and Adrienne would meet, Mickey would appear, racing towards her, warbling, 'Oh Billy Billy Billy Billy Billy,' like a silly ingénue in a thirties movie. According to Adrienne, it came from an old film called *Warlock*, where Richard Widmark cradles his dead brother in the street crying, 'Oh Billy Billy Billy Billy Billy.' A childhood game they'd played. Re-enacted now by Mickey to project, perhaps, a closely shared past into the present?

In the end it got so irritating that Rick began to change their regular eating venues. For a blissful three days they managed to give Mickey the slip, but it was too good to last. Mickey, professing nowhere to stay, promptly turned up to share the bed Adrienne had in a corner of her friend Ruby's apartment. Next evening a card awaited Rick in his dressing room. *Oh will* you *have dinner with* me *tonight? Please say you will.* Underneath, a greetings message: *I want to shine in your heart all year and for all the years to come.* She wrote in conspiratorial tone that Mickey had told her she'd kept repeating Rick's name in her sleep, adding *I'll bet he* loved *that!*

That coming weekend, after his Sunday matinée, Rick and Adrienne were due to leave for Princeton, where they would stay on campus with an old friend of Rick's, returning on Tuesday for the evening show. The matinée performance over, seated in his dressing room, a tense unhappy Adrienne told him dully that she couldn't go.

'Why?'

'I just can't.'

'There has to be a reason.'

But she wouldn't tender one, other than to say, 'I'm under a lot of pressure right now.' As he fastened his big coat, 'I love you,' she whispered.

He looked at her. Holy God. Casablanca. Ilsa. 'If you loved me, Adrienne, you'd be going out that door with me.'

On the train, he spent a miserable hour and a half trying to figure it out. Right out of the blue, it had totally unnerved him. What had gone wrong?

Tuesday evening brought the answer. Another little dressing-room note. In pencil. Telling Rick she'd been wrong not to go with him, that she loved him and what had happened that day had been due to unfair pressure brought to bear upon her, but that she was true, unwavering, and the rest was now up to Rick.

That entire weekend, Adrienne afterwards recounted, Mickey had dogged her all round town, pressing her ceaselessly to tell him what Rick meant to her, until finally, in tears on a street corner, holding on to a phone booth (she was wearing roller skates), Adrienne told him she loved Rick.

Less than a week later, after the evening show, Rick was on his way to take a shower backstage, when, like a shock, a dark-haired woman stepped into his path.

'I'm Alice Rader,' the voice said.

Adrienne had let Rick know her mother was in town and wanted to see the show. Indeed, he had arranged the tickets. Regaining his composure, Rick enquired how she had liked the play.

'I can see what it *means*,' she replied, closing out any contact, smile, handshake or hello. Rick could see hardly anything of Adrienne in her face. But that wasn't so surprising. Many people had told Rick he didn't really look like either of his parents. Alice's mouth was thin, taut, the facial skin drawn tight, with a nose uncommon long and pointed, down which were staring two dark eyes, the image of a late-twenties photograph of Edith Sitwell Rick had seen in a magazine. He at once thought of Sam, his father, singing the old Durante favourite, 'It's My Nose's Birthday Today'. And yet, Rick saw a kind of raw beauty there in her. She must once have been a good-looking woman. So this was Adrienne's mother.

Adrienne went off for a family supper leaving a grateful Rick to dine alone. Now, seated in a cosy little place near the theatre where a pencil-moustached Chilean called George played piano, he ordered cognac with a big slice of cheesecake and pondered on the meeting. Why this response to him? She'd not been able to conceal it, let alone contain it. Why had she introduced herself in that way? Like she was already prejudiced against him? After the pressure Mickey had put on Adrienne, had he spoken with Alice? Is that why she'd made the trip from Chicago? Rick had looked forward to meet and make friends with her, let her see how happy he and Adrienne were together, but the way she'd greeted him had surprised and jolted him. As sudden as a street sign warning on a corner you were just about to turn forcing you to slam on the brakes. NO ENTRY! That malefic stare set her at her own prescribed distance. For what reason? He sipped at his drink and thought. Had she determined to take up clubs where Mickey had failed, and if so, why? Possessive mother? Resented him being with daughter? He couldn't come up with any other ideas.

Alice Rader was not to cross his path again for three solid years nor speak to Adrienne for two. As it was, she repaired next day to Margie's – her niece and Adrienne's cousin – beside herself with fury. 'I'm going to smash this,' she had boasted. 'Oh yes. I'm going to smash this,' Margie had told Rick some time after he'd been introduced to her by Adrienne.

Rick was to 'meet the family' one by one over a period of four years. Adrienne had shown him a snapshot of them all in younger days, holding spaniel puppies. Patrice, the eldest girl, fair like Adrienne, then Karen, dark-haired with pretty eyes, Mickey (holding two puppies), and Adrienne. The youngest, Donna, not then born. When Rick finally met her, he was struck by her youthful beauty. In looks more like the mother than the others, but without the nose. The last he was to encounter was wordless Bill, 'Mr Mum's the Word', the father who could never look Rick in the eye.

On the MGM flight, a smiling hostess loomed over him, breaking his reverie. 'Do you want me to set up your table for lunch?'

'Oh. Sure,' he said and nodded. 'Forgive me. I was miles away.'

Lunch on MGM Grand was not unlike dining on the *Orient Express*, except more private, with several enclosed and beautifully appointed glass-panelled booths for four. In one of these compartments Rick sat alone, with the feeling he was the only person on the flight, shut off with his thoughts and clucked over by super-service mother hens. The full-size table with its dazzling white cloth was duly set with flatware, the cut glass promptly filled with sparkling Chardonnay, all administered by a she with a friendly smile. He sipped at the wine. 'Friendship,' he reflected.

Adrienne and he had two main friends – Broadway Jack Biaggi and Ruby Gonella – as different again as chalk from cheese. Ruby was an Italian-American, like Jack, but there the connections ended and there was little love lost between the two. Neither beautiful nor pretty, Ruby was by no means plain. Hair auburn-brown, eyes either side of a hook nose glassy-dark, teeth sound, though the uppers a mite discoloured, Ruby made her looks count. She dressed attractively, used make-up sparingly, expertly, was always 'well turned out'. Queen of the heavy-handed wisecrack, with a voice of sing-song, 'ain't I cute?' disingenuous-ness, she struck Rick as just *too* cutesy to be really cute. Married once to a Dane, he had abandoned her after a handful of weeks, never to return. Ruby maintained he had married her solely to obtain a US work permit. Her broad, overt manner differed from Alice's, which was measured, studied in every word and turn, but to Rick, neither woman was easily accessible to contact. A seeming reluctance, or perhaps inability, to display open emotion; to give heartily or *from* the heart a piece of themselves, even in greeting. Ruby and Alice. A duo perhaps who mistook emotional generosity for weakness. He could discover no compassion there. Though different in style, it seemed to Rick they had a common denominator: *performing* themselves, rather than *being* themselves. Performances that none the less pressed Adrienne into the role of, in Ruby's case, admirer, in Alice's, disciple.

Because of her friendship with Adrienne, Rick had more than once made the effort to get through to Ruby, not the least one summer in London when, at short notice, she arrived to stay for a few days in a flat he had rented in Sussex Gardens on the north side of Hyde Park. On this particular evening, he'd escorted Ruby and Adrienne to the old San Marino where they had dined al fresco opposite the Queen Victoria pub on the corner of Sussex Place. While Adrienne slipped downstairs to powder her nose he talked to Ruby squarely, trying to sidestep her loquaciousness to get to the person Rick felt was holed up somewhere inside. Get her to give some answering signal, a wink, a true-eyed smile, a beginning of a friendship. Instead, Ruby was poleaxed to muteness. For one brief moment, one tiny beat, there was, he thought, a hit, a contact. Then it vanished. Like the snowflake on the river, a moment white then gone for ever.

Rick wondered, as Adrienne returned to the table, could it be she was afraid she would be hurt, that it was fear beneath what Rick felt sure was her defence? Fear of giving, of opening up, being made vulnerable? Or perhaps *this* was the real Ruby, and that was that. He let it go there, gazing at Adrienne, she who desired the heart of love, seeking the way to deliver herself. But he could not help but be conscious that her love words when they were alone were poached from him, that timbre of her voice overlaying the patent of his own endearments, and he wanted to say, 'Those are not yours. They are my words. I want you to love me with words of your own.'

After eighteen months of being together while he was filming in London, in high summer, Adrienne had written from New York asking him to marry her. Elated, he began to lay plans for some time the following year. That next winter he appeared in a play in New York which, though getting a cool critical reception, did well at the box office. Almost imperceptibly she didn't seem to be so near his elbow. Around this time Rick became aware of Adrienne's friendship with someone called Lucy Boyden, a girl she worked out with, whom Rick was to hear of but never to meet. Although he did come face to face with Karen, the second sister, while she was taking a short break in New York. Dark hair and eyes with pretty smile and downy hair from knee to ankle. 'Carpetshins,' he'd thought. Over lunch, in the apartment he'd rented for the duration of the play, she had opened up to an astounded Rick and an agog Adrienne about her girlscout-leader history and the fact that she was a practising lesbian. Her marriage to some Hispanic guy long since dissolved, she took delight that cold spring day in recounting how Alice, consumed with curiosity, had visited Karen's scout camp where, nodding at Karen's trailer she had said, 'Well we all know what's going on in there.'

'And was it?' asked Rick.

She stared at him as if he were mental. 'Of course,' she said.

Adrienne, eyes shining, had pealed her sweet silvery tinkle of laughter.

In that first year and a half, each day for Rick and Adrienne was a continuing of their idyll. Just themselves. No Alice, no family, and Mickey, praise the saints, off to a dancing job in Europe. Occasionally they'd see Jack, Ruby, Margie and her boyfriend Buzz. But their days had been for themselves. She rarely worked out, except in bed. Each warm morning would begin when he'd wake to that hard, loving grasp around his cock, hearing her breathe, 'King's very stiff this morning,' before, gazing deep into the Mongol eyes, he'd begin with her.

Placing her pretty knees beside the tiny ears, her legs high up over his shoulders, he'd do it to her, after minutes, pulling her down sideways, the leanness of his hips smacking against the tight round hardness of her bottom, completing the half circle by laying her face down now, pinning her, her head turned out, his cheek on hers, each slapping thrust forcing the tiniest gasp as he milked her nipples, her hands on his hands, finally tonguing the delicate ear and guiding her into a kneeling position before taking her from the bed – to bend, hands on a chairback, her knuckles clenching white, from whence she'd turn silently, stretching one leg up beyond his chest, his head, till she was straight from toe to toe-end and he would do her deep, her arms looping softly about his neck as she sucked upon his lower lip.

After, she'd return to the bed, fixing him with that unblinking gaze, and he would stand amazed at how she'd slowly open up her legs to the ten-to-two position, then, smiling, take the stiffened King right to his root.

Standing pearly naked from her bed, at her belly-end there was no hint of lips or slit or mound, even. Just that sweet little slate-grey triangle. But when she scissor-split, the big groin muscles levered her apart to bare the deepest axe-wound known to man. The sweet and sticky Venus trap. King's Bermuda Triangle.

After an hour or so of touch and thrust, she'd dress, go to the neighbourhood store, buy herself a bran muffin and pick up the *New York Times*. Back in bed, she'd fight to keep the crossword, then finally share it with him till they'd crack its last secret, when they'd rise and shower, sometimes together, and while she kissed him under a lashing spray, he'd soap her breasts, full and slippery, her cute little buns, and the muff, inside and out, till she was squeaky clean, ready to meet the world.

Lunch as a rule was local (Mitchell's, Nero's or The Hub) but now and then a foray to the snazzy, thirties-style East Side would bring them to Le Cirque, Le Cygne or to La Caravelle where she'd drink him glass for glass and, at their table, kiss him brazenly. 'Adrienne,' he'd begin, embarrassed, and she would cut him off, her face full into his, laughing gaily.

'You're never going to stop me doing it, Rick. You're never going to stop me doing it,' laughing more as he would lilt in baby fashion, 'Oh dear.'

Merry as a grig, she'd scintillate beside the double-breasted, debonair Neilsen, vibrant, shining, turning many a head. Once, leaving Le Cirque, he had grabbed her at the top of the long exit between the tables and danced her down it, singing 'How Could We Be Wrong?' At a table near the door a woman clapped her hands together. 'Oh, only in the movies, only in the movies,' she laughed to her escort. 'Who *are* you?' Rick heard her call as they'd swept on out, whether to himself, to Adrienne or their quickstep togetherness he couldn't determine. Though it must have meant Adrienne, for the Rader-girl she radiant *that* day, baby. She radiant.

Exultant, she punched him as the cab rolled up. Inside, 'And you dare to complain when I kiss you, Rick Neilsen!!!' Reaching out, 'Come here you piece of human wonderment,' she said and draped herself around him, teeth nipping sharply through one pinstriped shoulder. 'Man flesh,' she growled, switching her gorilla bite up to his cheek. 'Man flesh.' Then she was on his mouth, giggling into it as she kissed and kissed and kissed at him. Occasionally, Rick caught the cabby's eyes staring from the rearview mirror. If the poor bastard had had a lousy morning, he must surely be enjoying this afternoon.

It had been all beer and skittles then. Well . . . . almost all. In between seeing the odd movie, they'd go bowling or watch the Mets on TV, until Adrienne decided Rick needed more constructive exercise. She bought a pair of racquets and took him to the

90th St Y for his first racquetball lesson. She explained the rudiments, showed him how to serve and, after a ten-minute knockabout, they began. Though a novice, Rick had always been good at hand-eye coordination games. In three sets he trounced her, dropping his serve craftily into the corner where, nine times out of ten impossible to retrieve, it drove her almost to distraction.

Outside, walking by the reservoir, she complained bitterly. 'You're not supposed to do that.'

'What?'

'Play that way.'

'What way?'

'The way *you* played. Dropping the ball in the corner like that.'

'But that's what you showed me.'

'Yes, but you shouldn't do it all the time. It spoils the game for the other person.'

'Oh, you mean the game's not about winning?'

'Not like that. It takes away all the fun.'

Boy was she upset. And she was right, he thought. She'd wanted him to admire her prowess, her athleticism, and he'd destroyed her credibility as a spunky little sportsgirl by unmercifully creaming her.

Stupid of him. He *had* spoiled it. 'I'm sorry,' he said softly and seriously.

'It's all right,' she quavered and he could see from her tears that he'd hurt her.

'You *fool*,' he cursed at himself.

'I wanna go home, I'm cold.' A whimper. It made him feel utterly wretched. Now they were both unhappy. They never played racquetball again. She asked him a few times but they never got around to it somehow.

Always in the past, whenever he was through with a New York job, he'd take Adrienne to Europe but she wasn't coming this time. She'd hooked herself a part in a play, an off-off-off-Broadway production somewhere down in the Village. Good for her! They'd meet up when Rick returned in four to six weeks. In the month or so prior to his leaving, he saw less and less of her as she spent her time working out with Lucy Boyden.

Three days before his departure (the landlord having secured a date with the theatre to bring in a new tenant), Adrienne returned to the apartment mid-afternoon. She was uncharacteristically quiet. Leaving her be, Rick slipped into the bedroom to begin packing. No sooner had he done so than great breaking sobs echoed from the other room. Rick stopped dead. She never wept, certainly not like this. She only cried hard under real emotional upset, like that first time at the Stone Resort when she'd decided one chill winter morn that Rick didn't love her, the silly monkey.

Racing through the hall he found her perched on the sofa's edge. 'Adrienne. What's wrong? Sweetie, what's wrong?' He wrapped her in his arms, her own not opening in return, remaining clasped round her body.

'I'm just . . .'

'What? Tell me . . .'

'Just . . . never gonna get a job!'

'But you've *got* a job, honey. You start Monday!'

'I mean a *real* job!'

He pulled her head down to his shoulder. 'Come on, every job's a real job, my angel,' he said gently. 'However bad it might seem, if you don't play this like it's Chekov or Tennessee Williams, then it won't be any good.'

'You're right,' she said and stood, wiping her eyes. 'I have to pack, too.' In a small voice, 'I can leave my trunk with Margie or Ruby.'

Their last night they spent at Margie's on a makeshift mattress on the floor in a wreck of a room used as a store-cum-workshop, cans of paint and rubbish everywhere. In the morning they made love amid the mayhem, her strong legs bent, wide open at the knees, her feet planted firmly on the springless mattress, the face wan, the body listless. He stopped and she looked up at him, her face both quizzical and sad.

'My darling,' he said softly, 'I have to go to London. There are things I've got to take care of. They want me to do a theatre season but I'm not going to because I don't want to be away from you. There are two other people I have to meet and one of the things I'm going to do is kick my agent's ass so he gets me a big piece of work that'll buy us a real New York apartment, not that Club Paradiso for roaches we just vacated. I would've kept it on for you till I get back but it was already leased to somebody in the next theatre production.'

'I know,' she said.

He rose and fetched a small envelope from his bag. He took out some bills. 'Here's a few hundred bucks,' he said. 'It's all I can manage right now.'

She took the money with a small, 'Thanks.'

He took her in his arms. 'Look, its not as if I'm abandoning you. I'll be back in six weeks, four maybe.'

'It's OK. I can stay at Ruby's. It's OK.'

He chafed all the way to Kennedy. Two big pay days would take care of everything. As an actor he had a sterling reputation, but reputation doesn't buy your breakfast. He dwelt on an echo of her last words to him. 'OK, OK.' Well, they didn't sound OK and he didn't feel OK.

In London, he struck it lucky. Calling an old friend, Marina Hood, he was offered the use of her flat in Paddington. She left two days after he got there to spend the summer in Italy, and he had the place to himself. He saw his lawyer, had one or two meetings with some theatre people and had not long finished fixing a lunch appointment with his agent when the phone rang. It was Big Bob, the self same agent, a huge, red-faced, hirsute American. 'Rick, something's just come up which might interest you.'

'Yeah?' He could just see Big in shirtsleeves, tie and suspenders, hunched over the desk, eyes closed, lips stretched baring forty-seven rows of teeth, in an attitude of very painful constipation, his 'phone attitude'.

'A couple of guys are here from the States. They own a theatre out west, eleven hundred seater. You could do anything you want. Your choice.'

'How long would it be for?'

'It's a six-play season. Yours would be the second slot. One month rehearsal, one month playing and that's it, starting around two months from now. Also, they pay well.'

'OK. Let's meet with them.'

'Fine. I'll set it up and call you back.'

The lunch went well. Rick came up with a play, and a part for Adrienne. He would direct it and he knew he could get a really good performance out of her. Disappointed looks from the Americans. 'Couldn't *he* be in it? He was the attraction for the theatre.' All right. Agreed. Smiles all round, handshakes, cognac and coffee. Rick walked with Big back to his office. The more he thought about it, the more he liked it. He could direct *and* appear. Adrienne would be free, they could be together on and off the stage and she would have that real job she craved. They'd do the play, he'd do a movie, they'd get married and live happily ever after. 'My Blue Heaven.' Yeah!

In the office he asked Big if he could phone New York. Big nodded. 'Sure, use the office next door.'

He made two calls, to no avail. Margie didn't know where Adrienne was. Ruby didn't know where she was either. He didn't know the name of her play or of the theatre. He had no other number for her. He walked over to the window and stared down at the tops of little red buses beetling their way down Oxford Street. This was nuts! Where was she? In all the days they'd been together, for the first time he felt afraid.

He made four further calls over a three-day interval. From Ruby there was only the answer-machine. He left no message. Margie had still heard nothing. Rick left her his Paddington number. He'd been almost three weeks in London and no word of or from her. At the fifth attempt, bingo! Margie had a number, somewhere in the Village. He scribbled it down on a copy of *The Times* tearing it off the bottom of the page. 'I was just about to give you a buzz,' said Margie. 'She only called a little while ago.'

'Did she ask if I'd called?'

'No, but I told her and gave her your number.'

'What did she say?'

'Oh, that she'd been working hard on the play and that she'd try to call you soon.'

He thanked her and hung up. 'Try' to call him soon? Why try? Why not just fucking do it? He picked up the torn piece of paper and dialled. The low, lilting song of her voice repeated the number he held in his hand. 'It's me,' he said. 'I've been trying and trying to get hold of you. Where the hell have you been?'

'I've been working on the play . . .' The musical notes drained out of her voice. She hadn't called him 'Sweetie', or *anything* and he began to listen for tell-tale signals, subtle shifts.

'You could at least have left a number with Margie. How was I supposed to reach you?'

'I told you I was busy.'

Not pausing to ask where she was staying or how the play had gone, he went straight into it. 'I'll be coming into town soon. I want you to marry me.'

The answer was small, flat, but emphatic. 'I don't want to get married.'

The sounds of the street life faded. He stood paralysed, deaf to all but the transatlantic hiss at his ear. 'Adrienne, last summer . . .'

'I don't want to get married.'

'But you said—'

'I don't want to get married,' she said firmly.

He gripped the receiver tightly, trying to steady himself. 'Right. OK then,' he said harshly before smashing the phone down. Snatching up his jacket from a kitchen chair he tore from the apartment and down the three flights to the street. 'Fuck you!' he roared, wrenching back the door to slam it like a thunderclap behind him, on his way to the nearest pub.

For a week he refused to call her, going out to Père Michel's or the Bombay Palace to eat, until a growing anxiety put an end to appetite, leaving him only to walk and drink. The walks grew shorter and the drinks longer, until finally he consigned himself to a chair by the phone, waiting for her call. It came on a Friday at one pm. Or so he thought. Grabbing at the instrument his heart sank as he heard the wheedling tones of his agent. A big TV movie Rick had made the year before was being given a press ballyhoo in New York and Phoenix. 'Would you go, pretty please?'

'When?'

'Next week,' came the reply. 'Hotels, limos, per diems, the whole schmeer.'

'Fine,' he said, leaving Bob to fix the details. Now he could go to New York, see Adrienne's play, see *her*, go to Phoenix for some press bullshit – maybe take Adrienne, woo and re-seduce her under a desert moon. On his way to lunch he had a dreadful coughing fit on the street which was followed by a total inability to focus, a frightening sensation of drifting, of leaving his body. Rick shook his head, straining for perspective, trying to gather his senses. Paddington Station loomed above him, like a hideous morgue, a gothic death chamber (what it looked like, anyway, he decided later). Feeling himself laid bare by some strange force, he began to tremble.

Rick had been married once before. To Daisy, another striking blonde, by whom he'd had a son, Pete, now in school Stateside. The marriage effectively had lasted less than three years. Out in California, towards the end of their courtship, Daisy had got involved with somebody else. Rick, about to leave New York to join her, had had a similar horrifying experience on a Saturday around noon in someone's backyard out on Long Island where, suddenly, he couldn't focus on anything material, except a leaf on a small tree. He stood there, eyes riveted on the leaf, which alone held his identity secure within its small serrated shape. Each time he tried to shift that focus on to house or patch of grass he felt what he imagined was his soul, etherized, drifting inexorably from his physical shell. Transmigration. So back he'd go, nose to his leaf, holding on to an arterial life, stitching himself in, knowing, should he come out of it, he'd capitulate and lose himself altogether. He remained transfixed before the leaf for half an hour. His bemused hosts asked, 'Would he not sit down, take some tea, a drink. . . ?'

'No, no.'

At length the local quack was summoned. 'Have you taken LSD?'

'No.'

'Or any drug?'

'No, no.'

'This is a very LSD-like symptom.'

'Sorry. I gotta go back outside.'

'Wait a second, young man.' Magic black bag opened. 'I want

you to take these.' Two minuscule red pills and inside minutes, an exhausted peace, and relief on the faces of his hosts. Four years later, after he'd married Daisy, she told him all about that time. It had happened one weekend, by a lake, up in the mountains, in a trailer, about nine o'clock on a Saturday morning. He calculated. Nine o'clock LA, twelve o'clock Long Island. ESP or quantum physics, telepathic transfer particles, or whatever the hellfire fuck it was, had all but paralysed the shit out of him, at the exact moment she was opening her legs and transferring her heart.

Now here it came again. The Transmigration Tango. On this Doomy-Friday Paddington Street, and no quack with his little red pills. Holy Moly. Wait! The Archery. The little pub opposite Père Michel's restaurant near Bathgate Mews, just two streets away. In the bar he sank four large armagnacs in quick succession along with a beer chaser, his eyes as riveted on the pump handle sign ('Burton Ale' it read), as the Australian barmaid's were on him. One more drink, then he took in the room. All well. No drift, no etherizing. Only little terrors running in his cups as he thought back to those last days in New York. She only cried like that when under severe emotional pressure. Her quietness. Her coolness. Her economy of words. The marriage refusal. The absence of contact. He *knew*. Transfer!

'Trouble?' the barmaid enquired.

Turning to where the voice had come from and seeing a pair of softening eyes, Rick realized he must look just how he felt. About seven and lost. 'Oh sure,' he said. 'Trouble.' In store.

In a tiny Greenwich Village theatre, before a painfully small audience, Rick watched Adrienne playing opposite an upper middle-aged actress – lines perfectly known, but no heartbeat. Not her fault. The piece itself dulled the brain. He'd got the theatre address from Margie. It was Saturday, the last performance. Outside, he'd waited the best part of an hour to catch her, without success. Had she seen him, and sidled through some other door into a backstreet? Disappointed, he rode a cab uptown. Courtesy of the studio's publicity department, he was staying (ironically) at Wyndham's Hotel, behind which Adrienne and he had once stood locked in their first embrace. On Sunday, around eleven, he called her. No reply. Then Jack, then Buzz and Margie. Same. Margie played the organ at some church, he knew, and Jack was probably out on Long Island. Finally, Rick called Bob Cash, a producer friend of long standing, leaving a message on his answerphone.

Throughout the day he called the mysterious Village number. Still no Adrienne. Rick was to have dinner that night with the publicity big chief. He decided to leave further calls until Monday. At ten am he got her. Oh, that voice! How was she? 'Fine.' He'd seen the play, thought she'd been good. 'Thank you.' Would she meet him for lunch? Pause, then quietly, 'Yes. Where?' A moment's hesitation, then, 'The side entrance of the Plaza – at noon.' Fine, she'd be there.

Right on time, at the foot of Central Park South, he watched Adrienne make her way towards him, dressed simply in tight, pink, three-quarter length pants, sandals and white T-shirt, exposing the young brown arms he ached to have about him. A luscious pink and white meringue, he wanted to devour her. 'Hi,' she said quietly. 'Hi,' he said back. No offer of a hand. No kiss. 'You're never going to stop me doing it, remember?' he wanted to say, but all of a sudden was too unsure. Holy Jesus, what had happened? Here was the two-year love of his life standing passionless before him. Wordless too, except for 'Hi.' The kind of greeting you would give at a play-reading to an actor you'd never met before. Where was her heart, the chipmunk smile, that seal-kiss that was his and his alone? A fearful strangeness kept them apart, he anxious, she wary. Christ! He wanted to shake her angrily into the abandon of a public fuck.

Instead they rode a cab down Lexington to the Ile de France without holding hands. At the table, inwardly quivering like a fiddle string, he asked quietly if she had met someone else.

'Yes.'

'Did you sleep with him?'

'Yes.'

'Was it good?'

'Yes. I enjoyed it.'

'Then I don't think there's much else to say except . . . Could I have the bill please?' he called softly to a nearby waiter, leaving the open bottle of wine untasted. His heart and soul were in his boots. On the way out, Rick thought back to their first meal together when he had confessed his love for her. That, too, had ended without a morsel eaten or a drop being drunk. Full circle.

On the street she said, 'Thank you. You taught me an awful lot,' and stuck out her hand. He ignored it and she walked off quickly through the lunchtime crowds. Full obliterating circle.

At Wyndham's he hit the bar next door swallowing three glasses of straight Hennessy in quick succession to dull the shock. Dear fuck, he'd been right. His instinct had been right on that damned London street. The quantum physics javelin had speared him. Six months ago desperate to marry him, minutes ago the crossbow at point blank range.

He took the elevator and, as he approached his suite, heard the phone ring. His heart leapt. Could it be. . . ? It was Bob Cash. Still in a daze, Rick told him of the movie publicity, the promotion trip to Phoenix.

'That sounds great. Is Adrienne with you?' Silence. Then he told Cash the story. 'Jesus. D'you have a number for her?' He did. 'Would you mind if I called her? Let me try to find out what's going on.'

Rick fumbled in his pocket for the number. 'Now I've got a play, an eleven hundred seat theatre and no Adrienne.'

'Did you speak to her about it?'

'The play? No. And don't you,' he warned.

'What are you going to do, Rick?'

'I'm not going to call her. Maybe write her a letter when my head clears a little, except I don't have her address.'

'Lemme see if I can get a hold of her,' said Cash. 'I'll get back to you soonest.'

With no appetite, he sat in the room, waiting for Cash to call. At ten thirty he gave up and took a cab uptown to a bar on Second where he knew Broadway Jack worked the odd shift. To Rick's relief he was on that night, greeting him like the prodigal and mixing him a bullshot. 'Lemme get rid of these geezers at the bar then I'll close up and we can sit and gab,' he said sotto voce. Within the half hour they were seated in two comfortable chairs in the little space at the back, lights dimmed and the door blind pulled down low. Rick recounted the episode in the Ile de France. 'Phew. Well, whad'ya know?' Jack murmured. 'She was in here. Late. A couple of weeks ago, you know? They have guitar playing and singing in the back sometimes. She was with that whatsher-name gym friend o' hers?'

'Lucy Boyden.'

'Lucy. Yeah. Then I didn't see 'em no more.' Rattling the ice around the glass he took a long swig of Bourbon. 'Whad'ya gonna do buddy?'

Rick shrugged.

'Gotta talk to her, pal.' Jack looked across at him darkly. 'Gotta have an explanation. She owes you that. Who is this geezer and what's goin' on? Is this a fuck or for ever? You went the whole nine yards for her for two years. Come on Rick. She can't just walk out on you without you knowing why. That's just bullshit.'

At eight fifteen next morning he was jangled into wakefulness. Groping for the receiver he heard the soft, warm tones of Cash. 'Hi. Sorry if I woke you, but I'm just on my way to the office. I spoke with Adrienne late last night, but after I got through I thought it was too late to call you. Are you there? Rick?'

'Yes.'

'I think everything's gonna be just fine. I thought you'd like to know.'

'Come on, Bob. I didn't come up the East River in a banana skin. She's involved with somebody.'

'Aah, there's been a somebody, yes, but it's not important, Rick. He's not the big new thing in her life. Look, OK, she's had a doozie little fling. We all do that at some time in our lives. I think she just doesn't know how to handle it with you, that's all.'

'Then why didn't she tell me he wasn't the big new thing in her life?'

'Maybe she wanted to. Who knows? You didn't give her much chance to, aah, talk at length.'

Silence. Then, 'Well what did she say?'

'That she loves you but she needs some time on her own right now; time to let things settle so she can be able to deal with it. I think she's right. Write her that letter. I have her address. Do you have a pen?'

The address in Greenwich Village was Lucy Boyden's. Lucy Boyden. ' "Curiouser and curiouser," said Alice.' He wrote the letter, sending it Personal Delivery.

Two days later, he found a little note under his door. She had passed by the hotel but could not come up. She felt so dirty. Instead, she had walked round the park. Maybe she would come by tomorrow. She made two more attempts to see him, but Rick was never in. Then, late one afternoon, three knocks brought him quickly to the door. 'Who is it?'

Muffled, 'It's me, Adrienne.' He swung the door wide, and Adrienne ran the three short steps into his arms. 'I love you and I'm sorry,' she sobbed and clung to him, her body shaking. After the phone call from Europe, she told him, she'd felt deserted, depressed, alone. There had been this guy around, a sound engineer. Things just happened. She wasn't in love with him. She never mentioned his name and Rick never asked. In the end they made love. She whispered, 'I'm scared,' as she came naked, timidly towards the bed.

Scared of what? he wondered. That it might not work? Might not be as nifty as Mr Sound Engineer?

But it did work and, after the three-day promotion trip to Phoenix where all he did was think of her, they began to see each other on a twice-weekly basis at a French restaurant on Sixth, near the park. There he told her he had called Norman Martin, who had the same apartment down in SoHo they had used just recently. He had agreed to lease it for a year. Rick didn't like the apartment much but there was little time, not too much money and beggars can't be choosers. It was nothing special, one of hundreds, which constituted a huge grey oblong spanning an entire block. The ghastly corridors with their coiled neon ceiling lights put Rick in mind of a house of correction. He remembered an old movie on TV entitled *Inside the Walls of Folsom Prison*, and here it was, in Downtown Folsom, where he and Adrienne would spend the next three and a half years amid weirdos, nutters, AIDS virus holders, bickering Jewish families and seventeen billion roaches.

She did not move in with him right away, and every time Rick saw her there was a tell-tale smudge beneath each pretty eye. Adrienne was under pressure and he did his best to make things easier for her by trying not to make any demands. There was, of course, the problem of the play. Rick hinted he might drop it as he was honour bound to commit within the month. Two days later she called him from out of town. 'Yes,' she said.

'Yes what?' he asked.

'Yes to the play,' she intoned softly. 'I really wanna do it.' She told him she wanted to come back to Folsom but first she needed a complete break. She was going to Wyoming to stay a month with Karen who was counselling at a camp. 'It's so peaceful there; that big sky. After that I'll be ready and we can be together.' She left the following weekend clutching her copy of the script.

Two days later a cheery wee note waited in the mailbox, sending Rick a reminder that she loved him, and to please write her in Wyoming c/o Karen, so there'd be no mix-ups in the mail. The last time they'd spoken, Adrienne had been so tense and withdrawn, Rick had asked her if she was 'on anything'. Her postscript told him she knew she'd behaved 'weird' but drugs were really not her. He sent off an immediate reply, mailing it first class that same morning to the address she'd given him. Two weeks passed without response.

Rick occasionally met up with Margie and Buzz, the last time at Pedro's Chilli Bar, somewhere over on Second, where he mentioned the Wyoming trip and their plans to settle in Folsom. They were an oddly matched pair. Buzz, who, not long ago, had possessed a full beard, now wore only a moustache. He seldom smiled. Deep dark eyes and a short nose set in a grave face gave him the appearance of an early agrarian. Were he to have stepped into a clearing wearing animal skins, sat down under a hibiscus climber, plucking the *New York Times* and a pair of hornrims from his furs to read quietly while peeling a banana, you might not have been surprised. Margie, humorous, bright spirited and more delicately featured than Adrienne, had the unmistakable, Rader, broad, bone-cracking jaw and similar cranial outline. Sister-daughters, easily.

As the waiter cleared away the plates, Buzz looked at Margie then at Rick. 'I think you oughta know,' he said, 'Adrienne isn't in Wyoming. She's in New Jersey, at a beach house without a phone.' Rick's heart stopped. 'She told Margie she was going about a month ago. I just thought you should know.'

A week later Adrienne called, some time in the late afternoon, obviously from a public payphone, Rick could hear traffic and an echoing breadth of sound like she was near a parking lot outside a shopping mall. 'Hi, Sweetie. I just wanted to call you and see how you are.'

'Fine,' he replied. 'How's the great outdoors?'

'I'm having a great time, yeah.'

'Good. I'm glad. How's Karen?'

'OK. She's really busy. There's such a lot to do here.'

'I'll bet, under that big Wyoming sky.'

'Yeah.'

'Can you see it from where you're standing?'

'Oh yeah, it's really beautiful.'

'Well that's strange.'

'Why?'

In a voice both musical and matter-of-fact he told her. 'Because you're not in Wyoming, you're in New Jersey.'

There was an ear-splitting silence as the cool winds of Wyoming quietly swept the Jersey shore. He could hear, he fancied, the tumblers clicking in her head.

'Oh, my God,' she capitulated. 'I feel so ashamed.'

'Is that so? Well, if I were you I'd go fuck my lover in a canoe. Oh wait, you can't can you, let's see, of course, you're in New Jersey, not Wyoming. Stupid of me, I'm sorry.'

'I'm not with anyone, I'm here with Lucy.'

'Really?'

'Lucy's been in love with a married man who told her he loved her but was just using her, screwing her.'

'I know the feeling.'

23

'Rick, it's true. She decided to take a break to see if she could end it and I came down here with her.'

'There never was any intention of going to Wyoming, was there?'

'No.'

'Then why lie to me?'

'Oh Rick. I'm sorry, I don't know. I guess I thought if you believed I was with Karen . . .'

'I wouldn't think you were with anyone else, right?'

'I guess so. I guess I didn't want you to know I was so close to town, I didn't want you to be worried or upset.'

'A month off is a month off, it doesn't matter where you take it, I wouldn't have bothered you, but deceit is deceit and a lie is a lie.'

'I know, Rick, I know and I'm sorry. Look, I gotta go, I've no more money.'

'OK,' he said, simply.

Then, with a throbbing catch in her throat, 'Rick, I love you, I love you and I feel so awful, I'll call you in a couple of days. Please be there, promise me? You'll be there?'

'We'll talk soon. Bye.'

'Bye. I love you. There's no one else, believe me, Rick. I'm sorry and I love you.'

Click.

He hit the street with his head buzzing. Just what was the story here? He walked disconsolate through the bright lights of the theatre district until he found himself outside the old Belasco theatre, where he had made his first appearance in New York. It was dark and empty. Rick stared at his reflection in the glass door. You're a hell of man when you want something, Neilsen. He stopped over on Sixth and sat near a fountain, staring across at Radio City Music Hall. Was Adrienne simply putting her lover on hold while she took the leading role in a play? If so, this was quite a juggling act; a lot of balls in the air here.

Ten days short of her month's sabbatical, Adrienne rang again. 'I'm coming into New York tonight,' she told him. 'Lucy wants to see her lover.'

'Do you want to see yours?' he asked.

'Yes.'

'When will you be here?'

'Around eight.'

'I'll see you then. Let's have dinner.'

'I'll get there as soon as I can. I love you.'

Inside a week she had moved her belongings into Folsom and there they were, 'Just Molly and me'. The loving was the same – with tiny differences. No more would she reach out for King at early light. Nor ever was the crossword fetched again and huddled over – except by him to fill in time some afternoons. Lovemaking could not take place now before nine am. 'I need my rest. I've signed up for classes at Hunter College and I'm working out.' The Giaconda smile seemed flat, little of the wanton left within it. Or was it his imagination? So most mornings at nine, nursing a two-hour erection, he'd coax her gently into the wakefulness that would turn her eyes to the bedside clock to check if he was too horny too early.

2

IT WAS STILL AM New York time when the MGM flying palace touched down at Kennedy. Rick reached Folsom on the stroke of noon, tired and glad to close the door behind him. Dropping his bags in the hall he went into the living room to fix himself a drink. In the doorway he halted in shock. Before the piano in an April silence stood the slimline Alice, clad only in panties and bra.

'Hello, Rick.' The voice was low, husky, close to that of his lover. Alike yet not alike, she stood before him. Here I am, proud to show you me. Whether it was some movie-type backlit slant from the window, the blue of April sky that washed around her figure, his own tiredness, or all three, she looked young. Firm and delicate, shy, almost – pants tights, bra high. Curiously attractive in diffused sunlight. The mother of his lover.

'Oh, Alice. Hi,' he said. Now many a man full puffed in ego might have interpreted this as a come on – daughter out, mother smiling in her scanties, thunderstruck thesp in doorway, two minutes later sprawled on the sofa in glutinous kiss, fingers inside the knicker elastic. But Rick read it fast now. This confident, unabashed stance simply stated, 'This is my place just as much as yours and I'll come and go as I please, *and* in underwear if I wish. Still, I know you can see what a flat belly I have.' Christ!

'I'm a little jet lagged,' he said weakly. 'Guess I'll crash for a while. D'you know what time Adrienne will be back?'

Spreading her feet slightly, Alice gave him a small look. 'In about an hour I think. She's at class.' As she spoke the spell broke. It had all been a trick of the light.

Rick glanced at his watch. 'I'll see you all later then.' So saying, he dipped into the bedroom with his bags, closed the door and stood. Fuck! How long would she be here for this time? Any bets

26

on the duration of the second Eisenhower administration? For two years now she'd invited herself at will to the apartment. Sometimes for weeks. With notice given through Adrienne, always just a day or so before. Spending as much time in New York as she did with her husband; even when there were no auditions. Rick felt she hung around in fear that she would miss out on anything exciting that might happen professionally with himself and Adrienne. And whether there'd be anything in it for her. Very occasionally, he could feel a sympathy. But not for long.

From the sanctuary of his bedroom, Rick heard his semi-permanent house-guest burst into Mahler song-practice. He collapsed on the bed pressing the knuckles of his index fingers to his eyeballs. Welcome to the omnibus edition of *Alice Sings*. He mused on famous murders and the words of a classic golden oldie sprang into his head. 'When I grow too old to dream, I'll have you to remember.' Remember Doctor Buck Ruxton and his 'Brides in the Bath?' He would sing to them, marry them, do them in and then saw them up in the tub. Rick's father had always maintained Buck's signature tune should have been, 'When you grow too cold to scream, I'll have you to dismember.' He winced as next door the voicebox vibrated to a piercing shriek. Rolling on his back, Rick gazed blankly out the window at clouds bunched gloomily above the East River. 'Gag me with a spoon,' he groaned softly.

He thought back some two years to one of the first Folsom dinners she had appeared at. The Ming dinner. Just himself, Adrienne, Alice and Bob Cash. Alice had been introduced as Adrienne's cousin and, having taken her seat, immediately refused the proffered glass of wine. 'Oh no, no no. The ketones aren't good for you, you know.' Yet, whenever there was champagne in the offing, it was never refused. She would not drink much, but down it would go, with ne'er a mention of a ketone. But then, fizz was the swig of stars, wasn't it? He could not quite recall the line from the Book of Timothy. Was it 'Drink no more water only wine for thy stomach's sake'? Rick raised his glass and quoted one he knew well at Cash. ' "Drink, for you know not whence you came or why. Drink, for you know not why you go, or whence." '

'What's that from?' asked Cash.

'*Omar Khayyam*,' Rick replied and they drank. Adrienne ventured only a timid sip, the same Adrienne who in Le Cirque, Le Cygne, La Caravelle and all the best fish restaurants in Paris and the Midi had drunk him glass for glass through château-bottled clarets, Gewürztraminer and Dom Pérignon Rosé. Her very own and certain person. With that kiss, that laugh, that look in her eye.

It was Bob's first encounter with Alice and she did not disappoint. While she held forth on freedom and Nicaragua, Rick studied all the little prison windows on the opposite wall of the Folsom yard, thinking, 'Everybody wants to be free but perfect freedom is an illusion. There comes the inevitable moment when we are no longer free. Obligations and priorities. Our obligation to the other, like it or no. Nobody is ever free, really.' He looked over at Adrienne – his first obligation and his first priority, for whom he would relinquish freedom, and happily be chained. Her eyes were riveted on Alice. All her values were based in the mother. Since she'd reappeared in Rick's life, it had been all 'Alice says, Alice thinks, Alice really knows,' from Adrienne. On almost any topic Rick's wife appeared to hold no opinions of her own. She would never enter discussion or take any position. Never. But Alice's pronouncements on ecology, geology, politics, religion, life itself, though dressed in cliché, were, to Adrienne, Tablets from the Mount.

It depressed and irritated Rick, for Adrienne read a lot and had an active mind. Way intelligent enough to form her own judgements. What was it then that kept her silent? That persuasive yet restrictive voice? Nursing at its back heaven knows what thoughts or secrets, ever prepared to lend support with subtle shifts of tone and inflection. Low, melodious, encouraging. Nonetheless, its directives, cunningly concealed in friendly observation, kept Adrienne off balance. Her Master's Voice.

Like the voice of Saruman, Tolkien's Wizard of Many Colours '. . . all that it said seemed wise and reasonable, and awoke desire in others to seem wise themselves. For those whom it conquered, the spell endured when they were far away, and ever they heard that soft voice whispering and urging them . . .' Whenever Alice showed up, she brought, for Adrienne, her little sets of rules, clichés and judgements. Guides that Adrienne would afterwards mimic out, following obediently in their wordsteps. Even when Alice was not there, she had a presence still. Trying to tackle Adrienne, as Rick had once or twice, on the value of these oft recanted lyrics, brought only the tight-lipped, obstinate response of 'Alice-really-knows'.

In a sudden change of tack right out of nowhere, 'I'm a counsellor,' Alice revealed, hands raised and fingers fluttering. 'I deal with people's problems all the time and I find helping them is a very rewarding job.' Rick groaned to himself. Christ! A counsellor now. What was *this* all about? Just as suddenly the scales fell from his eyes. Of course. Stardom! She had to be the centre of attention. She needed to perform. She must be the star. Underneath the veil on all these hats of authority she changed around, *that* was the common factor.

As she paused (for breath or change of subject), Cash stepped smartly into the breach as Rick enquired about his latest project. Cash was set to produce a Noël Coward play in London, with, he hoped, a front-line English actress.

'She's promised me she'll do it,' said Cash. 'And I'm just praying she doesn't get offered some blockbuster movie in the next two weeks 'cos she's going to be goddam marvellous in the play. It wouldn't be a disaster if she couldn't do it – there are other actresses who could play it well enough, but not like she'll play it.'

'You think she will?' asked Rick.

'She's told me she wants to, but won't give a definite yes till the end of the month. I've got my fingers crossed. Toes, too!'

'Good luck!' Rick toasted, three wine glasses were raised, and a very quiet voice began a modest dissertation.

'I think the most extraordinary moment in my life,' Alice started off, 'was when I was in a roomful of people surrounding Mother Teresa, who stopped when she saw me, signalled me to come forward, and for two and half hours, we shared an enlightenment. I'm absolutely sure we shared a connection.' Two and a half *hours*, mooned Rick, silently. What were all the others doing in the meantime? Oh, of course. Taking pleasure in watching *two* living saints. With 'Some Enchanted Evening' playing in the back-ground.

Cash looked on in open-mouthed amazement. Adrienne nodded gravely, and Rick got a laser flash of Alice. Shit and derision. Ming! Yes. Straight out of *Flash Gordon* – Ming the Merciless. The eyes and conk she had already. With the black widow's-peak skull cap and the Fu Manchu 'tash, she was a cinch for the next remake. A cube of half-masticated chicken almost sealed his craw. Rigid, he dared not breathe to choke the shriek of bottled mirth for fear of corking the trachea. Instead, he raced to the bathroom and, propelled by an Indian 'whoop', the offending lump shot from his throat and, with one rubbery bounce off a faucet, ricocheted away behind the bath, doubtless to the enthusiastic cheers of the SoHo Roach Club, gathered back there in their usual numbers.

For a minute he sat on the edge of the tub breathing slowly. Then went to the sink and washed his hands, talking to himself. 'Now, you know Ming is in there and you mustn't laugh.' Adolescent nonsense though it was, his glee was quickly stifled by the certain knowledge that Ming would be around tomorrow and tomorrow and tomorrow. In his one-bedroom apartment. Under his feet. Chasing after stardom.

Returning to his seat, Rick apologized for his abrupt departure.

'Frankly, I didn't think the meal was all that bad,' Cash said cheerily.

'Asshole,' Rick said with a grin.

Rick had nodded off at the memory of the Ming dinner revelation. Now he awoke to silence and the sight of his grip on the bedroom floor, the bedside clock showing ten to three. He unpacked, dropping some laundry in the basket in the bathroom. There was no soap that he could find, apart from one sliver on the tiled platform of the shower. Putting away some folded shirts he spied an open letter on top of the chest of drawers, from Alice to Adrienne. It was the end that caught his eye. *I really admire how clever you're being. You're a real smart cookie Adrienne, do you know that?* Feeling his heartrate rise, he prowled into the sitting room. Of the Diva there was neither hide nor hair.

He cased the joint. It was grubby and in need of a good tidy-up. He went to the hall closet, pulling out the old red vacuum and checking his watch. Three pm. As he went about cleaning, the tiny motor on wheels hummed happily away, following him about like a little red goblin. He smiled as he remembered Sam's tale of the Goblin when Rick was just a child. A good amateur middleweight boxer, his father had borne a certain resemblance to Ronald Colman, with his dark good looks and pencil moustache.

The saga of the Goblin had been preceded by Dark Friday, the curséd day that Blackjack, Sam's younger brother, had been dispatched by his dreaded wife to follow Sam's example and borrow from the local butcher a set of chimney-sweeping rods and brushes, thus saving money by doing the job himself. Now Blackjack had a quick and furious temper which could take exception to almost anything at any time. But Blackjack lived in mortal terror of his wife, christened by Sam, 'The Bleck'. And so it came to pass that, on a late Friday morning, the brushes were secured and the task begun.

Shortly after lunch the same day, there came a knock at Sam's front door. It was his father. They exchanged greetings, the old man asking, 'Are you busy?'

'No,' replied Sam. 'Not particularly, why?'

'Come with me for a minute, there's something I'd like you to see.'

Curious, Sam put on his coat, accompanying the old man down the street to his home, which adjoined Blackjack's. As they approached they heard a stream of snarling curses, an apoplectic cadenza with an all-too-familiar ring. His father stopped and pointed heavenwards, smiling broadly. 'Look,' he said. Sam lifted his gaze and they both began to laugh, softly at first, then more openly.

Silhouetted against the winter sky, with the face of a Kentucky minstrel, was Blackjack, dancing in rage upon the tiles, the whites of his eyes flashing maniacally as he smashed a succession of halfbricks down the flue, while hurling curses at the cackling duo below.

'Everything started off well,' the old man told Sam, wiping his eyes, 'until the brush-head became stuck.' In his zeal to free it, Blackjack had unwittingly turned the rods in the wrong direction, succeeding only in unscrewing the head which had jammed halfway up the chimney. Fetching a ladder, he had taken to the roof where they now beheld him, a raving Vulcan, entertaining all the street. Well, not quite all. Some little time later his spouse returned to find her abode thick with soot and brick dust. Neighbour after neighbour pricked up ears, riveted to hear Blackjack receive the blistering volley of threats and abuse that straightway followed The Bleck's primal scream. Made to scour the house for days, Balckjack was in the doghouse for weeks.

Sam, Blackjack and their father had all worked in the same light-industrial plant, which manufactured aluminium ingots to specification. On one late shift, lit by the glow from a roaring furnace, Sam revealed the seed of a plan to his silent brother. 'We take a small metal drum, line it with fireclay, fill it with coking coal, stick in a carborundum pot, put in the scrap aluminium, melt it down, pour it into a mould and bingo! Aluminium ashtrays in the shape of a leaf. All we have to do then is shine them up with the electric buff and they're ready for sale. Bob's your uncle!' Blackjack listened, riveted, while Sam explained further. 'We'll have a mould made, but everything else – drum, fireclay, carborundum pot – we'll whip from the plant.' They would set up their own little operation in the big wooden shed at the bottom of Blackjack's yard.

'Mmm. Great idea,' Blackjack said. 'But what about a fan? We'd need a blower to heat the coke to melting point.'

Sam had a red hot brainwave. 'Easy,' he said. 'The Goblin.'

'What goblin?'

'The Goblin. *Your* Goblin,' Sam grinned. 'Just the job.'

'Aah, yeah,' Blackjack nodded. 'Now why didn't I think of that?' Then, 'Well, I don't know.' He shifted nervously.

'What?' asked Sam.

'Well there's just one snag. It's her pride and joy. If anything should happen to it . . .' he faltered.

'What *can* happen?'

'OK, but all the same,' he said warily, 'we'll need to wait till she goes to the stores.' She. The terror of his life. Whose prize possession was the spankingest carpet cleaner in the world to date – the Goblin.

And so, every Saturday as she closed the door behind her, setting off to shop, the Goblin would be filched from its nesting place below the stairs and hijacked down the yard to where the carborundum cauldron glowed in readiness. Switching it on to 'blow', they beheld the coke take fire like dragon's blood. The melt was swift, the pour swifter, and as they surveyed the shining little leaf-shaped ashtrays cooling in their rows, they recharged the pot and began the process all over again. Later the Goblin would be whisked back to its lair, with The Bleck none the wiser. Until one fateful day, between melts, they decided to take a half-hour break around noon, leaving the Goblin beside the makeshift furnace. After tea and sandwiches, they restoked the fire and again filled the pot with scrap metal. 'You're a wonderful contraption,' sang Blackjack, giving the Goblin an affectionate pat, blissfully unaware that, in the interim, the machine had filled with combustible gases from the furnace. On contact with a wayward spark as he switched it back on, there was an almighty BANG! and the thing blew apart like a joke cigar.

The force of the blast lifted Blackjack off his feet and across the floor plastering him against the planking of the shed where he stuck momentarily, white as a sheet, before sliding helplessly to earth. Horrorstruck, he pointed a trembling finger at the Goblin. The steel case-pins holding it together had been straightened like the fur of a terrified cat. The vacuum cleaner lay smouldering at both ends. 'Jesus Christ,' he wheezed. 'She'll go mad. I've had it.'

'No you haven't,' Sam mouthed without conviction.

'You don't know what she can be like.'

'I'll tell her,' Sam offered.

'No fuckin' chance!' Blackjack staggered to his feet, imagining the nightmare face of The Bleck ignite in fury. After the brushes episode he was wiped out of brownie points.

'We've got to fix it,' he babbled.

Sam looked at him incredulously.

'We've got to. It's more than my life's worth if we don't.'

They set about the casing like the Wright brothers trying to

33

repair a P38 with a pair of Stillsons. But, inside an hour, they had plugged it into the mains and – lo and behold – it worked. The steady hum was greeted with an enormous sigh of relief from Blackjack. Seizing a handful of cleaning rags, he rubbed feverishly at the chromium. 'There,' he said, surveying his handiwork. 'She'll never know.'

'Right, we'd better get it back.'

'What about the melt?' said Sam, nodding at the pot.

'Fuck the melt. I prefer to live.' Peering furtively round the corner of the shed, he examined the house for signs of life. The pathetic charade reminded Sam of Thurber's cartoon 'House and Woman', and he began to laugh.

'What the hell are you laughing at?'

'You.'

'You bastard,' snarled Blackjack.

Sam was still laughing as the Goblin, swathed in sackcloth, was hugger-muggered up the garden path by an ashen Blackjack. Discovery by The Bleck this time, he knew, would mean the chatré.

'He got away with it,' Sam remarked at a much later date. 'She never knew. God knows, but *she* never knew. Still,' he laughed, 'for months after, every time she vacuumed, Blackjack would stop and listen fearfully for the whine of a failing motor.'

Rick stooped to pick up a bunch of panties and odd socks by the alcove which housed the TV and the hi-fi. He grimaced. Having to pick up Ming's divested undies was not in his contract. Couldn't she at least aim them at the laundry basket for heavens' sakes? Using his fingers like a pair of tongs, he dropped the soiled underwear into a plastic bag. Underneath a wrinkled pair of tights on the coffee table, Rick spotted a small black book, with *Diary* embossed in gold on the front cover. He flipped the pages, crammed with comments on family and others he knew not, and then suddenly saw his own name: *A good host. Doesn't mask. Interesting.* This last, underlined. Followed by something like, *Whenever he and Adrienne talk about being in the theatre and movies, I can't bear it because I want it so much.* This last line savage with exclamation marks. Five he counted. There it was. In print. Alice's secret! The root of her prejudice towards Rick. And her two-year vow of silence against Adrienne – from that very first meeting. Rick almost laughed out loud. Instinctively he'd held a suspicion for an age, but here it was, clear under her own hand. Adrienne was now the family star, and the anguish was consuming Alice. Sad, envious, resentful, unhappy Alice. An Alice to feel sorry for. But an Alice to be mindful of, Rick thought, and reading no more, he placed the diary back upon the coffee table.

Like icy, baby feet of mice, a childhood thrill of horror ran up his spine as he remembered opening a 'forbidden' book that had been left to gather dust in the lumber room of his grandmother's apartment by an uncle who had gone off rather late in the day to get married. There was a mask, which he believed to be a real face, worn by one of the 'People of the Black Peacock! It was bony, cold and brutal with a curved beak. As a child, Rick was absolutely certain that the masked figure standing at the throne of stone was searching for *him*. He recalled how quickly he would turn the page, heart thudding like thunder in the dim light of the tiny bedroom. Then, almost against his will, he would sneak the book open again to recoil at the masked face that held a fearful fascination for him.

He stood rapt, thinking on the letter. *You're a real smart cookie, Adrienne, do you know that? I really admire how clever you're being.* Then the diary. *I want it so much!!!!!*

Almost immediately there was the turn of a key in the lock and there she was. Honey blonde in a red satin jacket, faded jeans with a tomboy glow in her eyes. They stood for long enough locked in a tight embrace, kissing and tracing one another's bodies. With her hands kneading his bottom, 'Oh how I've missed you,' she purred with that low voice, 'you and your cute little bunses.' He got a big, smacking seal kiss, then, 'Where's Alice?'

'I don't know,' he said. 'Out someplace.' He led her by the hand to the bedroom, a caravanserai where, hungry, thirsting, they refreshed themselves with love that yet was gentle as the smallest breeze, as soundless even.

After, staring at the ceiling, arms around each other's shoulders in the old pals position, she asked him about the movie. 'One actress a sweetheart, one totally self-involved, crew terrific. Usual mishmash. Director OK, but distant. Didn't bother me, but it's amazing how they can't seem to realize that a little quiet encouragement would just be that much more productive. Maybe they're afraid of being considered soft or wimpy, who knows, but I don't think so. More a case of directors being into themselves in this country. Self is the style. The easy, bedside manner, you hardly ever see here.' He yawned and clicked his tongue. 'I think it should be mandatory for all aspiring directors to be actors for one year at least. It would make them realize what it's like, could only make things better, better than this constant running battle, star director versus star bitch or asshole or, at best, who can outdo the other in the outfits they appear in each day. Baalburg's just like that, one big showboat plant.'

She frowned. 'Baalburg?'

'Where they worship gold and the graven images they themselves create.'

She laughed and, with her head cradled in his shoulder, told him of her doings of the past weeks – the fruitless auditions, the workouts, the courses she was signing up for. He listened, stroking her body. Her dreams were important to him and he helped her with them. He really believed she had a movie future with that Bergmanesque face, that voice, those eyes. 'You know, you never called me once in six weeks,' he said inside a small silence. 'It's not as if it costs you anything.'

'Didn't I? Oh sweetie, there's three hours' difference there. I'd be either asleep or working out.'

'All day, every day?'

'Oh well, sweetie, you were always calling me.'

'And sometimes I found you.'

She gave him a hurt rabbit look from the mud-greens and nuzzled him. 'No fair.'

'Sure it's fair.' He kissed her nose. 'It's just nice that it's reciprocal sometimes, you know?' He rose, stretching his long, lean body before the window.

She watched him from the pillow. 'It *is* reciprocal Rick. You know that.'

'I know, I know.' He smiled, looking over the East River towards a break in the clouds.

He took a warm-like-needles stinging shower, towelled himself down vigorously and, dressed in fresh clothes, returned to their own version of the Goblin.

'What are you doing?' he heard her call.

'Cleaning the apartment, what do you think?'

'It's not that bad, sweetie.'

'It's filthy, Adrienne. I've already had to pick up after three pairs of your old lady's bloomers and socks, here.'

'Rick.' From the corner of the doorway she threw him a small frown of disapproval.

'Also, there's no soap and there's other stuff we need.' Shutting off the Goblin he disappeared out the door. 'I'll see you shortly.' He didn't mention the diary.

After a lightning tour of the local Korean supermarts, he had a cool beer at the corner, relishing the cacophony and smell of old New York. Even a cheesy whiff of Sodom and Gomorrah was preferable to antispetic Baalburg. 'Turds are all right,' he reflected, 'and pink ribbons are all right, but turds and pink ribbons don't mix. As he stepped from the elevator he was pleased to hear an industrious hum and found Adrienne in the bedroom, scouring away with their vacuum cleaner.

In the next hour they got the place shipshape, shouting pieces of information to each other from opposite ends of the apartment.

'Joe Alder's having a play-reading at his place, day after tomorrow. He asked me to ask if you would do it.'

'What is it?'

'New comedy.'

'Any good?'

'Yeah. I think it would be fun. D'you wanna do it?'

'Sure.'

'Oh good, sweetie. I'm gonna read too and Alice is coming.'

The lump in the mashed potato. He pulled a face in the mirror, then laughed.

'What?' she called.

'Nothing.'

'I said I'm gonna read too and Alice is gonna be there.' She shut off the Goblin and came into the bathroom, watching him as he cleaned the sink. 'Rick, don't tell anybody she's my mother.'

'Adrienne, I . . .'

She hurried on, 'Nobody knows she's my mother.'

'Joe does.'

'He doesn't.'

'Oh come on, sure he must.'

'No, he doesn't. Just say that she's a cousin or a friend. Please, Rick.'

'Come on, Adrienne.' He leaned his hands on the basin and stared at the soap dish. 'I'm hardly going to go trotting round a room full of people chanting, "This is Adrienne's cousin or friend, I just forget which." '

She tried her little smile as he gazed at her reflection in the bathroom mirror. 'Just please don't call her my mother.'

He turned on the taps. 'Your secret's safe with me,' he said swilling out the brush. She walked up behind him planting a kiss on the back of his neck.

There was a full house at Joe's. Two writers, one of whom had written the piece to be performed, and an assorted cast of about a dozen. After introductions and some small refreshment, they sat in an improvised circle while Joe and playwright spoke briefly about the characters and plot. Rick sat watching Joe. He was an odd character. Born of Pennsylvania-Irish coal-mining stock, his face was at once open and intelligent, with a shock of brown hair, sharp hazel eyes, short nose and a behind-the-bite-smile. He lived for theatre, adored being in musicals. He had spent last summer in stock doing Gilbert and Sullivan. Rick always pictured him in thigh boots, button tunic, rapier and spaniel wig, camping it grandly through *HMS Pinafore*. A brilliant administrator, he would have been perfect as a nineteenth-century actor/manager of musical comedy.

They started the read and Rick felt his body tense as Adrienne began her role. Her theatre voice lost something of the energy that was naturally in her own. The low tones disappeared and the voice wobbled in a middle register that lacked character and force. A

38

speech defect on the 'r' sound turning it often into a 'w' didn't help, but she loved the lifeblood of it all so much that Rick wanted to gather her in his arms, to hold her tight and tell her, 'Never mind theatre, sweetie. Just wait till they hear that throaty movie voice and get a load of that neo-Bergman head up there on their screens, then you'll show them.'

In an accident-prone role, the leading woman twittered like a dazed bird, scatterbrained and very funny. Once, at a line where she had everyone rolling with laughter, Rick caught sight of Alice, sitting upright, hands clasped and lips compressed, staring straight ahead, like the portrait of Whistler's Mother. It made him feel curiously depressed knowing that, what was for him an afternoon's lark, she would die to be asked to do. Rick all at once felt sorry for her. Seeing Adrienne looking at him he smiled. 'Rick,' she prompted merrily and, 'Rick,' said Joe. 'It's your line.'

'Oh. Sorry, sorry,' he proffered, picking it up lightly amid laughter. When it was over, they didn't stay long. Joe wanted to open the play at a little out-of-town theatre and eventually, to bring it into New York, but Rick knew in his heart that the piece did not have the pith to make it.

In the elevator, Adrienne looked brightly at Alice. 'Well, what did you think? Did you like it?'

'Yes,' she said with an affected ease. 'Yes, it was . . . quite nice.' Behind her eyes, the diary screamed.

The day after Joe Alder's reading, Alice was due to catch a pm flight back to Bluebell Road. Hearing her stir in the adjoining room, Rick got up, showered, dressed quickly and slipped out. On the fresh, early morning street, in a storefront window, something caught his eye which stopped him in his tracks. He went in, found an assistant and, pointing to the object, left a small deposit then departed, walking for close on an hour, dreaming. Finally, he picked up *The Times*, sipped a bitter, black coffee in the Chelsea Hotel, filled two brown paper bags with groceries and headed back to Folsom. On his return, Adrienne passed him word that Alice was to stay another week. Ay-gad! 'Fine,' he said. He could put up with it OK, but when she was around, Rick was aware always of her en-passant observation of him. Whenever he gave himself some wine, or freely cursed, or waxed relaxed, he felt this *heavy presence*, like the continuous bearing of a grudge. A scent of something. Like a dog smells fear. It was there. Not paranoia, not invention, and it disturbed him, made him uneasy. Rick didn't dislike Alice (although he certainly could do without her. And Mickey), rather he wanted *her* to like. Not him particularly, but *like*. Having fun or feeling groovy. Dump this Whistler's Mother disapproval drag.

The night before she left, Rick took Adrienne and Mom for a champagne dinner at the St Regis. But it still didn't break the ice of that permanent restriction. Could Alice not laugh like Adrienne? He would love to see her throw back her head and let go. Like his own mother used to. He couldn't believe she hadn't ever. Sipping his drink, *So go get on a plane, Alice,* he silently implored. *Go home to Bill. Feed him. Go to the movies, take vacations, have friends over, and give us a break. For a month or two, anyway. Please?*

3

O N A BRISK, LATE April morning packed with urgent city sounds, the sun smiled down on Folsom, summoning dreamers to the roof. Rick waylaid Adrienne outside the bathroom door, propelling her gently to the sitting room, into the middle of the big Boukhara carpet, bathed in sunshine, and turned her naked body round to face him. 'How . . .?' He smiled into her upturned face.

'How what, Rick? Come on, I wanna get ready.' She shifted but he caught her arms and took a breath.

'How would you like to be a June bride?'

She looked hard at him then dropped her eyes.

He waited a split second then said, 'You're supposed, I think, to say something like "Why Rick, this is so sudden." Or something, whatever.'

She remained silent and still.

'You asked me first. I kept the letter,' he whispered with a crooked smile.

After a moment, she replied, 'Yes, yes. OK.' As he took her in his arms and held her she began an over-his-shoulder qualification. 'Except . . .'

'Except what?' he murmured.

'No one must know we're married.'

'Wh . . . why not?'

She clutched at him, hiding her head in his shoulder. 'Oh, I don't know. It's just . . .' She kissed his chest. 'It's just that . . . people get a handle on you and I don't want anybody to get a handle on me. You know?'

'No,' he said slowly, taking her hands from his shoulders. 'No, I don't know.' Grabbing up his towel, he strode to the door.

'Rick,' she called and came trotting after him.

'You needn't worry,' he said softly, 'I won't ask you again,' and slammed the door behind him.

'You bet I won't,' he muttered angrily as he spread the towel on the flat, tarred, boiling roof that burned your soles. Bile rising in his throat, he mimicked her, ' "Don't want people to get a handle on me". So go stick your handle up your ass!' he rapped out fiercely as he lay back to bake under a pollution-screened sun, while honks and squeals of traffic flew up like jeers. 'As far as it'll fuckin' go!'

He must have been up there near on two hours before a little buzz upon his lip foretold the coming of a sun blister. With a small curse, he fumbled after the Blistex. Dabbing at his mouth he saw her sandalled feet, her hard, strong legs as she stood before him in the short, white dress he liked so much, the sunlight a corona round her honeyed hair, eyes sparkling but serious under the long dark lashes. Surprising himself he spoke. 'First bullshit from you, now a blister, damn!'

'Oh, sweetie,' she commiserated, her thighs swelling as she hunkered down beside him. 'Here, let me.' She rubbed a little salve over his lips, talking softly as she crabbed round him, knees spreading, the lips of the fur-burger innocently parted, the left fuller than the right, the base of an asymmetrical fat little W straining against her tight mauve pants, a dampened bead at clitoris height.

Oh scissor round thighs about my ears, olive beauty clamping out all sound leaving only taste of salt and cream as I am taken in, drawn up, finally to rest, bright apple, sparkling in each blackness circled by the irises of mud-green eyes. Woman and I are one.

'I came up here to find you. I'm sorry, sweetie, I didn't mean to say what I said. I guess it just kinda took me by surprise. It was stupid and I just wasn't thinking. I'm sorry. Of course I want to marry you, I want to spend my life with you, you great big wonderful man.'

The last was a phrase he had told her his mother had always used to his father. Every time Adrienne used it to him he wondered how much she meant it, though it always pleased him to hear it. She lifted her face to his. 'It's just . . .' she smiled, showing even teeth.

' . . .Oh, in a year from now, I want a *real* wedding with all my friends and family. I want it to be a really wonderful day.' She gazed imploringly at him. 'You know?'

He thought, silent, yes, of course she would. Who wouldn't want that? But he wanted too – things to be more concrete, her to be more solid about the thought of marriage. But perhaps he *had* just taken her by surprise. . . *So, waltz her round the park and tell her what she means to you!* a voice encouraged in his head as a second voice upbraided, *As if she didn't know.* He smiled guardedly, saying nothing, putting his big paws on her shoulders.

'I love you,' she said in a low whisper.

'Oh? And what about your "handle"? How does *it* feel?'

'Come downstairs and I'll put both hands on *your* handle. Then you'll see how it feels,' she breathed, giving him a big, cool, open, wet seal kiss. He took her by the hair and pulled her face back, looking at her.

'Oh, yeah? Then I want to walkie-talkie with you around the park.'

She backpedalled, squealing with delight as, grabbing up his towel he chased her angel body to the elevator.

Hand in hand, they strolled across Sheep's Meadow towards the skating rink. 'Someday I'd like to have babas,' he said. 'Your and my babas, well one anyway. A wee breadsnapper. It's one of the main reasons for marrying. Family. When you've been with someone for a very long time, it's what you usually do, the final act of love. And I love being with you, just being around you, hearing your laughter and kissing that face of yours. And I'm concerned for you, for what ails you, for your work and dreams, if you're happy, if your clothes suit you, if you're enjoying your dinner. All this is part of the love I bear you and all that makes you happy I long for. And I'm happiest when I see you happy because . . .' he measured out the words emphatically, '. . . you're my first priority. You, come, first. Before my father, even. My loyalty to you, my support for you are absolutes. For me there are objectives. Making your life as happy as I can, trying to do my best, most of the time, being loyal to you above all others, supporting you when you're down, shouldering the part of any burden you find hard and talking to you first about things of worry and concern, so others, near or strange, are not privy to the workings of our bond, our love for one another. That should be *our* mystery, belonging to us alone. And that, when we marry, is the unspoken troth I'll pledge you. Help me to keep it as I will help you. When I hurt, try to understand, when I err, remonstrate with me, if I stray, reprove and, if, going out the door, I ever once forget to kiss you, kick me with a reminder. Goes like this:- 'Hey you! Haven't you forgotten something?' She laughed and squeezed his hand, and he grinned at her. 'So, no more of your handles, OK?'

'No handles.'

He stopped her there. Overhead, eavesdropping leaves wagged and whispered, washing sun and shadow down upon his face and hers. She looked like Eve in Eden. She laughed again and her eyes blazed brighter than the music from the carousel blaring out 'The Last Time I Saw Paris'. 'I'll make you happy, and proud, you'll see.'

'Not more that I am now. You couldn't.' He nodded in the direction of the carousel. 'Wanna get married in Paris? We could have a wedding breakfast at Lipp' – the brasserie she loved in St Germain.

'No, no. Here, right here, Rick. Soon. Whenever you want. Oh, sweetie.' She stopped and looked at him long and fair. 'I love you. And I feel just the way you do.'

'OK, beloved, you're on,' he sang out. 'Let's go.' And arm in arm they tripped towards Fifth Avenue while the carousel, loaded with screaming poopers, barrelled out, 'If You Knew Susie'.

Nearing Folsom, he stopped. It was still there, in the little window. 'How would you like a long weekend at the lake?'

Her face lit up. 'Could we? Oh Rick, could we?'

'Well, it's almost your birthday isn't it? I thought it might be a nice present, along with this . . .' He turned her by the shoulders so she could see the thing for which he'd left the small deposit.

On display in the window of a bright boutique was a three-quarter length, figure-hugging, lilac dress, fashioned from the lightest, finest wool.

She caught her breath and stared. 'Oh, Rick. It's beautiful.'

'Well, don't just stand there,' he laughed. 'Go try it on.'

'Really?' she sparked.

'Really.' He browsed among the fashions until she emerged from the changing booth and stood, artlessly, before him. A child of nature. Woman and dress.

'You can't wear underthings in this,' she whispered urgently and stood back, breasts, belly and thighs tightly sheathed.

'Turn around,' he said. From her lovely shoulders, down her back and over that perfect, provocative bottom, the material hugged and contoured, breaking halfway down her buttocks to hang perfectly just below her calves. A nereid painted in lilac. 'I'd marry anyone in that,' he breathed into her ear.

'You'd look pretty silly in it, sweetie,' she bantered, skipping backwards to the booth.

'We'll take it,' he smiled to the beaming assistant.

'Doesn't she look heavenly?' she eulogized. 'Just breathtaking.'

'As long as you ain't Miss Piggy,' he thought, feeling sorry there and then for all the women in the world who couldn't wear it.

Upstairs in Folsom, she tried it on for real, pirouetting before the big mirror in the sitting room, hurtfully beautiful. Princess Aura. Ming's daughter, longing for Flash Gordon. A sudden rat-a-tat-tat at the door startled Rick. 'That's Jack,' he said brightly.

She caught hold of his arm, fingers gripping very tight, her eyes sharp and gleaming. 'He mustn't know we're getting married,' she whispered urgently and, seeing his expression, at once softened grip and voice. 'Not just yet, sweetie, that's all, so we can have our real wedding.'

'Oh, come on here, Jack's an old friend . . .' he began.

'Please, Rick.'

Blowing out a sigh, 'OK, Adrienne.'

Taking her hand from his arm, he moved to answer the insistent knock, swinging the door wide open. 'Jack.'

'Hey, big guy.' Hand outstretched, Jack breezed in. 'Good to see ya, pal. Just stopped by on the off chance.' Seeing Adrienne he spread his arms. 'Radski,' he laughed, using an informal derivative and kissing both her cheeks.

'Hi, Jack,' she smiled as he stepped back.

45

'Holy cow.' He grinned and shook his head. 'What an outfit. Goin' dancin'?'

Quickly, 'No, Jack,' she said, 'Rick just bought it for my birthday.'

'Knockout,' he admired. 'Just knockout. I wish ya the health to wear it Radski.'

Thanking him, she glanced sweetly at Rick. 'Guess I'll leave you guys to it while I go get changed.'

As she vanished into the bedroom, 'What an outfit!' Jack repeated. He looked at Rick. 'Real high-class hookers don't come better dressed than that, pal.'

Rick spluttered with laughter. 'Oh, come on, Jack!'

'No, no, seriously, I mean it, buddy. That is some piece of merchandise.'

While Rick broke open a bottle of Tokay, he asked after Susie, Broadway's half-Chinese sweetheart, listening as Jack relayed the minor dramas of the past few weeks. A gregarious, generous man, he reminded Rick of a slightly older John Garfield in *Body and Soul*. Charming, polite, he was easy to like with his broad smile, the polished teeth like gravestones. His nose was almost straight, just the merest hint of a hook, the eyes dark blue and the hair parted and greased back, Italian style. Years ago he had worn a Jimmy Connors fringe but Rick had made him get rid of it, and sweep it back. Result – The all-Italian guy. But it was the eyes you came back to. They could twinkle, crinkle, crease with laughter, but there was something else that showed at times. A cold cast that would flash a sudden warning. Not often used, but there it was.

Rick told Jack of their plan to go to the lake.

'When?'

'In about a couple of weeks, around mid-May.'

'Best time,' nodded Jack. 'Not too hot, not too crowded, and, as Adrienne appeared in shirt and jeans, 'Maybe me and Susie'll come up for the day and see what's cookin'.'

'That'd be great,' Adrienne said.

'Do they have a band up there?'

Rick frowned quizzically. 'Sometimes on a Saturday I think, why?'

Jack looked at Adrienne. 'Then you can wear that outfit,' he smiled. 'Watch a few of the old fossils retire with heart flutter from the dance floor when they realize what they're missing.'

Within ten days Alice was back, this time with Bill in tow. Adrienne sprang the news on Rick just two days before the arrival, saying that they would be staying for a long weekend. He had made a chicken curry in preparation and, on their entrance, was treated to his second sighting of the The Housebound Husband. The first had been at an overnight stay in Chicago while Rick and Adrienne were en route to the Rockies. Rick had taken them all out to dinner. Bill had not looked at him once. Rick was again amazed at how teensey he was. Tubby with a face that might have been given a tiny pinch at jaw and hairline by a giant thumb and forefinger, he could have measured hardly more than five foot three.

At dinner, wine was again refused by Alice with light condemnation. 'The ketones aren't good for you, you know.' During the evening and, indeed, the entire time they spent in Folsom, Bill never spoke to Rick once, nor ever once looked at him. To her credit, Adrienne did her best to bounce a conversational ball, but it was just three-way-pitty-pat.

Rick toyed with the idea of opening a bottle of something fierce, and swigging it from the neck before shambling to Bill's side to sit, breathing curried absinthe over him before slurring, 'How are things on planet Mongo these days? Same old fire and brimstone eh? Tell me, tell me, tell me' (drunken, low key, conspiratorial enquiry), '. . . er, do you . . . er, ding Ming's thing? You know? Get the old leg over? When's the next time? Can I watch?' Uproar! At his small private titter, two of the three glanced his way.

The word 'Mom', applied to Alice was taboo, a guarantee that she would suffer a broken-winded vapour, then an instant mild stroke. The title precluded her from being offered thirty-year-old leading lady roles. She was fifty-five or thereabouts. Therefore her father, to Adrienne, became Bill, Never Dad. It was Bill who offered, via Adrienne, to take them all to Sunday lunch to say thank you for the weekend digs, a lunch which produced for Rick neither word nor flicker of an eye from his prospective pa-in-law. The weekend closed, as it had begin with 'Mum's the word'.

On the Friday following that weird weekend, Rick picked up an early morning message Adrienne had left upon the coffee table on her way to Hunter College. *Could you meet Joe Alder in the Ginger Man at noon? (He says you know where it is). If you can't make it, he'll understand. He has a one-thirty midtown appointment.* Rick glanced at his watch. Quarter after eleven. He called Joe. No answer. He guessed what it would be about. The play-reading, and the pitch to mount an out-of-town production. Knowing he had no intention of doing it, Rick none the less showered, dressed, and copped a cab up Tenth to Lincoln Center and strolled across Broadway to the Ginger Man. It was hot. Not humid; just a good hot Gotham May day.

Twelve-o-five, at the bar, Joe was there and it was as he'd guessed. About the play. Thirsty, Rick ordered a beer, then said, 'Sorry Joe, I have to be in love with something if I'm going to do it.'

'I didn't think you would.' Joe couldn't hide his disappointment, 'But, I had to ask, you know? Between ourselves!'

'Sure,' Rick said. Then, as the bartender tuned the TV to some militaristic aerobics channel, 'Look, Joe, I hate it here. Let's go eat someplace. Wanna slide over to Rockefeller Center?'

'It'll be a zoo, Rick, and I have a one-thirty appointment.'

'I know,' Rick flashed Joe his crooked smile. 'We'll get a table,' he promised. 'With a sunshade. Right next to the fountain. Or I don't know Rosie.'

'OK,' Joe sighed, and they headed for Central Park West.

Passing Tavern on the Green, Joe said suddenly, 'How are things with Alice? She's staying with you, right?'

'Don't remind me,' Rick said dully. 'The woman is part of the fixtures and fittings. She's never away from the fucking place. If I hadn't met her husband, I wouldn't believe she had one.'

'God,' Joe said, 'I know exactly. She kept inviting herself to stay at my apartment. Time after time. Auditioning for parts half her age. At one audition they told her, "Sorry there's been some mistake. We're seeing people for the role of the mother in the afternoon." "Oh no no no no no, there's no mistake. *This* is the role I'm up for." Really weird. Sometimes I'd come home and not speak or be just plain rude, "This is my apartment, Alice. I need to live, to relax here." And she'd say, "Oh, I can just sleep *here*, in the corner by the fridge." ' He exhaled. 'She's something else. I have this partner, Jimmy Waterman, guy I was at high school with. About a year ago, Jimmy and I are out in the Mid-West with our own show for a couple of weeks or so, and Alice insisted we stay with her. I figure, why not? It's my turn. So we get to Chicago, and it doesn't take Jimmy five minutes. "This woman is totally nuts," he says. When we're introduced to Bill, I think to myself, I know him from somewhere. And then it dawns on me. This is the guy she was with in New York, two or three years back. I thought he must be her lover, because he was wearing a wedding ring. She had never mentioned anything about them being married. Anyway, we're given this room to share, quite comfortable, and there, on a chest, is a wedding photograph, obviously of Bill and Alice. Nineteen-fifty-ish. Nice photo. So next morning at breakfast I ask, "Is that your wedding picture in the room upstairs?" She becomes immediately hyper – "Picture? What picture? I don't know. There are so many pictures in this house. What time is it? Oh, I have an appointment." And leaves the room. Jimmy gives me the long stare. That first day we get back from the theatre earlier than expected, and there's a woman in the house with two young girls. Twins.'

'The Drone Twins,' murmured Rick, still dwelling on the wedding-ringed dwarf-husband.

'Who?'

'Claire and Sarah. Monotonic voices. They look like double Peppermint Patties from the *Peanuts* strip.'

'It's true,' laughed Joe, 'they kinda do look like that. Well, we've barely said Hello when Alice bundles them all out the door and off they go. "Are they family?" Jimmy asks. "No, no, no, no, no," ' Joe mimicked. ' "They're just friends. My little friends." That night we notice the wedding photo's disappeared.'

'The woman is Patrice, her eldest daughter,' Rick said. 'And the twins are her grandchildren. Come on, Joe, her next birthday cake has to come with a built-in sprinkler system.'

Joe screwed up a corner of his mouth. 'One afternoon they took us somewhere in the car, I forget where. Alice and Donna were yakking about something, when Donna suddenly said, "Oh Mom!" Instant silence. Alice became bent out of shape. "That word! Ooooh, that word! How many times have I told you don't ever, ever use that horrible, horrible word!" '

'What was Bill doing through all of this?'

'Nothing.'

'Tell me,' said Rick.

'Mom and mother are words which just cannot be spoken.'

'*Dites-moi, bébé,*' Rick grunted.

'Not even by Donna, who's the only child of theirs she admits to.'

'Then how does she explain the first four?' Rick laughed in disbelief.

'As "friends", and' Joe assumed his Alice tone again, ' "people who have passed through this house at various times." That's how she referred to Patrice.'

Rick stared at him, incredulous.

'They're all "friends". All except Adrienne. She's the odd one out. Alice told me she's the daughter of a close relative of Bill's – maybe his brother, who shot himself. Apparently, Alice took her in and became her legal guardian. Adrienne's her ward.'

'What?!!!'

'I'm telling you, Rick.'

They emerged into Central Park South, turning left to walk towards Fifth past the horse-drawn cab ranks. 'She wrote me this letter,' Joe said. Apparently she'd wanted to clear something up with me when last we'd met, but hadn't had the chance. First there was some stuff about her being Adrienne's legal guardian for a few years. Said she'd made some comment to you about Adrienne's father, but realized you didn't know because Adrienne shot her a meaningful glance and you looked amazed. She wasn't going to mention anything to me, but she thought she should clear it up 'cos if, in the world of showbiz, she's seen as a twenty-four-year-old's mother, there would be serious casting problems. It finished up saying something about her talking to an actress friend who plays parts ten to fifteen years younger than herself and who wouldn't dream of revealing her real age. Finally she says every woman in showbiz suffers from age discrimination. That was about it.'

Rick put his hands on the post of a stoplight and placed his brow against his knuckles. 'This is fuck-king pre-pos-ter-ous.' He straightened up. 'It's horseshit!' The light changed and they crossed the street. 'Total unmitigated horseshit!'

'I'm not saying I believe it, but Adrienne does look kind of different from the others,' Joe insisted.

'Yeah. She's better looking,' Rick said, suddenly aware he was raising his voice. 'Which is one reason I'm . . .' He was about to say, 'going to marry her,' but shut it down in time.

'Rick, I'm only—'

'Wait, Joe, wait.' Stopping in front of the Plaza Hotel, Rick drew a deep breath. Over Joe's shoulder he could see FAO Shwartz, its windows crammed with toys of all sizes, while in the little square between, a ghetto blaster blared as four black guys breakdanced to an applauding crowd. He exhaled slowly. 'Adrienne told me, long ago, there'd been a grandfather who'd blown his brains out with a shotgun. And that there was a cousin, I thought she said, who'd shot himself at eighteen. Now, if that's *her father*, he must have been married at just seventeen. And if all this is so, there's just one question I'd like to ask.' Rick stared evenly at Joe. 'Where's the mother?'

They crossed the street, turning past Van Cleef and Arpels and on down Fifth, Rick mute and far from happy. Halfway down the block, 'Joe,' he said, 'she's got five children, the eldest's almost forty. I've seen the photographs, with the kids all in a group. Holding spaniel puppies. That they are siblings, *all*, there is no doubt.'

'Something odd did happen though,' Joe said. 'Karen turned up that first week we were there. She had an exhibition of her paintings. She and Alice didn't hit it off at all. There was a very strained atmosphere in the house, like Alice didn't want her there, maybe because we were around, I don't know. Anyway, when we were alone one afternoon, I asked her, as nonchalantly as I could, about the family. But I guess I handled it rather clumsily, for she just wouldn't get into it other than to say, "Alice is definitely my mother," in a pissed-off sort of way that made you feel she'd been through all this before.' He paused. 'I never spoke to Bill much, but he and Jimmy got on quite well. They were both golfers, although when Bill said he didn't play anymore, there was a kind of wistful look in his eye. Jimmy said he felt the decision had been made for him. Anyway, we had to drive back to New York for a few days, and Bill asked him to bring his clubs along with him and he'd arrange a game with some of the guys at work.'

'What did Jimmy feel about Boring Bill?' Rick asked.

'He liked him,' said Joe, 'though they talked only generally. About work, and so on. Jimmy's a marketing man. I think he relaxed Bill, allowed him to expand a little.'

'And?'

Joe grimaced. 'He reckoned here was one unhappy man. Leading a life he didn't want to lead. The joke is, Alice is always going on about ecology, and here's this guy talking about his work at a mammoth industrial plant which spews all this shit into the atmosphere.'

At the Rockefeller Center, Rick guided Joe down the steps into the multi-restaurant area, towards his favourite corner, seeking and finding Rosie. She put them by the fountain, right under a broad, blue and white brolly, smiling as she took their order. Two salads, one glass of Chardonnay and an iced tea for Joe. Under the sluice of water that ran down the high wall, Joe took up where he'd left off. 'When Jimmy and I got back to Chicago, about a week later, Karen had gone. Donna was back in school, so we were given her room. That's where Jimmy uncovered all these photograph albums, and one morning we went through the whole lot. Masses of snapshots of the young Alice, smiling and bottle-feeding an array of infants. Jimmy said, "I'd like to write on each, 'Congratulations on the birth of your new friend'." ' Joe took a long sip of iced tea. 'I was spending most of my time at the theatre, but Jimmy was able to get in a few rounds of golf with some of Bill's friends. He said he got a quite different picture. Of a nice guy. A different person at his work. Hard working, well-liked, bright and intelligent.'

'If Bill's so bright and intelligent, how come he doesn't say something about what's going on?' Rick said. 'It's got to be an embarrassment to him.'

Joe pursed his lips. 'I think he just turns a blind eye.'

'If he does,' Rick said, 'he's . . .' He stopped. 'Or maybe . . .'

'Maybe what?'

'I don't know. Maybe it's just completely out of hand now.' Rick found himself thinking of a line from Anaïs Nin's *Diary of Henry and June*. It isn't strong women who make men weak, but weak men who make women over-strong. Alice had the family in her thrall. And the strange thing was, Rick knew she had no guts for confrontation. Like Adrienne, if push came to shove, she would run.

'I think he really loves this woman.' Joe stared at his plate. 'You know?' He looked up. 'Something must have happened with her in the Sixties. New freedoms, women's lib, all that. And here's this woman with five kids born over twenty years, the last in nineteen seventy. She can't always have been like she is now. Look at all those smiling pictures of the bottle-feeding. Maybe she was a good wife to Bill, and that's the memory he loves and cherishes. She stuck with him at the plant, went to Central America in the middle years, bore all those children. She's shown her loyalty. Now he's showing his. She made sacrifices, now it's his turn. You know what Buzz told me? It's the past that's hated. Not the family but the past. She sees them all going off and doing what she wishes she could do. But the world's changed and now she wants all that lost time over. Time has to stand still, and the years roll back so she can begin at the beginning. So no older children, no husband and no boring family life must be allowed to get in the way. I think *that's* the something that happened.'

Rick pondered. 'So that's why the facelift. So she could pursue these younger roles.'

'She had a lift?'

'Adrienne told me.'

'Wow! I thought her skin looked kinda tight.'

'As a frog's ass, Joe. And that's water-tight.'

For a moment they fell silent.

'And all these names she has,' Joe continued. 'Alice Rader, Alice Baker, Alice Gray. She's got as many names as children.'

'So if one isn't working, she can change her identity for the next audition,' Rick said.

'That's it,' Joe replied. 'Bill had a business dinner when we were there, but she wouldn't go.'

Again Joe mimicked her with his hands splayed out. ' "No, no, no, no, no, I never go any more. Men made passes at me under the table, so I always carried a hat-pin. To jab them with. And when they cried out, I'd ask, 'Is something wrong?' " '

'Jesus,' Rick breathed.

'The last night we were there she gave a party. More to impress us than to entertain, I think. Halfway through the evening, with Alice playing the star like mad, Jimmy said something that burst the bubble, and Bill actually laughed. Out loud. It was just like school. Bill was dismissed. Sent out of the room for laughing.'

'And he went?'

'Oh, yes. Right away. They do her bidding, Rick, all of them. They see it, that they're puppets, but they do it. Just jump at the pull of the strings.'

'Star-mother as dominatrix,' Rick murmured. 'Devourer.'

Joe glanced at his watch. 'Jeez Louise. It's almost one-fifteen. I have to get going. I'm gonna be late. Thanks for lunch. I'll call you soonest.' And, hopping between the tables, he was gone.

Rick left a good tip for Rosie before walking slowly back up the steps to Fifth Avenue. Lifting his eyes to the heavens, he saw the dark bronze sculpture of Atlas towering above him, the banded globe that was the earth set for aye upon his shoulders. 'I know just how you feel, Matey,' Rick called lightly upwards.

Back at Folsom he found Adrienne seated at the little oak dining table, spooning Häagen Dazs chocolate chip ice-cream out of a pint tub.

'Hi, sweetie. What did Joe want?'

'Me to do his play.'

'Are you going to?'

54

'No.'

'Oh, Rick, are you sure?'

'Yes. It's just not developed enough.'

'I think it could be really good. Why don't you ask him to make some changes and you'll think about it?'

'Maybe,' he murmured, pouring himself a glass of white wine from the fridge.

'Oh, my birth certificate arrived. Alice mailed it with her letter. I didn't tell her why I wanted it.' They needed it for the marriage papers. His hand froze in mid-pour. Shit! The birth certificate!

'Can I see it?' he asked, innocently.

'Sure.' She took the paper from the envelope. 'Here.'

He unfolded it with thumping heart. A hospital in Chicago, Illinois. Adrienne Louise Rader. Parents: Alice and Bill. A flood of relief.

She spooned down the last of her ice-cream. 'What do you want to look at my birth certificate for?'

'Just to make sure you're not lying about your age.' He winked and she smiled her chipmunk smile at him, coming to sit sideways on his lap. Wrapping his arms tight about her sweet hard body, 'You poor wee thing,' he whispered, but she caught the tiny charge of emotion.

'What's wrong, sweetie, what's wrong?'

He almost said it, almost told her, then bit his tongue.

Alarmed now. 'Rick, what's wrong?' The mud-greens trained upon his face. 'I want you to tell me what's wrong.'

He couldn't, fearing he'd hurt her, hurt himself, start something that couldn't be stopped. 'Nothing,' he murmured hoarsely. 'It's nothing.'

She opened up her legs and straddled him, bringing her face close to his. 'Tell me this minute.'

'It's just . . . sometimes . . .' he uttered the truthful lie, 'when I see your beauty, it takes me by surprise, takes my breath away . . . like the first time.' In a tremble, he began to say, 'I love you', and her mouth crushed out the sob of the last word as she held his head tight with her hands, tasting him, salt and all, her lips wet with passion as gently he undid her blouse.

Joe Alder rang sometime later. 'Is Adrienne there?' he asked, gingerly.

'No. I think she's up at Ruby's. Why?'

'It's you I wanted to talk to, Rick. I just wanted to make sure Adrienne wasn't around.'

'What's wrong?'

'Nothing's wrong. Well . . . depending on how you look at it. Rick, I found the letter, it's just as I told you and worse. . .'

Rick stopped him. 'Joe. I have some information for you.'

'Go ahead.'

'This afternoon I saw Adrienne's birth certificate. A hospital in Chicago, mother, father, dates, ages.'

A heavily pregnant pause. 'And?'

'Legal guardians can't have their charges' names put on US birth certificates with themselves created mother by some hospital official in Chicago.'

'Alice and Bill are her parents?'

'Alice and Bill are her parents.'

From the other end of the phone came a soft whistle.

Armed with her birth certificate and his passport, in the early part of the week they picked up the necessary documents and filled out the marriage details. Surrendering the papers, they waited, seated, with other soon-to-be-weds until their names were called, for the forms to be returned to them. Rick could see in the corridor all these faces. Unlikely looking duos, black, white, mixed, Hispanic, shifted nervously outside shoe-box rooms, waiting to be spliced, or garotted, he reflected. To judge by their complexions, some gave the impression they were the victims of arranged marriages, appalled by the choice of partner to whom they'd just been introduced, clutching wilted flowers.

Adrienne sat slightly apart from him, brooding. Earlier in the day he had told her they were having lunch at Pearl's Chinese Restaurant with Benny, his accountant, and that, naturally, Benny had to be privy to the goings on.

'Why? You promised.'

'I didn't promise anything. The only people I'm telling are my father and my accountant. He has to know, Adrienne. There are such things as income tax, bank business, benefits and non-benefits, all of which are altered by the state of marriage. If you didn't know that before, then you know it now. And if you don't want to go through with any of this, all you have to do is say the word, no one's breaking your damned arm.' Mad, he went into the bedroom and slammed the door, realizing as he did so, he had locked himself in. Now he would have to ask, from the depths of his anger, that she open it. Shit and derision. 'Why not just get married and be happy?' he shouted without meaning to.

'I am happy.' A muffled retort from the other side.

'Well you don't seem it, look it or act like it.'

'I am happy. It's just, I've told you, I want a wonderful day, I want us to have our own house, to have my family and friends to. Open the door, sweetie.'

Pause, 'I can't.'

'Please.'

'I can't. It's stuck.'

'Oh.' There was a push, a thud as she put her shoulder to it, then a thumping crash as the door flew open and she came skidding into his arms, falling to the floor with him as she began to laugh, and he began to laugh, as she kissed him, her darling girly-giggle reverberating inside his mouth.

4

L ATE SPRING MIDTOWN WAS splashed with yellow cabs, dollar-honking their way through the city. Benny was at the table nearest the door, almost abreast the little bar where Pearl herself often stood, Chinese, but too American to be inscrutable. Heavy crêpy curtains obscured the diners from outside view. The room was white, bright, bubbling with noise. A mild-mannered and gracious man, Benny took great pains over his work. His conscientiousness at times exasperated Rick to the point where he would enter the office and say, 'Don't explain anything. Just show me where to sign and then let's go eat.'

Chosen mostly by Benny, lunch was ordered. Rick watched, amused, as the businesslike folder was produced, Benny wetting the second finger of his right hand with his tongue before turning to the relevant pages.

His accountant had the most enormous ears Rick had ever seen on a man, like a giant fruit bat. His hair was knit close to his skull, and a gerbil's eyes could not have glittered more inquisitively. He was, Rick recalled his father saying of someone similar, 'Fourteen months old before they knew whether he would walk or fly.' Poring over the papers, Benny displayed a deceptively youthful ingenuousness as he sat backlit by the afternoon sun. 'Studying for his bar mitzvah,' Rick thought, and he smiled.

'I'd like to be the first to offer my congratulations,' Benny said. 'May you have a long and happy life together. Shalom.' He lifted his glass.

'Locheim,' said Rick, as he and Adrienne did likewise. They all drank. Then Benny got down to business. He went through what benefits there might be regarding taxes, consulting first Rick then Adrienne with his sharp accountant's eye, before going on to discuss the joint account he'd opened. Adrienne sat silent and expressionless throughout.

'So tell me,' Benny said at length. 'Where is the wedding to take place?'

'We're not sure yet.'

'Where are you going on honeymoon?'

'Probably Paris.' Rick looked at Adrienne.

She shrugged her shoulders.

'Let me speak to someone I know,' Benny suggested. 'I think he can make the whole thing easier and nicer. I'll call you, my friend.'

Rick thanked him and once more Benny lifted his glass. 'I feel very happy for both of you,' he said. 'May you prosper in all things. Again, Shalom.'

True to form, Benny called next day with the name of one Leo Werfeld. 'He's a nice guy and should be able to help. Anyway, give him a call.'

Rick promised, asking, 'Would he be able to put together a contract for me?' His first marriage had ended in ghastly publicity and endless wrangling.

'I'm sure,' said Benny. 'Talk to him about it.'

'OK. Thanks.'

A pause. 'Uh, Rick, was Adrienne feeling all right yesterday?'

'Yes. Yes, fine. Why?'

'She just seemed . . .' Another little pause. 'I don't know. She just didn't seem too happy to me.'

'No,' Rick said. 'She's quiet, Benny, that's all.'

'I guess she is, I guess that's it. OK. Call me soon will you, my friend?'

Leo Werfeld's office was spacious, with glass-fronted darkwood cabinets crammed with leather-bound tomes. Rick sat in a comfortable, antique-style armchair facing a huge leather-topped desk behind which Leo held sway, a modern Doge of Venice, framed by streams of light, searing between blind ends and curtain edges at the far wall and shafting down the room like quivering lasers, sealing Doge and visitor between their blazing tracks.

As they talked, this steady, calm, grey-suited sage, nodding behind heavy, dark-framed spectacles, effortlessly organized his world. A judge, a friend, would, in her chambers of leather and mahogany, perform the rites. All would be well. A restaurant, even, was close by, God's own, for the nuptial feast. A contract would be fairly struck to shelter both from unseen harm, 'Ah, yes indeed'. Jerome was summoned, a discreet and proper scribe, to sit with them between the shafts of light and set down the conditions. Should Adrienne decamp within a five-year span, then twenty-five per cent of Rick's earned holdings would be hers. When they parted company, Leo the Seer, Lord Oracle, insisted that upon the day he would himself appear as foremost witness, 'The *ancien régime* Johnny-on-the-spot,' he said.

Deaf to the thunderous roar of traffic, through the Gotham jam and jostle, down Madison, Rick floated in a serpentine of dreams, deathless and dancing through a wonder of summer, capering over the fields of Elysium, lost in the mists of love.

That evening he escorted Adrienne to P.J. Clarke's where, a little over five years ago, he had taken her on their first dinner date, after singing 'I Can't Give You Anything But Love, Baby' to her in a jazz club up the street, where she had giggled, sitting near the edge of the bandstand. He remembered clearly what they had ordered - chilli, cadillacs (the famous P.J. bacon cheeseburgers), and white burgundy, left untasted on the table as, suddenly, he'd belled the cat and told her that he loved her. Through all the agonizing that it took in the telling, Adrienne neither spoke nor moved but watched him with unblinking eye, as if in a trance. Her appetite quite banished by shock, discomfiture and embarrass-ment, he presumed, his own evaporated. He made apologies to her and to a thoroughly bemused waiter, who asked, 'You're not even gonna drink a little of the wine?' Rick paid the bill and they departed, the waiter gazing after them with slowly shaking head. Outside, cursing his rashness and stupidity, he hailed a cab for her when she stopped him, turning him to face her and, under the white globe light of P.J.'s, on the corner of Fifty-third and Third, she kissed him, for the first time. His first seal kiss, a real humdinger, wet, open, warm (it was winter) and worth a thousand abandoned dinners. Again she kissed him and again until, at last, they crossed the street, her hand in his, the touch a thrill beyond ecstasy.

Stopping just before Wyndham's Hotel, she led him up a flight of steps and on to a sort of public forum, guiding him behind a high green trelliswork fence, where they kissed softly and gently and deeply for minute after heart-racing minute. He was totally, completely, helplessly, in love. Spellbound. This was how it happened with him. He had known this kind of love a few times before, but never so big, so instant, so exciting as this. Yes, this is how it happened, and he was aware of the dangers. His ardour would not dampen, nor his fire fade. Indeed, he felt her moving in its flame, roasting in the blaze of it.

Now, as he looked at her across that self-same table five years on and more, it was exhilarating to feel that, not only was that fire still there, but burned hungrier and yet more fiercely. He smiled and she smiled back. 'Us desire you,' he said softly.

'Oh, sweetie,' she dropped her little, broken-fingered hand on his, 'Us desire you, too.'

He toasted her and talked of that first time; then, 'I wanted to come here tonight to tell you as I told you then how much I love you, how much you mean to me, how much your happiness means to me and how important your dreams are to me, and their fulfilment. I want everything for you that you would wish yourself, but . . .' He stopped and took a drink, watching her eyes flicker at him in the dim light.

'What, Rick?'

'I don't want you to marry me if there's the slightest doubt in your mind. That you may not be sure somehow it's what you really want.'

'I'm sure.' She regarded him squarely.

'I still have as strong a love now as I did back then in this very room. Stronger even.'

'So do I. Just the same. Nothing's changed.'

'Yes,' he said, 'yes it has.' She looked at him, frowning slightly. 'I don't know if you know it, or sense it, or whatever, but there are times when you, seem to . . .' He paused, wondering how to phrase it, staring unseeing at the blackboard with its chalked menu, letting his eyes drop to the chequered tablecloth before going on. 'Kind of drift away from me, recede somehow, ebb, separate, like there was no spark or sparkle of excitement in me for you, that I'm strong on security but short on thrill, a doll you can keep and play with in your room and, at other times, find tiresome.' He mentioned the 'handle' episode, the dress with Jack, the lunch with Benny, not calling him on the movie. 'Now all these may seem niggling little things but they worry at me, make me feel that you don't have concern enough for me.' He tilted up his head to find her eyes level, steady, reassuring.

'But Rick, I do. When I say I love you I mean it. I do love you. I do want to marry you. I do want to have our child. I've told you about not wanting people to know we're married. It's not about not wanting to be married to you, it's that I want a wonderful day with my friends and family. We can marry now and have a proper wedding next year when there's time, so let's just go ahead. That's all it is. If I was quiet in Pearl's the other day, its just that I'm not really into all those figures and stuff and I'm not gonna sit and pretend I'm in raptures.' In a hurt tone, 'And you do sparkle for me, you know that. I feel the same for you but I'm five years older than I was when we met. I've changed, of course I've changed – I'm not so girlish, not young like that any more – but I love you, you big dummy, and that's never changed.' At that, two broken little hands reached out in affirmation.

The evening, warm and wonderful, strayed into shadow only at the mention of the contract and his conversation with Leo. He steered away from it at once, deciding to deal with it when he had the papers in hand. 'Blithe,' he sighed happily, 'I feel blithe,' as they strolled over to the West Side up Fifty-fourth. Almost at Seventh, they stopped.

'What?' she asked.

'Don't you know?'

'No. What?'

He had not been past since it closed, had expected a boarded-up shell of a building, but the empty space shocked him like the passing of a friend. He stared at the brick coloured carpet of rubble, all that was left of a palace of jazz. 'Jimmy's,' he said softly, leading her over the broken stones to where, he was sure, the bandstand once had stood.

'Oh. Was this it? Was this Jimmy's?'

'Yes,' he said softly, as though words might drown a far-off ragtime strain and memory of Dixie.

'Yes, this was Jimmy's.'

At Jimmy's he had sung impromptu with the best jazzmen in all America. Where two famous horn players, one black, one white, had thrilled him with their music and their words. Leaving the place one night, he was stopped by a hoarse voice and turned to see Roy standing alone outside the door. 'Hey, ever thought of making a record?'

'No.'

'Well, you should. You sound good, man.'

It had bowled him over and his heart had leapt as high as the praise he did not know how to accept.

'Ya oughta do somethin' with that voice of yours,' Roy continued. 'I'm tellin' you, you sound good!' They were wonderful words from men who never flattered. Actors would flatter, but never men like these, and Rick felt thrilled to bits, heavens to Betsy, for music was his first love, always.

'If music be the food of love, make mine a foxtrot on toast,' he announced to a smiling Adrienne, then, stretching out his left hand, 'Suicide,' he murmured. 'He always worked this end of the bar.' He told her the story.

Suicide Charlie was known by no other name. Lean, hatchet-faced, monosyllabic, he was a curmudgeon who had had an endless running battle with the floor waiter – Phil the Greek – whom he affected to detest. His pet phrase, uttered in a dry, long-suffering rasp at each evening's end, was, 'All ashore, goin' ashore.' Underneath, though, Rick suspected a soft centre, but even had there not been, he liked him anyway. Long since dead, Suicide Charlie had been a character. Rick, curious, once asked Phil how he'd acquired the nickname.

'Oh, Charlie,' he had laughed. 'Well, Charlie liked to gamble, liked to play the horses you know? One time, when he was young, he lost a fair amount and couldn't come up with the dough so a collector was sent to the bar where he worked who told Charlie if he didn't have the money in twenty-four hours he'd better commit suicide. Now Charlie was the favourite bartender of one Cockeye Dunne, who happens to be sitting at the bar that night. Cockeye Dunne and a guy called Brennan were famous Irish gunsels of the day – Dunne later went to the chair, ya know, jokin' with the priest to the end about the high cost of electricity.' Phil grinned at the memory of the well-worn story. 'Well, Cockeye turns to the collector and says, "Who the hell are you?" The collector says, "Mind yer own business," at which point Cockeye pulls out a gun, sticks the barrel right up this guy's nose and says to Charlie, "You pay him one goddam nickel and you'd *better* commit suicide, Charlie." Then, to the guy who's staring literally down the barrel, nearly as cockeyed as Cockeye, "You. You ever come back here, you're a dead duck. Now beat it." So it was Suicide Charlie from then on.'

'And he never paid?' asked Rick.

'Never,' said Phil, laughing. 'Not if Cockeye Dunne told ya not to. This was Brooklyn in the old days, Rick, ya know?'

It was dark in the levelled space, only the lights from the parking lot splashing on to the street as he sang, 'I Can't Give You Anything But Love, Baby.' And they danced, her head on his shoulder, his cheek smooth against hers, oblivious of the jagged ruin under their feet.

5

O N THE BUS TO the lake, she had slept all the way. How different her face looked in repose from the face which had frozen at the sight of Leo's contract dropped on the Folsom dining table not two days before. He had tried to explain it as security for both of them. She sat in silence, not even looking at the paper.

'I went through something once,' he began. 'The shit, the rancour, the malice, the poison. I never want to experience that again.'

'Well, that was then. This is now. Why can't we just trust each other?'

'Because I've heard those words before.' He had too.

'Not from me.' Her voice quavered. She was near to tears. 'It's just so dirty.'

Two unhappy faces, still as stone, bent over that which lay between them, like Pandora's box. 'Marriage is so beautiful,' Adrienne said, 'so sacred that to have to sign something like this takes away all the trust.' She faltered and the tears broke. He picked up the typewritten sheets and slipped them back in the envelope.

'It's OK, it's OK,' he said, very gently. 'We'll just go ahead and get married and I'll tell them to forget the whole thing.'

She looked up, eyes smeared with tears.

'No. No, I'll sign it. I'll sign anything you want.'

'I don't want you to sign anything,' he said.

She stood up and hugged him, her wet cheeks leaving little damp patches on his shirt.

'Oh, Rick. Trust me. I wanna live my life with you. I want to be so proud of us. You'll see!'

The bus shuddered over a pothole and she stretched her body in sleepy protest. Listening to her gentle breathing, he remembered her words, 'Marriage is so beautiful, so sacred. Trust me. I want to be so proud of us, proud, so proud.' Only no one is to know we're married. Now that's real All–American proud. Rick looked out the window at serried ranks of trees, marching up rolling hills into farthest distance. 'Not long now,' he said in a gentle whisper.

So, the pretence had to be kept up for a year. Why not then wait for a year? Why not make it September or spring? No, she wanted to do it now, so too did he. There was a lot at risk for him, Rick thought, as they rumbled through the Adirondacks towards the Stone Resort. So why? Why risk it? Why not get out now, cut his losses, sling his hook and go? Becoming part of Adrienne's family wasn't exactly North America's most thrilling prospect, especially after hearing what Joe Alder had had to say. He sighed. Well, wasn't it George Eliot who'd said 'marriage is like an exploration of pleasures and pain and an abundance of someone else's relatives'? But for all the persuasive arguments against, he felt, as he always had, that Adrienne was worth the candle. Underneath it all, she had the strength, that, in the end, she would come through for him. As she had over Ming and Mickey at the start.

From a tower window, Rick and Adrienne stared out at a beauty that seemed to belong to them alone. The great stone building at the lakeshore crowned above the splendour of a deep green forest panorama sweeping away south as far as the eye could see. Northwards and eastwards loomed conifer-clad crags, while from the small chapel across the rustic bridge, past the blooming rosebeds and stables, broad meadowlands fell away to the west. Summer in its youth. Her still, angelic profile gently edged behind him out of sight.

> *And by came an angel who had a bright key,*
> *And he opened the coffins and set them all free.*
> *Then down a green plain, leaping, laughing they run,*
> *And wash in the river, and shine in the sun.*

They competed at tennis, putting, paddle tennis and a funny quoits-like game played with red and black slates pushed by wooden sticks up a numbered concrete pathway. More often than not, he won. More often than not, she was silent. During play, by the lakeside, even at mealtimes, she seemed to retreat into a world of self. She won the women's section of a short mountain race while he photographed her. But she would not swim across the lake with him, something she had always prodded him into doing with her before. Nor would she dive for him as she had, gladly, in the past, then swim quickly back to the teak decking, where lobster people sunbathed, to kiss and talk and laugh with him. Some lively lines of Betjeman's seemed bloodless in recall.

I see the lake, running with light, beyond the garden pine,
The lake whose waters make me dream her mine,
Up to the top board, mounting for my sake,
For me she breathes, for me each soft intake,
For me the plunge, the lake and limbs combine.

Their love-making alone remained the same, quiet and unhurried. Sometimes strong, at other times gentle and prolonged, his finger rotating round her little button as, silently, she strained for orgasm. The nine am rule was still in force, and sometimes he'd imagine the loving was endured, taken under sufferance. But, if she ever felt that, she never showed it. Like a magnet, she drew him to her. A silent force, she awaited him in an attitude of total sexual surrender, legs open, mouth ready for the kiss, lending him her body, her being. Her eyes watched him throughout. Watched him with that unfathomable smile. And when it was over, it was she who was finished with him. Until the next time.

After their tête-à-tête in Clarke's she was again, it seemed, remote and drifting. But he was determined not to ask any more questions, not to disturb his precarious universe. What further could be, would be, said? She'd given him her pledges there in Clarke's. That should content him. Perhaps she, like Rick, was mulling things over, taking final stock.

Late that evening, leaving her asleep, he walked the track that hugged the waters of the long, black mere, along a path, deep darkened by the leafy branches spreading wide from overhanging trees. At the pebbly beach where sometimes fishermen stood to cast their lines along the deepish banks at noon, he stopped still in a dangerous moonlight. Words rippling through his head, mirroring the winking pulse along the darkling shore. *What beckoning ghost, along the moonlight shade / invites my steps and points to yonder glade?*

Rounding the corner he saw the lights, so close now, of the Stone Resort. The moon, illuminating his watch dial, showed him it was midnight. Counting the floors he tried to figure out which room was theirs, thinking on, *Flaxen hair, green eyes and lilac dresses / A June bride / Except, no one must know we're married*. Mounting the wooden steps toward the doors, he gave a last look to the silvered lake, then to the sky. One cloud slid like a long knife across the high moon. If it should go wrong . . . June and lilac bring me hope.

On their last day, Jack and Susie arrived, changing in Rick and Adrienne's room before descending to the lake to sunbathe. Rick gazed around at the shining waters, the trees, the holiday people, the towering crags, listened to the splashings, the call of waterbirds and the laughter of floundering bathers in the merry merry month of May. Again refusing to dive or swim with him, within minutes Adrienne slipped into the water, stroking towards a moored raft where she lay on her back, staring at the cloudless sky, the sole inhabitant of her little island. When, sometime later, Jack and Rick swam out and heaved themselves aboard, she rose immediately, plunged in and made back for the shore.

'Something I said?' Jack called out as she cleft the water.

As he turned back towards Rick, smiling wryly, the two men were suddenly caught, eyeball to eyeball. It was an instant of dead giveaway where all Rick's insecurity and agony of doubt were revealed. He looked away towards the stone cliffs which reared in splendour above the dark trees at the far edge of the lake. 'Beautiful here, isn't it?' he said, at the same time thinking, 'You fatuous idiot!'

The raft undulated as Jack walked over to him, and gripped his arm for a moment. 'Sure is pal, sure is.' Then, 'Guess I'll take Susie for a walk, I'll see you in a while.'

Rick watched as his friend powered away in a swift, easy crawl. He sat down on the raft, legs akimbo like a baby in playpen. Seeing Jack and Susie stroll off into the trees, he had an almost irresistible longing to run after them, to blurt it all out. 'Listen. I want to marry

68

Adrienne but I can't. The answer's no. I'm going to drive with you back to the city tonight. It's all over. I'll explain later.' But then his eyes fixed on Princess Aura, anointing her body with oil. Sending him salutation with a single wave before she lay down by the sparkling waters. And he knew he never could run away like that.

At one, they ate alfresco in a little hollow close to the resort where many salads with meats hot and cold were set out on buffet tables under tall trees. The afternoon was spent playing doubles, which they lost, and on the putting green where Adrienne emerged a worthy winner. Later they played baseball catch, Adrienne imploring Jack to, 'Show me how to throw like a man.'

Dinner, for Rick and Jack at least, was a spirited affair, many tales, much laughter, the day ending with a twilight lakeside walk before Jack and Susie drove off down the long and curving driveway. As the engine note receded, Rick turned her face up to the moon and looked at her in the gathering dusk. Her features sparkled with the merest dusting of mother of pearl, while, catlike, half hidden under heavy lids, the wanton eyes shone, smoky, dreamlike, ghosty. 'I love you, you great big wonderful man.' Her voice was low and throbbing. In a stillness heavy with the fragrance of eventide, under a brilliant mantle of stars, she closed her eyes and parted her lips. 'Kiss me,' she whispered.

As soon as they got back, he fixed their wedding date with Leo, and she hit Rick with a real curveball.

'I have to be back in the city on the seventeenth.'

For a full five seconds, Rick stared at her. 'What the hell for?'

'I promised the school I'd be a counsellor for the kids' class this summer. The usual guy's going on vacation.'

'Well, tell them you've changed your mind.'

'I've tried. I can't get out of it. There's no one else. I promised them.'

'But . . .' he did a depressing sum, 'that only gives us eight days for a honeymoon, including travel.'

'I know and I'm sorry, sweetie, but we'll see each other back here and we can go to Paris later in the year. She looked at his crestfallen face and ran to put her arms round him. 'Oh, Rick, we'll have the best eight-day honeymoon anyone ever had.'

★

'Zip me up?' Half dressed himself, he stepped out of the closet and did what she asked, burying the catch of the zipper under the lining seam at the neck. 'Thanks, how do I look?' she breathed.

'Brighter than the day. It is the east and Juliet is the sun. Arise fair sun and kill the envious moon who is already sick and pale with grief that thou, her maid, are far more fair than she.'

She feigned a blushful shyness. 'Alas, sir, how shall I reply?'

'Nay, and thou knowest not, wench. I must speak for thee. My bounty is as boundless as the sea, my love as deep. The more I give to thee, the more I have, for both are infinite.'

He kissed her and she murmured in his ear, 'You clever sweetie. How do you know all that?'

'One of the benefits of a university education,' he whispered in return as she punched him playfully in the chest.

'Don't forget to put your pants on,' she giggled.

'I'd get married in a puce jockstrap and lilac fur boots if necessary.'

She laughed. 'It's just necessary you get dressed.' Then, pointing at the bedside clock, 'Come on, Rick. Look at the time.'

Following instructions given by Leo, half an hour later they stood outside the judge's residence, Rick baking in tie and blazer in the fierce June heat, Adrienne, sheathed in lilac, fingers in his palm, cool against his. Mounting the half-dozen steps to the portico, the push of a polished brass bell summoned a shape they could barely make out through the etched glass-panelled door with its iron grille. 'The Château d'If,' Rick thought, as the doors swung back and the floating shape became woman, who, neatly dressed in grey, led them through a quiet hallway to the appointed place where Leo and her honour the judge, awaited them.

After the briefest of introductions, they repaired to an inner sanctum accompanied by a fresh-faced, grey-flannelled clerk, press-ganged from some office desk to be a second witness. It was exactly as Leo had described – tooled leather, mahogany, a polished Princeton cabin hidden at Manhattan's edge. Leo and fresh-face took up their positions to the right, in front of them, and as the judge moved to her desk and picked up the ritual book, Rick realized he was standing on the wrong side, on the left where

Adrienne should have been. About to say so, he was pre-empted by the judge's opening remarks.

'This is a very solemn moment and the words and undertakings that you are about to give to one another should not be spoken or given lightly.' Rick found it difficult to look at Adrienne directly with Leo and young grey-flannel sitting in his eyeline like a pair of pissed-off tailors longing for five o'clock.

He heard his own and her 'I do', then the famous line ending in 'A ring is given and received.' It took just a second to sink in. Oh, fuck my old granny's boots! Pants he was wearing, hadn't forgotten. Ring, there was not. 'Urh,' he said and the judge's head snapped up.

'No ring?' she accused.

'No. Er sorry, afraid not. Forgotten it.'

He felt the ghastly shame of being exposed in front of the class for not doing homework. Wringing a sparkler from her hand, the judge passed it over. As Rick took it, he spotted Leo's stone-grey eyes snap like camera shutters in a mini-second to record 'JERK'. He placed the ring upon Adrienne's finger thinking, 'Wrong side, no ring, JERK, what next?' Imagined headlines above his mugshot in that stupid naval blazer, 'Seafaring man held in theft of priceless gemstone. Arraignment expected soon. Unknown tailors to testify. Fledgling lilac ape-girl disappears, key witness last seen swinging from branch to branch in Battery Park. Happy New Year.' All it needed now was Ming, with extra-terrestrial cause and impediment, to zap through the nuptial doors, screeching she was forty years too young to be his mother-in-law. Christ, he hadn't thought of that. She was now his mother. If word got out, she'd have a bilateral cerebral. Oh well, those whom God hath joined together, let no Ming put asunder.

What remained of the ceremony passed without mishap and Rick invited both Leo and the judge to an impromptu wedding lunch. With these two strolling on ahead, Rick stopped with Adrienne under a broad-leaved tree. Smiling naughtily from behind, hands on her shoulders. 'You belong us now,' he whispered.

Virtually tearing herself away, she spun to face him. 'It's going to take more than a ring and piece of paper to keep me with you if I don't want to be.'

'Come on,' he said. 'It was a joke.'

'You don't joke about things like that,' she said and walked on.

He knew she didn't mean it. Perhaps she felt she'd surrendered her independence. Her life had always been her own with Rick, of that there could be no doubt. But maybe that was it. He thought, as he caught up with her, he'd talk to her later, lay any fears she had to rest.

The restaurant Leo had suggested could not take them, but a second close by did. Italian, it was cool inside and they sat at a round table in the middle of the marble-paved floor, Adrienne edgy and unsmiling as she was introduced to the maître by the judge as Mrs Neilsen for the very first time. The waiter was slow in arriving to take their order. Leo nattered away discreetly with the judge, leaving the happy couple to savour their first few married moments.

'I can't stay long,' Adrienne murmured. 'I have a workout at three.'

He sat open-mouthed, then forced a smile. 'Come on. You're kidding.'

'No, Rick. We leave for Paris the day after tomorrow. This is the last chance I'll have to work out.'

'Adrienne,' he breathed, 'This is our wedding day.' Which was as far as he got for, at that moment, the waiter appeared.

She barely touched her pasta and refused dessert. When the bill came, Leo wanted to spring for the meal but Rick wouldn't hear of it. 'Thanks for everything,' he said. 'And,' he smiled to the judge, 'thanks to you for the kind loan of a ring.'

'That's not the first time it's happened, I can tell you.' Everyone laughed except Adrienne.

They shared a cab with Leo, and it was not until they were outside Folsom that Rick was able to ask, 'Why didn't you tell me?'

'What, sweetie?'

'That you'd be bouncing your ass around a gym at three o'clock on your wedding day, that's what, sweetie.'

She changed like lightning, then, off to collect her bike, 'Oh,

Rick,' soothing, in a hurry, 'I'll be back before nine. We can go out then.' She put her arms through the loops of her gym bag. 'I love you. You great big wonderful man.' She gave him a smacking kiss then vanished until nightfall, while he sat alone in Folsom, bursting with incommunicable news.

Wandering into the bedroom, he slipped off his jacket and tie. Her wedding dress lay on the bed. Going to hang it up, on an impulse he pressed the fabric to his cheek and at once began to dance, waltzing through hall and sitting room, to stop finally before the mirror, still clasping the lilac softness to him, while his missus, the lilac ape-woman, somewhere in the sweating city swung from bar to bar. Maybe I'll go swing from bar to bar, he thought. After all, wasn't that what people did on their wedding day, made merry, sank a few? Laying the dress down gently on the sofa he went to the fridge. His shoulders sagged. Not one refrigerated swig. Not even a beer. Her words in the leafy shade wafted back to him. *It's going to take more than a ring . . .* What ring? He smiled ruefully as he saw again the look on the judge's face. He hadn't looked to spend the day this way. Alone. Not unhappy. But not happy. Preoccupied. *Pas seul.* And you shouldn't feel that on your wedding day. Should you? He wound the windows open wide, sat at the piano and began an old New Year's song, his wedding present to the whole of Folsom. In a deep sonorous voice, slowly he sang, 'We have no beer / We have no beer today / We have no beer / But we know where to get it. . . The phone rang. It was Jack. 'Hey buddy. Great day, huh?'

'It sure is,' Rick said.

'What's up? Takin' it easy, pal?'

'Yeah,' he answered. 'Yeah Jack, I'm just taking it easy.'

Chicken, he thought they'd eaten that night, around nine. In a place she took him to. Where she'd laughed when the frozen mushy Daquiris she'd ordered had half paralysed his sinuses.

They had a pre-Paris dinner the following night at Mitchell's, a fish restaurant in SoHo. Just Rick, Adrienne, Jack and Susie. They'd set out to walk from Folsom, the girls stepping out ahead, Rick and

Jack following just behind. 'What a night I had on Friday, pal,' Jack murmured from the side of his mouth.

'What happened?'

Jack rubbed at his head. 'I'm tendin' bar in Jimmy's disco out in Queens. It's gettin' near closin' time, the place is thinnin' out when these two guys walk in. Arab-lookin'. Loungin' at the bar. Real arrogant, one of 'em dead pushy. Drinkin' Coke and lookin' around like they own the joint. The pushy one takes a shine to this blonde who's sittin' over in the corner with her boyfriend. Chick was beautiful, Rick. Tall, great set o' knockers on her, and the pins . . . boy!' Jack smiled. 'Could have gone for her myself, pal. Anyway, when the boyfriend goes to the john, this Arab goes over and starts chattin' her up – wants her to dance with him, starts tryin' to pull her to her feet at the moment the boyfriend returns and tells him to get lost. The Arab guy turns nasty, shoves him down in his chair, and the geezer jumps right back and knocks him on his ass. Suddenly, the second Arab slams down his glass and moves like greased lightnin', and I get it in one. This is the minder. Big fuck, Rick, and fast. Before I can call Jimmy, he's right in there with Tony, his partner, and two of the bouncers on the door. It takes three o' them to finally get a hold of the minder, while Jimmy half-nelson's Casanova through the foyer, who's screamin' out how he could buy and sell the place and what he's gonna do to them for this. A minute later, at the bar, "I'm up in the office", Jimmy tells me, "and I get a buzz from the door. Two guys don't wanna pay full admission 'cos it's late. I say fuck 'em, they have to pay. One of 'em gives a lot o' mouth – says he owns half of Iran or somethin' – but they're not drunk so they let 'em in. I have the feelin' I'd better keep an eye on 'em for a while and sure enough, I was right.' Jack paused, raising his voice against the roar of a passing truck. 'I'm just about to call last drinks when one of the bouncers runs in. Tells Jimmy they're on their way back. Five of 'em now, from out a white limo in the parking lot, and two of 'em have sticks or metal bars, he couldn't be sure. Jimmy's on his feet before the geezer's through talkin'. "Gimme the bats, Jack," he says. We always keep a few behind the counter,' Jack informed Rick. 'Just in case o' trouble. I lay hands on three of 'em and Jimmy says, "Here," and gives 'em to the bouncer. "I'll need you too, Jack," he says, and in fifteen seconds we're out on the steps. Three bouncers with three bats, Jimmy, Tony and me. They're about thirty yards from the door when Jimmy yells, "Go," and the three bat-boys go after 'em, with Jimmy, me and Tony followin' fast behind. One look was all it took, pal, before they each did a Carl Lewis back to the limo, without a blow being struck.' Jack ran his fingers gently through his hair. 'Until,' he said, 'the mouthy fuck picks up a rock and throws it. I duck, but the fuckin' thing hits me in the side o' the head.' Jack's eyes darkened. 'It's been a bad night, Rick. Down on the usual attendance, and the tips real low. Now here's a whack on the nut into the bargain. While the little rat still has the door open, I grab a bat and with one swat I smash the side window. They're all screamin' at the driver, but before he can get it in gear, I crack the windshield with one pop and shatter it and the bat with the second. Three home runs, buddy. Then off they shoot with a squeal of tyres to wherever they're goin'. Fully air-conditioned!'

As they closed on their partners near Mitchell's, Jack whispered, 'Don't whatever you do mention this in front of Susie. She'd go fuckin' nuts and I'll never hear the end of it.'

In the restaurant they sat at the corner table in front of a cabinet full of silverware, an antique pendulum clock ticking away on the wall above their heads. Both women were quiet. Susie reserved, serene, her sweet, mild, oriental face's soft complexion and dark eyes framed with shining, jet black hair. Sipping at some newly opened wine, he thought back to Jack's Queens episode.

Jack's father had been a hard working man who now eked out a living after suffering a debilitating heart attack that, over the years, had impoverished the family and made him bitter and angry. All his hopes were rooted in Jack ('Sonny Boy' he called him), and Jack knew that it hurt his father that he was not getting a foot in the door. Modelling and slinging shots until three in the morning in a mammoth club in Queens were bringing in some bucks but it was tiring work and it was small potatoes. It would have devastated Jack to know what none of them at the table knew that night, that his old man was as good as dead already. Only twenty short weeks to live. That was the damnable thing about the dreaded, it was so silent as it stole upon you.

Jack raised his glass. 'Have a great time over there you two. I only wish we could be there wit' ya'.

Susie looked across the table. 'Yeah, I hope you have a great holiday, Adrienne.'

'Oh, thanks, thanks. I'm sure we'll have a good time, it's really beautiful there right now.'

Jack took a swig of his amoretto. 'Are you still gonna get that machine, pal?'

Rick had been talking about picking up an exercise machine they had in Macy's and taking it to Europe. It was a good machine. Jack had one. 'I can bullshit my way on to the plane with it, we've got first-class tickets. But how do I get it to Kennedy? It's too big for a taxi.'

Jack thought. 'I can bring the jeep into town, ya know? We'll tie it on the top. I got some rope.'

'Are you sure?'

'Come on, anythin' for you Ace.' Jack winked at Adrienne. 'Then he's got no excuse for not beefin' up that lean bod o' his. You can stand over him, makin' sure he works out every day, right Radski?'

'Right,' she said quietly.

Jack beamed. 'You'll come back a moose, Ace. Have to watch how we talk to ya.'

They strolled home from Mitchell's side by side, her hand not in his, joined yet out of joint. Rick looked at Jack and Susie out in front, hands clasped and swinging down the lane. That's how we should be, he thought, aching to chime with happiness and whisk the three of them into the local watering hole to announce the nuptials to all and sundry, breaking open flagons of the best, cannikins a-clink, cheered with revelry and song. Instead, here they were strolling back through the Village to the 'Dead march in Saul' and there was something he couldn't keep pace with, something diminishing, fading out of sight.

6

THEY ATE BREAKFAST on the plane, Adrienne asking for tea and Rick sinking a Buck's Fizz. While she was in the bathroom, the seatbelt sign went on and the captain's voice informed that they were passing over Gay Paree. Rick craned over her seat to peer out the portside window. He could see the winking ribbon of the Seine on this bright morning, and scanning wider found it – there – so tiny, like a small black toy that might spill out with the contents of a box of Shreddies. La Tour Eiffel, where, once upon a summertime, some five years since, they'd sticky-kissed at its turret-top, then, eschewing the elevator, dizzied down the great iron helter-skelter to dance back to the streets of Paris. The Rodin Museum, which she'd loved best of all, and Closerie des Lilas, where Rick loved to take her to dine. Inside and out. And – oh! – after the Louvre, the sole and turbot lunch at Lipp-on-Sunday (upstairs where not so many went, yippee), started off by a rich crab salad washed down with chilly, earthy fragrance of a vin d'Alsace.

Hailing a taxi at Charles de Gaulle, off they sped towards the city. As they neared the avenue Foch, the Arc de Triomph, Rick sat up. The gateway to Paris! There, at the magic turn into Champs-Elysées, Fouquet's, the famous café restaurant, where soon the bourgeoisie would gather for millefeuilles and coffee, lounging in cane armchairs upon the sidewalk, while round the corner, down its flank on avenue Georges Cinq, alfresco tables soon would be dressed up for lunch, white linen blazing a reflection from the climbing sun. Across the wide thoroughfare, hidden away in rue Chateaubriand, Atala, a hotel they'd stayed at once. The enormous twenties bathroom with its antique fittings. And that sudden surprise view of high-walled garden, always deserted. No, wait. Once he'd seen a woman there, paper-thin, face obscured under a white and broad-brimmed summer hat. Standing alone by a wrought-iron chair, holding a single rose and sipping at pale wine. Remembering a love? In a secret garden. There was one, too, at the other place he'd taken Adrienne to stay – at l'Abbé de St-Germain. Dix, rue Cassette. Oh, those musky morning fucks, before the arrival of café complet. The green-year days all to themselves in the wide-awake walkable city, stopping for lemon-crêpes at little kiosks, with the bonus of a Grand Marnier in your own wee glass, before, maybe, a movie, then over to l'Opéra and Café de la Paix, *real* French bourgeois (steak tartare and salade niçoise prepared at your table) and where there were no garçons. Only women. *Très serieuses* in black, with white cuffs and collars. All looking like that English actress with the French name. Professional matrons, gliding under cloud-borne cherubim blowing silent trumpets in a sky-blue ceiling garlanded with painted flowers. And a tapdance away, down the boulevard, a late summer sun dwindling down on sidewalk cafés, tubs full-fat with ice and oysters. Ricard, Kier, and Deux Magots. Gingham-tabled bistros (memory of one near Centre Pompidou, where once a cracking time was had, the reason for it quite forgot).

Paris. The sight, the breath, the smell of her. Sexy, *bébé méchant*. The pair of them had slept half the day away but the city was warm and sunny still, when, near to his home, they stood upon the Pont Neuf, catching the babble of excitement rising up from the tourists cruising on the stream beneath, pointing Paris landmarks each to other. Wordlessly, they wandered hand in hand until they came to Notre-Dame. A sidewalk café, drinks, then on by alleyways they knew so well, and into St-Germain. On the way, he stopped her by the picture window of a pâtisserie. Shining glass shelves crammed with every imaginable sweetmeat. 'Look,' he said. Rick watched her eyes grow wide with Tiny Tim longing and she turned to him with a little wounded moan. Why can't she moan like that when I put my cock in her? he thought. Lo, the joyful crumpet sounds.

'Oh Rick. Can we?' she began.

'They're just closing up, Adrienne and anyway, we're on our way to dinner.'

'Oh, but . . .' He swore he saw a tear in her eye.

'Tomorrow. I promise you, tomorrow. We'll have our own little home wedding dinner. Anything you want, even surprises.'

'Oh, goody.' She hugged him, casting a last, lingering glance back at the window as they crossed towards the boulevard that would bring them to the doors of Brasserie Lipp.

It sat, next evening, in the middle of the dinner table – a huge, red, raspberry cake, plastered with gleaming gelatine, enough for a children's party. She had watched Rick lift it out of its box like it was a cheque for a million dollars, but he would not permit her the teeniest bite. 'Not till you've eaten dinner,' he said. Obediently, she disappeared upstairs to take a shower while he prepared the table. Happy as a child at Christmas, he unwrapped the goodies and set them out – Russian caviare and Scotch smoked salmon purchased at Macy's, in New York, two days before, when he'd picked up the exercise machine with Jack. Fresh mozzarella, tomatoes, a basil plant, spinach fettucine and home-made basil sauce, he had bought from a little charcuterie off boulevard St-Germain. A bottle of Dom Pérignon for starters, while, for the mozzarella and fettucine, he had fetched three bottles of claret from the cellar, for tasting. A Montlabert '75, a Cantemerle '78 and a bottle of prize Bordeaux – a 1970 Château-Lafite. A five-course wedding feast, with some of the best wines in the world.

Slicing some brown bread in the kitchen, he took it into the blue room, noticing as he set it on the big, oblong, cherrywood dining table in the near corner, that the phone light was on. It hadn't rung, so she must be up there talking to someone. He wondered who it might be. Rick skipped upstairs following the sound of her laughter to the bedroom, where she was just putting down the receiver. She rose to her feet. 'Oh, Rick, isn't it great?' She took his hands, 'Mickey's coming.' The full atonal orchestra exploded in his skull. 'He's bringing a girlfriend, a dancer.'

'When?'

'Tomorrow, in the morning. They're travelling overnight from Holland. He can be here the whole time we are. Isn't it great? Rick, I hongy,' she pleaded in baby voice. 'Is it cake-time yet?' and ran downstairs. He followed slowly, a slough of despond starting the bake of an iron-clad turd in his bowel. Like unto Alice, a single word ventured against brother Mickey would be met by a po-faced Adrienne.

'I just wish you'd told me before,' he said, not even tasting the fettucine.

'Oh, Rick, I was going to. I called him from New York to say we'd be here but he didn't know whether he could get away. I wanted it to be a surprise.'

'It's certainly that,' he conceded, the mental picture of Buck Ruxton, smiling eyes on Mickey, bath and chainsaw running.

She nibbled swiftly through each course towards the cake that waited, a red well of hypnosis that each few seconds drew her gaze. Greedy, needy, horny gaze. Mouth full of oily tangy fettucine, Rick felt the sudden hot desire to fuck both cake and her. To plunge King firmly in the centre of the gleaming gel then ravish her, she in her turn ravishing the cake, gobbling down the sticky delight. Wild raspberrries. Oh, to be such an object of passion to her as that lucky-to-be-so-devoured confection. He got a sugar-sweet and slimy kiss before she helped him clear away.

As they settled in the old Victorian armchairs to play backgammon, he found himself wondering what Mickey's girl would be like. Not a sailor in drag, he hoped. As the blue-grey sky darkened, the pieces were put away and she went upstairs, leaving him standing in front of the mirror savouring the Lafite. Disappointing, it wasn't a patch on the Montlabert. He felt rather than heard her arrive at his elbow, to remove the empty glass from his hand and lay her honey head upon his chest.

'What ya thinkin' about? Come on, what?'

'How peaceful it is at dusk with the lights on the water.'

She swayed, her loins gyrating slowly against him.

'Lights on the water,' he murmured, dreaming himself back to the ballroom on the QE2 where, on their first trip to Europe, they had danced into the early hours until the band would play no more. Dazzling in their quickstep, they were Fred and Ginger afloat under stars, clasped in the follow-spot, chased by the rotating overhead mirror-ball speckling them with refracted petals of light. 'Oh the light, the light, the light fantastic.'

She lifted her face and her voice asked, while her eyes commanded, "Kiss me, you fool."

He laughed faintly. 'No.'

The lids opened slightly, allowing her to focus. 'No?' she cooed gently in a long, upward inflection.

'No,' he said quietly. 'Wrong. It's not "Kiss me, you fool".' They spoke in whispers, her belly continuing to rub warmly against him.

'What is it then?'

' "Kiss me, *my* fool". Know who said it?'

'No. Tell me.'

'Theda Bara.'

'Oh. But wasn't that a silent movie?'

'Subtitled.'

For a second, Beauty beheld the Beast before the lids once more began to close, the lips parted and 'Kiss me, my fool,' she bade as his mouth came down on hers. Round they turned and round, tightly together, growing heady and giddy as here, now, in a silent fandango, they span, the thermodynamic and his heat-seeking missile locked in their timebomb quickstep of death. Breathless, they stopped, swaying as they tried to stay steady, she reaching down between his legs as he held her tight little breech in his hands. 'Take me upstairs,' she breathed.

He heard the internal phone buzz and feigned sleep, while she slipped quickly from the sheets, yanking on shorts and a tanktop on her way to press the release button which opened the big front door. A patter of feet on the stairs, a door flung wide, shouts and cries, then the awful shrilling trill, 'Billy Billy Billy Billy Billy. Oh, Billy Billy Billy.' He buried his head in the pillows. You didn't need a spoon to gag on this one. On tiptoes, he went to close the bedroom door. A few minutes later he heard muffled voices from the kitchen, caught the faint aroma of coffee.

It was a full hour before he went downstairs to greet them and was introduced to Katrina. With those painfully thin arms and wren-bone shoulders dancers often have, she stood about five foot six. She had, he was surprised to find, a simpatico face. Nice, sensitive eyes. The mouth might have been a little thin and she had small, uneven teeth. But Rick liked her on sight. He gave them the whole bottom half of the house for their stay with its Empire bedroom and sunken bath. While Adrienne showed them the way, Rick opened the fridge to find the smoked salmon wolfed, the cake plate empty and, on the table, more than half the remnants of last evening's wine quite gone. 'He was so hungry,' Adrienne revealed some little time later. 'Poor Mickey, he hadn't eaten for two whole days.'

For the next five days, Rick was tour guide of a gilded honeymoon for four. His suggestions that Mickey take Katrina to the Louvre or visit the Rodin Museum were dismissed with a flutter of fingertips. 'Oh, no. No, no. I want to see my sister.'

Why did he put up with it? he thought after Adrienne had asked for a thousand francs for each of them.

'So they can get back, they've no train fare. They'll send you the money.'

'I thought Mickey was a lead dancer in a company. Doesn't he get paid?'

'He doesn't get that much, and he phones Alice a lot.'

He stared at her. 'Gimme a break! That's what he does with his salary?'

'He gets lonely.' Adrienne flashed him her hurt rabbit look.

'So, let him find somebody and go fuck his brains out. Why should I have to finance someone who's totally self-supporting? Or should be. It's times like this that make me ache for the reconstitution of the draft.' He held out the cash. 'Here. Take it.' She hesitated. 'Go on,' he said dully.

'Thanks,' she said.

Climbing the stairs to muster them for lunch, Rick stopped at the blue room door, fascinated. Mickey was at the piano, in concert, being photographed at close range by Adrienne while the young dancer sat in the corner like a spare prick at a wedding. The singer-composer's voice rose in mounting tremolo, while he sang of dark romantic lands of fairytale, in a struck, dead-serious posture. As Mickey caught his eye, Rick felt naked, mortified at being trapped in an exquisite discomfiture. Like farting in a public silence. Mickey struck a last deafening chord, then rose gravely from his stool and went to the long oak server by the mirror and picked up a shining little goblin head he had fashioned out of papier mâché the previous summer. As Adrienne gazed fondly on, he stared into the coloured glass embedded in the goblin forehead, and began a faint incantation. Rick wondered what the dancer girl made of it all. She smiled and shrugged her shoulders and he smiled and shrugged back.

'Nosebag time,' he bellowed. 'Come on. Lu-unch!' noting gleefully that the goblin skull had leapt at least an inch in Mickey's hands.

'Oh, you broke it. You broke my spell. Fuck you.' In sudden treble pitch, a very familiar echo. Alice.

The honeymoon was over. Rick and Adrienne stood in the bedroom clasped in each other's arms. 'Sure you've got everything?' he enquired softly. She nodded her head against his shoulder. 'I'm gonna say goodbye at the door,' he said. 'Mickey wants to walk you to the taxi.' He had made such a palaver over it that Rick was happy to let him get on with it and, anyway, he had always hated farewells. 'I want you to do something for me,' he said rocking her gently to and fro in his arms like you would a sleepy baby.

'What?' she whispered.

'You know I've told my father we're married? I'd like it if you told Mickey.' He did not know why he said it. It had not been premeditated. Instinct, he supposed, the same instinct that told him, in this moment, he was taking a fatal step. The first turn of the kamikaze propeller. Surprisingly, she offered no resistance, her body did not stiffen or tense even. Her only reaction was a small, 'OK', and she stayed in his arms kissing him until it was time to go downstairs.

'I wish I didn't have to go back. I wish I hadn't said yes to looking after all those poopers,' she had protested at the last.

'I wish you hadn't too, sweetie,' he sighed, 'but what's done is done.' He raised up her chin with the knuckle of his index finger. 'I'll see you soon. It won't be long.'

She kissed and held him. 'I love you, you great big wonderful man.'

It was only four hundred metres or so to the cab-rank and he stood at the big green door waving until she vanished from sight among the crowds that thronged towards Notre-Dame, Mickey nattering ceaselessly into her ear. It was a beautiful cloudless day, a soft breeze drifting through the giant elm across the way in a mere whisper of leaves. Music was coming from somewhere. Chopin. An étude, light and delicate.

It took him some seconds to realize the music was coming from the blue room. Katrina was playing. He went in and sat, listening until she finished. Her touch was soft and sure, very lyrical, the melody wafting through the open windows above the bustle of the Seine. A sudden surge of emotion made him want to stand in the window, as the sky darkened and the wind rose, and howl Adrienne's name into the eye of the storm, so that his voice, like the blind Rochester's at the end of Jane Eyre, would be borne upon the air and carried to her ears and she would come, heart in her mouth, to love and care for him.

The girl stopped playing, leaving him gazing out the window. He did not look round immediately, aware that foolish tears were in his eyes.

'I'm sorry, do you mind if I play?'

'No, no. Not at all.' He turned to her. 'I was enjoying listening to you. You play very well.' He smiled. 'I've always wanted to play like that.'

'I'm not really very good,' she said apologetically.

'Oh, but you are,' he replied. 'You are. Please, play some more.' She did as he asked while he remained at the window, dreaming away to himself, until she had finished the piece. 'How long have you known Mickey?' he asked.

'Not long.' She had come to the company some weeks back and they had struck up a friendship.

He asked about her family. They lived in Italy. Her father was Italian, her mother from Germany. 'So, I'm Italian.'

'You look German', he said.

'I feel Italian,' she smiled.

'Are you in love with Mickey?'

She raised her eyebrows and cocked her head to one side. 'I don't know,' she said slowly. 'I think so. I may be.'

Somehow he felt enough in her trust to say, 'Be careful.' She did not ask him what he meant.

'I am careful,' she considered. 'Or, I try to be.'

Leaning out of the window he caught sight of the returning Mickey marching down the street with a face as black as thunder. Excusing himself, Rick went to let him in.

Swinging back the door as the buzzer rasped, he beheld the young Dorian Gray, eyes bright, face now wreathed in smiles.

'Well,' Mickey said, 'Well, congratulations. It seems I should call you . . .' Rick waited, willing him to say it, but try as he might, he refused to vomit up the word 'brother'.

'Thanks.' Rick capped the awkward silence. 'I wanted Adrienne to let you know. While you were away I've been listening to Katrina play,' he said closing the door. 'She's very good. Just goes to show – life's full of little surprises.' He watched Mickey's back as he walked away towards the stairs, wondering what was the expression on his face. But he already knew.

That same evening, over dinner in the Café Munich, hidden away up a winding street across the boulevard from rue Cassette, Mickey finished off his ham in Sauce Madère. Adrienne's midday bombshell had temporarily floored him, but he had taken the mandatory count and now was smarting, the grape having flushed his dander up. Leaning back against the shining red leather of the booth, 'I hope you realize, you got the best,' he started sharply and, before Rick could venture a response, 'I know you're her lover,' he continued. Husband, actually, thought Rick but let it pass. 'I know you are.' Fingers splayed, eyes glazed, he was the oracle, keeper of the flame enthroned before the door of secrets. 'But there are things you will never know about her, *can* never know about her, if you live with her for the rest of your life, will *never* be able to understand about her.' His voice became quite piercing and from tables at the centre of the floor, nosing diners slewed to look.

Embarrassed, Rick failed to grasp the strange unnatural subtext. Looking down, he saw his knuckles were white, knew his face was red. 'Listen, Mickey,' he said. 'You can never really know anyone else, no matter how intimate the relationship. Any one of us, at any moment can be betrayed by our nearest and dearest and cast adrift. Adrienne and I got married because we both wanted to. Because we're in love.' Mickey didn't say a word. 'I know all I want to know about Adrienne, and she knows all she needs to about me. Any future revelations, I hope, will only make our life together stronger. You see, she's happy, Mickey, and I'm happy, and that's all my wife and I really need to know.'

'There's just so much about her that—' Mickey again began but was cut off as Rick asked the waiter, 'L addition s'plait.'

On the way home, Mickey babbled about the ballet company and the administration's intransigent attitude towards him. Rick hardly listened. He was thinking of Katrina, the sweet pianist whom Mickey had seen off on the train earlier. How did she figure? Of course, not at all. If Mickey had cared for her in the slightest, wouldn't he have left with her? They passed the grey domaine of St-Germain-des-Prés with Mickey still wittering, and turned down towards the Seine and Notre-Dame. Apart from the judge, just how many fuckers did I wed here? George Eliot's abundance of relatives. Dear octopus, he thought. Yeah, never step outside the Nautilus, Captain Nemo, giant squid'll get ya and them suckers is covered in suckers, Captain, you bet your sweet life.

Bag packed, Mickey was busy at the sitting-room cabinet, in jeans and a lavender shirt, pouring himself a large gin and tonic to brace himself for the return trip. Half an hour later, seated outside Deux Magots, he asked Rick for a further loan.

'I'm sorry, I can't. I only have two hundred francs on me.'

Quickly, 'Two hundred would help.'

Rick forked it over and saw his brother-in-law on to the train. At least, thank God, he was going. Off to the flat green Netherlands, with a half-bottle of Cissac '78 decanted into a beer bottle, ripe Brie, bread and a Granny Smith in his bag. Hanging out of the window of the moving carriage, Mickey flapped his hand in farewell.

An hour later, hands sunk in pockets, Rick mooned along the Quai d'Orsay. How can you keep a marriage secret? How can you marry and not want it known? What Rick had done had been deliberate. Mickey would, of course, betray their secret. Reaching his front door and fishing for his key, Rick laughed softly. Jesus, he was even financing the call he had no doubt would be put through. In a matter of hours Alice would know she was his ma-in-law. *Oh boy.*

In the living room, he headed straight for the armagnac Napoleon, to pour himself a stiffener. He laughed as he picked up the bottle. 'So that was why the gin and tonic.' It was as empty as a whore's promise. Rick wound slowly up the stairs and walked into the blue room to be alone with thoughts of her. At the windows, in the fading grey light above the Pont Neuf, he closed his eyes, feeling her about him. Like a ghost, her conjured voice came whispering.'Kiss me, my fool.' He put on the lamp in the window, sat at the piano and index fingered the horse's teeth. Over his shoulder the pale gold lamplight glowed about the Ibach as he figured a soft easy tune, gazing at the painting of the ploughmen on the opposite wall. Solitary confinement in his own little San Simeon. 'June. I'm a married man – a *single* married man. Yes.' A slight shock, someone had spoken. No. Surely no. A noise though. Within the house? He listened. 'Eventide,' he breathed softly, looking up. On his left, solid on the wall, the big mirror seemed dark, smoky, only the ghost of a light at its farthest corner. As Rick doused the single lamp, the mirror flashed a wink from the edges of its bevelled eye. There was a strange quiescence. Nor tick from room nor breath in summer silence. Something though. Vibrance? A warning? Closing the lid of the Ibach very quietly he went over to the mirror. As he leaned on the server beneath it, his hand touched something. It was the ghastly goblin head Mickey had fashioned. The faceted glass in its forehead twinkled at him like a probing eye. He shivered and turned it away using finger and thumb.

Unable to sleep, he called Adrienne at four am – ten pm New

York time. She answered right away. He asked her how the flight had been.

'Oh fine, fine, but I'm still a little tired. I was on my way to bed when you called.' She asked about Katrina and Mickey and he told her of the embarrassment in the Café Munich.

'I've really had enough, Adrienne. It's just too damn tedious. Worse than that, it's sick.'

'Oh, that Mickey,' she sounded genuinely annoyed.

'I saw him on to the train and, quite frankly, could barely resist cheering.'

'I'm sorry, Rick,' a little pause, 'it's just that he's going through a lot just now.'

'Yeah, my goddam money.' Cheers from the peanut gallery.

'He'll pay you back, Rick. I know he will.'

'There's no more Adrienne, that's the last. That's it!'

'You're right, you're right.'

He was always right when she had nothing else to say. He rang off after telling her he would call her at least twice a week and that, 'It would be nice to hear from you once in a while.' She promised he would. Less than a week after she'd left, Rick received a thank-you card from the sweet piano girl, together with a hundred guilder note.

7

D URING THE LAST year's comings and goings, in and out of
Baalburg, he had talked with a business manager name of
Dan Nagel, about doing a theatre evening there. 'It would
be a great shop window,' Dan insisted. Rick had not been so sure
but the more he thought about it the more excited he became at
the possibilities.

While involved in his last movie, before his marriage to
Adrienne, Rick and Dan had talked to an LA management, who
were definitely enthusiastic. They had a small theatre in Hollywood, ready and available, and asked Rick for an outline. 'It's a
kaleidoscope,' he told them, 'designed to whet and sustain the
audience's appetite with constantly changing styles of drama,
poetry, music, anecdote – the whole schmeer.' What he had really
meant was that you'd have to kick incessantly at a Baalburg
audience's ass whose attention span, brutalized by television, was
likely to last less than seven minutes in a theatre.

'Looks like it's on,' Dan crowed over the phone to Rick in Paris.
They would provide the theatre, advertising, everything else. Rick
would have to pay the band. At six hundred per man, that meant
three thousand balloons a week for a five-piece. Manageable,
given reasonable attendance. 'Whad'ya think?'

'That's what I was about to ask you.'

'I think it could really take off,' said Dan. 'D'you want me to talk
to them some more?'

Rick thought. Dan was a Baalburgian, versed in its ways. 'Could
we get them to pay the band?'

'I don't think so, but I can try.'

'Would you?'

'Sure.'

'OK. Call me.'

'Will do. I think it all sounds great.'

If Rick did this, it would be at very short notice. He would have to get cracking right away. He telephoned Adrienne at once and, amazingly, found her in. She even liked the idea of the show. 'I'll come out with you,' she added.

In the next four weeks he worked out steadily in his gym and beavered away at the programme. He called Adrienne constantly, as often as not getting the answerphone. Then he'd wind up the old gramophone and send some scratchy Crosby or Victor Sylvester playing 'You're Dancing on My Heart' ready for her return. She never referred to any of these romantic serenades and, to his enquiries as to where she had been when he had called her late, the answer was always the same: 'I spent the night at Ruby's.'

The week before he was due to leave for New York, Rick paid a flying visit to London. Insurance policies had to be signed at his lawyer's office, there was a lunch with his wine broker (investment purposes), also his son, Pete, planned to be in New York with his mother. Rick wanted to be sure he could spend time with him there.

He'd arranged to stay with old friends just off Holland Park Avenue and had barely settled in when he got a phonecall from his broad-toothed agent.

'Rick, I've got a great project for you. Give me your address there, I want to bike it over right away.'

'Bob, I'm planning to go to LA.'

'Please Rick, read this first. It's perfect for you, just perfect. And listen to the deal. Two hundred and fifty thousand pounds and I think it's the best role in what's virtually a four hander. I'm really excited about it. The director is Hector Scunner, flavour of the month guy and he wants you subject to a meeting tomorrow which should be a formality. Promise me you'll read it tonight.'

'OK Bob.'

'Great. His phone number and the information where you should meet him I'll put with the script.'

Rick read it that night. It was good. Real good. The one o'clock rendez vous was an address in Soho.

Next day, at one, the cab dropped him off somewhere in Dean Street. Here was the number, Rick pressed a button, gave his name speak-easy style and was admitted. A dark girl at the desk motioned to him to go upstairs, where, in a large sombre sitting-room a man stood alone, with his back to him.

'You look like a Scunner,' Rick said quietly. He'd forgotten the fellow's first name.

'Yes, yes. Hector. Shall we sit down?'

They settled themselves in two chairs at a window. Harsh sunlight. Striking Rick full in the eyes, half blinding the left one, the weak one. With apology he asked to move, at the same time taking in the oddness of this place, this room. Secondhand armchairs from auntie's parlour squatting beside small tables, a tattered Chesterfield, plump and overblown, carpets and curtains that had seen much better days. One consolation. An upright piano with remarkable touch and tune as on examination Rick rattled through 'Give My Regards To Broadway' while Hector went in search of the gents. On the stroke of his return, a sturdy black girl with fat gold finger rings and strong features, brought a menu, asked what they'd like to drink. A bottle of Merlot was agreed and Rick gave Scunner the three second once-over as Hector clocked the menu.

Though the man appeared nondescript, timid in manner, the face yet had the cunning cut and pallor of a civil servant. Someone you imagined might've run a youth scheme on a city council in Battersea or Camden. The role was tailor-made for Rick. They talked for more than an hour, Hector finally let slip that the person he'd really wanted for the part was 'busy making big Hollywood movies'. Rick knew of him. A man who'd been washed up for years. Short nose in a leprechaun face. He'd be making big Hollywood movies when Rick became President of General Motors. If Hector's revelation wasn't insensitive enough his parting shot was a gem.

'Of course all this is incumbent upon who it's on offer to at the moment giving his yes or no.' Who it's on offer to?! In the midst of the tattered Edwardiana, Hector dropped the name. Fuck me drunk! Big Bumfleet! But Bumfleet was bus-pass age. To have full threat and power, and also have you believe in the love scenes, the movie required this pivotal role to be played as stated – forty-five to fifty years old, an age Rick could easily scale up to. But with the character looking in his seventies, the film would lose all credibility. You might as well retitle it, 'Grandad's Been Caught Wanking Again'.

At once Rick reached for his *Herald Tribune*, its crossword yet undone. 'That'll be all for me,' he said, knowing right then there was no way back to a thing he would have been so brilliant in. Barely was he on his feet before Hector was doing an Indian dance all around him babbling 'I'm only trying to be honest with you. I'm only trying to be honest with you,' in spinning repetition like a worn seventy-eight with a stuck needle. Jottering before him like a beater, a ghillie. This was a frightened man. And you don't make good movies if you're running scared. Hector was cacking his wee tartan breeks and Rick was no more than a supernumerary in his drama. A back-up idea. The stop-gap should the geriatric Bumfleet not come through. Rick had always, always trusted his own instinct. All he wanted now was to be out, away and clear. Halfway to the door, 'Good luck with it,' he said to the jottering ghillie, then was gone, nursing the anger sealed within him. JEE-ZUZ!

Twenty minutes later, he was ordering a bottle of fizz in a place opposite the theatre where an ambitious, plump little thesp had squandered a decade-plus in a humdrum thriller. A place changed now, fashionably awful. Twee. In-crowd. And, dear fuck, to seal it with a kiss, here they came. In the doorway, receiving a royal welcome, stood two Rick knew full well. Cueball Buick, the Kingmaker, and N.H. Klax, the scribbler. Buick, a lesson in smoothness and guile. Klax, ever straining for *le bon mot*, too clever by half.

Face with that peculiar, raw, sore-eyed look, Cueball was blinking and nodding, while Klax affected a nonchalance which didn't quite come off. Just a shade too studied, as he waited, tall, hirsute – the long wildebeeste face with full puffin lips (a tiny lacteal seepage ever at the corners) buttoned over shining porcelain monstrosities that might have been knocked together by a thick-fingered apprentice in his first week's bash at dental mechanics.

The pair set off for a far corner, Buick in the lead, not so much strolling as sashaying, the flat feet splayed, flapping in time with the nodding head; Klax following in puppy-sashay, imitating the hands-in-pockets Cueball, accompanied by the maître and two waiters, fussing like East River tugs about the *QE2*. The Odd Couple, Rick thought.

They were seated, and the thumbs-up signal was given. Thumbs-up, blinks, nods, winks. The Buick trademarks.

Determined to avoid the ghastly charade that surely would follow if they saw him, Rick slipped out to the foyer where a pale-eyed hatcheck girl stood forlorn. It was pissing with rain outside. Rick went over and sang gently into her ear.

> *Auntie Mary*
> *Had a canary*
> *That lived up in the leg of her drawers.*
> *And when it came down*
> *For half-a-crown*
> *It won the Victoria Cross.*

He winked and she laughed as he dove through the door and into a hack which had just pulled up. Collapsing inside, 'Fuck. Me. Gently,' he breathed. He'd been made to look a fool by the wee Scunner. You just don't behave like that. Ever.

At six pm Rick Neilsen was in pensive mood, snug inside the Notting Hill pub where now he stood, enjoying a pint of Fuller's India Pale Ale and dreaming of kissing his wife.

Two evenings remained to him in London, and Rick felt the need for company. On an impulse, he called Marina Hood, his friend in Paddington. After a dozen rings, he was about to hang up when Marina answered. 'Sorry,' she said. 'I was in the bath.'

'Is that Mrs Hood?' Rick adopted a mild home-counties' twang.

'Yes . . .'

'Mrs Marina Hood?'

'Yes. Who is this, please?'

'Sergeant Verges, Paddington Police. We've received complaints from a number of persons that a call-girl service is being run from your premises.'

A bemused laugh filtered gently down the wire. 'Did I hear you say *call-girl* service?'

'That's exactly what I said, and,' sterner now, 'I can assure you, Mrs Hood, that this is no laughing matter.'

Refusing to be intimidated, a clear English country voice rang back. 'Now look here, officer—'

'Sergeant.'

'*Sergeant* . . . I can only tell you this allegation is quite unfounded, and these . . . persons, whomever they may be, are quite, quite mistaken.'

'I'm afraid not, Mrs Hood. You see, I happen to know one of the parties personally. Perhaps . . .' he paused, reverting to his own voice. 'Perhaps we could discuss it over dinner, Marina?'

There was a stunned silence before she shouted, 'Rick! Rick Neilsen, you foul fiend!' Then, in a shrieking laugh, 'Oh, Rick, you beast. I thought I was about to be taken down to the station. You sounded so damn convincing. You bastard.'

'It's what I'm underpaid for. Listen, let me make it up to you. If you're free, can I take you to dinner?'

'Rick, there's nothing I'd love more, but there's a big party at Rosie's and I have to go,' she said. 'Why don't you come? It'll be great fun and we can talk for ages.' Before he could reply, she trotted out the address.

He wrote it down, cursing inwardly. Major parties, Rick abhorred. Trapped, 'Marina,' he said, lamely, 'you know how much I hate—'

'Do come, *dear* Rick,' she begged and, fool that he was, he went.

'This is it right here, Gower Villas.' He paid the cab fare and looked around the street. On the far corner, a tatty little Indian store was still open, selling everything from newspapers to bananas and beer. On the side where he stood, a long line of white-painted late-Victorian dwellings stretched away down a slight incline. The racket led him to the number Marina had given him. The door was open. Passing through a hallway of utter desolation, he mounted two flights of dingy stairs to the second floor where he stopped in an open doorway. To the left and right of him, two enormous rooms simmered with a babbling multitude. Rick had never seen so many weirdos in his life. Together in one place, that was. Stuffing themselves with pasta, delicatessen meats and breads heaped upon a long refectory table, red and white plonk flowing free. It was like a zoo. Monkey and parrot house combined. The whole thing cried out for a stun grenade. Some of the inmates Rick recognized. No mistaking the figure helping itself to the baked lasagne. Big Fat Doug, The Grouper, called so for his lips and his unhealthy appetite. Enormously wealthy, The Grouper was very careful with his money. It was rumoured he could peel an orange in his pocket. Once, bumping into Rick in an airport lounge, The Grouper had asked, would he like a drink? A modest half-bottle of wine was ordered, whereupon The Grouper plonked fifty per cent on the counter leaving Rick to cough up his half – and the tip. 'I never leave tips in airports,' The Grouper had stated.

He was now squiring the young dark-haired creature standing at his side, wearing a red suit and pill-box hat that made you want to call for Philip Morris. She reminded Rick of that peculiar-looking woman always in Woody Allen moves, the one with the mouth that out-Raye-d Martha. Hanging on to The Grouper's other flank and never taking his eyes off him was Din Din. They were both in the music biz. Songwriting. If The Grouper was the fat end of the business, Din Din was the very thin end. Rick had been present at one other gathering, three years or so back, when Din Din had brushed past him, snaking through crowds muttering, 'Where's Doug? Where's Doug? Is Doug here yet? Where's Doug?' As if, in the relief of finding him, his own identity would be regenerated. In his happy limpet-cling to The Grouper, Din Din was once more saying it with music, back in harmony. Right in the thick of it, dressed in black, from head to toe, stood the hostess and zoo keeper, Rosie – admitted élitist, dark as a Romany, voice a drawl, known as Rosie the Riveter after her talent for bringing people together. Her hair, long, steel-grey and parted in the middle, gave her a Disney-like Joan Crawford look. Close by her, nursing a glass of white wine, stooped a gloomy soul with a pout. A bubble-curl wig and concertina topper on him and – hey presto! – Harpo Marx.

Procuring some vino, Rick squeezed away from the table to come face to face with a pink-cheeked individual, about five foot six, totally bald. 'Hello, Wick,' it said. Yet another Anglo with the inability to form the 'r' sound. It introduced itself, 'Julius Berkie. You may not wemember me.' But Rick did. They'd been introduced by Marina, years ago. Julius was 'an authority on antiques', whom Rick remembered as a 'proper little blackhead'. He had half a floor in one of those emporiums near Stamford Bridge.

'I'm bald, fat and ageing, now,' Julius piped.

'You mustn't worry,' Rick returned kindly, 'you were bald, fat and ageing then.' Detaching himself, Rick saw the girl again. She'd walked past him twice as he'd lurked by the door. Pale, blonde, open-faced. Wandering lost, through the press of bodies. Ah, the flush of desire to lead her by one fragile hand, and cradle her in some cosy little corner. Were there one to find.

In the roaring whirligig some shards of showbiz bobbled about. There, a glimpse of Susie Lyme, squeezed into designer pants straining to contain the swell of dumpling-tum she never would be rid of, chattering away to Plughead Rob, her aide. These two now joined by Zach, Susie's betrothed, brilliant corn-cob smile whacked between two man-tan cheeks, looking more Engelbert than Humperdinck. Behind them cavorted a guy in a green satin clown-suit. It was pure Wedekind.

Over at the bar, Rick picked up on two figures he'd met years ago, independent of each other. Arnold the Impresario, and Ivor the Surgeon. Unfortunate tale there. Little Arnold Pulitzer, he of the famour schnoz – he reminded Rick of a daschund – his wife a mercenary, his sex-life a misery, holding what appeared to be a tight-lipped conversation with a prissy-looking silver-haired Ivor Severn-Clives, Welsh, plump as a corgi and who loved playing God. With an Oxford accent. The surgeon who'd performed the 'simple op', sliced his way through Arnold's particulars, with the prediction that Arnie's libido would very soon attain Casanovic dimension. Casanovic turned catastrophic, as Arnold, emerging from etherized haze, found to his horror, he'd been all but castrated, his mercenary wife quickly passing on sentence of cock-death in whispers to her friend a few mews' doors away. 'He could hardly before – now he can't at all.' Spoken not without relief. She'd married him only to swan it in a world of celebrities, and Arnold knew plenty of those.

Now, for Arnie, no smokes, water with his meals and nothing in the pencil. Evenings of cards, TV or Dick Francis as substitutes for the conked-out acorn. Small wonder Arnold was tight-lipped. Ah, there now with them, the wife of Severn-Clives, tall, statuesque, blonde. Some years back, bored with the God-corgi, she'd been conned into bed, poor creature, by an Italian restaurateur who'd mounted her on several post-pasta afternoons before shooing her back to Severn-Clives, who, on discovery of the bouncings, had made her life a hell. She was now his emotional prisoner-sans-parole. Of her infidelity, I. Severn-Clives cruelly kept her in constant reminder. Which would induce hysteria from time to time, to Severn-Clives's satisfaction, she'd revealed to an acquaintance over lunch in a Wheelers restaurant. His retribution. Poor woman. Rick hoped the conversation was about the bungled op. Wished Arnold would crown God-corgi with a platter of linguine.

Further off in the motley, chortled the ego-puffed Ned Traup, whose wife-to-be Rick, at her shy anxious plea, had bedded. Inches before her marriage. At a Friday late-night party, she'd given Traup the slip. One heart-racing whisper saw it done. 'I only ever come here to see you.' Her naked, bold confession. Made in a bare-bulbed shabby hallway of a drab North London House. Outside a bathroom. Where the water from an Ascot slow as geriatric pee took half an hour to quarter fill a chipped enamel tub. A minicab flight to Victoria. To the home of a Napoleonic War expert. Who gave his sitting room over for the two bare-arsed beasties tremblingly to unlock their lust. Therein. A mound arching, a shaft breaking. As he undressed, turning away lest lightning flash of the Polaris should put the wind up her, over his shoulder, Rick admired her parts. Pre-wifely thighs so shapely,

Hoyden bum so young and rounded under prettiest of knickers. A maid of stunning ripeness. Readying sofa. Then herself. For thespian insertion. From pillow case, her eyes on him. Wig-wammed in his blanket on a Persian rug. His prick the shining pole. A last guilty stand. Only guilt no match for weak lust's swollen meat. 'Oh, come to bed, Rick, please.' One eye slightly lazy. Giving her a dreamy, mid-orgasmic look. Come deliver my horn. Across the brown Sheraton room to kiss soft mouth and stiffening paps. Remembrance. Of hands upon her, levering wide the knees, the outer lips following in quick obedience, showing the little hidden ones within, opening so shyly to his touch. 'Rick.' A tiny whimper as the shining aubergine was put to them, stretching them into a sucking mouth that soon would ripple down the head, locking tightly underneath the spongy ridge, lubricant and warm. One more small, 'Rick', as Nature now demanded that she be a giving girl, he her taking tiger. A quivering thrust, and sweet pink membrane ran like lava, burying all the head. A gasp. A cry. His name sobbed out. Under dark polished wood, framing the charge of the Scots Greys at Waterloo. Prepare to receive cavalry, my love. Here comes your shining Lancer. After, warm-breasted, spent, 'I never was loved so strong and deep as that. My God, Rick, where did you *get* that?'

Cradling the glorious fullness of her bottom, 'Same place you got that,' he smiled.

Long since divorced from Traup, Rick wondered what had become of her. And if she was getting it deep. And strong. In happiness. He hoped so. A grand girl. A real pearl. With a belly like a cream-sweet dream. But there! O Gad! The portrait of Anus! The bespectacled Anus Grange, the portrait painter, head shorn neatly at the sides, under a slick, raven growth on top, the thickly gelled black bristles giving the bullet head on his gangly body the look of a wet distemper brush wearing pebble glasses – like one of those cartoony characters – what were they called? The Simpsons. Yes, except dark. Filling his glass with wine was his in-the-swim companion, the lisping Keith Penn – dubbed by Marina, 'Penethia'.

Owner of a prodigious sexual appetite, The Anus thrived on

gossip. It was plain nuts to say even 'hello' to him. Penethia had remarked to Rick on their one and only encounter, regarding The Anus, 'You know what he's known as round London, don't you?'

'No,' Rick had replied.

'The Simpering Viper,' Penethia lisped with glee, a sort of sibilance, followed by a vowel: 'Tsuh, tsuh, tsuh.'

Rick had inwardly recoiled, thinking, Should this be your lover, who needs betrayers? Betrayal was a word The Anus adored. It was a theme of his. How often in this world he'd been betrayed. At that precise moment, The Anus, delighted by some tickled fancy, exploded into mirth. Even within the bedlam, heads swivelled. The laugh, something between ass-bray and death-shriek, was shock to some, mortification to others. Jeez! A blue beard pinned beneath the spiky, rounded skull dealt you the image of Bluto in the Popeye cartoon. The Anus and Penethia – a pair to be avoided. Absolutely. All it craved now was the reflux. Of Hector the hiatus hernia. Enough was enough.

Much as he liked Marina, Rick couldn't wait for her. She would be miles late anyway. Setting down his glass on a small table, he prepared to flee. Almost at the door, a very familiar voice stopped him in his tracks. 'Rick. My dear old thing!'

A hundred and twenty degree turn to his right brought him face to face with . . . 'Binkie,' he cried. There, in a smart grey suit and Wykehamist tie, was Binkie Blythe-Carrington, the one and only. Racing enthusiast, romantic thriller writer under the pseudonym of Desmond Dance, and straight from the pages of P.G. Wodehouse. Eyebrows raised beneath the domed, slanting forehead, above it a thinning head of reddish hair, below a noble Roman nose supporting a pair of heavy, horn-rimmed glasses through which a pair of deep brown eyes danced merrily. The clipped ginger moustache now had a dapple of grey in it.

'Rick, my dear old thing, how amazing. Only today I was thinking of you, wondering what you were up to, and here you are. Simply amazing. My you look well.'

'So do you, Binkie, so do you. What are you doing in this dreadful place?'

'Killing time, old thing. I've just dropped off a manuscript and felt the need for a restorative. I have to meet this woman tomorrow. Lila, she's called, believe it or not. Can't remember her second name – works for a woman's magazine. She's interested in serializing my next book. What taste. How's Adrienne?'

'Fine. She's in New York. I'm flying back next week.'

'Give her my best, will you?'

'I sure will. How's Maggie?'

Binkie's face clouded. 'A thing of the past, I fear.'

'I'm sorry.'

'It's all been quite ghastly.' Binkie swallowed his wine. 'Christ,' he said. 'I wonder how they managed to get the cat to sit on the bottle.'

'Wait till you try the red.'

'Have you eaten?' Binkie asked. 'The stuff on that table looks as though it came from Safeways.'

'I was just about to stroll across the park to the Khyber Pass.'

'Do you fancy some company?'

Squeezing past chattering new arrivals on the stairs, they emerged into a light summer evening, and took a bus to Notting Hill Gate. They got off by the park gates near Millionaire's Row and Binkie revealed a little more about Maggie. 'I cannot tell you what that woman's done to me, Rick. It's simply unbelievable. I've been out of the country quite a bit over the past two years. Each time I return I hear these stories about her. She's been seen with this "Brian" creature. Minor public school. Very, very minor,' said Binkie dismissively. 'What a Charlie.'

Rick smiled. A Charlie was Binkie's condemnation of anyone who hadn't been to Winchester or Eton. All other schools were nowhere as far as Binkie was concerned. Even Harrow was beyond the pale.

'Inevitably, things became somewhat strained between us, and she starts seeing less and less of me. I press her about this Brian johnny and she denies anything's going on. Except, ah-hah! One lunchtime I'm driving down Kensington Gore, when I see her walking with what I take to be this Brian. Hand in bloody hand. I park like lightning and race up behind them yelling "Got you, *got* you! Caught red-handed!" I'm yelling, she's screaming, he hails a cab, and they race off. I call her that evening, she refuses to talk to me. I go round to her flat, she pretends she isn't in. I can't tell you what a cow she's been to me.'

Maggie was a Canadian. Fairish hair with a tinge of red in it, light blue eyes, infectious laugh – always in a hurry, always late. Rick and Adrienne had spent a memorable weekend once with her at a place Binkie owned 'somewhere in the country'. Memorable, to Rick, for one unexpected slice of eroticism. Binkie had met all three of them at some pub near the station, then driven them to his country seat, a house without character, set in fields, drearily furnished and with plump, white chickens pecking about outside. They spent a thoroughly wretched weekend, getting out only once to a lunch Rick gave in a restaurant on a funny little street dwarfed by some towering church or cathedral, maybe. The meal was pretty filthy, and during it, an ugly little spat erupted as Binkie and Maggie had a disagreement over what seemed to Rick to be nothing at all. Mounting a blistering attack on her, Binkie swiftly reduced her to silence. Mercifully, they were the only people in the place (which, having tasted the food, hadn't surprised Rick in the least). Maggie sat limp and crushed. Adrienne's face was frozen in silent anger.

'Binkie,' Rick said. 'Don't speak to Maggie like that, she doesn't deserve it.'

'Old thing, I'm just making it clear . . .'

'Then do it somewhere private. If you carry on like this, Adrienne and I are going to have to leave.' And leave they all did, a few minutes later, after tepid coffee drunk in uncomfortable silence. Binkie suggested a stroll round the cathedral, 'It aids the digestion, old thing.'

Rick and Adrienne allowed their luncheon guests to go on ahead, so Binkie could begin a lame apology. 'Ghastly lunch,' Rick said. 'I'm sorry.'

'I hate him.'

'I meant the food. Sometimes Binkie opens his mouth without engaging the brain, that's all. It's called temper. I've got one too, you know?'

'Maybe – but you wouldn't have spoken to me that way.'

Suddenly, Adrienne stopped, clutching at his arm, alarm in her face. 'Goll. Oh Goll!'

'What's wrong, sweetie?'

'Rick, I have to pee.' They looked up and down the pathway. No one. Only Binkie and Maggie, arm in arm now, receding into the distance. 'I should've gone in the restaurant, but we left too fast.'

Rick gave a gentle laugh, 'No big deal. How about over there.' He pointed to a recess at the back of the cathedral.

'You don't understand, I have to take my pants off. I need to go real bad. Promise me you'll keep watch.' He moved to give her a hug and she squealed. 'Oh, don't squeeze me or I'll go right here!' Scampering from the pathway, a desperate, 'Keep watch!' floated back as she whipped off her pants, hunkering down in the shadow of a buttress, gathering her dress up to her waist, knees wide apart.

Eyes peeled for interlopers, Rick saw the silver jet shoot what must have been four feet. Jesus, what an awesome little turbine! He gasped, half in laughter, and her head snapped round. 'Is there someone coming? Rick, keep watching!' As she spoke, the jet stuttered into long spurts, like a huge ejaculation. He stood marvelling, until she finished, hypnotized by the milky flex of pull–relax that swelled then settled the perfect muscles of her legs, as she yanked her pants back up. It was one of the most erotic sights he had ever witnessed, and it had prompted a giant erection he was fighting to conceal, hand within his left pants pocket.

'Wow, I never knew a woman could pee like that . . .'

'Come on, Rick,' she frowned. 'I needed to go real bad. I told you.'

'Like it had the Hoover Dam behind it,' he laughed and she thumped him hard on the chest.

'You shouldn't have been looking, you asshole. You were supposed to be watching out for people.' The voice dwindled to nothing, and he brought her to him, held her close.

'Hey, hey. Come on. It was beautiful. Everything about you is just crazy beautiful. Don't you know that you . . . you lover, you.'

Feeling the sudden rude stiffness against her, she stepped back with a sharp intake of breath, her mouth open, her eyes round. 'Rick Neilsen! You big horny toad!'

'Could it have been bottled, I'd have drunk it.' He kissed her on her so-straight nose.

'No, you wouldn't have,' she pouted.

'Yes, I would,' he said right back, and meant it. For if angels did such things as pee, he'd seen one.

The rest of the weekend passed very slowly. There was some half-hearted blackberrying so Maggie could prepare a pie for the Sunday evening meal, which was another disaster. Adrienne was unable to touch the high grouse on her cold dinner plate. A dish of corned beef and tomatoes was hastily produced by Maggie as a substitute, while Binkie finished Adrienne's portion. 'It was practically humming,' a shuddering Adrienne told Rick in bed. 'I nearly went into the gag reflex.'

'All right, all right, Adrienne,' he groaned, the half digested game-bird churning in his gut. She gave a huffy grunt, turned over, and fell into an immediate sleep. Rick tossed unhappily for hours, the souring contents of his stomach fermenting into dragon-breath.

Binkie chewed ruminatively on a piece of chicken tikka. He and Rick were the only people in the Khyber, outnumbered by four waiters. 'Week in, week out I called her, old thing, telling her till I'm blue in the face, I'm in love with her, that I want to have children by her. The one time she does see me, I prostrate myself on the fitted Wilton, begging for a mercy fuck. Nothing doing. Well, in the end one can take only so much. I heard she was about to give a dinner party and that this Brian was to be there. So I fixed it.'

'Fixed it?'

'Yes. You see, a good friend of mine, Moira Clark, lives in the same building. I got her to buzz me in through the main entrance and on my way up to her flat, I stopped off at Maggie's door and spiked the works with super-glue!'

'Binkie!'

'Yes, absolutely, I did.'

'What happened?'

'Maggie arrives at her doorstep, laden with groceries and, of course, can't get in. She puts two and two together, twigs that I'm upstairs and calls the bloody police, who come hammering at the door. My good friend Moria opens it, they ask if I'm there and can they speak to me? Naturally I deny all knowledge. Moira backs me up manfully, as it were, and there's nothing they can do except leave. Afterwards, Moira turns to me and says, "It was you, wasn't it?" Of course, I come clean, lower a few stiff drinks, trot out the whole woeful tale. She hears me out, then makes an appointment for me with this hypnotist/psychiatrist johnny she knows. Like a fool I agree to see him.

'Three days later I turn up at his rooms, feeling like an absolute bloody idiot. To top it all, the man has a serious speech defect. I can barely make out a word he's saying. He motions to me to sit on this sofa next to his desk. I do what I'm told, like a good boy. Then, do you know what? He tells me to take off my trousers. "Under no circumstances," I reply. "You have to take off your trousers," he says. "Let me assure you, I shall do no such thing," I counter. He stands up and advances towards me. I was totally convinced he was about to put me under with the lidless stare, then shag me. It wasn't until I was halfway down the stairs that it dawned on me that what he'd really said was, "Take off your glasses" '

A breeze carried the smell of new-mown grass as the two men strolled back towards the Serpentine bridge. Binkie bade Rick farewell at the top of Exhibition Road, near Queensgate, where the bronze figure of the Balaclava'd Ernest Shackleton, polar mitts and all, gazed stoically ahead from its niche halfway up a red-brick wall. Queensgate. More memories. There Rick had had his first London flat. Number seventy-eight. Fourth floor, no elevator, and a ghost in the bedroom. It had visited Rick around three in the morning, the hour of the wolf. No figure or shape. Just a mist, whitish, about the size of a basketball. It hovered at the bottom of the bed, then slowly drifted towards him. He spoke to it. 'I'm not afraid of you.' He *was* afraid, of course. 'What do you want?' The haze intensified. It seemed to pulse and surge like an infant struggling to speak. But no words came. Groping in the darkness, Rick switched on the light. Nothing. Off. Nothing. Blackness.

He arrived in Gotham on a hot July afternoon. She had known he was coming and was waiting for him in the apartment. They had made love barely five minutes after he closed the door behind him, and he lay panting now under the spinning blades of the ceiling fan. 'That var good,' he whispered into the tiny ear peeping through the tresses.

Giving him a slanting, naughty smile, 'You was hongy boy,' she breathed, kissing him as he cradled the fullness of her bosom in his hands, milking gently at each bud with thumb and forefinger.

'Speaking of which,' he said, turning himself to kiss her nose and gaze down on the mud-greens, 'I could eat a horse.'

'Didn't you eat on the plane, sweetie?'

'Hardly anything,' he answered. 'I'm ravened. Let's go to Raga.'

'Rick, it's only six o'clock.'

'So?'

'Can't we just wait for a hour and go to Nero's? I don't wanna eat Indian in this heat.'

'Best time. Every Hindu knows.'

'Well us no Hindu, us desire pasta. Pretty please?'

Nero's was their local Italian. Rick was not crazy about the place but dehydrated from the flight and remembering they had New Amsterdam on tap, 'OK,' he laughed. 'You get your wish.'

'Oh, goody. We'll get ready at seven. Now come here and kiss us some more.' She moved to him, opening up her body and that cool, wet mouth. He gently squeezed the compact perfect bottom and she drew back to look at him.

'You velly full,' he murmured.

'I know,' she rapped aloud, smacking his rump softly with her free hand. 'Velly, belly, belly full. You sperm whale you. You bad boy.'

8

IT WAS ALMOST AUGUST and the evening was hot and humid. Nero's was jammed except for one or two open tables just inside the door in the bar area. Almost at once, Adrienne lifted an arm in greeting. 'Oh, Rick, there's Ruby and Mort. He's her new boyfriend! Let's go over, maybe we can eat with them.'

Before he could reply, she moved off towards a crowded corner, Rick in tow, edging through gossiping groups to halt before Miss Wisecrack and her brand new escort. A golly-gosh gush of 'welcome back' greeted Rick, then something wisecracky, cueing Adrienne's giggle, then the introduction of her beau. 'This is Mort Green.' Rick took the proffered hand recording 'no grip' at the precise moment his three-second eye-snap of the upturned face consigned each detail to the photographic memorybank.

Mercifully, there was no room to sit, and Rick and Adrienne retreated to plonk themselves down at a small table opposite the bar. 'What were Ruby and lover-boy doing here?' Rick pondered as he studied the menu. This wasn't their area. Odd. And that they should be here at this particular moment. Coincidentally puzzling. He examined the memory printout of Mort. Balding, light brown hair in sparse crinkly clusters, glistening droplets of perspiration on frontal pate areas, the lines of the forehead crabbed in a tight knot above the nose, a sharp downturn of mouth, and no expression in the eyes. What name was it Rick's father had used for a face like that? Vinegar Puss. Yeah! Mort. That was him exactly.

He chuckled and Adrienne looked up. 'Whad'ya laughin' at, sweetie?'

'Oh, I'm just feelin' happy.'

'What about?'

'About being back, being here with you. Hearing your voice. Gazing into those oh-so-pretty eyes.'

Reaching for his hands, she let him have *that* smile. 'I love you, you great big wonderful man.'

While they waited for the food she told Rick of her plans to follow him to California with Greg Farben, a gay guy, according to Adrienne, who'd arranged for her to do a clutch of TV and movie interviews. She'd met Greg on a theatre project she'd been involved in, and now, turned agent, he was to represent her. 'California-here-I-come' time! Farben called her day in, day out, with a nonstop motormouth routine which would draw small waterfalls of mirth from Adrienne. A sample of the Farben wit (concerning a supposedly horny man): 'he's got a chicken in 'is pants, he's got a chicken in 'is pants.'

Rick first clapped eyes on Farben when Adrienne had invited him to Folsom for a drink. He was immediately struck by the man's eyes. Watery-blue behind thickish lenses, darting ceaselessly about him out of a pale blob of a face. Hair a short fairish tangle, and, under the threadbare failure of a gooseberry moustache, the incessant mouthworkings punctuated by an intermittent hubble-bubble of a laugh. Uriah Heep on speed, Rick thought and zeroed back on Adrienne, her eyes bright with California dreaming. Rick only hoped she wasn't in for a big letdown. Hollywood was a dirty business.

Inside a week, Pete arrived. Adrienne and he were old pals. The three of them spent every summer in Italy, and every New Year in Paris. They would sing together, swim, frisbee and sail together, play liar dice, Uno, Trivial Pursuit. On two or three occasions when he was about nine, Pete had begged to sleep in Adrienne's bed, while Rick dossed in the *salla*. He would hear Pete's laughter as Adrienne blew giant-fart kisses against his neck, hear them sing until sleep came. In the morning, with Pete still in Morpheus' arms, quietly she would come to where Rick lay, sprawled on a mattress on the black and white stone courtyard overlooking the sweep of sea and golden sands and there, by a wall decked with morning glory, in the shadow of a thick-leaved lemon tree, she would let herself be taken in the day's first heat.

Now, for the first time, Adrienne distanced herself from them a little. Perhaps it was all this childminding she was doing. Well, this was the last week. Soon they'd be in LA.

Rick took Pete down to the South Street Seaport where they snacked among the dozens of stands laid out in a huge ovular eatery mall. Away in the distance the Statue of Liberty propped up a bright blue sky. Rick bought Pete a Mets shirt and cap on their walk round the pier. As Pete looked at Liberty, Rick looked at Pete. Sandy haired, he had soft blue eyes, a pale complexion, nose with a slight curvature, and eyebrows darker than the hair. It was a very photogenic face, easily given over to delight, but Rick at times caught in those eyes the stretch of the waking Black Dog, the Terror Demon, sower of panic. What kind of world would he and his inherit? Global warming compounding the crack in the Antarctic Larsen shelf. Catastrophic flooding. A race up to its ass in salt water, starving and carcinomaed through the ozone hole. Skeleton governments squirrelled away in lead-lined caves, high and deep in far-off hills, or under the Greenbriar Hotel in West Virginia, with years of food supplies, rubbers, and a telecommunications system doomed to last not half a year. And still uncertain about what to do. World famine. Yanks and Canucks living on wheatie-bars, the Chinks on rice cakes, except the paddy-fields are ten feet deep. Every satanically versed Islamic fundamentalist cobbling together bombs and death-gas to obliterate Israel before the Negev desert becomes Dead Sea II. The Pope still holding out on prophylactics, his dying words, 'One rubber erases you from Paradise'. While on the slopes of Everest, the last company of Gurkhas battle it out with Bigfoot for the remaining edible clumps of radioactive Himalayan daisies. The Second Coming had to be by 2020: 2020 vision – only it's gonna take some miracle this time. To feed the multitudes. Would you believe three billion tons of gefilte fish and unleavened bread? A week. There'd be no Second Coming. The Saviour's got to be MIA. Once crucified, twice shy. I mean – who'd want to save this lot? The only path left for the Human Monster is the primrose one to Arthur Balfour's pit.

Pete turned towards him and Rick slipped an arm round his shoulder.

'What's up, Dad?' A frown on the face under the baseball cap.

'Nothing, son, why?' Rick smiled.

'You looked sad, all of a sudden.'

'Did I?'

'Are you?'

'What?'

'Sad.'

'No.

'What then?'

'Just thinking.' Rick gave Pete's shoulders a squeeze. 'Want to see some monsters?'

Together they ambled through Central Park, headed for the Natural History Museum. The baseball diamonds were in full swing, teams of kids and older men acting like it was Shea Stadium. Hims Ancient and Modern. As they crossed towards the path that led to one of the West Side exits, a chorus of squeals and yells announced the arrival of a group of children, spilling down a sloping bank and spreading across a grassy hollow to open their packs for lunch, their chaperones in close attendance. The guy was probably mid-twenties, brown hair, kind of good looking. The girl he recognized by the single cry of 'Luuuuunch, children,' even before he saw her clearly.

Pete smiled up at him. 'It's Adrienne,' he said.

'Shhh,' Rick breathed, then, 'Let's sneak up and surprise her.'

Her co-minder was busy with a second group as Rick and Pete skirted the little dell and snuck up on her shoulder. 'Boo!' they shouted in unison.

She jumped and whirled round, her eyes wide in shock. 'Oh!' she said.

Rick had expected a 'Hi, sweetie!' and a palsy-walsy fifteen minutes while the poopers had their faces in their lunch pails. But there wasn't a spark of welcome in Adrienne's face. Irritation rather. Not without a hint of aggression. 'What the hell are *you* doing here?' she said.

'We're on our way to the Natural History Museum,' he said quietly. 'How about a hug?'

'Oh, Rick, not here.'

'Why not?'

'The kids. You know how they can tease.'

Rick held up his camera. 'Wanna have your picture taken with Pete?'

'Rick, I can't, I'm busy.'

'It won't take a minute.'

'I can't. Look, I'll see you later. Have fun, Pete.'

Rick took the photo of Pete, alone in sportive Mets gear, while Adrienne, her back towards him, fastened on her group. They hadn't been married two months and she'd taken a six-week job as a 'counsellor', looking after kids for a few bucks a week when there could have been a wonderful sunny honeymoon in Yurp. It just didn't make any kind of sense.

In a great vaulted room within the Natural History Museum, Rick and Pete studied a towering facsimile of the creature that had ruled the earth sixty-five million years ago. Rick looked up at the pitiless eyes and jagged teeth of Tyrannosaurus Rex. 'Fun seeing Adrienne in the park, wasn't it?' he said.

Pete's four-day stay had gone like lightning, and forty-eight hours later, Rick was being driven through the baking heat of Los Angeles, past mangy tracts of land, parched and sere, straddled by hundreds of oil pumps levering up and down like nodding donkeys. Bisecting soulless suburbs of stucco and cement, the limo dropped him off at last at the old Lantern Hotel near Hollywood Boulevard, Avenue of the Stars. Door opening on to an outside stairway, his suite comprised an enormous sitting room with dining area, partially concealed kitchen, big bedroom and bathroom. Surrounded by the four walls of the white two-storey building, the pool sparkled in the sunshine, hemmed by wide green Astroturf, on which cream-coloured tables and chaises longues were neatly arranged in groups. Roses, hydrangeas and bougainvillaea everywhere. Palm trees, like sentries, casting jagged shadows.

The theatre, about half a mile away, was poky, without character (like most of LA), but workable. The owner was the very double of Zero Mostel. Completely bald on top, he'd grown the hair on the left side of his head nearly a foot long, training it over to the right, and plastering it down with pomade. A fascinating sight, it reminded Rick of George Armstrong, a stills photographer on a movie Rick had made some time back, who'd worn his hair in a similar style. If a sudden wind sprang up, the person standing at George's immediate left would be given forty lashes.

Rick put the assembled five-piece band through its paces (there would be rock, swing and comedy numbers), worked out the lighting, the sound problems, and in one week they were ready. He'd done a lot of press and TV with Dan Nagel, the show had been reasonably advertised, now it was up to the first night. The morning before the opening Rick bought two cases of wine – champagne and Chardonnay – and a slew of grub and fruit from Greenblatt's on Sunset.

Adrienne was due in that afternoon *avec* Le Farben. At around four there was a pounding at the door, and before he could get to his feet, Adrienne burst in, pushing him back into the room. 'Wait, wait there,' she insisted excitedly. 'Don't move, sweetie. Close your eyes.' Grimacing, he obeyed. A beat then, 'OK, you can look now. Sur-priiise!' Point-blank, Rick gazed into *Nightmare on Palm Street*. Holy shit! Mickey! Just how he converted his spasm of instant horror into a smile of welcoming delight would forever remain one of Rick Neilsen's most inspired feats of naturalistic acting.

'Mickey's on vacation,' Adrienne trilled. 'He can stay almost a week. Won't that be fun? Yea!' In that moment Rick could happily have tied her tits together. Instead he found himself uncorking a bottle of champagne as Talkman began his *Daily Variety* gabble. *Ay*-gad! Mickey, small relief, was to bunk with Farben, in the single room Rick had reserved on the other side of the building. 'That should prove interesting,' he thought.

Next day, Rick hired a car from Rent-A-Wreck, so Adrienne could motor in comfort to all her assignations. She could also collect Rick at ten fifteen each evening after the show, when they would have a late supper *à deux* in the suite, with Mickey, Motormouth, old Uncle Tom Cobley and all. The three of them attended the afternoon preview, which went smoothly enough. Then came the good old Hollywood ballyhoo opening –

Twentieth Century Fox searchlights raking the skies, house papered with celebs and friends of Dan Nagel, and afterwards an open-air wine and food bash in the garden area out back. As the press photographers and TV guys organized by Dan homed in, Rick beckoned Adrienne to join him.

Slipping through the crowd she whispered in his ear. 'I don't want to have my picture taken, Rick, it's *your* night.'

Before he could speak she was gone. Watching her rejoin the other two, he caught sight of another figure standing next to them, someone he hadn't seen in four or five years. The Moke! Charlie Mokem, manager of numerous music groups. Old Liverpool-Irish good-guy. Rick waved and The Moke raised his glass. After the photographers had fled, Rick sought him out. 'Charlie, you son of a gun! I'll be darned. You're the last guy I expected to see. How are you?'

'Fine, fine. You were great.' Charlie gave his familiar rasping laugh. 'The show was just great. I saw the ads in the papers and knew I couldn't miss it, bein' yer number one fan an' all.'

Rick stared at the tomato juice in Charlie's hand. 'What's this rubbish you're drinking?' he asked.

'I'm cleaning up my act, Rick. Doctor's orders.'

'Come on, you're kiddin' me!'

'No, I swear.' Charlie looked at his watch. 'Jesus, Mary and Joseph, I gotta go. I'm on a six o'clock flight for San Francisco termorrer, I've gorra breakfast meetin' with the lads, then I'm off to Chicago.' He adjusted the fedora Rick had never seen him take off. 'Listen, I'll be back here in a couple of weeks or so. I'll give yer a call, I'd love to talk with yer. Great show, just great. Good luck with it.' Rick shook his outstretched hand, then Charlie was gone, weaving his way through a knot of people standing near the door.

In the morning Rick got a call from Nagel. Television reviews excellent, NBC ecstatic. The *LA Times* disappointing. Well, they'd just have to wait and see.

From that moment on, Rick saw practically nothing of Adrienne, from the moment she left their bed in the morning to be promoted round LA by Farben until she picked him up at night. The theatre was dark on Mondays, Rick having opted to play a

Sunday matinée instead, which ended at five. That first Sunday, at six, Mickey was brought before Rick by a worried Adrienne. 'He's not well,' she said quietly.

'What's the matter with him?'

'It's my heart,' Mickey chimed in. 'It's jumping all over the place.'

'Do you have pain?'

'No, but my heart's racing.'

'Perhaps you're in love?'

Adrienne snapped at him. 'Rick!'

'Let me see.' Rick took his pulse. Classic. 'You have arrhythmia,' he said.

'What's that?' Mickey looked alarmed.

'When the electrical impulses that control the heart go haywire. It can only operate at seventy per cent of its capacity. You can't get your breath properly.'

'Yes.'

'You have pills, don't you, Rick?' Adrienne said. 'Can't you give Mickey some?'

'They're beta blockers, Adrienne. Not much help, I don't think.' He looked at the startled rabbit. 'You can take two if you want.'

'Please,' Mickey begged. 'What is this ay . . .?'

'Arrhythmia,' Rick shrugged. 'It's not life threatening. It'll probably pass in a very few hours,' he said. 'If it doesn't, go see a quack.'

Despite overall favourable reviews, by the end of week one they were playing to two men and a dog. Each evening, Adrienne would pick him up and drive him home to supper. She was quiet about her interviews, and seldom asked how things were going. On the Wednesday of the second week at ten fifteen, she didn't show. Rick paced the theatre front for almost half an hour before legging it home.

Adrienne was sitting with Farben in the poolside twilight. She leapt forward to her feet as soon as she saw him. 'Rick! Oh goll! What time is it?'

'Late,' he said. 'Where were you?'

'Oh, sweetie . . . I forgot.'

'Sure.' Before she had a chance to speak, 'I'll see you upstairs,' he said. 'Goodnight.'

He was pouring a glass of champagne in the kitchen when he heard her come in and go to the bedroom. 'Rick?' she called. 'Rick? Where are you?'

He took a pull at the chilled fizz, staring at the fake wood kitchen cabinets. 'In here,' he said.

'Do you want me to fix you something to eat?'

'No, thanks,' he said. 'I'm not hungry.'

'Oh, Rick, it was such a long day. I was tired, that's all. It won't happen again. I promise.' He took another swig. 'Rick?'

'Yeah?'

'Sweetie, I love you.'

'It's all right.' He managed a short, tight smile. 'Why don't you go to bed?'

'Are you coming?'

'Soon. You go on ahead.' Rick gave it a couple of minutes, then took the half-empty bottle and quietly slipped out to sit by the deserted pool.

Sweetie, I love you. But so few smiles now. If she was not happy, he could not be. What was wrong? Eyes fixed on the bright blue water, Rick recited lines:

> *Time, bring back*
> *The rapturous ignorance of long ago,*
> *The peace, before the dreadful daylight starts,*
> *Of unkept promises and broken hearts.*

She was asleep when he got back to the bedroom. He was careful not to wake her, putting the light out on her lovely, sleeping face.

In the morning, the place beside him was empty. It was almost eleven. He knew Adrienne was free until the afternoon. Showered, dressed and hungry, he went to the fridge. About to open the door, he heard her laugh, and padded to the window. Easing back the curtain, Rick watched the beauteous spunky body powering up and down the water, while Farben, baggy shorts reaching to his knees, sat at the edge of the pool. For a change, he was talking. And as Adrienne stood up in the shallows, Rick, eyes riveted on her darling smile, felt himself a spy.

At the beginning of the third week, Rick was forced to pull the show. The houses were so poor the management couldn't meet their overheads, and with Rick paying the band three thousand a week plus rehearsals, he was out fifteen grand. After the closure he had four days of TV and radio talk shows to do, after which he and Adrienne could have some time together. Alone at last. Until Adrienne gave him the news. 'I'm going back with Greg, Monday. I have to sign up for the new college term and I *gotta* get back to working out. It's been almost a month.'

'Why the hell don't you tell me these things?'

'I thought you knew.'

'Who am I? The Amazing Randy? I'm not fucking psychic, Adrienne!'

'I told you.'

'No, you didn't.'

'Oh, sweetie, it's only four days, I need that time to get prepared. Classes start in just over a week.'

Out of the blue he got a call from The Moke. 'Bloody shame about the show, Rick. Listen, I'm back in circulation. Fancy a bite termorrer?'

'Sounds good.'

'I'll pick you up. Eleven thirty OK?'

At eleven thirty on the button, Charlie pulled into the forecourt of the Lantern, hunched behind the ivory steering wheel of his vintage shining-black mint-condition Cadillac. He was wearing the perennial grey-green suit and the old fedora he sported outdoors and in – even at dinner. The medium blue eyes behind the big thick lenses would squeeze themselves to asterisks when Charlie laughed his rasping laugh. And the years spent in the good old US of A had done nothing to soften the Liverpool-Irish accent, still there, thick as peat. At least some things never changed.

Rick stuck his head in at the right front window. 'Morning,' he said, and got in.

'Bit early fer lunch. Fancy a drive?' Charlie backed the Caddy through the Lantern's forecourt.

'I'm your guest.'

The roadster swung into the street, a few minutes later turning left on to Vine to cruise past the white stone tower of the Methodist church on Franklin, then taking the road that hugged the freeway to where they would cross the bridge which led to Lake Hollywood.

The lake was a man-made tree-lined reservoir. A long road traced round it, passing over the dam wall the halfway point from where you could see odd parts of Los Angeles lying in a carcinoma of smog. They'd walked barely ten yards before The Moke got right to it.

' 'Oos the girl – the one yer were with on the first night?'

'Adrienne? My sweetheart, Charlie.'

'She's an actress, right?'

'Right.' A bend in the road brought them to the left shoulder of the lake.

'Yer not plannin' ter make it permanent, are yer?'

Rick paused. 'No,' he lied. 'Why?'

'Just wonderin'. 'Oos the little geezer with the glasses?'

'Her agent.'

'Thought as much.'

'Before you ask, the other's her brother.'

'Is tharra fact?'

A horn sounded and a city parks truck rumbled past, a couple of dungareed artisans lazing in the open back. 'Why?'

'Well. You know when the press wanted the photos – at the first-night party – and you called her over to have her picture taken and she wouldn't?' Charlie scanned the expanse of water. 'It's none o' my business, but them two shook their heads at her.' He loosened the knot in his tie, undid a coat button. 'Yer don't mind me talkin' to yer like this?'

Rick breathed in the lakeside air. 'Like you say, Charlie,' he said, 'It's none of your business.'

'I know. Sorry. But if I were you I'd give it all some time. Don't for fuck's sake get too involved there.'

116

Rick kept silent.

'It was a great show, Rick, great. But if I'd known beforehand I'd have tried to stop yer doin' it. This is not a theatre town, Rick. The fuckin' RSC even got its arse kicked out of 'ere four weeks before the end of its run. Nobody goes any more. They even have trouble with musicals here. It's not a theatre town any more. Why didn't sombody tell you that?' Rick held his peace. 'You should be doin' movies, not messin' about with—'

'Impossible right now, Charlie.'

'Why?'

Rick quickened his stride, as though he wanted to escape his answer. 'I can't work without being given the chance to *do* something. I'm not a painter or a composer, Charlie. I can't set things down without the tools of my trade. They come in lots of little words written on lots of little pages in between two soft covers and they're called roles. And I don't got me one, right now. Nor a magic wand to create me one. You just have to wait for that to happen. It takes patience and control – waiting for your pitch. Listen, Charlie, just the other month this chortling mogulite comes up to me in the Four Seasons in New York. He's got this gammy leg and a cane with a gold and ivory handle. "I'd just like to shake hands with the best actor around," he says to me. "You really believe that?" sez I. "I certainly do." sez he. "Then why don't you front me in one of your movies? Let's do *Under the Volcano* together." Ever see a cripple sprint? This man was A Team material, Charlie. Amazing pace off the blocks.'

Charlie laughed. 'Come on.'

The two men halted for a moment at the centre of the dam face. Rick leaned against the parapet, gazing sightlessly down past trees and tiny dwellings into the gorge that spread its jaws on to some wide unknown sector of the sprawling city. Hazy little patterns of sameness, a massive grid of pink painted turds vanishing into the distant pall of a vast orange death-cloud. 'I told you this is not a theatre town,' Charlie said. 'Jesus, Mary and Joseph, what the fuck are you doin'?'

In a voice just above the level of a small roar of water coming from some drain-like affair in the middle of the lake, Rick began a lilting self-mockery. 'I don't know, Charlie. I don't know anything, see. I'm dumb and I'm blind. No head. Just heart, Charlie, that's all I am. Big-hearted Arthur, my mother used to call me. It was a warning I mistook for a compliment.' Rick laughed. 'No head, see?' A swallow wheeled along the parapet, soared, hung, then with a stretch of scimitared wings dove away below them.

Charlie fixed his eyes on the gorge opening out and away towards Hollywood. 'It's all down there waitin', Rick. You're approachin' the prime of yer life, for Christ's sake. You gorra get rid of this pain-in-the-arse label yer got. 'Cos that's not you, I know.'

'Labels stick, Charlie. Like shit.'

'Come on, you know what I'm talkin' about – gerrin' inter them movie-business cliques.'

'I'm no good at that, Charlie. It's not my game.' Rick started walking back towards the car.

'You remember what Marilyn Monroe said after she got the big contract?' Charlie spoke directly to his back. ' "That's the last cock I'll ever have to suck." Your problem is, in her place, you'd've said it without the fucking contract. You gotta get out there and hustle – be Nicely Nicely Neilsen, otherwise it's going to be "Hallelujah, I'm a Bum" before you know what's hit you.'

'That's it, Charlie, keep it funny.'

A blur of wings, a dive, and Rick stared down the dam wall, following the geometric sweep of the blue-glide swallow, marvelling at each thrilling arc, wondering were he to swing out over the parapet now, locking on for a petrified second before letting go, would it be possible to joyride down the concave wash, a swallow-inspiration rocketman, sledding at its bottom through a switchback dale of new-grass smells, before the brake slid him under lily-pads of leaves, screening out the light.

No. This was no spirit waterslide. Just a concrete lesser version of that huge glass ice-green scoop of a building curving down on mid-Manhattan. There, as here, it would take but one small rubber ball bounce before the journey into space would rejoin Earth our mother with an over-ripe melon splatter at the feet of all those hopefuls beetling their way down Fifty-seventh Street to ICM. Acting their little socks off before a pogrom of superannuated restaurant-haunting prats. Instant Constipated Mediocrity. His voice belled above the canyon like a trumpet before Jericho. 'All we are say-ing, is give us a goal.' He looked at his friend. 'You remember that one don't you, Charlie?' he said softly.

The Moke lifted his hat without removing it, and mopped his brow with a big square hanky.

'Ever go to church, Charlie?' Rick asked as they neared the Caddy.

'What would I wanna go to church for?'

'Well, you're an old Liverpool-Irish Catholic, aren't you? Don't you believe in God?'

Charlie stared ahead through the pebble lenses. 'No, that's all a fuckin' fairy tale. What about you?' he asked back. 'What do you believe in?'

'Me? I don't know anything, Charlie, remember?'

'You're in some fuckin' mood and no mistake.'

'Why, I'm in sparkling mid-season form, my dear Chas. Remember the actor who was told he was a cert to win the Oscar?'

'When?'

'Oh, years ago.'

'No, who was it.'

'I forget. Well, when the name was announced, the guy was halfway down the aisle before he realized it wasn't his. At which moment he pitches face down on the carpet crying out, "I knew it, I knew it, there *is no* God".'

Charlie put the Caddy in gear. ' 'Ow about a steak at Musso and Frank's?'

'Sure thing,' said Rick. 'You really don't drink any more?'

'No.'

'Amazing.'

'You said it. I was doin' two bottles of Bacardi a day a fuckin' year ago and not even noticin'.'

'So why did you stop?'

'One fuckin' leg blew up ter twice its size. The quack told me I 'ad a year if I didn't chuck it.'

'I needs must imbibe instanter,' breathed Rick.

'That's your motto?' Charlie laughed, thick lenses flashing like diamonds in the California sunshine.

'No, Charlie, that's emblazoned on the family crest. *Nunquam miratus, semper spe depulsus.*'

'What's that mean?'

'Ne'er surprised, e'er disappointed.'

Charlie let the ivory wheel spin in his hands. 'Sometimes I wish there was a God,' he sighed. 'Jesus, Mary and Joseph.'

The first call Rick received back in New York was from Joe Alder. 'I got tickets for the Mets game tomorrow afternoon. You and Adrienne wanna come?'

'Hang on a sec, Joe.' He could hear the whine of the blender from the kitchen as Adrienne mixed herself a protein drink. She stuck her head round the door as he bawled her name. 'Joe's got tickets for the Mets tomorrow,' he shouted. 'It's a day game, can you make it?'

She thought for a moment. 'Sure, that'd be great.'

Rick lifted the phone to his ear. 'Yeah, thanks, we'd love to. What time's it start?'

'Three.'

'Why don't we meet up here around one? We can have a salad or something, then take the subway.'

'Swell. See you then, Rick.' Joe's brother was a big wheel in the Phillies triple-A setup down in Florida. Rick knew they'd be good tickets. Probably right on first base.

Just what they proved to be. They had a worm's eye view of the action, including two shouting matches between the Mets manager and the first-base umpire. Joe bought peanuts and crackerjack, Rick and Adrienne ate popcorn, drank Coke and beer, and they all sang, 'Take me out to the ball game', in the stretch between the sixth and seventh inning. All the things you do at a baseball game. The Mets, alas, lost, but it had been a great day out till the end, when Rick and Adrienne got separated from Joe in a crowded exit gate. The subway was packed and they stood all the way to Manhattan. Two young guys were eyeing Rick from a slight distance and finally one of them pressed forward and leaned in on him. 'Excuse me, but you're Rick Neilsen, aren't you?'

'Yes.'

'I just wanted to tell you I'm a great admirer of your work.'

'Thank you.'

'I'm sorry, I didn't mean to bother you.'

Rick returned the smile. 'It's no bother, you're welcome.' Time was when he'd have got a big hug from Adrienne along with a whispered, 'I love it when people say that.' Standing right next to him, she acted as though she hadn't heard a word.

Tomorrow was his birthday. One more candle. Oh, well.

In the morning he waited eagerly for the tiny three-word whisper in his ear. 'Happy Birthday, sweetie,' followed by a barrage of wet smacks as his face was kissed off. Nothing. She rose, showered, dressed, took up her shoulder-bag, wheeled out her bike and rode uptown. He tiptoed round the apartment, checking all the likely, then unlikely places for a card. Zero. Maybe she was buying one now. Probably.

He didn't see her till just after seven. Still no word, no look, no sign. He hadn't eaten all day, waiting to share his celebration time with her. 'Let's go to Mitchell's,' he said brightly.

'Oh, Rick.' She gave a little sigh. 'I don't wanna walk that far. Can't we just go to Nero's?'

'OK,' he said. 'Sure.' There was one free table at the bar-end, in the corner. They ate almost in silence, Rick still waiting for a sprung surprise. At the end, determined not to look hangdog, he ordered coffee and a sambuca. 'Make it a large one!' Adrienne looked at him unsmiling and he gave up. 'Do you know what day it is?'

'No.'

'Don't you know what day it is?'

This time she shook her head. 'No.'

'You're sure you don't know what day it is?'

'No, Rick, I *don't* know what day it is!'

Coffee and Sambuca arrived and Rick set the spirit aflame to roast the beans. 'Today was my birthday,' he said softly.

Suspended animation had been only a phrase to him, but now

he was able to observe the real thing at close quarters. Some four seconds ticked by while her eyes opened in a silent scream, then the hinge mechanism which kept the lower mandible pinned to the upper malfunctioned, and Rick swore he heard the thud as it hit the table top. A progression of mangled, churning sounds, then actual words were formed. 'I'm sorry. Oh, God, Rick, I'm sorry. It's all been so busy. What with California, college and working out. I'm sorry.'

'It's OK,' he said.

Here came the hands, laid on top of his own. 'I'll make it up to you, I promise.' He blew out the flame on his liqueur and her hands cupped his face as she leaned across to kiss him. Long and tender. 'Oh, sweetie, I'm really sorry.'

He smiled. 'It's OK,' he said. 'It's OK.'

It was a smart label. Saks, Fifth Avenue. Standing at the foot of the bed, Rick opened the box. Peeling back the corner of soft tissue, he lifted out the present and held it against his body. A dark, tweedy multi-coloured heavy sweater. Quality. He pulled it over his head and shoulders and looked up with a grin.

'Right size, huh?'

'Betcha. Great sweater.' Rick stood before the mirror. 'Sure is.'

Jack grinned. 'Two hundred buck number, pal.' Then as Rick stared at him, he added with a wink, 'Fifty dollars in the sale.' He took Rick by the shoulders in a small hug. 'Wish ya the health to wear it, buddy.'

'Thanks, Jack.'

As he slipped the garment off and folded it away, 'What did Adrienne get ya?' Jack asked. Before Rick could manufacture a reply, there was the rattle of her key in the lock.

'We're in the bedroom,' Rick called.

'Oh, hi, Jack,' she said as in she came, clutching an envelope.

'Look what I got from Jack,' Rick said, motioning at the box on the counterpane.

She stroked at it with one hand. 'It's beautiful,' she murmured and, turning to Rick, held out her little offering. 'Here,' she said quietly. 'I'm sorry.' As Rick opened it up she looked at the bemused Jack. 'I forgot his birthday,' she said, then burst into a wailing laugh, 'And I'm never going to be allowed to forget it!'

'Not true,' Rick said. 'It's forgotten already.' The card was white, with three little brown monkeys in the attitudes of Hear no evil, see no evil, speak no evil. Rick opened it. 'It's your birthday, do whatever you want', read the message. Adrienne had put three exclamation marks behind it and added a huge HOORAY!! – HURRAY!! she'd spelt it. In her distinctive handwriting her greeting to him said: *To my love, on his Birthday. Have many more, be happy! Healthy! and love me as much as I love you, forever!* Placing the card on the rolltop desk, 'Thank you.'

She kissed him, before checking the bedside clock and grabbing up her shoulder-bag. 'Oh Goll, it's almost noon, I gotta run, I'm late.' She stopped in the hall. 'I love you and I'm sorry.'

Both men stood for a moment after she'd gone just looking at each other. 'Come on,' Jack said. 'Let me buy you a drink.'

Jack baled out after one margarita while Rick ordered a second. Swallowing it down, and turning to leave he found his way barred by a rotunda of a man, about five foot seven, early forties maybe, small eyes, button nose, and good teeth exposed by a wide smile pressed into a pink-fleshed cannonball of a head. Greying hair above it, giant butterball of a torso below, Rick couldn't begin to guess the weight. 'Mr Neilsen?' The man's expression turned grave. Oh-oh. Who was this? The IRS? FBI? So far as he knew, he'd paid his taxes, hadn't throttled Ming. Yet.

'Yes?'

A chubby paw emerged. 'My name's Frank Goldston. We live in the same building.'

A nut, has to be, thought Rick, at the same time shaking the other's hand. It felt like a veal baseball mitt. The stranger volunteered his apartment number. 'Oh, you're in a different cell-block,' Rick said flatly.

'Yes. Yes they do have that look, don't they?' At the cream-teeth smile, Rick had a fantasy flash: Adrienne had sent him as a kissogram birthday surprise. 'I'm a great admirer of your work,' Goldston continued. 'I've written a screenplay.'

Thank you but my birthday's over.

'And I'd like to talk to you about it.'

Oh, please God, no. 'Yes, well I'm kind of busy right—'

The veal mitt flew to a little leather case on a barstool. I just happen to have a copy with me, go on, say it, Rick screamed internally. Right on cue, the guy said, 'I have a copy right here. There's a great role for you in it.' He recited a name. 'Here, I'll write it down along with my home phone number. I hope you'll like it. I'd really appreciate it if you'd call me sometime and let me know what you think.'

Suddenly, Rick saw him differently. A vulnerable man appealing on behalf of his art. Rick took the piece and smiled, but not too warmly. 'Thanks,' he said. 'Er . . .'

'Frank.'

'Frank. I'll read it as soon as I can.'

'I wanna bike.' On her way to morning class at Hunter, Adrienne was standing in the sitting room doorway pulling on her shoulder-bag.

'You've got a bike.'

'I mean a real one. So we can go biking in New England with Mort and Ruby.'

Jesus, what a prospect. 'Adrienne . . .'

'Will you buy me a bike? For my birthday?' Her birthday had been back in May, for which she'd received a lilac dress and a twelve hundred dollar long weekend at the Stone Resort.

'How much does it cost?'

'About six or eight hundred dollars.'

He went to his briefcase, took out a blank corporation cheque and signed it. 'Here,' he said. 'Happy double birthday.'

'Thanks, sweetie.' She smiled, and the hug and kiss came strong and warm. She gazed into his eyes. 'You too.'

'Me too what?'

'You too bike. So we can have fun together.'

'Oh. Oh sure.'

That evening, Adrienne got a phone call. Karen Carpetshins was to be married. 'When?' asked Rick.

'This coming Saturday. Wanna be there, sweetie? Alice and Bill are going, and Patrice and Dom.'

'No,' he said, deadpan. 'I'll just stay here with you.'

'What do you mean. *I'm* going.'

His voice was all concern, 'But your classes. Your workouts. What about them?'

It sailed miles over her head. 'Oh, they're no problem. I'll catch up. It's Karen's wedding. You don't get married every day.'

'I'll drink to that.' In deep draughts, he thought. Oh, it's gonna be such fun. Yea! He remembered the fun of his own wedding day. Alone in this very room, waltzing an empty dress.

'I gotta call Alice,' she bubbled. 'Sure you won't come, sweetie?'

'No,' he smiled. 'No, you take a nice break with your family.' Any place Alice was, he could well do without. Rick had met Jim, the soon-to-be-bridegroom, on the trip out West with Adrienne. Apparently the mother had denounced the relationship and electrified the neighbourhood with the racy news that her son had been 'mesmerized by a lesbian'. She ain't seen nothin' yet, Rick mused. Wait till she claps her lamps on Ming.

Adrienne was away for almost a week, calling him only with the news of her return. He read Frank's screenplay. It was hilarious. A tremulous New York comedy about a magic book, the occult and a sweating terrified writer's confrontation with the Angel of Death. Terse, very funny dialogue – the kind of comedy movie producers *should* be making. Class stuff. A real surprise. Rick met with Frank a couple of times and they talked at length about the plot, the style, the music, even. Rick felt it should be a mixture of *Scheherazade* and Bobby Hackett's *Caravan* with the Angel of Death doing a little Phil Harris in the nightclub scene.

'Why don't you direct it?' Frank said excitedly.

Rick gave his crooked smile. 'Never work,' he said.

'Why ever not?'

'I'd do it brilliantly, make a huge success, bring it in for under four million dollars and no studio would ever forgive me.' Frank laughed and he and Rick agreed to keep on meeting.

On Adrienne's first day back she informed him they would be

playing softball on Sunday in Central Park. 'Just a group of people that get together to play and have fun. Ruby and Mort will be there.'

Rick's heart sank. 'OK. I'll give Jack a call. He likes softball.'

'Let's not ask Jack.'

'Why not? It's just a bunch of people having fun isn't it?'

'Yes but . . . there may be too many.'

'Then we can double up. Some guys can take an inning or two out.' She looked really miffed. 'Come on,' he said. 'Jack's a friend,' and went to the phone, trying not to show how pissed off he felt.

On the day, Rick and Jack were on opposite sides to Adrienne, Ruby and Mort. When Rick's team were at bat, Adrienne asked if Mort could borrow his glove. 'Sure.' On each occasion, the glove was taken without so much as a word. At the bottom of the fourth inning, Rick ambled back to the side benches where Jack had been standing, watching.

'What an asshole,' Jack breathed.

'Who?' Rick laughed.

'That geezer you been lettin' use your glove. You shoulda seen the over-the-shoulder look you just got.' Jack watched the fielders take position. 'He's with that Ruby, right?'

'Right. Why?'

Jack made a single clicking noise with his tongue, then spoke the words without a pause. 'I was just wonderin' what the big deal was with them and Adrienne.'

Rick sat on the bench as the pitcher lobbed one over the plate. 'Well, they all pal up and go to the gym together.'

'Yeah, and I'm Pee Wee Herman.'

In the change around at the top of the seventh inning, there was a sudden commotion. Racing after the crowd of shouting players, Rick saw a black guy who'd been watching the contest caught in a knot of pursuers, headed by Mort. Rick took hold of Adrienne's arm. 'What the hell's going on?'

Slightly out of breath, 'My purse was taken,' she said.

'What was in it?'

'Nothing much. Couple of dollars. The keys to the apartment.'

'Damn.'

'Mort's got him.'

'Why didn't you call me?'

'Mort was nearest.'

Protesting innocence, the black guy was allowed to leave, clutching a small holdall, which Rick discovered minutes later no one had asked him to open. The game over, 'Let's have lunch with Ruby and Mort,' Adrienne said, as they gathered up their belongings.

'Let's not and say we did.'

'Rick, we—'

'Nope.' He looked at her levelly. 'On the one day we can be together, I want to have lunch in the company of my woman.'

Walking over towards Ninth they were both silent. God knows what she was thinking. He was recalling Jack's words of an hour or so ago. *What's the big deal between them and Adrienne? . . . Yeah, and I'm Pee Wee Herman.* Why did she even have time for somebody like Mort? Or am I saying why does she like people who don't like me, he thought. But no, the guy was totally disagreeable. And discourteous to boot. As they left the park behind and hit the roar of traffic, Rick heard another roar, that of the voice inside his head shouting his frustration and uncertainty.

Laden with late Monday morning shopping, Rick placed the brown bags against the apartment door. As he reached for his keys, he could hear her guitar. She was singing. He leaned his forehead against the red-painted door, straining to catch the words, 'Are you somewhere feeling lonely, or is someone lovin' you . . .' She never sang to him any more like she once had, summer and winter. Never sang her song for him. No more 'Stood Out in the Rain'. Now, it was for herself she sang. Now it was all 'You've Got a Friend', or that Peter Gabriel thing, 'In Your Eyes', or the one she was singing at this moment. Thinking of someone else? And whether it was a tape, or she was playing herself, she'd stop the music whenever Rick came in. And now, here he was, groceries at his feet, standing silent, waiting to hear 'Stood Out in the Rain', like a child aching for a thing it couldn't have.

Taking up the bags, he let himself in. Passing by where she sat on the sofa, he went into the kitchen to unload. She put her guitar away at once, and seated herself at the little oak dining table, gathering up her notebooks. 'Hi, sweetie. Been buyin' up half of Balducci's, huh?'

'Yep.' No embrace. He decided not to put everything away, and sat opposite her, in the big armchair between the small server and the library table. 'I feel like a Bic pen,' he said.

'What are you talking about, Rick?'

'Bic pens' – She looked at him like he was nuts – 'are the cheapest and the best,' he went on. 'Like me. I've been out of real work for six months, it doesn't cost that much to hire me, I really deliver, and I can't get one goddam decent job.' He sat there, waiting for her to say something, anything. But she didn't. In the silence he heard an echo of Hector Scunner. 'I'm only trying to be honest with you.'

After a while, with a 'See you later, sweetie,' she got up and left.

Seated in the sudden quiet, he closed his eyes. After Daisy, Rick's love had lain fallow for four straight years. Until the moment the green-eyed catalyst had thrown wide the doors on a warehouse of pent-up love. A hoarded love. A complete, singular, smouldering intensity. Kept quietly stoked.

He had been the lover from that first so-thrilling winter kiss. Adrienne his sure responding object of desire. The true enchantment. His beloved. There were many in the wide world like him, male and female. Lovers. And many, many more beloveds.

Joe Alder had once remarked, 'The thing about the Raders is they're all so ordinary. Nothing exceptional about them.' And although there might have been much about Adrienne that was unremarkable, she was, to Rick, the very opposite. The sparkling target of his heart. Not a clouding of suspicion before or since the marriage could by one millimetre derail the locomotion of his passion. The quality, virtue, value of love are mapped out by the lover alone, and to the essence of those words will the lover adhere. What was the song? 'I'd rather be a hammer than a nail.' Most everybody wants to be the lover. Now, behind the mud-green eyes, was his love a thing intolerable to her? Subconscious fear – perhaps even hate for him, and his love, growing there like a lesion.

128

Did she feel the hammer of that love nailing her down to where she couldn't move or breathe, silence her only retreat. Is that how it might end? When they would be like all those other people they'd always sworn they'd never be like? Himself left with not one plea-bargain, craving any possible relation with a false enchantment. How soon would that be? That new loneliness?

Rick sat in limbo. An image growing and darkening about him. A Steinberg painting – the one set on a music score page, with blind mankind in bureaucrat formation at the edge of the abyss, each file waiting turns to topple, their wondrous achievements and crimes against their fellows and the planet, scattered haphazardly under a treble clef of meaningful, meaningless symbols. The whole shone over by an *e pluribus unum* golden-dollar sun, burning above a smear of unreal clouds, behind which, blackness. The image unlocked the meaning of Arthur Balfour's chilling words – *The energies of our system will decay, the glory of the sun will be dimmed and the earth, tideless and inert, will no longer tolerate the race which has, for a moment, disturbed its solitude. Man will go down into the pit and all his thoughts will perish. The uneasy consciousness, which in this obscure corner has, for a brief space, broken the contented silence of the universe, will be at rest. Matter will know itself no longer. Imperishable monuments and immortal deeds, death itself and love, stronger than death, will be as though they had never been.*

Black Dog! Instantaneously, the clammy zero hand reached for his throat. Jesus, he was going to have a panic! Unwittingly, he'd let slip the lock. Ego defences momentarily unmanned, the gremlins, with billowing banners of despair, sprang forward to lay kindling round his dread.

Booze needed now, and how. Find fellows, fulsome women, quickly. Drink with Doctor Omar while the sun hovers yet at the yardarm to hear the hoary sage cry out, *Come my lad and drink some beer.* Wrong doctor, but the right idea. Surely it was Johnson. Lash-lacing at one loose shoe, the thong broke – *The line broke, the monkey got choked and they all went to heaven in a little row boat. Clap hands, clap.* The black Ferris wheel rotated in his head, spinning out words of Socrates: *Death is one of two things. Either it is annihilation and the dead have no consciousness of anything or, as we are told, it is really a change, a migration of this soul from one place to another.* 'Migration time,' he jabbered trying to halt the murderous Ferris, close down its images with idiot verse. *Each new, forever day, some hug of company provides/A business lunch, a dinner, interposing taxi rides/A book, a fire, an instance of desire, a little hope/so lucky, oh, so lucky not to be an Ethiope, sans hope.* Then what the fuck is luck without your hope? 'The pit indifferent to hungry or well fed, has just one purpose, to receive its dead.'

The elevator descent was a space trip to Ganymede. Rick sweated in the stillness remembering a time he'd asked Juan, in this same tin travel-box, if he, like Pablo, liked a drink.

'Nah,' had come the flat retort. 'Just eat. And pussy.'

Like a deadly summons, there was a sudden dry, knocking sound from within the elevator as, slowly, it ground to earth. To earth. Ashes to ashes, dust to dust. Knock knock knock – *Someone came a knocking at my wee small door/Someone came a-knocking I'm sure.* I'm sure, I'm sure. *Only yourself and myself, the father and I are one.* Not long now. Till you will never even know that you existed. Lost for ever. Dreadful sorry, Clementine. Screams. Good.

In the Watering Hole he swilled down one drink, quickly ordered a second, then a third, aiming them like bellows at a last-gasp glow, forcing it to burst into contented flame. He'd got it! Stopped it. Just in time.

Inside fifteen minutes he was in sparkling Buck Ruxton form and humming. All well, once more. Still, he tested the waters with atheistic judgement. – *The hand lies open, the heart is dumb. The soul that held my substance together like a hard gem in the hollow of my own power will, one day, totally give in. – I am alone. Thou art alone. The father and I are one.* Poor Tom Merton, electrocuted out in India, far from old Kentucky, a standing-lamp across him where he lay cold, alone with his burns, on a bed, in Delhi. But here, the waters were clear, not a clouded ripple, nor threat of hidden tentacle. The ego gone to ground, momentarily secure, in the hollow of his own power. The gremlins put to rout, he contemplated lunch as, smoothing down his ruffled plumage in the glass, 'Consider Fleabag, who was once Samson with balls like you,' he confided to a bemused but smiling barkeep.

9

THEY WERE WATCHING *Gaslight* on the boob when Adrienne informed him Alice would arrive the next morning for a two-week stay. Rick sat up with a pained expression. 'Why is it I'm never cued on immigration?' He flopped against the sofa. 'It would be nice, just once, to be given due warning.'

'Come on, Rick, it's no big deal.'

Rick thought he heard Boyer say 'You're not feeling well again today, are you, my dear?' before he closed his eyes.

Twenty-four hours later found him on the same sofa with Adrienne on his left, and, next to her, Alice. Perhaps as a warm up for Alice's auditions which Rick suspected were 'go-sees' (you just turn up on spec), Adrienne had begged him to read *Dial M for Murder*, and here on the Folsom sofa they perched ('Did you ever see the picture of we three' he thought), thesping away. Alice, natch, playing the Grace Kelly role. Margie had seen Alice act. When Rick asked what she'd been like, Margie replied, 'If I were that bad I'd want someone to tell me.' It was true.

Next morning, as she was leaving, Adrienne let it be known there were some Saturday meets coming up, and from now on she would be at workout every Sunday.

'Jesus Christ, Adrienne, I hardly get to see you as it is.'

'It's just till the end of the year, sweetie.'

'Yeah, sure!'

Busy chopping onions for a Friday evening nosh, Rick heard the phone ring. From the kitchen, he caught Adrienne's pleading tone. 'Oh, no, don't whatever you do, call her my mother.'

Poking his head round the kitchen door, 'Who was that?' he said.

Just a friend of Mickey's Alice and I met in the corner deli. Bit of a creep. He's gonna stop by for a while this evening.'

'Why invite him if he's a creep?'

'We didn't. He kind of invited himself.'

'Well I'm not feeding him dinner, Adrienne.'

'Rick, he's only gonna be here a few minutes.'

With jumbo shrimp curry simmering on the hob, Alice was camped on the carpet talking with Adrienne, while Rick, sprawled shoeless on the sofa, watched the Mets taking a beating. Around the bottom of the seventh inning the doorbell razzed. Adrienne ran to answer it, revealing an individual she introduced as C.O. Jones.

'Smells like a Cairo bazaar in here,' he said, squatting down on the Boukhara next to Ming. Adrienne hadn't been wrong about him. For close on half an hour, C.O. yakked ceaselessly to Ming and Adrienne whilst dropping smart-ass comments about the apartment, the Mets and the kind of couch-potatoes who watched them. You're sailing mighty close to the squall, mister, Rick thought beadily. 'You know the type,' C.O. added. 'They usually don't wear shoes.' It took all Rick's willpower not to rise and firmly escort him to the door. As the Mets got hit for another home run, 'OK, guys,' C.O. said, 'I'll leave you to it.' Pausing at the sofa end, he tweaked Rick's big toe. 'So long, Spud,' he yipped. That did it. The silly little straw that broke the control of Rick's frustration about Adrienne, his marriage, career, his birthday, Saturday meets and Sunday workouts all at once. Exploding from his pink-patterned hammock, he grabbed the offensive little prick by his coat lapels and smacked him hard against the passage wall. As he drew back his fist the voice roared in his head, 'Don't do it! Don't hit him!' He pulled the punch to no more than a dig in the bread-basket. Jones gasped and buckled as Rick hauled him to the door and thrust him into the corridor, with Alice and Adrienne shrieking and swooping after them like seagulls at a feed. 'You come back here again,' Rick roared, as the Wizard of Oz Strawman wobbled his way to the elevator. 'I'll tear your fuckin' head off!' Half of Folsom felt the tremor.

'Rick!' Adrienne's voice thick with reproach, as they regrouped in the living room.

'Don't Rick, me,' he rapped back at her. 'I don't have to take that kind of crap on my own turf! Not from anybody!'

Ming simply glared.

'You shouldn't have hit him.'

'He shouldn't have touched me, Adrienne.'

'He didn't touch you.'

'He did, and he got what he asked for. It was only a poke in the ribs for Chrissakes!'

Over Adrienne's shoulder, Rick could see the ballgame. A line drive loaded the bases for the Mets. Sensing victory out of defeat, 'You wanna eat?' he asked, with a half-hearted nod at the kitchen.

'I don't think either of us is feeling very hungry,' said Adrienne, leaving the stage to her mother.

The I'm-struggling-to-regain-my-composure voice then passed its judgement, 'There are just better ways of dealing with it, Rick. Better ways of dealing with it.'

Silently, he cursed himself. He bopped a stupid little clown, and in the process opened himself up, primed the missiles, made himself a target. And there sat Alice, with a gleam in her planet Mongo eye.

Confirmation of this was received next morning, when Rick rose to go to the bathroom. Through a crack in the door he beheld his wife, still and attentive, under instruction from Mother Church yet again in bra and pants, her hands upon her daughter's naked buttocks, the head weaving slowly from side to side, eyes fixed on the other's, voice a percolating whisper. '. . . and ever they heard that soft voice whispering and urging them . . .' Rick caught some words, 'Anger . . . scary . . . rest of your life . . .' before, at a small sound from his side of the door, abbess and novice, they broke smartly apart. Rick sat on the bed. If he got into anything vital now, she'd never listen to him, he felt sure. Instead would focus all upon his outburst. Now that the voice of Saruman had been at her she would have no independent thought of her own. He'd painted himself into a goddam corner.

For the next three weeks, Rick hardly saw Adrienne. Ming had gathered up her underwear and fled the apartment. There were a couple of Saturday meets, followed by Sunday morning-to-afternoon workouts. It was on the second of these Sundays that the mystery calls began. Always around a half-hour after Adrienne's departure. When Rick answered, the phone would be put down. On the third Saturday after Ming, they were watching the New York marathon on TV. Suddenly Adrienne stood up. 'I wanna go see it,' she said.

'It's almost over Adrienne,' Rick laughed. 'What's the point?'

'I wanna go.'

In the cab, he gave Adrienne's thigh a thrillpinch of thumb and finger that once would induce a giggle and a seal kiss, but she shook herself free. 'Please don't squeeze my muscles,' she snapped.

Rick rammed his hands in his pockets as the cab neared Columbus Circle. They reached the crowds at the finish line to learn that the race had long since been won. They stayed, none the less, for a half-hour or so, watching the intermittent arrival of the club runners and the younger competitors.

'OK,' he said at last. 'That's that. Let's go.'

'I – can't, sweetie.'

'What do you mean?'

'I promised to meet Ruby and Mort here.'

He exhaled deeply. 'News to me.'

'Rick, I told you.'

'No you didn't, Adrienne. What you said was that they'd be here watching the race.'

'I told Ruby I'd meet them here.'

'Where?'

She gave an irritated little shuffle. 'Well, here, somewhere around the finish line.'

'Look, the race was over an hour ago and we've been stood here for half that time. Let's go.'

'No. I wanna try and find them and, anyway, I wanna see more of the marathon.'

He started to speak but she was already moving off through the crowds. He trudged behind her like her valet. On and on they went, stopping at intervals over the next hour as the yuppies and the hairy-assed brigade breezed by, pursued by the panting, early middle-aged and, finally, doddering into view, the van of the wizened greybeards. He imagined teams of drovers in the rear, red-tongued charioteers, urging them on with whips and curses through a diversion just short of the finish and into the abattoir where, along with Rube and Vinegar Puss, they would be processed, canned and distributed to the needy.

Ten minutes later it was getting dark. 'Adrienne,' he said. 'How much longer do you plan on staying here? Till midnight and the last bathchair? Come on. I'm hungry and this procession of geriatricos is making me nervous about how much time I have left.'

'What are you talking about?'

Half to himself, 'Beginning to dwell on mortality, that's all.' Then, 'How about a little candlelit dinner? Just me and you. We've been here two hours now, it's enough already, gimme a break, I'm starving.'

She hit him with a frown of disapproval. 'Come on, Rick. Lighten up. *You* should be in the marathon.'

I'd do it alone tomorrow if your countenance would shine upon me, he thought.

He followed her through the jostling throng until they reached Ninetieth Street and were standing on the bank of the reservoir. Adrienne seemed to be checking the participants rather than scanning the crowds. 'They're really fit, these people,' she said, 'and it's the fulfilment of a year's dream for them.'

'Yes. So you've said.'

Rick watched, aghast. Faces drained, a herd of shattered lemmings staggered past, two with eyes rotating in their skulls like dying Catherine wheels. 'Look,' he said. 'I think it's fine that people should want to keep fit. I've run round a few parks and lakes myself, with and without you, as you well know. I'm just not all that wild about spending the entire evening watching Grandad Incorporated bow-legging by. Let their nearest and dearest welcome them home. I mean, it's not as if you or I even knew anybody in this sweating farce.'

'It's not a farce.'

The crowd were chanting, 'Come on, come on, go on, go on,' the words translating inside Rick's head to 'It's gone, gone, gone,' of 'You've Lost that Lovin' Feeling'.

As he gazed at Adrienne's chiselled profile, he felt rejection, like a hard stone in his shoe. These days he had to rack his brains to find ways to solicit the old regard, even resorting to baby talk – 'Does it lub us?' 'Yes it lubs you' – but it never said so itself, only in the morning, going out the door when nothing more could happen. On the evening's return just 'Hi, sweetie,' and when he would reach out for her, 'Oh, wait, wait wait wait. Guess what I did today. Three double-back . . .' and he would listen, patiently to the revelation of some twat-splitting, workout routine. Then, 'What's that smell? Oh, yum. Let's eat. Are the Mets on TV?' 'No.' 'Then let's get a movie. I'd like to watch a movie.' Keeping him at sweet arm's length. No cuddles, no soft, deep embrace, no gaze into mud-green eyes, or from them.

The flap and slap of a thousand sneakers brought him back to Nightmare in Central Park, as Rick offered up a silent prayer for a Fifth Avenue fanfare announcing the arrival of the gilded invalid carriage bearing the rattling bones of the oldest jogger on the eastern seaboard, a Social Senility placard clutched by gnarled hands proclaiming the magic words, *Take heart my dears, I'm the fuckin' last*. Shit and derision. They must have stood silently in a cheering host of everybody's marathon relations for at least another half-hour before finally shuffling off for a frosty dinner in a place he couldn't afterwards recall.

Next morning brought with it one of the wonders of the modern world. Adrienne had no Sunday workout! Frank had invited the two of them to brunch at the Mardi Gras, a creole restaurant in the Village. It had live jazz. Rick knew a couple of the guys. Feeling slightly fluey, he sent Adrienne on ahead, and on his arrival half an hour later was incensed to find Ruby and Vinegar Puss sharing the same table. Pushing away his empty plate, fizzog bearing its customary scowl, Puss vacated his chair and pointedly left the restaurant just as Rick sat down and offered his apologies to Frank. Throughout the meal, Ruby had a little half-smile on her face. Rick couldn't figure it out. Surely the abrupt nature of her beau's departure should have sent her scurrying after him. So what was so funny?

Afterwards, waiting in the Folsom lobby for the elevator, Adrienne let him know she had a meet in upstate New York this coming Saturday and would be staying the weekend with someone called Lara. A friend, apparently. The following week, she added, she'd be spending five days in Chicago at a family reunion. It took place every year. First year in six Rick had ever heard of it. 'There's gonna be over ninety of them.' Plus Buck Ruxton and his magic saw, Rick fumed inside a black wish.

Inside the apartment he let her have it. 'What the hell were *they* doing there?'

'Who, Rick?'

'Ruby and Mort.'

'I invited them,' she said, and waited frozen-faced for his response.

'Well, you had no fucking right to invite them. It was a brunch Frank gave for us alone, and you just don't go inviting every Tom, Dick and Harry just because you feel like it. It's plain bad manners.'

'They're not Tom, Dick and Harry, they're my friends.'

Rick moved up two gears. 'And I'm your goddam fucking husband,' he rapped out. 'Remember me? The husband who hardly ever gets to see you? Who, anytime he does have the opportunity of a few moments alone with you finds Ruby and that twisted-face asshole making up a four for bridge.'

'Mort's not a twisted-face asshole.'

'Baby, he would need massively serious cosmetic surgery just to set his face straight.'

'He just doesn't smile much that's all.'

'Bull-*shit!*' Rick took a deep breath. 'Here's a little scenario for you. Right? *I* get back after my own little personal honeymoon in Paris. *Who* just happens to be sitting in the same restaurant on our first evening out? Ruby – and Mort, scowling. At softball, Ruby – and Mort, scowling. Who's at gym workouts? Ruby and Mort. At the Indian restaurant we took Buzz and Margie to? Ruby – and Mort, scowling. Who gets his hair cut by you in our bathroom and leaves *me* with a scowl? Mort. And the Mardi Gras this morning.

Mort and his scowling exit. And Ruby sitting there with a grin from ear to ear. What was all that about?'

'I don't know, Rick.'

He punched the words out at her. 'Have you been telling them things about me?'

She shook her head without focusing on him. 'No, of course not. What do you mean?'

'I mean have you been saying things about me to them?'

'What things? No.'

'Things like,' he gave a pained, soap-opera rendition. ' "It's not going so well with Rick. I'm unhappy. He's nasty to me." Things like that, Adrienne. I'd just like to know what the fuck is going on here?'

'No, Rick, I . . .' She started to cry. 'I don't know what you mean. They're my friends, that's all. Like Jack is with you.'

'Like Jack is with *us*, Adrienne. I have *never* felt friendship from Ruby altho I've tried helluva hard a lotta times to show friendship to her. For your sake. She's been in this apartment times without number, for dinner and socially. And when she broke up with that Danish guy. I think I've been in her apartment about four times in my life and I've never eaten there. And as for that disagreeable appendage of hers, every time he looks at me I see nothing but downright hatred. Well you can stick *that* for friendship. What I want to feel, Adrienne, is *your* friendship. Your love.' He stopped, aware that he was trembling.

'I do love you.' She didn't make one move towards him.

'It sure looks like it!'

Eyes glassy with tears, she at last looked at him. 'I love you.'

Rick said slowly. 'It's impossible to love a man you are ashamed of. A man you're not prepared to publicly call your husband.'

'I'm not ashamed of you. I told you I want a big day with all . . .' Tears ran down her cheeks.

'Fuck big days,' he said in a choke. 'I'd sooner have a little life.'

'Rick,' she cried, but he was already out and down the hall, on his way to some gin-joint, there to lick his wounds.

It was Armistice Sunday. Adrienne was in Chicago. Rick dressed himself slowly in his dark grey chalkstripe, carefully knotting an old regimental tie. Unlocking his briefcase, he opened an envelope marked in Sam's handwriting, 'Murdoch's last letter'. The grandfather Rick had seen only in a photograph. His mother's father, L/Cpl Murdoch Storrie, Argyll and Sutherland Highlanders. He'd been a miner. A coal-face stripper, working in low cramped seams, with the wee pit ponies. A rough, tough job. With no knowledge of music, he played the melodeon with instinctive brillance. Often he would ask of a street musician if the fellow could play such and such a tune. On being told 'No', he'd demand, 'Here, gie me the damned thing and I'll play it.' And he would. To delight the wife who was always at his side. Agnes. With her wonderful singing voice, the woman he loved dearer than life.

Gingerly removing the letter, Rick opened it. The years had faded the ink to sepia, the scrawl of words tapered from bold to thin with each hurried dip of a post office pen. It was in two halves now, a ravaged little Dead Sea scroll. Clattering through the plastic tape boxes Rick found the *Variations*, and put it on. As 'Nimrod' began in gentle sadness, he pieced together the letter. God, that music. 'Moving' was no description. It was indescribable. The heart of the enigma. It just numbed you. Slowly, quietly, he read the words aloud.

Folkestone
20/10/17
Dear Wife
Agnes, just a note to let you know I arrived at Folkestone alright and I am now waiting on the boat to take us over. Well love, I received your letter with PO for 2/6 and also another letter just as I was going to get ready to go away. I know you will be wondering if I got it or not. Well, Agnes, I was happy to have that last letter from you. It was a nice one, I went away very cheery over it.

Well, Dear Wife, I could not get writing you sooner otherwise I would have done so. We left Edinburgh at 1.45 pm and arrived in London 4.30 am. You see that was about sixteen hours in the train. The Zeppelins held us up for a bit on the main line to London, and when we did start it went for miles and miles with all lights out.

We heard when we arrived the train in front of us escaped neatly, one bomb dropping about 100 yards in front of it.

Well dear, never mind knitting gloves, for I got issued with a pair before I left. Well, Agnes, I must again say your last letter just fairly gave me new life again, and I shall never think of nothing else but you the whole time I am away.

Kiss Mary, Archie and Flora for me Dear and I will kiss you for it when I return.

from Daddy

Love to all,

Agnes XXXXXXXXXXXXXXXXXX

Mary XXXXXXXXXXXXXX

Archie XXXXXXXXXXXXXX

Flora XXXXXXXXXXXXXX

Cheer up Agnes love.
I will write and let you know my real address when I know it myself.

God bless you Aggie and bless you he will.
I always pray for you and the children
XXXXXXXX
Please send me a writing pad if you can, love.

She never heard from him again. He was only twenty-six when he was killed in no-man's-land, retrieving the wounded, an act for which Siegfried Sassoon had been awarded the MC. It was a duty Murdoch Storrie carried out many times, under fire, with death his only reward. When I am laid in earth remember me, remember me. Rick looked again at the scrawl of words. So utterly simple – a brief litany of peace and love a man had tried to carry with him as a prop against the murder and desolation to which he must return. To no-man's-land. He heard 'Nimrod' through once more and put away the letter asking a silent blessing from no one in particular for Murdie, and his Agnes. Climbing into his dark coat, his big scarf red as a Flanders poppy wrapped about him, he headed off to where he knew hardly anyone would be. The Dorset Hotel, close to the MOMA. It had two restaurants. A big and a small. Heaven knows why they kept the big one open when hardly a soul used it.

In a bright November sunshine, he walked the whole way, timing his step to an imaginary band playing, 'It's a Long Way to Tipperary', while he reflected on those terrible losses suffered at Loos, Passchendaele, Vimy Ridge and the Somme. Murdie had fought through and survived all that simply to be ambushed at last by the outlaw of averages. Leaving behind, to torture Aggie's memory, a round bronze plaque with his name on it next to a lion and a laurel-wreathed figure of Britannia, *He died for freedom and honour*. Surely he and countless other brave men died in honour. But they were dispatched to that dreadful death by The Donkeys. There's an unmistakable pompous arrogance peculiar to overprivileged incompetents. 'Chortle photographs'. Staff Officers. In shining boots. *So* enjoying it all, haw-haw-haw. Plastered with a fruit salad of medal ribbons for each HQ they'd served and been served by. 'Isn't it fun to be off to the war!' one titled militaristic clown had gone into print as saying, like he was off to Royal Ascot. It surely is, mister, when you're washing down roast capon with your claret back at Brigade HQ. At Loos, on the second day, a force of nine thousand eight hundred British infantrymen were sent over the top to charge the German trenches and machine-gun emplacements. Most of them never got halfway to the wire. In three and a half hours their casualties numbered three hundred and eighty-five officers and seven thousand, eight hundred and sixty-one men. Bodies left to hang on wire for weeks, a cold rôtisserie of rotting scarecrows, traversing machine-guns blasting the survivors in the back as they retreated, until the German commander Lüdendorff ordered the carnage stopped, with the words, 'These British, they fight like lions'. To which an aide replied, 'True, but they are lions led by donkeys.' Not a single German received a scratch.

Douglas Haig took over the command of British troops from Sir John French. The same Haig who had failed his Staff College examination, who had been hopelessly out-manoeuvred in autumn exercises not two years before the outbreak of war, and who stated only five months before Loos, 'The machine gun is a much over-rated weapon and two per battalion is more than sufficient.'

Entering the Dorset, Rick passed by the bar and small restaurant to his right and strolled through the lobby to the main dining room. No maître. Waiterless. Deserted. Maybe they had closed it after all. Slowly, he walked by the parade order of empty tables with their pinkish tablecloths and chair seats, loosening his coat and unwinding the long scarf as he went. He stopped at a table near the far wall, placed his things on a vacant chair and sat down. Moments later a face appeared at a kitchen-door porthole window, bobbing and peering as though trapped in a giant washing machine. Then the door swung open and the maître, neat and smiling, wished Rick a pleasant Good morning.

Greeting him likewise Rick asked, 'May I have lunch here?'

'You certainly may, sir.' A menu was brought and two waiters materialized to quietly clear away the other places. There was a gravity in their movements, as if they knew what day it was. Rick ordered very simply – some pasta and a glass of wine. Staring at the platoons of empty chairs filling this silent meadow of a room, each stark white wooden frame a headstone for regiments of slaughtered men, Rick whispered again the words from Purcell's *Dido and Aeneas*.

'When I am laid in earth remember me, remember me.' Two hundred thousand in unmarked graves. Half a million never found. At any chosen point it would take four days and three nights for the British dead alone in line abreast to pass.

Apparently all Murdie ever said about the war was, 'The shellin's the worst – that's the *real* hell. That and hearin' the whistle. But ye just take up your rifle and get on wi' it.' The whistle. The signal to once more go 'over the top'. Rick kept the great big faded photograph of him, standing before the Folkestone tennis courts in tunic and kilt (in which the Scottish regiments then fought – so fiercely, the Germans dubbed them, 'The women from hell'), his glengarry set at a rakish angle over burning eyes. Rick grinned at the memory of Murdie's crooked smile. His 'Dear Wife Agnes' loved him all her days. 'To live in the heart of those you leave behind is not to die.' He never did, for her.

The plate of pasta was placed in front of him, along with a glass of red. Rick barely touched the food, but drank the wine, longing to be set within his own wife's heart. Instead of wasting slowly in this growing desolation. Well, today was about desolation. He fancied he heard a ghostly voice. 'You just take up your rifle and get on wi' it.' The plaque. There should have been a separate minting for Haig and French and others. With a donkey replacing the lion, and a clown with cup and ball, Britannia. Instead of which, Geordie Five, father of the shooting partner on Haig's whisky estate, made the bungling ass an Earl! In the words of old Charlie, 'Jesus, Mary and Joseph!'

10

THROUGH THE REST of November and half of December Adrienne spent only two full weekends at Folsom. The first, looking after Ruby's dog while Ruby was away, the second, playing host to Dom and Patrice, there on a break from Chicago.

Patrice had the best singing voice in the family. Similar colour hair to Adrienne's, a wide smile revealing perfect teeth, and a bulbous nose that was quite different from Ming's. Conko, Rick thought. Dom with his flat, expressionless face and furry, thick black hair atop a ramrod body, put Rick in mind of a totem pole wearing a shorn Busby.

After Rick had taken them to lunch at the Park Plaza Oyster Bar, at some street market in Greenwich village, Adrienne quickly asked him for eighty bucks so Dom could buy a microscope.

'He needs it for his work, sweetie.' The weekend cost Rick six hundred balloons.

Every weekday now Adrienne would leave the apartment at nine am, returning between eight and nine in the evening. The baseball season long done, each night she would bring home a video and watch it in bed. In five weeks she and Rick went out only twice. Once to a Peter Gabriel concert at Madison Square Garden where the warm-up group made such a deafening racket you had to shout to make yourself heard. Rick bought himself a beer, Adrienne a soda. He tried to take her hand, but she sat with both stuffed in her green jacket pockets, hunched against the iron balustrade of a stairway, her body three-quarters angled away. For almost half an hour he sat, his arm draped round her, gently rotating his fingers in her shoulders, without response. The rows of seats were thick with couples. Heads together. Shining faces in the flickering light. Putting his mouth to an ear, 'Where are you?' he lilted in anticipation. 'I'm trying to listen to the music, Rick!' You could have heard it on Jackson Heights.

Pissed off, he headed to the refreshment area, then suddenly took the elevator down and out of the building, stopping in at Charlie O's, right next door. Ordering a beer, he sat crooning quietly. 'A fine romance with no kisses. A fine romance, my friend, this is.' He had had to get out of there. Away from the woman he loved. When all he'd wanted was to sit and listen, with a rub of cheek, a squeeze of hand. Like those all around them were giving and getting. Wemmick Castle nods and winks. 'Which *you* ain't gettin',' he murmured.

' 'Scuse me?' returned the barman.

'Just another beer, please.'

'Comin' up, my friend.'

Non-communication. Is that the way so many love songs fade, die? A pair of differing heads in different sand? One shutting out, the other shutting out the dread of being shut out? Rick sat unmoving, buried with his thoughts. To return to her side now would diminish him. He prized his love too high to be a fawn. And she hadn't wanted his nearness back there, that was for sure. For whatever reason. Maybe she just really *was* into the music. Personal thing. Yeah. Everything would be all right tomorrow. All at once a giant children's choir bullied in his head:

> *That she doesn't want you, you are afrai-aid,*
> *That she doesn't love you, you are afrai-aid,*
> *That she's going to leave you, you are afrai-aid,*
> *That there's nothing you can do, you are afrai-aid.'*

Where is your self to be found? Always in the deepest enchantment you have ever known. But. What was it he had read somewhere? When we are falsely enchanted, we desire either to possess the enchanting being or be possessed by it. We are not free to choose by what we shall be enchanted, either truly or falsely. In the case of a false enchantment, all we can do is take immediate flight before the spell really takes hold.

Rick stared into his glass.

An hour later he was in bed. On her return to Folsom, Adrienne said nothing and neither did Rick.

Their second outing was on a Wednesday to Le Cirque Imaginère. It was lashing with rain and Adrienne was late. During the intermission, the English company manager introduced himself to Rick. 'Time you did something on the London stage,' he said after they had shaken hands.

'He's right,' Adrienne added later.

The following morning she left New York to spend five days in Chicago. She didn't call once. On her return, Farben began to show up on the occasional evening exhorting Rick to return to the London theatre. At the end of one of these intrusions, 'Look,' Rick stated flatly, 'In the event it's escaped your attention, I'm an inveterate New Yorker. I have little or nothing to do with London. In any case, I don't wish to be apart from Adrienne.'

'I'd come over and see you.'

Regarding her without expression, 'You mean like in the Cancer Ward?' Rick said, and the subject was dropped.

Another weekend was spent with Lara. Again there'd been no Sunday mystery caller, neither when Adrienne had been in Chicago, nor on the two Sundays she'd stayed at Folsom. Because whoever it was knows where she is? Five days remained before Rick had to leave for Paris. Adrienne would follow less than a week later. A sudden bright idea! What if he invited Buzz and Margie, and Dom and Patrice? There would be only Pete and Rick's father, Sam, in the house. Maybe Adrienne would feel happier with family about her? That night Rick put it to Adrienne. Her face lit up and at once she called Patrice. Placing her hand over the mouthpiece, Adrienne whispered, 'She says they can't leave the twins.'

'Tell her to bring them.'

'Oh, Rick, they wouldn't be able to afford it.'

'Tell her I'll pay for the tickets.'

'Really?'

'Really.' In forty-eight hours it was all set. Including Buzz and Margie, who would pay their own fares. Working out the final costs, Rick got a call from Adrienne.

'I called home this morning and spoke to Donna. She feels so left out.' A short pause. 'Rick . . . can she come too?'

'Sure. But I gotta get these tickets done now.'

'I'll call collect and tell her it's OK. Oh, Rick, I love you, you great big wonderful man.' That night she came home bubbling with excitement. 'You've made Donna so happy. She says to say thank you to you. She's *thrilled* to be coming. Oh, we're gonna have such *fun*.' Yea! Adrienne gave him a smacker of a seal kiss. Rick gazed into her shining eyes. She was happy. He was happy. Simple as that.

They were standing in a gift shop down near Canal Street. Adrienne was showing Rick a display of little trinkets. Silver and polished stone. The silver were Chinese. Each talisman meant to bring good fortune, children or long life, the assistant told them. The stones were North American Indian. Of animals. Wolves, and the like with arrow motifs where their hearts should be. The assistant was trying to explain all this while Rick's gaze was fastened on something else, and he pointed, 'What are those?' he asked.

The assistant, dark with a hint of Apache about him, produced a thin eighteen-inch long silver sceptre encrusted with semi-precious stones and crowned with a huge rough-cut crystal. Beautiful. Laying it on the counter, he reached into the display case for a thick rod, also pure silver with criss-crossed patterns and a convex polished crystal at its tip. 'Here,' said the friendly Apache. Pulling off the detachable base, he handed the instrument to Rick. 'Look.' Rick put it to his eye. It was a kaleidoscope. He laughed. Glittering regalia of fairy tales.

Outside, Adrienne manoeuvred Rick to a clothing store. 'They have a couple of dresses here I wanna try on,' she told him. 'I want you to see them. They're *so* beautiful.' Rick waited outside the changing booth till she emerged. There was a black dress and a blue. If the black was incredible, the blue was sensational. The way it hung on her almost knocked Rick's eyes out. Adrienne focused on him. 'Well,' she breathed. 'What do you think?'

Concealing his reaction. 'They're beautiful,' Rick said simply. 'But . . .'

'But what, sweetie?'

'I just don't think they're you, somehow.' Her face clouded with a deep disappointment. As they walked up the street, 'I've got to get a present for Dad,' Rick said. 'But he's so difficult to buy things for. His needs are so few.'

'I know where you can find something for him,' Adrienne said. 'Come on.' She led Rick to the open-air market on Canal Street. Dozens of wooden stalls stretched away down the hill. 'Get him a warm scarf or gloves or something.'

'Let's take a look around, maybe we'll see . . .'

'Rick, I can't. I have to work out. I'm late already. I'll see you tonight.'

'Make it early then, will you? I leave tomorrow. I'd like for us to have dinner together.'

'I'll try, sweetie.' On tiptoes, Adrienne gave him a lightning peck, and vanished in the crowds.

Mooning round the iron-wheeled barrows for an hour, Rick couldn't come up with anything better than Adrienne's original suggestions. He bought Sam a good blue woolly scarf, and the warmest pair of fur-lined black leather gloves he could find. Then he went back for the trinkets plus two furry-rabbit glove puppets for Claire and Sarah, Patrice's twins and, with a final rush of blood to the head, the rod and sceptre. Lastly, the dress. Rick knew, the moment he saw her in it, that she must have it.

From Paris Rick called Adrienne on three or four occasions around eight am her time. There was no answer. The day she was due to arrive, in the wee hours the phone rang. 'Rick,' Adrienne's voice was faint. 'I missed the plane.' Before he could reply, 'There was a lot of traffic, I only missed it by fifteen minutes or so. I'm on the same flight tomorrow.'

A church bell clanged five.

'Rick, I'm sorry.'

'Can't be helped now. I've tried to reach you a few ti—'

'Rick I'm at the airport right now. I'll call you tomorrow when I get in.'

'OK. I love you.' A pause.

'I love you too, sweetie. Listen, I gotta go, I've no more change. See you tomorrow.'

Click.

It was the first time he'd ever known her to miss anything. She *always* left herself time. Traffic was never easy to Kennedy. Straining, Rick could detect none of the weird echoing airport acoustics behind the voice. Echo. Winds of Wyoming sweeping the Jersey shore. Slowly, he replaced the phone.

. . . So I've got three full days off. I can be there, right up till Christmas Eve,' the voice trilled. 'Promise me you won't let Adrienne know I'm coming. Thanks, Rick, I'm really looking forward to it!' End of call.

At the window Rick stared dully out at the waters of the Seine. 'Oh, for Doctor Ruxton,' he groaned, en route to the drinks table. Rick would be at one wifely side barely a day before Mickey would slot in at the other. On his way to uncork the armagnac jug, 'Buck, where are you?' Rick cried aloud. 'Shit and derision!'

Adrienne's call came around ten the next morning. Rick told her to take a cab and stepped out to buy some tea and the *Herald Tribune*. It was only a half-hour ride from Charles de Gaulle, and she must have gotten a taxi right away, for on his return, down the street, he watched as the yellow Paris cab drew up, and Adrienne got out. Shouting for her to wait, Rick did the fifty metres dash to the house in roughly seven seconds. Panting, he dipped into his pockets for some francs, only to hear Adrienne say, 'I've paid it,' as the driver slammed his door and drove off. Now here was something else she never did. Adrienne Rader was renowned for her thrift. She did not kiss him until they were inside the house, where, protesting exhaustion amid yawns, she at once retired to bed. She remained there till five pm. Taking to the street, her one kiss cold upon his lips, he wandered fuckless through the sidestreets to the haven of Deux Magots.

Next day, Adrienne was transformed. Her brother arrived. After the usual, 'Oh, Billy Billy Billy' performance, they disappeared leaving Rick to shop alone. There would be eleven people in the house soon, and the kitchen needed to be well stocked with food.

A whole cured ham, chickens, steaks, fruit, ice-cream, pasta and a ton of other stuff. Adrienne and Mickey he saw mainly at lunch and in the evening when he'd take them out to dinner. On none of these excursions did Mickey offer to buy even a beer. Why did he never have any money? Near bedtime, Adrienne would grow quiet. In bed she would retreat right to the edge of the monster mattress, body turned away till morning light, when love-making would be done against her bare bum, costing her neither kiss or cuddle. His gentleness. Her yielding. Sum total.

The day before Mickey was due to leave, Rick lay dreaming of other mornings, when Adrienne's hands had searched for him. Now she lay apart in a seven and a half foot square bed, and wearing goddam panties. He gazed at her half-Chinese eyes, long-lashed and closed, a flutter of movement beneath the lids. She was dreaming. Of what? Of whom? She began to stir into wakefulness, turning away, her back a tight flesh-coloured closed door. He waited for a moment before tracing a finger from her shoulder to her pants. Gently he began to slip them down, when suddenly, jack-knifing her knees in a bad-tempered spasm of energy, she fairly tore her panties off, slapping them down on the bedside carpet. Rick sat up in bed. 'Forget it!' he said, stripping back the covers. She was on him like lightning. 'Oh, sweetie, I'm sorry, I'm sorry. It's just that I'm so tired.' For a few minutes it was just like old times, her breasts and belly milky-warm against him, 'I'm sorry. C'mere, sweetie,' she whispered at him, opening up her body. 'C'mere.'

The words brought with them memories of Folsom mornings in times past, where, facing him, hands deep down and pulling on King, she'd steer him to the centre of the big Boukhara carpet. Stilling him to readiness, she'd slide behind him, one small tight hand easing between the buttock-gap to squeeze upon his testicles, forcing them to hardness, while the free hand, little muscles flexing along the olive arm, snaked around his front, slowly to rip him back, swelling King's head to purple, near to bursting as, mistress of him, she stroked and worked him with a cunning, changing rhythm that had him prisoner, trembling at the doors of ecstasy, the smiling reflection in the mirror asking her captive tiger, 'Does it feel good, sweetie? Tell me when you're getting near.' When he did, she would bend across the arm of the patterned sofa, in a slow arc, and in thrilling seconds he would put his milk in that sweet, pink tea-rose, laying open for him, slippy as a wet baby. On this memory-stirring Paris morning, she seemed available rather than desiring. Cradling King with her hands she put him to the inner lips, guiding the head inside and turning her bottom to settle it against the slapping thrusts. Barely three minutes later, Rick heard a thump, then a deafening chord accompanied by ear-splitting yells, as 'Mickey's New Song' was given a personal world première by the composer.

With a shift of her buttocks, Adrienne broke his rhythm, intent on following the 'melody' while Rick found himself recalling an ad he'd seen in the window of a Long Island fish restaurant, *Pianist required. Must have experience of opening clams.*

'Doesn't it sound great?' Adrienne breathed.

Grate, he thought. 'Yeah,' he said, attempting to withdraw. But Adrienne clamped wet and wanting round him, pushing her rear into his groin and he began to pound her to the Bedlam rhythm of the 'New Song' in a 'Ride of the Manic Orgasmic Valkyries', watching her over her honey-hair pick at the workout callous in her left palm, the whole plundering shag accompanied to the last gasp by shrieks and poundings from the floor below.

That evening, somewhere in the lower part of the house, Adrienne spent an age closeted with Mickey. Rick was barely awake as she slipped like a whisper into her side of the bed. Next morning he awoke to the smell of coffee, heard her rattling around the kitchen with Mickey. Half an hour later, Mickey was ushered into the bedroom to bid farewell. Wreathed in smiles he grasped Rick's hand, shook it hard and said, 'I love you!' and then left. Without Adrienne begging a single franc on his behalf. Between the sheets, Rick almost suffered a Festive Season vapour.

On Christmas Morning Rick crept soundlessly to the basement wine-cellar, where he'd hidden her presents — the trinkets she'd admired, her sceptre (along with his kaleidoscope), and the blue and beautiful dress. Like a child with a pocketful of mischief he sidled to the blue room, placed the rod and sceptre on a table and draped the dress over a Victorian armchair. Tiptoeing back upstairs, he quietly laid the trinkets, snug within their little boxes, on top of the dresser, then eased himself across the bed to where she lay, hooking his arms around her from behind to tenderly enfold her breasts and belly. Moaning, she tried to pull away, but he locked his arms hard about her at the same time laying his lips upon the tiny ear and whispering, 'First, you are the most beautiful creature in *the* world, and *my* world. Second, you will never, ever in this life meet anyone who will love you more than I do. And third, merry Christmas, and God bless you, my darling.'

'Oh, merry Christmas, merry Christmas, sweetie.' Rick kissed her, and she smiled and kissed him back. 'What time is it?' she asked.

'Ten. Come on.' Slowly, Rick pulled the lovely sleepy body to its feet, and led it to the dresser.

'Go on,' he said. 'Open them.'

'Rick. Oh Rick,' she cried. 'They're beautiful. Just beautiful. I love them. Thank you, sweetie.' And she brought up her lips to be kissed.

'Come with me,' he said.

'Where are we going?'

'Downstairs.'

'Sweetie, I've no clothes on.'

'So?'

'What if someone sees me through the window?'

'Then they'll have a more exciting Christmas than they expected.'

'Oh, Rick.'

'Come on!' Outside the blue room, 'Close your eyes,' he commanded, clasping her hands and leading her on to the Chinese carpet. 'OK. Now you can look!'

Inside two seconds Adrienne Rader's eyes grew as wide as Rick had ever seen them, before the sharp intake of breath. 'Oh,' she said lifting up the dress. 'Oh.' Holding it against her, she turned this way and that before the mirror, 'It's *beautiful*. Here! Help me try it on!' She fairly leapt into the dress panting, 'Zipmeupzipmeup!'

The disappointment of Canal Street turned to pure joy. Rick wanted to hug her till tears came. Adrienne whirled round to him. 'Oh, Rick Rick Rick.' She kissed him again. 'It's . . . the most incredibly beautiful thing I've ever seen.'

From the table, he handed her the sceptre of silver and crystal and blue and green gemstones. 'There,' he said. 'The Midas touch and it's complete.' Taking a step backwards, he gazed at her. The dress was an incredible amalgam of violets, mauves, blues and silver greys. The neck, round, angled down to between the breasts in a blue V of spiderweb net, the edges studded with tiny rhinestones. From breast to crotch was tight to the skin mauve satin with a silvered grey network of subtle washes like the lacteal cloud of spray that conceals the glory of a distant waterfall. From the crotch, it hung in heavier mixed blue satins almost to the floor. Behind, an almond-shaped opening exposed the back to mid-spine, the top half of the buttocks sheathed tight, the light satin biting into the crack like the grip of a jealous lover. The whole thing shimmered like a mystery when she moved. The dress was sensational. She, in it, no words could describe. Only her feet and ankles showed, yet to Rick, she was heedlessly, totally naked, putting the gleam of her sceptre to shame. The Barefoot Contessa.

Adrienne smiled and the thought of losing her almost broke his heart. She came slowly towards him, delivering a silver tap on each square shoulder. 'Thank you, my knight in shining armour. Thank you, my poet, my lover, my great big wonderful man.'

In minutes, they were in the mammoth bed. Her legs locked over his own, her feet inside his knees, she held her thighs as open as her eyes wherein he saw reflections of the best love they had shared. He loved her. She loved him. He *knew*.

Within two days, they were back to the edge of the bed routine. It was like spending your sexual and emotional life in a Link Trainer, Rick thought. Shut up solo in the dark, flying blind on instruments, instead of soaring with co-pilot and all-seeing eyes up into the wide blue yonder. Though depressing, he determined this stranger than fiction situation was not to become a misery. That there would have to be a showdown with her there was no question. It couldn't go on like this. But not now.

On the twenty-seventh, Rick made two separate airport trips to pick up Pete and Sam. To Rick's concern, Sam looked a little more frail since the last time they'd been together, but his spirits were their usual high. That evening, as Rick changed before taking them to dinner, Adrienne sat herself beside him on the big bed. 'Rick,' she said in a low murmur, 'I don't want you taking everybody out when they get here.'

'People on holiday like to go out, Adrienne, especially when it's someplace new. And this *is* Paris.'

'But you can't really afford it. Let's just eat in – please?' The mud-greens locked on to him.

'We'll see.'

That night, with Sam and Pete, they played gin rummy till late, Adrienne, easy and relaxed, mixed their personal tequila highballs. Twice! And unsolicited! Tomorrow the fun would begin in earnest. People time. He felt happy.

At the airport, Rick saw Dom first, totem-head and shoulders above the rest, standing with Conko and the girls – black-haired, pretty nine-year-olds with low monotonic voices. The Drone Twins, the Peppermint Patties. They were like programmed miniature androids, alien children from *The Midwych Cuckoos*. Rick had never heard them laugh. Bringing up the rear was a grave-faced sixteen-year-old Donna. After greetings, 'We want to buy something for Adrienne,' one Pattie droned, and while a small plant was purchased from a flower stall in the arrivals hall, Rick watched as Donna drifted off to lounge against a tall cylindrical advertisement drum, face clouded, unsmiling, remote. She hadn't spoken a word to Rick. Could this be the same Donna who, three weeks back, according to Adrienne, had been so excited to have been invited?

Rick put Patrice and Dom in the downstairs Empire bedroom. There was an adjoining bathroom on a lower level with a door which led into the long games room. You could play table tennis, darts, pool or snooker. There were free weights, two exercise machines, a sit up bench and a rowing machine. It had its own piano and a wind-up gramophone with stacks of old 78 records. Daguerreotypes of the Crimean campaign and the surrender of the

German High Seas Fleet to Earl Beatty aboard the battleship *Queen Elizabeth* adorned the walls. There was also a giant mirror in which to admire your 'boody'. A flight of stairs led down from the Empire room to the sitting room and kitchen, beyond which Pete and Sam were camped in a bedroom with its own private ablutions. The Drone Twins would bunk with Patrice and Dom.

In the upper part of the house, Donna was given the guest room next to Rick and Adrienne, leaving the top floor with the bath for Buzz and Margie. All but Donna for the most part seemed merry and bright; the house, along with Adrienne's dress, was much admired. Pete took the twins off to the games room, while Rick busied himself preparing grub in the upper house kitchen. Everything coasted along fine until just after six o'clock when the phone rang in the big brown sitting room. Adrienne answered it, her face lighting up the instant she heard the voice. 'Oh, that's great!' she cried. 'When?'

'Oh, Jesus, no,' Rick breathed. 'Not Mickey!' Worse. It was Ming. The phone was passed round to little squeals of delight. Ming the Merciless had invited herself! Would arrive on the morning of the thirtieth. Sans Bill.

'She can't bear to think of us having a good time while she misses all the fun,' Patrice laughed when the call was done. Rick nursed his drink by the fireplace, deep in thought. Ming! Dear Christ what a bummer. And she'd come without Bill. The Bill who's always complaining she doesn't spend enough time with him. Now she's giving him the festive elbow on the banks of the Great Lakes to arrow over to Paris. Across the room, Donna, smiling her first smile, caught Rick's eye and quickly looked away.

After dinner, Rick made some drinks, and everyone except Sam went down to the games room. While Pete and the Drones played table tennis, Rick put on some 'Tinkle and Slosh', the slow, slow, quick quick slow, of old Scarface himself, Victor Sylvester and his Ballroom Orchestra. All seven of them. He cranked the wind-up, lowered the needle, and, bumping into Adrienne as he turned, took her in his arms, sweeping her round the billiard table in the nifty quickstep he'd taught her on the *QE2*, while the strict tempo chimed out a delicate lively little number. As they whirled, there

155

was a light in her eyes. Radiant. He sang the words to her as she clung to him. 'The moon was high above, and heaven was in your eyes, the night that you told me, those little white lies.' A few seconds later, she dropped her arms and they stopped dancing.

In the morning, there was a group outing to some cloth and wool place. Conko had a loom at home and wanted to look at some materials. Rick made his last airport trip to collect Buzz and Margie and spent a quiet day with them and Sam, who had no particular interest in knitting, sewing, weaving or even creative knotting. The travellers returned at five, but Rick didn't see Adrienne until dinner. Loading the video camera she took Dom and Donna off to film them doing bits of a lousy movie script Rick had turned down. After they'd eaten, the company divided into four teams for Trivial Pursuit. Adrienne played with Donna, Rick partnered Pete. Once again Adrienne was bubbling and happy and the morning brought the surprise of her hands on King. Three days in a row now. The voice purred, low and provocative. 'Want me to make you come, sweetie?' She was a mistress of rhythm, had very strong hands, but the variance of once upon a time was missing. She masturbated him at speed like a maid in a hurry polishing a brass bedknob, his climax greeted with a smile and a lightning, 'I love you,' before she ran to the bathroom, as she did this morning, to wash the jet of sperm from hand and arm, before disappearing for the rest of the am.

Rick was alone in the upper house when the buzzer sounded. Picking up the internal telephone, he heard an elongated two-tone squeal, 'It's meeeee-eeeee.'

'Just a moment!' Rick buzzed the main door open, looked at his watch. Eleven-thirty. Opening the door, he moved on to the landing. 'Up here,' he called, and listened as the footsteps approached. She rounded the little half-landing. Brown hair, long coat, small bag. God, that nose. And those *eyes*. 'Hello, Alice,' he said, as warmly as he could, No reply. 'Why didn't you call? I'd have come to meet you.'

'Ohhhh Nonononono. I'm a well-seasoned European taveller.' She followed Rick into the brown sitting room. So many of the furnishings had been his mother's. Warm, comfortable, stylish. A swift appraisal, then, 'Nice taste,' said Alice.

'Everyone's out sightseeing at the moment,' he said. 'They shouldn't be long. Here let me take your bag and I'll show you where you'll be sleeping.'

'I'm quite able to carry my own bag thank you.'

Rick showed her to the guest room. 'You'll have to share with Donna, I'm afraid,' he said. 'Buzz and Margie are on the next floor. There's a bathroom up there, and,' he pointed to the sink, 'a washbasin here if you want to freshen up. Loo's across the hall and Adrienne and I are at the far end.' Alice placed her little bag on the floor. Not much luggage for a winter stay, thought Rick. 'Would you like some tea or coffee?' A pause. 'Or I can make you some breakfast.'

'Nononono. I'll just wait here until everyone gets back.'

'Suit yourself,' he said. 'If you change your mind, the kitchen's one flight down.'

Rick hadn't seen her since the C.O. Jones week. And here she was, according to Patrice, aching to join the fun. Sure looked like it.

Alice stayed in the room till the others returned. On cue, mother made her silent entrance into the kitchen. Adrienne was first up the stairs. Smiling, Rick turned to greet her but her eyes were not for him. Instead, they were fixed on Alice. The mother's arms slid slowly round her daughter's waist and clasped her tight. With Rick chained to the stove, Alice took immediate control of the family excursions, beginning that same afternoon. At around seven, Pete came into the blue room where Rick was playing the piano.

Grim-faced, Pete sat on the wide window ledge. 'What is it with Adrienne's mother?' he said.

'Search me,' Rick smiled at his son.

'We'd been walking for hours and hours, when I said, "Why don't we take the Métro?" You'd have thought I'd said something really awful. "Don't complain," she said. "We don't want any complainers. If you don't like the company why don't you go home?" "Yes, why don't you?" Patrice said.' Pete looked down at his feet.

'Then what?'

'Then Adrienne said it too. Just like the others. I couldn't believe she'd do that.'

Rick heard the footsteps on the outside stairs. 'Don't worry about it, Son,' he said quietly. 'Why don't you go tell everybody dinner'll be ready in an hour, then come up and give me a hand.'

'OK, Dad.'

Slowly, Rick closed the lid of the piano. 'No, you old bag, oh no,' he thought. 'You're not going to spoil this holiday.'

After a supper of roast chicken, salad and fruit and cheese, Pete went off with the Patties to the games room, while the adults gathered in the brown sitting room. Everyone sat round drinking and talking. Everyone except Ming who sat apart in a corner on the floor, in front of the television, talking softly to Donna, crouched at her side. Rick studied the profile. Beside her the portrait of Whistler's Mother was a study in warmth and compassionate benignity. Another session of videotaping was set up by Adrienne, and as she took Dom and Donna up the stairs, Rick went to the kitchen to fetch more wine. As he picked up the corkscrew, Adrienne appeared at his shoulder. 'Rick.'

With a sideways glance, 'Hi, stranger,' he said lightly.

Either she missed it or chose to ignore it. 'I think you should talk to Dom.'

'Why?' Rick said. 'What's up?'

'He's bought a knife.'

'So?'

'A switchblade. Because of what you said about being careful you don't get mugged in the alleyways here.'

Rick laughed. 'There's no danger, Adrienne.'

'You said there was. That's why Dom bought the knife.'

Rick put the screw into the cork. 'What I said, Adrienne, was that it's dangerous to walk round the sidestreets on your own after midnight. The only people at risk are half-drunk guys looking to get laid, and carrying a wad. There's no threat so far as Dom's concerned. No one's going to bother him.'

'I still think you should talk to him.'

'No,' Rick grunted as the cork was pulled. 'I'm not going to do that. Dom's over twenty-one. It's none of my business what he buys with his money.'

'Rick, I want you to—'

'I said no, Adrienne!' He got the beadiest of glares before she spun on her heel and ran up the stairs.

In the darkness, Adrienne's voice came quietly from the pillow. 'Rick?'

'Yeah?'

'Alice says Pete's been interfering with the girls.'

Stiffening, Rick went silent.

'Rick. Did you hear what I—'

'I heard you.'

'She thinks . . .'

'She thinks or she knows?'

'I'm not sure.'

'If no one's sure, then that's a goddamed *despicable* accusation.'

'Rick, I—'

'Which we'll talk about tomorrow.'

'I just—'

'I said we'll talk about it tomorrow, Adrienne. OK?'

'OK.'

Rick lay silent, unable to sleep. Adrienne seemed to have no such difficulty. She'd imparted this latest news as if it had been the conclusion of a geometry theorem. Alice says, therefore it is, QED. But surely there could be no such logic in the universe. Half an hour later, Rick stole from their bed and down to the brown sitting room. Switching on a single light, he fetched a bottle of beer from the fridge in the little corner bar and sat hunched in his mother's old chair, thinking. He would have to get into this tomorrow. Question the twins and Pete. In a cold anger, he tried to fathom it out. The sniping at Pete on the outing. Adrienne over Dom and his 'switchblade'. Now this rotten and, Rick was certain, groundless accusation.

Rick sipped at his beer. He would have to have it out with Adrienne the instant New Year was over. There was no other option. Choice, Adrienne, choice. Your mother or your husband. Ming or your man. Come on, say it for all to hear. 'This is my husband. Here is the man I love. He is my first priority. Yes, very soon now the cry would go up. *Prepare to receive cavalry! FIX bayonets!*

An hour or so before lunch, Rick found Pete as usual in the games room, at the pool table with the twins. 'Having a good time down here you guys?' he said.

'Pete's teaching us to play snucker,' one droned.

'They've picked it up really quick, Dad,' Pete said.

'He always beats us,' the other said ruefully.

Rick laughed. 'Just you wait till you've played a while.'

Pete was thirteen, they were nine. Rick remembered when he had been young and good at things before a captive audience. It made Pete feel important. He was heading his own little group instead of playing second fiddle to the grownups.

'OK. Have fun.'

'Bye,' they chirruped.

He left them to it. His role as head cook, bottle washer and general skivvy gave Rick plenty to do in the kitchen. He dropped in on the old boy on his way, determined not to breathe a word of Ming's accusations. Sam suffered from nervous dyspepsia and Rick didn't want him burping the New Year in with cans of Andrews Liver Salts. He decided he would tackle Pete and the twins later, separately.

Sam was camped on one of the two leather sofas in the brown sitting room, framed in the centre of the three windows that overlooked the Seine. Stick at his feet, he was massaging his knees. Rick knew he was in pain but would say nothing. 'Knees bad?' he asked.

'They stiffen up if I sit for any length of time,' Sam smiled. 'The joys of old age.' He reached for a cigarette. Sam and a gasper were never parted for long.

He exhaled a long plume of smoke.

'Ever thought of trying to give up?'

'Listen, brother. I don't drink, I eat very little, don't go to the

160

movies and an erection is out of the question. Leave me, if you will, to enjoy the one real pleasure I do have left.'

'Couldn't you cut down? Just a bit?'

Sam had heard it all before. 'I've smoked for almost fifty-five years. Since I was fifteen. And I have no earthly intention of giving up now. So there.'

'You know how bad it is for you . . .' Rick almost laughed out loud at how schoolboyishly like his own son he sounded.

Like lint from a lapel his father brushed it off. 'I might be sorry to get lung cancer,' he said, 'but I'd never regret smoking. Not for a minute. You know my philosophy; what's for you will not go past you. When you go, you go. The great big wheel keeps on turning and when it's your turn to get off, bye bye, out goes the light and that's all there is to it. In the meantime, life is sweet.' He cleared his throat. 'Where's the, er, the boiler?'

'The who?' Rick knew perfectly well who he meant.

'The old biddy.'

Rick laughed. 'Christ knows. I haven't seen her since lunch.'

'She's a bit of a boiler is she not, to be looking for leading lady roles?' Women past a certain age were, to Sam, 'boilers', (when a bird was no longer a chicken, it could not be roasted, but must be boiled.) He told Sam of the diary.

'Has the woman any talent at all?'

'None that I can see.'

'Is she still turning up for auditions on your New York doorstep?'

Rick nodded.

'Not so keen on domestic roles though, is she? Nor is Adrienne, come to that.'

Rick could have sworn he felt the sweep of an icy draught, then suddenly Ming was with them in the room. Without a word, she pulled Rick's mother's old rosewood chair into the centre of the carpet and took up the guitar which lay against the side of the sofa. 'I'm going to sing you a revolutionary song about Nicaragua.'

Fuck my old boots, thought Rick. He remembered his own mother and her jazzy happy warmth when belting out 'Some of These Days' while Rick had accompanied her on the piano.

Glancing quickly at his watch, 'Good God,' he said. 'Is that the time? Gotta check the stew.' He skipped the room to the first twang of the guitar, and a pang of guilt at abandoning his father. Up the stairs he ran two at a time and into the kitchen. Sanctuary!

Later, in the blue room, Rick placed the knives, forks, spoons, in an unconscious rhythm of 'she loves me, she loves me not', around the old Spanish table. Away each day, away each weekend, away at class, away at workout, away with Mickey, away at Ruby's, away with family, away at meets, away at Lara's, away in Chicago, away with the fairies and away to the corner of the – and as he said 'Big, brass bed' he laid the last three implements for dinner, like a man who was out to lunch.

Unable to find a bowl large enough for the beef stew, Rick slipped downstairs to the kitchen in the lower house. There was a silver soup tureen and ladle sitting on the old dresser which would be ideal. The Drone Twins had beaten him to it, and were sitting at the pine table, drinking soda. 'We have to go out in a minute,' said one. 'We wanted Pete to come but he's staying home,' the other intoned.

'Oh,' said Rick. 'Where's your mom and dad?'

'Upstairs with Alice and Adrienne,' they said together. Gramma was a word they had been trained not to speak.

OK, thought Rick. Now's as good a time as any. 'Are you having fun here?' he asked.

'Yes, we are.'

'We like Pete.'

'We really like Pete.'

Rick thought he could tell them apart now. Claire had a tiny red spot on the bridge of her nose. When it disappeared they would once again be indistinguishable. As well as inseparable. 'What do you do when you're with Pete?' Rick asked.

'We play snucker,' said Sarah.

'And pool,' said Claire.

'And table tennis.'

'And darts. But we're not very good at it.'

'Wow, you've been busy,' laughed Rick. 'Do you play any other games? Any . . . touching games.'

'You know, like tig?'

'What's tig?' asked Claire.

'Where the one who's touched becomes "it" and stays "it" till they touch someone else. Then it's their turn to be "it".'

They stared at him. He wasn't putting it very well. 'Er, tag?' he tried hopefully. They shook their heads in unison. 'What about catch? Do you play any catch games? Or wrestling?' Again two negatives. 'What about postman's knock?' Rick persisted.

Together, 'What's that?'

'Oh, never mind. Just a game.'

'We played hide and seek once,' said Sarah.

'And that's all? You don't play anything else? Like tickling games?' Two little heads shook and two clear pairs of eyes stared at him. One last probe. 'What about Pete? Is he nice to you? Is he kind?'

'He's our friend.'

'We'd like him to come home with us.'

The wee innocent things. Rick wanted to take them in a double hug and squeeze the delight out of them, but, in the same instant, could imagine the shadow of an intruder, creeping along the passage wall with a polaroid land camera to snap him in mid-Humbert fumble.

No one stayed to help wash up after the lightning pasta lunch Rick had rustled up. 'We'll leave it till you come back,' Rick said to Adrienne, as Ming led the party to the Eiffel Tower. He made Sam some tea, then challenged Pete to a game of snooker. 'Only if we play pool and table tennis as well,' came the reply. 'The two out of three winner is the overall champion.'

'OK.' They started with pool. Two minutes into the game, and three balls behind, Rick asked,

'You didn't want to go out with them all?'

Pete whacked a solid into a middle pocket. 'Not after yesterday, thanks.'

'You get on all right with Dom and the girls, don't you?'

Targeting another ball, 'Yeah, Dom's OK,' said Pete, 'and the kids are nice, but Donna's a bit of a pain. Every time you see her she looks like she's just lost another hundred dollars.'

Rick laughed.

'I only have to say the slightest thing and the women are all over me. Even Adrienne.' As Rick bent to take the shot, Pete went on. 'That really got to me, you know. After those summers we used to spend in Italy, when she was really great. It's like she's someone else now. When I think of how we used to dive and swim and laugh and sing harmonies together. And the holidays here, doing jigsaw puzzles on the hearth next to the Christmas tree and playing gin rummy. And remember when we did *Twelfth Night* on video, with me as Olivia, you were Malvolio and Adrienne Viola? That was fun.' Pete moved to the table as Rick miscued. 'I really love her, you know? But it's like she doesn't feel anything for me now. Nothing's fun any more. I feel like I've done something but I don't know what.'

'Well, her family's here, and I guess she's kind of busy with them,' Rick said quietly.

'No,' said Pete, 'it's more than that. She was like it before they came – like she's far away or something. I don't know.'

'But the twins are fun?'

Pete nodded. 'Yeah, they're OK. Only one to sink, then I'm on the eight ball – better get movin', Dad, or it's goodnight nurse.'

Rick lined up his cue. 'You're too good for me Fast Eddie. Pretty little things aren't they?'

'What are?'

'The twins – Claire and Sarah.'

'Kinda, yeah.'

Rick made a hash of his shot. 'Do you fancy them?' he said to the green baize.

Pete stared at him. 'Fancy them? What do you mean?'

'I mean . . .' You *idiot*, Rick thought, trying to rephrase.

'Dad. They're not exactly my age group.'

'I mean do you find them attractive?'

'Sure, they're attractive. They're cute.'

'Well, you never know.' Trying to dig himself out of a hole, Rick was slipping further into the mire. 'In a few years from now . . .'

'Dad, what's the matter with you?' Pete's face had the same two clear eyes as each twin. 'They're kids!'

Rick took a three-nil beating.

It was after seven when Ming and her troop returned. Inside five minutes he heard Patrice calling loudly from below. 'Gi-irls. Where are you? Are you alo-one?'

In the kitchen, Rick slammed the lid down on the stewpot. In Broadway Jack phraseologoy, it was wash-up time. 'Adrienne,' he shouted down the stairwell. The walls reverberated with the roar. She appeared in seconds, a wariness in her eyes. 'Got a minute?' he asked.

'Why?'

'We have to talk. He led her firmly by the hand to the empty lower house sitting room. They sat on a pastel-coloured sofa like strange, new-met relations, tense and distant. Rick ached to say a loving word, instead, 'That happy little chat we had in bed last night,' he began. 'What Alice said about Pete. I want to know where it came from.'

'What d'you mean?'

'I mean what does *she* mean? Did she say she saw anything happen?'

'No, no.'

'Did the twins say anything to her or Patrice?'

'No.'

'Then what the hell is going on here?'

'It's just Alice's feeling.'

'Did she say anything to Pete or the girls?'

'I don't think so. No.'

'So, she never saw anything, nobody said anything and she never asked anything?'

No answer.

'Well I've just talked to Pete and to the girls and none of them knew what the hell I was on about, thank God. But *I* want to know something. Like what the hell is the matter with this goddam mother of yours?'

Adrienne began to cry. 'Nothing's the matter with her. Alice

165

was interfered with when she was their age. Maybe it's that. She's never told anybody.'

'Except you obviously.'

'I didn't know anything about it until yesterday.'

Yesterday. Holy shit! What was the story with this woman? Nine times out of ten, Rick's fury might have melted. 'If Alice wasn't your mother,' he said. 'I'd kick her, Patrice *and* Donna into the Seine right now. But I'm warning you. If she steps out of line once more, that's *it!*'

'What do you mean?'

'What do I *mean*? Isn't it plain what I mean? An accusation is made based on Alice's feeling. Totally without foundation. Groundless! Adrienne, bypassing on such despicable nonsense, your mother is guilty of the most appalling and potentially damaging lie – about *children*, for heaven's sake. You've seen the girls. At every mealtime fighting over who's to sit next to Pete. And they're not half a day finished telling me they'd like to take him home with them.'

'You're right, you're right. I'm sorry, Rick.'

'So am I,' he said. It hurt him to see the tears on her cheeks, hear her voice like this. 'Go dry your face. There's a towel next to the stove.'

She did as he said. 'What about dinner?' she asked in a swift recovery. 'Everybody's waiting.'

'You go dish it up. I'll be along in a minute.'

Like a schoolgirl spared the rod in the headmistress's study, Adrienne fled.

Rick sat back in the sofa and looked round the little room, with its gilt mirror, marble table, Chinese lamps, Berber and Indian carpets and the many-coloured pastel sofas. On the walls, soft water colours. Everything for her. One painting of Millport Pier had faded over time, almost to advantage. Rick closed his eyes, feeling wretched. Minutes later, hearing a familiar clop clop dot and carry tapping, he got to his feet. Sam paused in the doorway, propped up by his stick. 'Aren't you joining us?' he said. 'Everybody's hungry.'

'I told Adrienne to see to it,' Rick replied. He took a bottle of Rioja from the corner rack and opened it.

'Are you OK?'

'Sure. Everything's fine.'

'I thought the lassie seemed a bit upset,' Sam paused. 'She doesn't seem to know what to do.'

'It's not that hard, Dad,' Rick snapped. 'Everything's ready. All she's got to do is carry the grub into the dining room and slosh it on the plates. Nothing too demanding.' He took a drink of Spanish red and tasted gall.

'I'll tell them you're on your way, then, shall I . . .?'

Putting down his glass, he squeezed Sam's shoulder. 'Sorry, Dad,' he said. 'I'm not mad at you. Tell them to start without me. I won't be long, I promise.' He saw the nicotine-stained fingers of Sam's right hand twisting on the head of his cane. 'Go on. Don't wait for me.' Father and son regarded each other, and Rick smiled. 'I'll tell you later,' he said.

Sam nodded and turned away.

Sipping at the wine, Rick contemplated the colours of the big Irvin painting that hung beneath the kitchen skylight. Wild, angry brushstrokes in the shape of the word YES almost obliterated by blood-coloured spatters and the pallid death-stamp of a white St Andrew's cross. So, there's a lassie who's upset and doesn't know what to do. Someone who never says diddleysquat is openly showing distress. Rick drained his glass. The whole chemistry of the house had changed the instant Ming from the planet Mongo had landed. Mongo. Rick recalled the *Flash Gordon* reruns. Those ancient black and white serial movies. The power-crazed Ming hell-bent on Earth's destruction through the Death Ray, and a devilish device to suck nitrogen out of the atmosphere, or else seeding the air with a dust called The Purple Death. Now, having survived the Tunnel of Terror and the Disintegrating Room, Ming was back. In Paris. Thirsting for revenge. Rick took a deep breath. 'OK, Flash,' he said. 'It's New Year's Eve, let's go.' As he headed for the stairs, sprucing his cheeks with his open palms, he noticed that his hands smelled of onions.

They were lapping up ice-cream as Rick tried, without appetite, to swallow his beef stew. He had made it with fillet steak, mis-take, and it was as tough as an old boot. Old boot, he said to himself catching sight of Ming sitting bolt upright, the Obergrup-penführer of the Chicago and District Waffen SS.

Princess Aura sat with buttoned lip and eyes cast down. Next to Ming, a mute Patrice then Margie. On his left, the Totem was swilling Gewürztraminer. Meanwhile, the twins were still arguing over whose turn it was to sit next to Pete.

Sam smiled at Rick. 'About time, too,' he pronounced.

Rick smiled back. 'Sorry about the stew.'

Donna managed a little grunt.

'It was a bit chewy,' said Pete. 'But I liked it.'

Sam ground the knuckles of his thumbs under his index fingers, something he always did when agitated or distressed. No one else said a word, like the air had been sown with The Purple Death. Rick looked about the table. A multiplication of Mount Rush-more. Dinner on Death Row.

11

THE DISHWASHER IN OVERDRIVE, Rick was loading the coffee tray when he caught sight of Adrienne vanishing upstairs with Donna and the camcorder. It was over an hour before they reappeared, when Rick, who'd been playing piano while everyone drank coffee, asked Adrienne to sing 'Musical Demon' with him. It was their party piece. She refused 'Aw, come on, sweetie,' he begged. 'Pretty please.'

'*No*, Rick. I told you. I don't wanna sing.' She left the room and Donna went to join with Ming, who lay on the patterned periphery of the Chinese carpet before an unlit fire. Sam, Pete and Dom were at the dining table, Buzz and Margie in the blue upholstered armchairs. Rick raised an eyebrow at Margie. 'Wanna play?' he asked, nodding at the Ibach. She was an accomplished pianist.

'Sure,' she agreed. He roped in Pete to sing the counter melody of 'Musical Demon', and as they sang, Rick's eyes fell upon The Boiler who was watching him with the lightest of mocking smiles.

Before the ring of bells which would herald the New Year, Rick opened the french doors behind the Ibach. There would be the usual firework display, and he wanted the whole gang to see and hear the whole shebang. It was mild for the time of year and the waters of the Seine shone like glass. All at once the city's clocks and bell-towers counted out the old year, while a thousand churches and carillons pealed welcome to the new as a bombardment of exploding colours slammed across the skies, flaring and reflecting in the river. 'Happy New Year, everybody', Rick yelled, before he hugged and kissed his wife, wishing her the best that health and good fortune could bring her in the coming twelvemonth. 'A happy New Year and many of them!' Rick greeted everyone alike

– even Ming – before ending up with Sam. 'And many may ye see,' he said gently to him, and as he took his father's hand, Rick saw there were tears in his eyes.

Adrienne spent the next hour hanging out the window with Donna watching the fireworks, while Rick dished out drinks and a final round of coffee. Conko and Ming disappeared, followed by a slightly weaving Dom, then Buzz and Margie. As Rick, along with Pete, cleared cups and glasses, he noticed Adrienne had slipped away with Sister Donna.

Rick, Sam and Pete repaired to the big brown sitting room where Rick put on an old Argyll and Sutherland Pipe Band recording. Twenty minutes later, amid reiterated New Year greetings, a skirl of the pipes saw Sam and Pete off to bed, leaving Rick alone. Turning up the volume and pouring himself a small tequila, he closed his eyes, listening. Aware of a presence, he turned to see Adrienne, a frown on her face. 'What's wrong?' Rick asked.

'It's Dom.'

'He's not thrown up on the Berber rug, has he?'

'No. He's saying things to Alice.'

'So what, Adrienne? He's a little bit gassed. People get like that while they're on holiday.'

'He's haranguing her. I want you to come and get him out of there.'

'He's benign. Just tell him to go to bed, Adrienne.'

'He won't go.'

'Then tell Min— Tell your *mother* to go to bed – they can talk it over in the morning.'

'I want you to come and—'

'Why is it,' Rick cut in, 'that the only time you see me or speak to me it's to do with something unpleasant?' Then quieter, 'I think it's high time you and I had a little heart to heart. In the morning. Now go down and tell him to go to bed. Or better still, your mother.'

Tight-lipped, she ran out of the room. Rick turned the music up even higher and locked the door from the inside. Ten minutes later brought Patrice knocking on a pane of glass in the door. Making a sleep mime with his head and hands, he went back to his music. Another ten and Adrienne returned, gesticulating at him to come down. Repeating his sleep charade, Rick left her, to go and refill his glass. What *was* this crap? Dom was tame, docile, weak. According to Adrienne the most he'd ever erred or strayed had been after the birth of the twins, when sex had become difficult, then ceased, and the passing of the months saw Dom trying to drink his way out of depression, picking up needy women in the aisles of supermarkets to get the hungry shag in backs of cars or lonely Mid-west rooms. Until discovery, Adrienne had told Rick. When Patrice, in a vapour, summoned Alice. Who at once had Dom put into counselling. Dom was Mr Meek. Alice was his Frankenstein. So. What was going on down below? Rebellion? Against the Voice of Saruman? Dom wasn't capable of that, thought Rick. Drunk or sober.

Shutting off the hi-fi, Rick walked out to the landing. Pricking up his ears, he listened. Nothing. No sound at all. Curious, he slipped downstairs, stumbling on the half-landing. At the precise moment he mouthed an oath, there came sounds of an altercation. On cue? Poking his head round the games-room door which opened to the hall, Rick saw Ming, a deck of cards spread out for solitaire under her feet. She had the tipsy Totem by his shirt-front, pushing him back and forth, at the same time squealing, 'Stop it! Stop it! Stop this macho stuff!' Adrienne and Donna raced their way past Rick, disappearing up the stairs.

'Adrienne,' he shouted to an echo of steps. 'Come back here!' But she'd gone. Rick turned his attention back to the protagonists. They might have been a pair in early summer-stock rehearsal. No, worse. This was lousy Arthur Murray. Someone being taught to dance and not being very good at it. 'Macho macho one step forward, women's lib, one step back. Adam's rib, two steps forward, macho camacho two steps back.' This was perfect Victor Sylvester stuff. Rick should have brought out the wind-up, stuck on 'Little White Lies' and counted out the time. The Totem kept repeating in inept rote, 'But I love you Alice, Alice I love you,' in reply to The Boiler's 'macho' squawks. And so it went on, backwards and forwards in a two-foot-space now-you-now-me.

'But I love you, Alice, Alice I love you.'

'Don't try this macho stuff on me!'

It really cried out for old Tinkle and Slosh himself, raising his baton over the seven magnificent metronomics of the V. S. Ballroom Orchestra while cooing in encouragement to the plodding duo, 'Shall we try it once more, lady and gentleman, please. Here we go then, with me now, a one, a two, a one two three four . . .

Manoeuvring Totem into the hall and up the six steps to the half-landing, Ming jammed her back to the wall, pulling Dom to her to hold him fast, to the continuous spewing of 'Don't try this macho stuff on me.'

While this farce was being played out, Rick shouted again and again for what must have been a full minute. Patrice appeared at his side. 'This is just plain fucking ridiculous,' he said angrily.

'Dom's behaving so badly to Alice . . .' she began, and Rick jumped on her.

'Dom's half bombed, that's all. Which he has every right to be. It's New Year. Look at him!' The disoriented part-oriental swayed, his arms flopping at his sides like a rag doll's, while Alice shrieked into his shirtfront. 'It's your mother who's behaving badly. She's been nothing but trouble since the moment she set foot in this house. The accusation made against Pete was nothing less than vile.'

Unable to look at him, 'It's just the girls are at a difficult age,' Patrice said lamely.

Jesus, thought Rick, this is like a conspiracy. Mad, he rounded on her. 'What the fuck does that mean? Pete's at a difficult age, we're *all* at difficult ages.' Rick brought the crosswires to bear on Ming. Here goes, he decided. We have lift off! 'You!' The words were harsh and lashing. 'In the name of God leave that man alone. He's less drunk than you are vicious, *you bloody fucking bitch!*'

The last four words, like lasered rockets, blasted round the stairwell. Instant freeze-frame. The little squabble stopped. Dom was still, Patrice still, as Ming's screech rent the air. 'Eeeeh've been called a bitch and eeeeeh'm leaving!' Unnaturally loud, projected like a weighted voice exercise, the echo brought the runners off their blocks with instant clatter of feet on stairs as Donna raced to Ming's side, Adrienne to within a yard of Rick.

In a trembling female basso the words rushed out. 'I'm leaving too!'

Rick stared at her for three blank seconds before, hearing Donna speak her name, Adrienne turned, and as one they took the stairs at breakneck pace, hugger-mugger up to pack their bags while Ming remained clamped to Dom, her 'macho stuff' routine sputtering like a damp squib.

Buzz appeared, naked to the waist, imploring arms extended in a too-late mediation, as Rick put an end to the pathetic farce. 'Oh, shut the fuck up, you old bag.'

Aiming Rick a last look of blinding hatred, Ming flew upstairs to gather her rags, leaving Totem sagging down the wall, macho as a spent match. Inside five minutes they were out the door, Donna, Patrice, twins and all. The Boiler led the sprint, as they hit the street like shit from a shovel. Adrienne, her little brown bag stuffed full, came last, brushing past Rick without a word. He called to her as she reached the door. She turned, her face totally without expression. 'Congratulations,' Rick said simply. 'You've got two assholes, sweetie and your mother's one of them.' Her reply was to slam the door.

'Do you mind if I stay?' The voice, from the stairhead, was Dom's.

'You're free to do as you wish,' said Rick as Totem followed him, a mite unsteadily, into the brown room. Rick filled two glasses with tequila, handing one to the Macho Man. 'Here,' he said, 'drink this.'

Downing it, Dom began a yell of glee. 'I've been de-Raderized,' he sang out. 'De-Raderized.' Taking one more snort, he buckled, and Rick half-supported him down to a deserted Empire room, leaving him propped against the bed. On his way back up, stopping at the brown room desk to douse the lights, Rick noticed two doorkeys placed there. Puzzled, he picked them up, checking each door on his way upstairs till he reached the third floor. The keys belonged to Donna's room and his own. Rick stared at the chest of drawers, two lying open. On it, the collection of silver and stones Adrienne had so desired lay strewn. Undressing, Rick collapsed into bed. He'd put a stop to Ming's shenanigans only to find his own wife an instant foe. His situation with her 'family' had always been hopeless. Like trying to tackle the Hydra with a steakknife.

By noon on New Year's Day it had all come out. It couldn't be kept from Pete what had been said about him. Buzz and Margie knew. Everybody knew. If Pete was indignant and upset, Sam was furious. Alone with Rick in the small downstairs sitting room, his father was in full spate. 'The evil, dirty old bastard,' he said, punching out the words. 'Had I gotten wind of that, immobile as I am, I'd have kicked her old arse all the way to Paris Airport!' Sam always referred to hateful men as cunts, hateful women as bastards. 'This'll never work. Your wife will never be back, and damned good riddance,' he said from his favourite armchair. 'I saw it all last night.'

Rick, drink in hand, regarded him from where he stood in the marble-floored kitchen. 'Is that why you had tears in your eyes?' he asked quietly.

'Good God, man, for five days you cook and set table for everybody while your wife buggers off in the daytime and at night she's running about wi' that damned camera makin' movies – and she and her sister hangin' out the window watchin' fireworks while you're doin' the donkeywork.' He paused to catch his breath. 'And here's a wife that never gave you a damn minute of her time, never even put that dress on *once* for you. As far as Adrienne was concerned, you might as well have spent the entire five days in the lavatory! I saw it a long time ago, Rick.'

'Then why did you never say anything?'

Sam lit a cigarette. 'Because I didn't want to be shown the door.'

'Eh?'

'Told to get on my bike.'

'Come on, you're my father.'

'Oh, I'm your father all right.' He blew out a long plume of smoke. 'But you might have told me I didn't know what I was on about, that it was none of my business.'

'Yes. I suppose I might've.'

'Then there ye go.'

Rick stared down into his glass. 'She's always told me, even as late as yesterday, that she loves me . . .'

'*Loves* you?' Sam echoed, with a small laugh as though he found the thought amusing. Shaking his head, 'Christ, you're just like your mother – a Robert Louis Stevenson damned romantic!' Sam seldom spoke of Rick's mother. 'Kid', he'd always called her. Kid. Who had suffered a dreadful death. With little fear, still less complaint. Every day, twice a day for seven months Sam had driven a round fifty miles to be with her. The day before the end, he had lifted her from her hospital bed to dance with him. In a white room. Ground-floor windows looking out on greensward, with trees. Magpies swooping. Magpies that she said brought pain. When her morphine wore thin.

At the last, fixed with heroin, 'I don't know what they've given me,' she murmured dreamily, 'but I wish they'd given it to me sooner.'

Dancing with him now, 'I love you, you great big wonderful man,' smiling as he held her, a 'don't give up *now*, Kid' bear cuddle encompassing the centre of his universe, a bundle of poor bones that had so short a time ago borne up a proud straight supple dancer's body.

Sam never accepted her sentence of death. When Rick had said, 'She knows, Dad,' Sam had rounded on him like a mortal enemy.

'She *doesn't* know! And if you ever tell her, it'll be the end between you and me. You hear me?'

'Loud and clear.' Silences. One last try. 'It just means none of us can say goodbye.'

'Because there isn't going to be any goodbye! She's going to beat this!'

She died the day after that last dance. On his birthday. I began with you, I end with you. Her last words to him, 'I'll see you on the other side.' His heart fled with her spirit. Sam never spoke of any of that time ever again. His Kid. And her final whisper had not been of fear or for herself, but for Rick. Her wayward boy. Murmuring *her* name for him, 'Look after Bobby,' she had made Sam promise her.

No doubt what he was trying to do now, Rick thought.

Sam's voice broke the momentary silence. 'Women are never driven by any other from the arms of the one they love. They fight. There's only one hand in this, brother.'

'I'll find out soon enough, then. I've booked a seat on a flight to New York the day after tomorrow.' Rick looked at the sad, unhappy figure of his parent. 'I'm sorry about the holiday . . .' he began.

'Never mind Pete or me,' Sam said evenly. 'We'll be fine. Whatever it takes you must get this sorted. What goes around comes around. They'll be actresses when I'm a parson.' Slowly, Sam got to his feet. 'Fancy a cup of tea?' he said.

What goes around comes around. Packing his garment bag, the Disney carousel began its rotation as Rick imagined he heard the order given. That Ming be pulled by the nipples from room to room and abused, then to the shrills of, 'Stop this macho stuff', yanked before an agora of swaying faithful to be labbered to death by Nubian eunuchs with stockingfuls of hot diarrhoea.

12

ON TENTERHOOKS DURING THE whole trip on the jumbo, unable to eat or sleep and uncertain about what he'd find at the other end, Rick began to try to paste some pieces together. He didn't like the way his thoughts were heading. Or the questions they were asking. Like why Ming hadn't simply gone to bed that night. Like why Rick was needed to subdue Dom. Like Dom didn't need subduing. He was potter's clay. Make any shape you wanted. Like Adrienne's flight on Rick's appearance. Like her non-response to his calls she couldn't have failed to hear. Like her immediate appearance with Donna at Ming's screech. Like the two keys left on the desk on their way out. To prevent themselves from being detained? Locked in by Rick? If that had been the case, then Adrienne and Donna were complicit. The moment had been premeditated. You don't act that way in sudden flight. Do you? A pack of other questions hounded him through sleepless torture all the way to JFK.

At last he saw the lights of Manhattan glistening in the winter's chill and prepared himself for landing. Orpheus descending. Abandon hope. Clearing immigration, Rick made a call. After a couple of tones, Broadway Jack answered. 'Ay buddy. Happy New Year. What's doin'?'

'Are you busy right now?'

'Right now? No. I'm just sittin' here watchin' TV.'

'Can you come and meet me? I'm at Kennedy. International arrivals.'

'I'll be there in twenty minutes.'

'Thanks, Jack.'

'No problem, buddy. Is everything OK?'

'Tell you when I see you.'

Half an hour later, gravestone teeth flashing in welcome, Jack gripped Rick's hand, and then his bag. 'Happy New Year, pal. Car's in the lot. This way.' They emerged into the barren, floodlit acreage of Kennedy, found the jeep, pulled out into the slip road, round to the main thoroughfare and sped away towards Manhattan.

It was freezing. There was little traffic and, as the jeep picked up speed, Rick gave Jack the run-down. When he stopped, they were almost to the Midtown Tunnel. Jack interrupted only once – at the mention of the marriage.

'Christ, Rick! When?'

'In the summer. Before we went to Paris.'

'Well, I'll be a dirty . . . that night in Mitchell's, when we all had dinner, you were married then?'

'Day before.'

Jack shook his head. 'And you didn't tell your oldest buddy? I can't believe that, pal.'

'I told you, Jack. I made a promise. Till we could have the big day. I kept to my part of the bargain.'

Jack whistled and hit the accelerator.

They were in Manhatten now. Passing close by Bellvue, the age-old nut factory, now closed for lack of city funds. The streets grey, dark. No one about. Not even nutters.

Looking at his watch, Rick saw it was ten pm, New York time. If she was out, she'd be back soon. If she was in, she wouldn't be going out. He smiled. 'I wouldn't mind a glass and a bite.'

'OK, pal. Where?' Five minutes later Jack found a parking space outside the Caledonian. In back, the restaurant area was almost deserted and they took a corner table. Excusing himself, Rick made a quick call to the apartment. He got her voice, saying, 'There's nobody here at the moment', and heard the message out before putting down the receiver. Back at the table, Jack raised his eyebrows.

'Nobody. Just the machine.' They ordered, and as the waitress left, 'I guess I should tell you then, right from the wedding.'

Once more inside the walls of Folsom prison, he counted the light blinking its way down from the fourteenth floor. The elevator slid open to reveal Pablo, the puffiness of hard drinking on his face. 'You have a nye Creama, Mr Neilsen?'

'Oh, I had a *great* Christmas, thank you, Pablo. A real lulu. And you?'

Pablo gave a squat shoulder shrug. 'OK. Good. 'S OK.'

The apartment was deserted, with signs of a sudden migration. Empty, filthy, silent – and with that peculiar smell you couldn't begin to imagine when you weren't there, but which was all too familiar on return. Something between gas leak and transient hotel. In the kitchen, the SoHo Roach Club was in full parade order on the dishes, munching on a sinkful of floating slops. He opened the fridge – scattered with junk food crumblings. The bathroom shabby, light not working. He changed the bulb, examined the laundry basket. A pair of panties lay on top. Mingish? Conkish? They weren't Adrienne's, anyway. He knew her every stitch, her every eyelash. In the bedroom, abandoned coffee mugs all over the place, on the floor, on the bedside tables. The bed was a mess. One black shoe lay on the floor. The dressing table was dusty, peppered with the trash of haste. It was like a single room in a doss house. All it needed was no curtains and a twenty-four-hour flashing neon sign ten feet from the window and you had the perfect forties seedy B movie. In a plastic bag hanging from the doorknob was a video from the store across the street, taken out two days before. *Sherlock Holmes' Elder Brother*.

They must have fled that day. Why? He peered into the bedroom closet. Clothes still hung there. His and hers. About to close the door, something he recognized caught his eye. On a shelf, stuffed in a pastel bundle, was the blue dress, his Christmas present to her. Again he saw the pre-season silver talismans she had so admired strewn on the Paris chest of drawers. Only the dress had been deemed worth keeping. So *that* was what was in the little brown bag on her departure.

He looked around some more. Her clothes, her trinket box were still there. Her bike, her guitars, her tapes. Where was she? *With lover of course*, sang the voice in his head. Back in the sitting room, even with the little golden light by the telephone turned on, he felt he was in the middle of an airport lounge. Athens. Or Madrid. Or somewhere equally horrendous. At five o'clock in the morning. Grubby and drab. With no one to bring you anything. Like news. His hand strayed to the telephone. But who to call? Ruby? Forget it. Farben? He didn't have his home number and, anyway, he could get him at the office in the morning. He knew she'd contact Farben and he'd ask Farben to get her to call.

He went into the bedroom to check the answerphone. Nothing. No, wait a minute. A voice, lilting and solicitous. 'Hello-o, Hello-o. Is there anybody the-ere? Hello-o.' A pause, then a click. Jesus H. Christ! It was Dom. He'd called to warn her. But maybe hadn't got through to her. He certainly hadn't called to speak to Rick. The rat.

Rick awoke at dawn, still dressed, sticky, parched and liverish. He showered, changed and took a walk around the freezing neighbourhood, buying a newspaper for its crossword – to help kill time until the city woke and he could make some calls. At ten-thirty he called Farben. 'Greg. Where's Adrienne?'

'I thought she was in Paris with you.'

'Well, she's not. I'm at the apartment.' He gave Greg the bare bones. 'So, if she calls you, tell her to call me right away.'

'You got it.'

'She may be at Ruby's, but I'm not going to call there. I'd rather she came here of her own accord. Or we can run to one another laughing on any street in town. I know she'll get in touch with you. Just have her call me.'

'It doesn't sound good.' Frank was chomping on a burger as they sat in the little eatery around the corner from Folsom. 'Why doesn't she come back to the apartment? She must be running out of clothes.'

Rick began to get nervous. 'Dom may have warned her I was coming in.'

'Why would he do that?'

'Covering himself.'

Frank excused himself to go uptown to see his lawyers. Rick

bought some beer and snackables at the deli and retreated to the apartment to stand vigil by the phone. It took thirty-six hours before it rang. 'Dom left a while ago.' It was Buzz, from Paris. 'Adrienne called him, asking him to bring all her clothes. But he didn't have time.'

'When did she call him?'

'About forty-five minutes ago.' Rick held his breath. 'Hello. Hello. Rick, are you there?'

'Yeah, Yes.'

'I think you should know. There was a tape made that night in the downstairs apartment.'

'What?'

'New Year's. There was an audio tape running. Pete discovered it. He was playing the machine after you left, and there it was.'

'What's on it?'

'Just Dom and Alice. Patrice, Adrienne and Donna were there, but there's only Dom and Alice on the tape. You can hear Alice playing solitaire, and Dom is just drunk. It's impossible to make out what he's saying. She's just sitting there, calmly annihilating him. The tape runs for just over ten minutes, and the number of times she called him a bastard was well above a dozen. Not exactly bedtime listening.'

'Keep it for me, will you?'

'I can't. Dom took it away with him.'

'He had no fucking right to do that.'

'Well, he's gone now.'

'Oh, swell.'

Sam and Pete had left the day before. He asked Buzz to give his best to Margie, then put the phone down. Pop goes Dom the weasel again. And Adrienne knew he was in New York. Otherwise, she'd never have called Dom. And who had told her Rick wasn't in Paris. Farben? He sat down. No, Frank, you're right, he thought. It doesn't sound good.

At seven-thirty, Farben rang. It was almost thirty-six hours since their last conversation. A day and a half. 'She's at Ruby's,' he said. 'I just spoke to her. Ruby that is. Adrienne isn't there right now. She'll probably be late back. She's working out or something.

Ruby said could you call her at nine o'clock tomorrow morning?'
All this last at diarrhoea speed. Rick thanked him and hung up.
She'd known he was in town for at least a day, he felt sure. So why
not have called already? None of this was making any sense.

At nine on the nail, he called Ruby. 'Oh, hi, Rick.' The gee-
whiz voice, madly overdone. 'She's not here . . . but she'll be back
in a little while, I'm sure. Could you call back in a half-hour?'

What the fuck *was* all this? 'I just want to meet and talk, that's all.'

'I know she'd like that, Rick. I know she'd *really* like that.' The
voice teeming with insincerity.

'Has she said anything to you at all?'

'No.' (*Gee-whiz.*) 'No. I know something happened with her
mother. But she hasn't really told me anything.'

Rick could just see her at the other end, in glassy-eyed ecstasy.
Natural enough, he thought, if she was protecting her friend. 'OK.
I'll call later, Ruby.' He walked around the apartment, the little
Disney voice needling him. She's not at Ruby's. She's just late in
arriving from wherever it is she *is* staying.

At the next call, he got Ruby again. 'Oh, just a minute, Rick,
just a minute. She's right here.'

He strained at the earpiece, hearing little murmurings, then, at
last, the darling voice – low, breathless, within it the ring of
sayonara. 'I was doin' doo-doo.'

This expression new, alien. It was an 'I belong with someone
else now' voice. The one, silly little 'doo-doo' utterance, more
than Ruby's teeming horse manure, confirmed that he was sunk.
Boom. The tin fish in the magazine. He felt himself shrinking,
decks awash, going down. He suggested they meet and talk.
Mitchell's would be quiet. It was fresh terrain, where they could
run to one another. Big, big hugs, held for ages, warm as pies.

The voice came back, controlled and quiet. 'All right, but you
have to hear what I have to say. I don't want you to say anything.'

Fuck my old boots. 'How long will you be?'

'About half an hour.'

'Okey-dokey'. He tried to make it throwaway, took a breath to
say something light-hearted and heard the phone go down with a
click.

In Mitchell's he was chafing at the bar. She was late. He stuck his head out the door. No sign. In a stew, he decided to go back to the apartment. Run for home, that's where she'd go, should be. He opened the door – of course all was empty and he stood trying to get a grip on himself. What the fuck was wrong with him? He ran back to the elevator.

About fifty yards from Folsom he spotted Adrienne coming down the sidewalk. Opening his stride, he raised an arm in greeting. She offered nothing in return. She was wearing her Germanic cap and Rick's old grey coat, which reached nearly to her ankles. Dismounted Uhlan, he thought. They stopped at the street end, each at a kerb, duellists without seconds. Her face was brutal. The eyes, ice-cold razors in a mask.

A roar of pouring, honking traffic pushed him towards her so she could hear his 'Hi'. She said nothing. 'I was at Mitchell's a while ago,' he shouted. 'But you weren't. I thought maybe we'd got our lines crossed so I went back to the apartment to check.'

'I have about an hour,' she said. 'I gotta go workout with Ruby.'

I'll bet he thought. 'OK. Why don't we go to the Hub?' He motioned over his right shoulder at a restaurant across the way.

'All right.' Together they crossed the avenue, streets apart. They went through to the back and sat under the leaded opaque coloured glass that framed the back wall. A dull, lazy drag of work sandals schlepping down the room brought a pasty-faced, frazzle-haired waitress to where they sat. A tired moan issued from pale lips. 'Help you?'

'I'd like a beer, and also a tomato juice, please.' He raised his eyebrows at Adrienne.

'Just water,' she said.

'We have Perrier or—'

'No. Just water.'

'With ice?'

'No. Just a glass of plain water.' A glass of plain water. I take nothing. You get nothing. Backer hanging in, star baling out. State what you feel, not what you crave, and to hell with The Ballad of the Sad Café. The waitress schlepped off. Adrienne remained frozen-faced. 'I can't deal with your anger,' she said.

He blinked, nice intro, fuck me gently, said nothing.

'Do you remember what you said that night?'

'Very clearly,' he countered. 'I remember what was said before that night too. Some things are said which cannot be passed over. Sorry. Go on.'

'There was so much evil in the house that night.' (I'll say!) 'What Dom said to Alice — and Alice was totally innocent — and what happened with the children.'

'What do you mean, what happened with the children?'

'I mean, it was terrible. The way poor Claire and Sarah were dragged into the street.'

'I agree. And who dragged them there?'

'What about the way *they* feel?'

'What are you talking about?'

'I mean the anger and disappointment they feel.'

He looked at her in disbelief. 'Adrienne, nine-year-old children don't react in that way. They might be wondering why they were woken up in the middle of the night, but that's all.'

'They've been really hurt and wounded by all this.'

'Horseshit,' he murmured.

'What?'

'I said that's all horseshit.'

'I came upstairs twice to ask you to help. Dom was drunk and he was saying things to Alice. We were trying to get him out of there and I came to get you twice and Patrice came once, but you'd locked the door and wouldn't open it.' She gulped for air.

'That's right.'

'You were up there playing your music and wouldn't help me when I needed it. There was such an evil atmosphere.' She stopped.

'Adrienne, whatever was *supposed to be*' — he hit the three words slowly — 'going on that night, it was an internal affair between Dom, Alice and whoever else wanted to get involved.'

'What hurt me the most was that when I needed you to help me, and I desperately needed help after Dom's harangue, you were completely wrapped up in your own anger. I had nowhere to go but you, and you weren't there for me.'

'I was there. Not angry, and listening to music . . .'

'You always talked about priorities. Well I certainly wasn't your first priority when I begged you not to confront Alice and Patrice.'

'Correction. I think, if you recall, I told you that afternoon that if your mother stepped out of line one more time, I would really go for her. And she stepped out of line.'

She swiftly changed tack. 'Anyway, I've been trying to understand why I chose to leave . . .'

The order came and Rick reached for his beer, all ears.

'. . . First there was such evil let loose . . .'

'Not from Dad, Pete or me,' he interjected quietly.

'I know what went on, I was there throughout Dom's madness – and I know that he wasn't the victim. He created the whole situation, he wanted it to happen – consciously or not – and there was no possible way of stopping him. I'd been trying to get him to bed for an hour before anything had even started.'

'All this Dom stuff is simply nonsense, Adrienne,' Rick cut in. 'It's no excuse to bring down a marriage.'

'I just couldn't believe you were so closed to me, and that your anger, justified or not, was the only thing that concerned you.'

'I've told you, I wasn't angry at the time you spoke to me. I was enjoying the music – but you do realize what you've just said?'

She looked up at him, blinking.

' "Your anger, justified or not." ' Slowly, quietly, he restated. ' "*Justified* or not." '

She made no reply.

'The whole sorry business could have been over in three seconds if your mother had gone to bed.'

She flared. 'Alice was completely innocent!'

'Really? Did you know there was an audio tape running that night? That some of that shit was recorded? Pete turned it on by chance two days later. Everybody's heard it. Dom comes over like a bumbling mushbrain while Alice is calmly annihilating him. Sitting there baiting him, according to Buzz. Fully in control, calling him a bastard. And when I finally came down to see what in hell was going on – that's when you and Donna disappeared upstairs, remember?'

'We were going to bed.'

He looked straight at her. 'Come on, Adrienne. You can do better than that. After waiting for me to "help" Dom to bed you leave instantly, all the hour-long concern for Alice forgotten. I must have shouted for you two dozen times in the next two minutes.'

'I didn't hear you. We were at the top of the house.'

'Wherever you were, I have one of the world's big voices, sweetheart. They could have heard me at the German fucking border. Buzz heard, and he came down. And you were going to bed and couldn't hear me? Yet at Alice's first cry of "I'm leaving", you and Donna are right at her side saying likewise. *Donnez-moi une casse*, Adrienne.'

She frowned.

'It means, "Give me a break".'

They sat in an agony of still life. He had not even raised his voice.

'I can't deal with your anger,' she said.

He sipped his tomato juice. It might have been chalk. 'I have a damned good right to be angry. As do my father and Pete. And when, by and by, did you ever speak to me about "my anger" before now – if indeed it ever was a worry for you?'

You could have heard a roach on its way across Broadway. Finally Adrienne almost whispered, 'Alice says something must have happened.'

'Your mother needs help, Adrienne.'

'There's nothing wrong with Alice. Alice is a good person. Bill wouldn't be where he is today if it wasn't for Alice.'

I'll drink to that, Rick thought.

'She really knows about people.'

'Tell it to the Marines, Adrienne. Her attitude to me has been unbending from the day we met. For a long time I thought it was to do with you and me, but no. It was to do with *her* and me. Because you were getting what she felt *she* should have been getting. A passport into showbiz. Even Buzz knows that. He and Margie got it in one. Years ago. At the beginning when Alice wouldn't speak or write to you for two years. Remember? Her reaction when she came to the theatre when first we were together? When I didn't know Buzz or Margie and she arrived at their apartment saying, "I'm going to smash this." '

'Alice would never do that.'

'Then how do I know? Ask Margie.'

'Alice would never do anything like that.'

'Christ, it's there in the diary.'

'What diary?'

'Your mother's. Last spring, up in the apartment. "I want it so much". That's what it said.'

'I don't believe you.'

'Then I'm not going to argue. Since you're so concerned about my anger, when did I ever lay a hand on you? Or even raise my voice? Never did and never would and you know that – you've *never* been afraid of me in that way. And at the same time you know I would be all over anyone who tried to harm you.'

Her face remained stony.

'You know, Adrienne, for long enough I couldn't work out why I was getting these poisonous looks from Vinegar Puss . . .'

She knitted her eyebrows.

'. . . I mean Mort. Or why he'd up and leave suddenly if I was around. On the plane back here, I got to thinking about a lot of stuff. After that brouhaha in the apartment with your brother's asshole friend, and about Alice's comments to you in the bathroom next morning. Concerning my anger.'

She shot him a look.

'Which I heard. I think that started the rolling ball. Hers and yours. Did you tell Rube and Mort that I was threatening you? Look at me, Adrienne,' he said.

She wouldn't.

'Did you?'

Silence. Her head down, he stared at the parting of her honey hair, a handsbreadth from the perfumed warmth he would never know again.

'Did you?'

'No, no.' She raised her head without looking at him.

'Otherwise there has to be another reason for an attitude towards me like he had. Every time he saw me.'

Silence.

'My anger? Come on, Adrienne. You knew all about me all those years before we married. It's not as if you discovered I was the Boston Strangler overnight.' He took a swig of beer, willing her to look at him, but she wouldn't. 'You know, if our positions were reversed, I might well be asking, "Why did you call my father what you did?" But you've made no reference to the words, "fucking bitch", because part of you must know that's how Alice behaved.' Rick cleared his throat. 'I could be wrong, Adrienne, but it's my suspicion you've stuck to the word "anger" because the morning after the stupid C. O. Jones fiasco, Alice planted it there. And yes, I behaved far from well. But if you'd loved me, couldn't you have forgiven me for that?' There was quiet. The only sound the clink of glasses being arranged up at the bar, the only thought in Rick's head. This is hell. After a moment, 'You know what your argument sounds like? "You wouldn't come downstairs to get Dom to bed, therefore I'm not your number-one priority, so I'm leaving you – for ever." In the past few years I could have, perhaps should have, spoken up about a lot of times where I felt hurt, but I didn't, so I'm not going to start now. You can't deal with my anger? Well. I can't deal with one-way traffic. You're not giving me or the marriage a single chance, Adrienne. It's sticking out a mile. If you could have seen your face on the Avenue a little while ago. Have you any idea what you looked like, Adrienne? What you look like now?'

Immediately, she began to cry.

'Please don't,' he said levelly.

The waitress appeared at the table. 'Everything all right?'

'Yes,' he said. 'Everything's fine.' She hovered, reluctant to leave. 'We're just planning our vacation.' He smiled.

'Oh,' she said and wandered off down the room, giving little backward glances. And that was when his head of steam ran out.

Wondering how she was fixed for cash, 'About money,' he began.

A grand cascade of tears. 'I'll pay you back.'

Pay him back? What the hell was she on about? 'Dry your eyes,' he said. 'You're keeping your gym-pals waiting. Adrienne. Let's go.' He paid the bill while she waited at a small distance. Strangely, he wanted to touch her (one last time – the last time?). He thought of those phrases in novels. *She had become a stranger to him.* The bolt went home only when it was you. There's not a thing on earth more chilling than your lover's disregard. The light of small shared things put out. A landscape of familiar pathways vanishing for ever, under a freezing snow.

In the two-minute walk to Folsom, her mood seemed to lighten. 'I'd like to pick up my bike,' she said. 'I need it to get around town.'

'Sure,' he said, a pinpoint of panic growing like ice-light as it strove to fill the void that grew within him.

In the apartment, he went into the sitting room, while she grabbed the bike, standing with it in the tiny hall, glancing at him through the doorway, determined not to be drawn into room or conversation. For the second time that week, she couldn't wait to clear the door. He offered no resistance, asked for nothing. He thought of what he'd meant to say, meant to ask. *I love you. Do you love me?* He knew it was utterly useless. He was wasting his time as he had wasted his breath in Sheep's Meadow. What was the point of mentioning the marriage? There never had been one.

'I'd like to pick up my guitars and tapes,' she said. 'I need my music.'

'Any time.' He stared at the wheel of the bike. 'Goodbye, Adrienne Louise Rader,' he said. A bell rang. On her bicycle? He didn't think it had one. Something rang. End of contest? Of story? 'Take care on that bike now.' It had been his daily reminder that she look out for herself.

There was nothing in the mud-greens. Only an ache to be gone. 'Oh, Rick,' she said. She'd expected a hassle, and her relief that it had been so simple almost made the two words real. She bumped through the door with her two-wheeler, and he fancied he could hear her sigh in holy freedom of release as the door closed between them.

It was a bare twenty feet to the elevator and he knew she'd caught his three words. 'Well, well, well.' He heard the elevator arrive, open and close. Then nothing. The mirror showed a stranded man. A scarecrow. Standing in a field of new-sown loneliness. He opened his mouth to scream but what he heard was, 'Thank you for your support. I shall always wear it.'

The previous evening was lost to memory and the morning remained a numbing blank. He moved across the freezing city, dipping into odd hostelries. A shamrock bar, a French auberge, the Roosevelt, the quiet Carlyle, till he was across on Lex, walking on the run, knowing cold not at all, but feeling icy fever, hungry without hunger, taking drink without thirst, hearing no voice and craving no fellowship. His life with her beyond aid, beyond hope.

He saw the figure sitting in the shelter of a church wall buttress. 'Can you help me?' the woman said as he passed. She wore a purple woollen cap, powder blue thick socks and old brown shoes. Behind the steel-rimmed glasses, the eyes were intelligent, the voice clear. A woman who should be taking classes at Hunter College. That's what she looked like. She couldn't be more than in her early thirties, surely. What in God's name had happened to her?

He stopped at the street corner and reached in his pocket for some notes. He took the two dirtiest ones and felt ashamed. There were two new ones. He back-tracked and held them out to her. 'Here you are,' he said.

She opened a small transparent plastic bag and, operating it like a surgeon's glove, took the money with it, so as not to touch his hand. 'Thank you. Thank you,' she said.

He held his paper in his left hand all the way back to the apartment, amazed by the clinical respect she had shown for his person, and by the way she had branded herself untouchable. Home, he dropped the paper, went immediately to the bathroom and washed his hands. He looked in the mirror. 'Pilate,' he said. A sudden car backfire on the street sent his nerves flapping in rags and he pulled the bathroom door tight shut behind him. Standing in the corridor, he laid his head to the wall, his voice whispering along it. 'You no longer have a wife. You are alone.'

The window in the sitting room was open and the winter wind blew the jingle of the hanging crystals like a taunt to where he stood, mocking him with summer memories. Crossing the room, he closed the window, stilling the sparkling glass with his fingers. There was a dry, dead quiet. He opened and closed the fridge, opened and closed the liquor cabinet. Shit and derision. There was nothing to drink. Nothing and silence. Silence and nothing. He sat, silent and inert. Grey ash, he thought. Death. Tumbleweed. In old western movies, that had always been an image of death to him. Tumbleweed – rolling away across an arid plain. 'That's it. It's finished. Gone. Gone.' He was fearful now, one arm across his breast, fingers kneading the ribcage, the other raised to his head almost looking to fend off a mortal blow. Body stiff-brittle, but everything in spasm, trembling. He was sweating slightly, and felt some wet on his cheek, but he wasn't crying. Too early for tears, surely – and too late to shut the sluicegate on the mill-race of fear, sweeping him to the sea, the whirlpool spuming in the distance, mind reeling, sucked towards the black hole, fighting to pull from the edge of the vortex in a desperate change of tack.

He groped for a Disney image, but none would come. He was shaking now and could no longer sit. On his feet now, grappling and battling the terror. Of death of the ego. Holy shit. He was going to have a panic. Here come the gremlins. Distant elevator drone. Crematorium hum, casket into frying machine. Must move. No staying still. Motionlessness equals death. Must get out of here. Right now. In the hall, grabbing at the big scarf and coat, which he could barely manage, having to kneel to fasten the faulty zip. In its frantic haste, the whole thing resembled a mad lifeboat drill. He flew from the apartment and stood quaking in the corridor stabbing at the elevator button. No sound. Nothing. Jesus. The overhead lamp was bluish-operating-table-end-of-worldy. 'Come on, come on. *Come on!*' No elevator. No sound. Nothing. 'I've got to have a drink.' *You're going to be all right.* 'I've got to have a drink.' He knew it wasn't so much a drink as a place. Warm watering hole, soft ambience with tinkling sounds of humanity. He began dancing from toe to toe like a first-night actor aching for a piss. Despairing the elevator, he raced to the stairwell, and hurtled, crooning panic ditties nine flights to the street.

There was a prison style grille-door at street level, near to the elevator, where you could escape. He did so, hot and slightly dizzy. Outside, an icy wind came belting from the East River, almost pushing him up the street. He clutched his coat at the throat. There is no argument with the inevitable; the only argument available with an east wind is to put on your overcoat. Who was it said that? An American? It didn't matter. He turned the corner, catching sight of his face in the pharmacy window. Christ, he was white! Thank God, no one was in the Watering Hole – just the bartender – the one who looked like Jerry Colona. Oh yes, damn. One other figure, somebody sitting at the bar corner, grinning. He would be sure to be grinning. Yeah. The bartender raised an eyebrow.

'Just a beer, a Bass.'

'Are you OK, Rick?'

'Sure, fine. Nothing a good shot won't cure.'

'Comin' up,' sang Colona, and at the same moment death of the ego surged and struck again. 'Aubade,' it said, and he tried to bat the word away, but 'Aubade, Aubade,' the gremlins chanted and the words of Larkin's poem ran like terror.

> *This is a special way of being afraid*
> *No trick dispels. Religion used to try,*
> *That vast moth-eaten musical brocade*
> *Created to pretend we never die.*
> *And specious stuff that says* No rational being
> Can fear a thing it will not feel, *not seeing*
> *That this* is *what we fear* – No sight, no sound,
> No touch or taste or smell, *nothing to think with,*
> *Nothing to love or link with,*
> *The anaesthetic from which none come round.*

Nothing to think with. Soon. Any time. The brain. That's all there was. Nothing spiritual. Just cranial mechanics. The catch in the throat at the first strains of a hymn, the well of emotion at the sorrow in an unknown face or at the stricken look of a lonely woman in poor shoes, or the fear of death of the ego – that primeval calling card in his early childhood, arriving without the priming of booklore or talk with adults, that first terror of the fact of finality which had sent him bounding from his infant bed and down the stairs to the arms of his mother, was nothing more than the amygdala's first punch – the part of the brain that deals with emotion, love, joy, pain, and also fear. Laying bare primitive emotions that occur independently of, and prior to, thought. Fear can strike without cortex control and can be learned without the cortex being involved. The cortex doesn't intercept at all; in fact, in rational regulation, is far too slow. Beaten squarely to the punch by a primitive Manassa Mauler. Yes, he knew what it was all right, and knowing didn't make it any better – only worse. The emotional reaction to the old sweet song, the darling face of love as it hummed to itself. The sad bag lady, the face smiling bravely in the cancer ward, the weeks-old ba-ba laughing toothlessly to itself in a delight of innocence. These were no manifestations of 'soul' or 'spirit' – only the lightning flash of the amygdala, where the gremlins lived; deep in the keyless mystery of the grey mush. Now one more stab as it nudged the cortex to produce another slice of Larkin.

> *. . . the total emptiness forever.*
> *The sure extinction that we travel to,*
> *And shall be lost in always. Not to be here,*
> *Not to be anywhere,*
> *And soon; nothing more terrible, nothing more true.*

Like a cold engine on a winter's morning, the cortex refused to be anything other than stubborn. He was trying to budge it, praying for a sausage machine throb of sweet responses, but, stuttering, it wouldn't engage beyond, 'Soon. Any time.'

> *. . . nothing to think with.*
> *Nothing to love or link with.*

He tried to curb the outward agitation, glancing over at the only other patron. God in Christ, Colona was prattling away about the Superbowl, to the grinning clown, with Rick's unfilled glass in his idle fist. He felt a huge ball of aggression like a whirling eddy in the mainstream of his panic. A raging desire to vault the bar and sack him like the quarterback Colona was blathering about, and pour the Bass himself. It seemed an age until the beer was drawn, and Rick could hear his heart thudding very fast. It was almost impossible to stay still. He clamped his hands at each side of the barstool, sitting rigid, gazing forward, a pale-faced scream in winter clothing. What if he had a heart block? Here, now? Fighting for breath on the floor of the Watering Hole – knowing that he was dying while the undrunk Bass sat frothing on the bar above him.

Colona at last set the glass down on the counter and Rick waited, aching, till he went back to talk to the man in the corner, before, with trembling hand, he picked up the beer and drank.

'Feeling better, Rick?' He came to in the empty Watering Hole, dimly aware he'd disposed of one further beer and at least three tequilas. The trembling had all but subsided and a smudge of colour had returned to his cheeks. 'A little. Thanks.'

'Good. I was worried about you for a while, there.' This, while changing a bottle at the shelf. 'Bad news?'

'I guess you could call it that.'

'Somebody pass away?'

Rick was silent. Then, 'Yes,' he said softly. 'Yes. Somebody passed away.'

'I'm sorry.'

Rick gave a bleak smile. 'Life goes on, you know?' Digging in his pocket, 'I'd like another of those. What about yourself?'

'No, no. Come on, please – this is with me.' Colona fixed a Cuervo and refreshed the amber Bass. At the tap, 'Family?' he asked. Rick gave a single negative twitch of the head. 'Someone you knew?'

Hiatus while Colona creamed off the stein with a spatula. 'No, someone I really didn't know at all.' He bit into the sharpness of the wedge of lime, then lifted the Cuervo and drank. 'Not at all.'

'Uh huh,' said Colona.

'No, I only really knew them after they were dead.' There was a deadpan air of Jack Benny and Ernie Kovaks in the exchange.

'And they just died?'

'Yeah.'

'Uh huh,' said Colona, completely flummoxed and deciding to leave it there. 'That's really weird.'

'Yeah. So they tell me.'

Half an hour later, he was back in Folsom, a deal calmer, but still wide awake. Bidding goodnight to Pablo, he stepped towards his door. Christ, what was that? He halted at once, ears pricked, throat taut, still as a tracker dog. From somewhere in the building Madame Butterfly shrieked her last. Fumbling with the key, he entered the apartment, stopping silent in the hall. Mad grief. He meandered to their bed, lowering himself upon it, her great big wonderful man, her poet-lover of such a nearby yesterday, just as the mystery sound-man brought *Butterfly* back to stereophonic life, driving Rick once more to the street, and turning his face uptown toward some grander locale. It was sleeting and cold. He had no idea what time it was. His watch lay on the bedside table. Or had he lost it? Shivering, he moved at a trot to get a cab over on Eighth. No chance. An uptown bus roared to the kerbside and Rick hopped on, taking a seat upfront. One lurching stop later, there was a minor crisis. A quarter had jammed in the money machine. The driver, a big black guy, gave the passengers their marching orders. 'Evuhbody offa bus. This bus no longer oprah-tiv. Evuhbody off.'

While the meek and muttering exodus formed a line, Rick advanced to the driver and nodded at the machine.

'All you have to do is give it a little smack,' he said.

'Offa bus,' the driver replied. 'This bus goin' a deepo.'

Rick lifted his hand. 'Look,' he said, 'all you have to do is—'

'Doen tuch dat!'

'—give it a little smack.'

'Bus goin' a deepo.'

Ric compressed his lips. 'What's the problem? This doesn't need fixing. It's easy.'

The driver sat hunched over the steering wheel. 'I'm just wonderin',' he said at last.

'What?' said Rick.

'Whether I should get out from behind this here wheel and kick yo' ass.'

Stop engines. Rick weighed things up as the head swivelled to

195

regard him. The guy was big. Big arms. But fat. And there was sleet on the sidewalk. If anybody overweight goes down, difficult for 'em to get up. Then the swift application of the toecap to the orchestras. Rick heard the recent Rader words, *I just can't deal with your anger*, and, with a gaze more pitiless than the freezing sleet, he let his eyes lock on the other's. His words were extremely calm. 'You come out from behind that wheel, mister, and you'll make the biggest mistake you ever made in your life.' Bringing his big fist down in emphasis, the money machine rattled and the quarter dropped. The driver didn't move. 'I guess that means everybody stays on the bus.' Rick laughed, and sat as the seething but silent operator piloted them on towards Central Park. As he disembarked, he could see the might-have-been headlines. Out of control thespian has waltz in the alley with innocent Harlem artisan'. The muck-rake gutter-slut in each New York daily on him like a rat up a drainpipe.

Still shivering, he fetched up on the corner of Sixth, by the Saint Moritz.

'Rick. My dear old thing!' The booming, umistakable trade mark.

Rick swung round. Ye universal Gods! There, in the middle of the sidewalk, arms flung wide, grinning broadly and inviting myriad New York stares, stood Binkie Blythe-Carrington. Rick's heart leapt a foot within him. 'Binkie,' he cried. 'Binkie. What the hell are *you* doing here?'

'Staying here, old thing. What else?' Eyebrows raised, Binkie pointed gleefully at the Saint Moritz. 'Got a free evening, world's my oyster, just about to dine. Will you join me?'

'Binkie, I'd love to.'

'Splendid. I say, what a stoke of luck.'

'Not here though.'

'Fine. It doesn't have to be here. Of course not. Do you have a place you like? Let's go there. I'm absolutely easy.' Rick turned to hail a cab. 'But perhaps we should have just one quickie here first? I mean, it's *so* convenient.' Binkie beamed at him, owl-eyed through the horn-rims.

Rick laughed. Unknown to Binkie, a 'quickie' meant something quite different in New York. 'OK. Lead on.'

They sat at the street end of the crescent-shaped bar of the Saint Moritz, Binkie bubbling at the bemused bartender as the drinks arrived. 'Excellent man. How splendid of you. Thank you so much,' before turning to Rick, glass aloft, 'To you, old thing. Here's how.' And, as the toast was returned, he drank deeply. 'Of course, you live here quite lot, don't you?'

'Quite a lot, yes. What are you doing here, Binkie?'

'As it happens, I've just finished another book and I thought I'd hop over and see my publisher and the fair Lila at one and the same time.'

'Ah . . .' Rick gazed quizzically at him.

'Of course, you haven't met her have you? I more than begin to wish *I* hadn't.' Binkie's face clouded and, after taking another large gulp of his whisky and soda, he began the saga of Lila, she who worked for a woman's magazine in London.

Binkie and Lila had met the day after Rosie's party last summer to discuss the serialization of his book, and almost immediately had become lovers. 'Then, in early October, I found out she'd been seeing a chap named, aptly, Roger. Well, a fair old bust-up ensued, ending in a fearful scene in a London restaurant.' After her 'Rogering', according to Binkie, he had graciously forgiven her and, for a time, everything in the garden was rosy. In November, she had moved to New York for a year, and now, after a couple of months, Binkie had flown in, to kill two birds, as it were. 'I must say I'm absolutely ravenous.'

Rick emptied his glass. 'Come on then. We'll go to the Yardarm. Old New York pub restaurant.'

'Sounds like heaven!'

As they bundled into a cab and settled back, Binkie smiled broadly, 'It's most awfully good to see you again, my dear old thing.'

'It's good to see you, Binkie, and looking so well.'

'That's terribly kind of you, Rick, but after recent events pure luck, I fear.'

'The fair Lila?' Rick raised an eyebrow.

'Absolutely, the fair Lila. Make what you like of this . . . Breathless with ardour, I arrive at her hotel, hot-foot and busting for a shag, to find a table *à deux* already set. After a lightning peck on the cheek and a stiff G and T, a flunkey appears and dishes up dinner, something going by the unlikely name of "Yankee potroast", during which, wait for it, old thing, she comes out with this grisly tale of how she's bestridden some ghastly, hairy-arsed, New York lawyer johnny, and enjoyed it! Bestriding and bestrode and what's more, and worse, each gruesome detail spilling from the lips and face of a Botticelli angel. Well, after the dreaded Roger it was all too much. I just sat there in a boiling fury, riveted by those bee-stung lips of hers and imagining what they'd been up to, or rather down on. So, immediately after pudding, I put her over the knobblies and treated her to Daddy's one-handed remedy – administered smartly to the naked rump and bloody right too. Which done, she canters off weeping, to the boudoir.' He paused and lit a cigarette, stopping suddenly, the spent match between finger and thumb. 'Do you mind if I smoke, old thing?' The face, with its large spectacles, was donnish but, behind Binkie's charm and propriety, his eyes had a remote set, revealing, albeit fleetingly, the harsh stamp of the English public school. 'I'm trying most awfully hard to give them up. About ten a day now, still, not good is it?'

Rick shrugged. '*Chacun à son goût,*' he smiled.

'As you say,' said Binkie, taking an appreciative drag. 'Well. I thought that would do the trick. I really did. You know, leave her a minute to pull herself together then slip in, give her a gentle, fatherly chiding and tell her all was forgiven so long as Hairy Arse got his marching orders, before mounting her royally, booted and spurred, while her glowing arse electrified the sheets. But not a bit of it, old thing. Not a bit of it.' Blythe-Carrington gave a wintry smile and blinked. 'Do you know she called the house detective, the whoring cow, and told him to summon the bloody peelers, who arrived within minutes, hammering at the door? Well, of course, I had just begun to cry out, 'What the devil's going on?' when, amid shouts of "Police! Open up!" and my reply of, "What the hell is this?" the door was thrown open by this master-keyed house hench-weasel, and these three enormously fat peelers burst past him with their revolvers drawn, sweating like pigs and with that hideously-furious red-necked look on them. Totally without style, old thing. Their leader an NCO, dead ringer for Herman Göring, all swollen and intimidatory, with piggy little eyes in a face like a pink blancmange. Obscene. I mean, imagine any of that lot in pursuit of a fleeing felon. Out of the question, old thing. One supposes that's why they carry those pop-guns, to bring down their quarry the easier way, like big game. Except the streets of New York aren't exactly Serengeti and, sooner or later, some benighted bystander gets one up the arse, or worse.' Binkie dusted ash from his knee. 'No. Ban all guns nationwide and, meantime, get the peelers in a sprinting and work-out programme. They remind one so much of German police here; overweight, aggressive and plain unhelpful.' Binkie smiled. 'Oh, while we're on the subject of German police, have you heard the two blue-prints for the new Europe?'

Rick shook his head.

'Best and worst,' said Binkie. The ideal Europe is where the police are English, the cooks are French, the lovers are Italian, the mechanics are German and the organizers are Swiss.' He paused momentarily, 'And the worst is where the police are German, the cooks are English, the lovers are Swiss, the mechanics French and the organizers Italian.'

Rick laughed, and a guttural Arab voice enquired from in front, 'Where you want?'

Leaning forward, Rick pointed, 'Over to the left,' he replied, 'By the next lights.'

They pushed through two sets of doors into an atmosphere thick with smoke. Neo Dickensian, with half-mullioned windows, and wooden tables in two ranks which filled one half of the room. On the other side, a long antique bar, mirrored its entire length, was stacked with bottles. The barman, Jimmy, with his ski-run hair style, was busy pouring ale as Rick and Binkie made swiftly for two open seats at the far end. A throaty voice behind them said, 'Well, hello.' It was Jules, the undermanager, a tall, statuesque redhead, warm and easygoing, the perfect hostess. After introductions,

Binkie said he was starving and Jules showed the two men into the back room, seating them next to a mirror against the far wall by a fat, antique wood-burning stove. Oak panelled and dimly lit, the room was relaxed and cosy. With a highlighted smile and a, 'Call me if you need me,' Jules left the two men to themselves. Within seconds, a friendly waiter arrived and they ordered food and a bottle of red which appeared almost immediately.

'So what happened with Lila?' enquired Rick, as the cork was drawn.

'Oh, yes. Er, Let's see, where was I?' Binkie frowned.

'Herman Göring had his gun out,' Rick prompted.

'Absolutely right. Yes. Well, at that precise moment, the fair Lila puts in a moaning, white-faced appearance at the boudoir door, hastily applied make-up I'll guarantee, and hench-weasel asks her, "Is this the man?" pointing at me. To which the slut croaks, "Yes. That's him," then feigns a dead swoon down the bloody wall. Hench-weasel and Göring rush to her aid and, as I'm saying, "Lila, darling, don't be silly, get up and let's be sensible about this," NCO fatty bellows at the remaining peelers, "Take him down to the Precinct and book him!" Whereupon, old thing, my hands are yanked behind my back and duly clamped with the old bracelets. "She's faking, can't you see? This is all a ridiculous charade," I say. Then, beginning to feel just a little worried, I try the old boy routine. "I demand to see my solicitor," I command icily, i.e. You don't know who I am but, when this is over, you'll all be pounding the beat. No dice. They naturally *would* not listen to reason. Thick as shit in a bottle, old thing, and twice as nasty.'

Binkie drew a breath. 'Have you ever fallen foul of the New York peelers?' Rick shook his head. 'Take my advice. Don't. They really are the absolute end. Göring screams, "Get him out of here!" and with the filthy, whoring slut feigning death on the carpet, I manage to utter a towering, "Jezebel!" in the doorway before being frog-marched down the hall and through the lobby on my way to Devil's Island. Well, now we're in the Precinct, old thing, an awful place, pure Franz Kafka – I'm interrogated endlessly. I ask to speak to a lawyer, I'm told to shut up. Questioned further. I ask again to speak to a lawyer, I'm told it's too late. I say, "I know my rights," I'm told I smell like a brewery, have my personal effects taken, along with my shoes, tie and suspenders and I'm flung into a dungeon with the words, "You'll see the judge in the morning," ringing in my ears as the door is slammed and the little peep-hole snapped shut. I mean, virtually clapped in irons. Well I can't tell you how wretched and angry I felt, and, as I vow vengeance with my hands in my pockets to hold up the bloody Oxfords, I hear a noise behind me and turn to come face to face with the absolute dregs of humanity – a cadre of foul, evil-smelling squaddies sporting Godless scowls who start to sidle towards me. It was pretty frightening, I can tell you. I tried the old blurb, you know, 'What are you chaps in for?' etcetera, but not a hope. Perhaps they'd never met a Wykehamist before, I don't know, but I was poked, pummelled and shoved to the floor. As I went down I was sure I was to be debagged there and then, my cheeks ripped apart like Christmas chicken drum-sticks, to be buggered endlessly until first light, appearing before the ten o'clock beak with the French pox, a round of applause and not to mention HIV positive. And all down to this filthy whore! Well, naturally, I yell as loudly as I can until the peep-hole snaps open, the Philistines retreat and I leap to my feet crying, "This is an outrage!" Whereupon I'm told to shut up, they're told to leave me alone and the peep-hole shuts again. I go back to my corner and sit down and pull my coat up round my ears. I manage to doze off only once and awake to find two of the bastards pissing on me. "Outrage!" again I cry. Same routine but, this time I go back and *stand* in my corner for what seems an eternity until the peep-hole opens and my name is called. I'm given back my things, re-manacled and transported to some beastly courthouse. In the process, it dawns on me that I have a very important meeting with my publisher at two pm that very afternoon but, by now, I'm almost past caring.

'Well, to cut it short, at about eleven-thirty that morning I'm up before the beak in my pissed-on suit, looking pretty disreputable, I dare say, while, a few feet to my right, I see the fair bloody Lila, dabbing at a pair of reddened eyes, courtesy of an all-night plundering fuck sans doubt, being supported by this troglodyte who's giving me the baleful stare. Göring gives, naturally, an outlandishly embroidered version of the evening's events after which I'm allowed to croak a few words about domestic spat, hideous mistake, etcetera, all completely ignored by the beak. I mean, it's well-nigh impossible to create the impression that you're Garter, King of Arms when you're looking like a sewer rat and smelling like a snake. Then the troglodyte asks for, and gets, a restraining order banning me from the orizens of the fair Lila and suddenly, as she grasps the hand of this trog and gazes rapturously up at him, the penny drops. This is Hairy-arse the Bestrider! Struth! The bare-faced audacity! Well, old thing, I'm virtually on the point of pealing out, "This is certainly not cricket," when the beak embarks on a monster castigation. "The fair and weaker sex must be protected from the pissed on and crumple-suited," etcetera, while expressing every sympathy through the troglodyte to Lila the anaconda. I'm admonished and fined two hundred smackers! So there it was, old thing. End of stewards' inquiry. Hairy-arse mounts the filly while I'm warned off the course, relegated to a beastly hotel room to watch Dan Rather and polish the fireman's helmet amid the encircling gloom. Sic transit vulva vagina.' He drained his glass and beamed. 'Speaking of polishing the fireman's helmet, have you heard the latest one, old thing?'

'No.' Rick waited, smiling.

'Regimental dinner. The port's going round. Everyone telling stories about their most embarrassing moment. Eventually, this fresh-faced young subaltern has the temerity to pipe up to the CO, "May I ask what was your most embarrassing moment, sir?" The mess falls silent for almost half a minute until, finally, the old boy begins, "I s'pose I, I s'pose er . . ." he wheezes, "My most embarrassing moment was when my mother caught me masturbating in the bath." There's a pause, then the young subaltern says, "Well, if you'll forgive me, sir, but perhaps that's not *too* embarrassing." Another pause then the CO, "Yes but this was last week." '

Rick rocked with laughter as Binkie replenished their glasses. 'A toast, old thing,' he crowed. 'To the Yardarm. Beats the Precinct by at least ten lengths. And to better days and sparkling women.'

They drank, Rick with a pang of envy, wishing he could

swashbuckle with such panache through the shards of *his* romance. He had been in love for years. Binkie got engaged to be married about once every six months. 'Binkie. What a story, what a cow!'

'Not a cow, old thing. As I've said, an anaconda; absolute crusher.'

'Holy shit.'

'Yes and in terms of Holy shit, the worst was yet to come.' Binkie winced skywards and Rick blinked.

'You didn't try to see her?'

'No. No no no. Ooh Lord no. After paying the bloody fine, I look at my watch and discover I'm barely ninety minutes away from seeing my publisher. I race back to the hotel, cast off the pissed-ons, shower, dodge into some fresh duds and race off. Of course I'm famished, fired with the mad rapacity of righteous indignation, and find myself diving into some Indian job on a corner. There, I order a blistering curry which almost gives me soft palate, wash it down with a bottle of filthy red and award myself a brace of armagnacs before hailing a cabbie and giving him the down-town address. And that's when it began.'

'What did?'

Binkie frowned. 'Well, I'd obviously been more upset than I realized. I was pretty agitated all round, had really been under the whip, so to speak. As I sat back, I experienced this awful feeling of *Weltschmertz* and the beginnings of the odd twinge and stab in the belly, followed by a purgatorial contraction and the first bowel-watering growl of woe. Talk about panic in the streets, old thing. I mean the last thing I desired was to have the *mauvais quart d'heure* in the back of a cab in my only other suit. In a cold sweat, I began to gasp and writhe, barking urgently at the cabby to hurry and, as I bent forward, of course, the absolute worst happened. I inadvertently let one rip, old thing, but, before I could get the sphincter under control, realized I had passed something of alarmingly soft consistency, round about cricket ball size. Well, naturally, I was appalled.'

Rick gazed at his glowing face.

'You see, I'm sweating *now*. Gad, I only have to think of it.' He went bravely on. 'It was the Devil's own job to hang on, I can tell you. Mercifully, we arrived in the next minute or so and I could feel the cabby's baleful glare boring into my back as I went waddling up the street, bum clenched and feet turned out like Chaplin, minus cane and bowler. Every ten seconds or so there was this crucifying bowel-watering growl and a pain like hara-kiri, and I'd be obliged to stop dead, with the old ring-piece pouting away. I mean *really* pouting, old thing. I totally understand what Peter O'Sullevan means when he cries out, "They're coming under pressure in the closing stages."

'The steps were the worst but, finally, I was off the street and at the receptionist's desk and, just as she said, "Yes, can I help you?" I got the old cutlass through the guts again and could only stand there, clenched and silent, grinning like an idiot. I remember thinking "A Dandy in Aspic" before it passed and I managed to croon out, "Binkie Blythe-Carrington. I have an appointment with Mr Mendell." "Oh yes," says she giving me a curious glance. "He won't be a moment. Won't you take a seat?" I said, "Thank you," and, in my best after-thought fashion, 'is there a lavatory I might use? I literally have to wash my hands." "Yes," she said. "Yes. Just there, around the corner to your left." "How very kind of you," I said, laying the jolly-boating on really thick and slid blithely from view to Chaplin down the hall to where it said "TOILET", mercifully empty and, mercifully, with a bolt which I slammed home. Whipping off my coat and jacket, I began, delicately, to climb out of the Oxfords. There was a washbasin, thank heaven and, great joy, a gleaming throne with waiting seat. Saved.'

Binkie took a swig and swallowed slowly. 'But oh, the best laid schemes of mice and men. Instead of clamping myself to the Royal Doulton, I decided to first rinse out the 'Y' fronts and flush away the cricket ball. To this end, I bent over the basin and, as I did so received the coup de grâce. The Colossus of Maroussi wasn't in it, old thing. I cried out and saw through the mirror, the throne, realized my arse was at an angle of forty-five degrees and, dropping the Y fronts in the sink, began to shuffle towards the vitreous china, in one of those Elvis Presley, jerky backward, clockwork-looking bosanovas, one sees in his movies. I flung out a hand behind to steady myself as I sat but, alas, missed the mark and, old thing, the beastly, *hideous* flap fell down just as the sphincter collapsed and a four-day Vesuvius of cack, including the Yankee Potroast spooned to me by that whoring cow followed, sans doubt, by the pm's curried chicken, with hydro-electric force, hit the flap dead centre and ricocheted away to absolutely everywhere as well as up my fucking back. With a howl I sprang to my feet and slammed the flap back up but, by then, control had quite gone and the next standing salvo hit my socks and boots. I managed to get back down to fully relieve myself, cursing bitterly at my inanity, when I was awoken by the sound of running water and, to my horror, saw the washbasin, choked by the Y-fronts, was now running over. I had to do an evil-smelling sprint to shut the taps off and clear the drainage, during which, another blinding hara-kiri and this time, in the frantic scramble back to the throne, the floor got it.' Binkie closed his eyes. 'The entire cabin blitzed with Yankee Potroast and the vengeance of Veeraswami. Well, that's it, I thought. Out first ball.'

Rick was holding on to his glass, tears in his eyes, shaking with silent laughter.

Blythe-Carrington smiled. 'Yes. I know, old thing, I know. Absolutely excruciating. Well there you are.'

'No. No,' gasped Rick. 'What happened then?'

Binkie popped a radish in his mouth. 'Well, naturally I was mortified at the thought of discovery, you know, the entire publishing house battering down the door to reveal me enthroned in boots, socks, shirt, Wykehamist tie and plastered with Delhi revenge. Again, cursing my idiocy, I rolled my eyes heavenwards and, Christ Almighty, it was up on the damned ceiling, spattered far and wide like a flock of high flying starlings. Perched on the front of the pan, I peered over my shoulder and shuddered. The wall was machine-gunned with it and the throne was a goner. No hope of cleaning this lot up. It would have taken squads of those johnnies, what are they called? Motormen? You know, on television here.'

'Oh, Roto Rooter,' Rick gurgled.

'Yes, exactly. Anyway, I thought quickly, and decided to do a crafty bunk. Only thing for it. I whipped off my boots and socks, and, skipping round my floor decoration, washed them in the sink. Swiftly did the tail of my shirt, then my back and arse and legs, drying them on the roller towel which, to reach, I had to stretch like a ballet dancer doing a barre exercise.

'I scrambled back into the Oxfords and glued my ear to the door. Not a whisper. I poked my head outside. No sign of life. What a relief. Tiptoeing into the corridor, I pulled the door to, catching one last flash of the smoking chamber of horrors – if you'd backed a dromedary in there it simply couldn't have topped it, I swear, and it stank like downtown Calcutta. I waited for a second, heart thumping away, then sidled like a fugitive along the passage wall, stopping at the end to peek round. All clear. The secretary not at her desk, Oh joy. In a sudden brainwave, I whipped across Reception and smartly down the steps into the street, jettisoning the Y-fronts into a garbage bin before running into a pharmacy which, as luck would have it, was right there on the spot. Breathlessly, I asked for a bottle of aftershave and, after paying, hung around the doorway dabbing it on to my face as if to try it out. Then, unobserved, I poured some on my socks then shoved the bottle up my coat, emptied some inside the Oxfords and on to the tail of my shirt, at which point I saw the assistant staring slack-jawed at me. "Hairy back," I cried, and leapt into the street, chucking the bottle in the Y-fronts bin before skipping back up the steps into reception. *She* was just emerging from an office, old thing, as I came charging through the door and she shot me a very quizzical glance. "Oh, I thought . . ." she began. "I'm sorry," I said gravely. "I had to go to a nearby hotel. I'm afraid it was just impossible for me to use your ablutions." Just then a door opened and there stood Mendell. "Binkie," he said, expansively, "Great to see you. Come in, come in," leaving a bemused receptionist holding a sheaf of papers.

'As Mendell ushered me in, I saw his nose twitch. I must have stunk like a polecat. Still, most Americans think the archetypal Englishman is half queer and swans around smothered in cologne anyway, don't they?' He dipped another radish in some salt and smiled.

'And that was it?' Rick shook with merriment. 'No one ever found out?'

'Well, put it this way, no one's mentioned it . . . Yet. You know, all the time I was in there, I half imagined I'd hear the hue and cry go up and find myself marched off with mop and bucket to publicly wash my sins away before the entire staff while, "Let not your anal dangers stray," was gently sung behind me by a sent-for priest.' Rick laughed as Blythe-Carrington tackled an enormous steak which had just been set before him. 'Goodbye to all that, thank God,' he said as he sawed away.

'Anyway, you're looking frightfully well, if I may say so, old thing.' Then, 'I'm sorry, how's Adrienne? How rude of me not to have asked before.' The congenial question came as a sudden shock.

'She's fine,' Rick lied perfectly in return.

'In sparkling mid-season form, I take it?'

'Yes.'

'She here, in New York?'

'Not at the moment.'

'Working?'

Rick shook his head. 'She's out in California trying her luck in the pilot season, new television shows, that kind of thing.'

'Do you think she'll get something?'

'I've no idea,' Rick shrugged.

'Might it make life difficult if she did, do you think? I mean, she there, you wherever.'

'Showbiz relationships are never easy, Binkie. It's an itinerant life. You're a traveller, you know the risks.'

Rick could feel himself getting testy and drank, glancing round the room. Damn. Why was he lying? Why didn't he tell Binkie? You've told me yours now let me tell you about mine. Because he had let it go too far without saying anything? Because he couldn't make it sound as funny? He drifted in thought. No. Neither. He just didn't want to go over it again. Over it, into it, whatever. Not here, now, anyway.

' . . Anyway, she had these enormous Charlies,' Binkie was saying.

'What?'

'Charlies – you know, Charles of the Ritz – tits.'

'Who had?'

'Lila, old thing. I've just been telling you.'

'Yes, of course, sorry!'

'And the most incredible nipples. Like rubber walnuts. The kind you could get your very back molars on.'

'Binkie!' Rick laughed.

'It's true, I swear. I'm an absolute tit man.' He paused, musing. 'I don't think women are anywhere near as obsessed with penis size as men are with breasts. An old psychiatrist I knew once told me that, down years of giving therapy to women in marriage collapses, not once had penis size been mentioned as a cause of breakdown or a source of disappointment, even. But men are different, aren't they? Much more involved with the physical. No two ways about it. Yes, that's what I shall really miss. Those whopping great Charlies.' He sighed wistfully, as Rick thought of Adrienne, having her bra and pants gently taken off, surrendering to her paramour with a very different sigh. So far as she cared, Rick could have King bronzed for the Smithsonian, entitled, 'Nine and a half dead inches. In shoving memory.'

'You've hardly eaten anything, old thing.'

'Hm?' He turned his gaze to Binkie who was owling at him over the remains of his steak.

'You're not eating.'

'I know.' Rick stared at the congealing hamburger. 'I shouldn't have ordered, Binkie. I had a huge, late lunch,' he lied again. 'All I really wanted was a drink.'

'Come to think of it, you do look a bit tired.'

'Do I?'

'Well, pale.'

'It's New York in January, Binkie.' He flashed Binkie his crooked smile.

'Yes, yes, I suppose it is.' He paused. 'Things are all right, between you and Adrienne I mean?' Crafty Binkie. Quick on the uptake. The "Absolutely," came back natural and easy.

'I'm so glad,' returned Binkie. 'You always seemed so perfect

together. Forgive the banality.' He laughed and launched into yet
another tirade against Lila, the Bitch-Goddess of mid-Manhattan,
then hearkened back to conquests of his Oxford days before, after a
couple of deep snifters, they bade farewell on the steps of the
Yardarm, promising to meet up soon.

13

RICK STAYED ALL THE next day, but the phone remained silent. Near four o'clock he slipped out for the *Times*. It was raining and miserable as he dodged into the Watering Hole for a Dos XX's and tortilla chips and chilli at the bar. He flicked through the paper, without really reading anything except headlines, before heading home.

The ringing started as he fumbled for his keys and dropped them on the tiled floor. Cursing, he got the door open and raced to the phone. It was Dan Nagel from LA. 'Listen, Rick,' he said. 'I have some great news. That script I sent you?' Rick had barely glanced at it. 'I just got a call. They're desperate to get you. Four hundred thousand for four weeks. All you have to do is get on a plane to Tucson, Tuesday. Rick?'

'Yes, Yes, I'm here.'

'You sound down. Is everything all right?'

'No. Everything is *not* all right. I'm in the middle of a complete and utter fuck-up with Adrienne and I just can't up and leave right now. Not till I sort things out.'

'Jesus. It's a great job, Rick.'

Yeah, for you maybe, he thought. From what little he recalled, his was a part any of fifty guys could play. 'Let me take a look at it and I'll call you.'

'OK, just don't waste too much time. I'd hate to lose it.' Rick found the script in his bag, dropped it on the coffee table and sat with interlocking fingers, staring at its cover. Four hundred thousand, huh? The Almighty Dollar. He had no idea how long he'd sat like that before the phone rang. It was Dan again.

'You have nothing to worry about. Everything's fine.'

'What are you talking about?'

210

'Adrienne. She doesn't want to split. She loves you.'

Rick sat up. 'How do —'

'I just spoke with Farben.'

'You shouldn't have done that, Dan.'

'Farben called *me*. He said there's been a little trouble with her family, but it's getting straightened out.'

'I don't get it. Why would he call and tell you that?'

'He didn't. He called to ask if I knew anybody who'd want to invest in his agency. He's looking for fifty thousand dollars. Then he talked about you.'

'Why hasn't he said anything to me? He knows my number.'

'He said he was going to. Maybe he's trying now. Why don't you call him? Meantime, can I say yes to the job?'

'No. I haven't finished reading it yet. I'll call you back.'

'OK, but don't leave it too late. It's Wednesday already.'

'Dan, I'll call you!'

'Today. OK.'

'Today.' Heart racing, he got a dial tone and in a minute heard Farben on the line. 'Greg, I just got a call from Dan Nagel. Saying Adrienne loves me. It's nice to hear it from him via you, but I'd rather hear it from her.

'She doesn't want to split, Rick, she wants to get back together.'

'Then why the fuck hasn't she told me?'

'She's going to.'

'Oh swell. Did she say anything else?'

'Er, Yeah, er . . . Lemme see . . . "I love Rick. Rick is the centre of my life. I can't imagine life without him." She'll call you at eleven. She's out till then.'

'Where?'

'I don't know.'

'You seem to know everything else.'

'Come on, Rick. I'm only trying to help.'

'Yeah, thanks.' Afterwards, he replayed their conversation over in his head. Come on, you big dummy. She's going to call. Just tell her you love her and the dishes are waiting in the sink. He searched for a record, and put it on. 'Every Night About This Time' – the Ink Spots. 'And as the band starts to croon our favourite tune, a tear falls on every line. Oh, how I miss you, every night about this time.' Singing along, hugging himself round the room in a slow foxtrot, he realized he hadn't eaten a proper meal in days. Hungry for a big plate of Nero's pasta, he took off the record and put on his coat.

The restaurant was full and buzzing with noise. Rick wolfed down a dish of pasta with a bottle of Soave. It was after nine-thirty. He ordered coffee and a sambuca, planning to leave soon. If she called early, he wanted to be there. He went home on dancing shoes, skidding across the shining streets to the music of tyres hissing in the wet. He put on the Ink Spots album again and listened to both sides twice before finally switching it off. Two minutes to eleven. He sat in the ticking silence. Eleven-fifteen. He began to get nervy, and paced the floor, wandering at last to bed around one-thirty, the memory of the happy Nero-hour turned to lead in his belly. During the night he threw up, kneeling mortified before the bowl, and didn't get to sleep until around five. The telephone didn't ring once all morning. At twelve he decided to call Greg.

'Adrienne didn't call, I know,' he said. 'She just stopped by here. She just this second left.'

'And?'

'Well, I still think everything's fine. She just wants to go away this weekend. Wants to think things out. She's going upstate to some friends of her's. Jim and Venetia? Do you know them?'

'Heard of them.'

'Well, that's where she's going.'

'That's all she said?'

'No. She said, "I really love Rick. I really love him but I just need some time before we get back together." And that was the first time, the very first time that I ever saw Adrienne cry.'

'Are you sure you weren't standing on her foot?'.

There was a pause. 'She'll call you Monday morning. I'm sure everything will be fine.'

'No it won't.'

'How can you say that?'

212

'Because I know her.'

'Well, I think I know her too, so let's wait and see who's right.'

'We'll talk on Monday morning, Greg. So long for now.'

Jesus, what a kick in the ass. Here yesterday. Gone today. Rick put on his coat, ran down the stairs, and made for the Watering Hole, but he couldn't go in. Instead, he walked round Folsom, two, three times in the steadily falling rain before returning. Maybe he could call up Frank, or Jack, see if they had the evening free. He checked the mailbox. Some advertising crap and a brown paper envelope, soggy and split open at one end. Addressed to Adrienne. Back in the apartment he tore off the mangled wetness and out fell a New Year's Diary (a platitude inside for every week) with an accompanying note. Starting right in about the twins' disapointment and anger – it was what Rick had heard from Adrienne in the Hub; now he knew where she'd got it from – about how Alice would just like to forget it all, but Patrice and the twins would have the consequences to live with, as would Adrienne. Then her admission that she'd been untrue to herself (wherever did she get *that* idea?). At the end she became Mahler's Woman in Anger. 'How can the sun shine as if nothing happened?' with Rick and Dom bracketed as alcoholic monsters capable of anything, 'Which boggles my mind.' Finally the sun shines, time moves on and her heart looks back in pain before limping along to catch up with the light. Wickedly insidious enough for Adrienne to swallow every word. This woman had a lot to answer for. Ay-gad! Rick left the letter on top of the piano and picked up the phone. Neither Frank nor Jack was at home. He went alone to the Watering Hole. If he'd wanted a drink before, he certainly wanted two now.

Rick made a face in the bathroom mirror. He'd sunk quite a few the previous night and now, trying to shave, couldn't keep the razor steady in his hand. He was buttoning his shirt when there was a knock at the door. Through the peep-hole he saw Benny, and undid the lock.

'Am I disturbing you?'

'No, Benny, of course not. Come in.' Rick ushered him into the sitting room and excused himself to pull on a sweater. From the bedroom he called out. 'What are you doing in the City? I thought you worked at home Fridays.'

Benny was removing his gloves and scarf as Rick returned. 'Elaine and I are baby-sitting for our eldest daughter. She'll be out of town today and tomorrow.'

'Can I get you some coffee?'

Benny consulted his watch. 'No, thank you. I've had breakfast, can't stay long – Elaine's downstairs in the car. I just dropped by to check something with you.'

'Sure.' Rick motioned to an armchair. 'Take a pew,' he said, squatting on the pink-patterned sofa. 'What's up?'

Benny gave one of his earnest looks, clasping his hands between his knees. 'Are you aware that a cheque for a substantial sum has been drawn against the corporation?'

'No.' Slowly, Rick sat up.

Have you issued any cheques at all lately?'

'No.'

'Well, it's your signature.'

'You sure?'

'Sure as I can be.'

'But how can that...? I thought you put a stop on any payments for a while.'

'As a precaution, yes, I did. But it's only temporary. To make it really effective it has to have your signature. And whoever cashed it was no amateur.'

'What do you mean?'

'I mean there was an attempt to cash it which failed.'

'I don't understand.'

'It was re-presented.'

'...I see.'

'You sure you have all your cheques?'

'Yes. I ... Yes.'

'You're positive?'

'Yes Benny. They're in my brief-case. Unless ...' He faltered at an image of himself opening the case. It struck him like a thunderbolt. 'Unless ...'

'Unless what?'

'I did give one to Adrienne, before Christmas, so she could buy herself a bike for her birthday.'

'How much for?'

'Nothing. It was blank.'

'And signed?'

'Yes.'

'Well it's been cashed.'

He bit his lip. 'I guess that's the one then.'

'I guess so. You have that joint account also, don't you, the one I set up for you?'

'Sure.'

'Have you checked it lately?'

'No.'

'I think you'd better do that right away. Soon as the bank's open.'

'OK.'

'Because I put a few thousand dollars in there for you just before Christmas. Let me know.'

'I will.'

'I'm sorry, my friend.' Benny stood up.

'No, Benny, no, thanks for telling me.'

Scrawling a number on a card, Benny handed it to Rick. 'Call me here when you've checked the account.'

'Sure.' He saw Benny out, then slowly sank back on the sofa, dropping his head in his hands. So *that* was why the tears. In the Hub. She'd thought he'd known about the cheque. *That* was what she'd meant by 'I'll pay you back'. It was crystal clear now. He stood up. He'd make some coffee, take his time. No sense in hurrying. He was pretty sure what he would find. Or rather, wouldn't find.

'There's thirty dollars in that account, sir,' the teller had said. Rick shuffled off into the street. When she'd asked for a bike for her birthday, it hadn't occurred to him she'd meant a gold-plated Harley-Davidson! He didn't stop walking till he reached Columbus Circle. The park lay bleak in its winter clothing. Scrubby and squirrel-grey. No thundering Wurlitzer, no skaters, no colours, no winter cries around the rink where they'd held hands. Just the roar of distant traffic over on Fifth. He shambled through some leaves. Looking down, his old white Nikes, now grey, were as old as he'd known *her*. White to grey. And fade to black. Crossing over to Madison, he called Benny from the Carlyle. 'Bare as Mother Hubbard's cupboard,' he said.

'Jeez,' breathed Benny.

'Way it goes. I'll call you.'

Slouching towards the Bemelmen Room to be born, he ordered a bullshot and sat at the bar. Holy fucking Toledo. Two bank visits and a disappearing act. She wasn't staying at Ruby's, he was sure. The whole thing stank.

He finished his drink and walked in a trance down to Lex. Turning the corner, there were the buttresses, and there *she* was again. He stopped and she looked up, regarding him. 'Why do you do this?' he asked gently. 'Sit here? Can't you get a job or unemployment?'

She answered him immediately. 'Weeell, I *have* nowhere. Look at me. And they stopped my unemployment.'

'Do you have any qualifications?'

'Oh yes. I took a PhD course at Chicago University. I worked a computer program in micro-electronics in West Germany. After the collapse of Air Force Intelligence there, I came back to this country. I'd learned German. Right away – for no reason – I was regarded as a security risk by the CIA – I'd always been pro-US and anti-Russian. Now I'm treated as a non-US citizen. I've been kicked out of Denmark, Sweden. I was in England for a while, but I couldn't get a job.'

Her eyes were hazel, not blue as at first he'd thought. The speech was fast, and clear. She was not deranged. Something just out of sync though, Rick thought. Maybe.

'I'm just waiting,' she went on. 'Now the situation's changed in Russia, things are bound to get better and I can leave.' So saying, she began to gather up her things. The hat was different today. Black. Her skin was clean, her face healthy looking and weather-beaten, her eyes clear and teeth good. She was older than he'd thought, not much younger than himself. 'I'm camping at the moment. I don't smoke, drink or take drugs. One night in Central

Park, I had my throat half cut. The only reason I'm alive is I can run fast.'

Rick gave her a five-spot and she took it gently, daintily almost, and stood. 'Well, I'm going now,' she said. Maybe he'd scared her by coming back and asking questions. Did she think he was CIA?

'Where to?'

'To get some lunch.'

Eyes fixed on her receding figure, Rick sang gently, 'We are the Ovalteenies, happy girls and boys . . .'

14

THE APARTMENT WAS a wreck. Rolling up his sleeves, Rick began to clean. The living room he did last, ending with the little alcove where the boob-tube, tapes and the hi-fi lived. There was something glossy leaning against the wall behind the television. He picked it up. The *Mets Yearbook*. He opened it. Given to Adrienne by Ruby. Just before Christmas, presumably. Inscribed on the flyleaf were the words, 'From your partner in crime and cookies'. Also inside the front cover were some photographs in a paper folder and a letter. He took the book to the table, setting it down and scanning the letter. From Jenny Devers, her old girlfriend of schooldays. It was chock-full of how beautiful Adrienne looked in the received photos, and how was her old flame Doug Seaman and was there anyone new in her life? No mention of Rick anywhere. Was she unaware of his existence? Hadn't been told? He put the book down and opened the paper folder, spilling out half a dozen snapshots. He'd seen the top one before. Of Mickey, 'looking goofy' in a Chinese restaurant, sitting next to the oddest-looking girl in Manhattan, and dabbing a napkin to his mouth. The last he'd never seen. Or, wait a second, had he? Central Park? That day with Pete? Was *that* him? A smiling good-looking, well-built geezer, Adrienne radiant at his side. Both in swimsuits. The photograph was recent. He remembered when the bathing suit was bought. He sat down slowly, gazing at the smiling couple. He with his arm hooked round her shoulders, hers hugged about his waist. When a woman is being touched by a man she is physically drawn to, there is a certain way her body presents itself, in a gentle, almost imperceptible incline, a pulse of sexual energy so often hidden in the quickness of life, but sharply revealed in a frozen print. Was this, then, the silent, Sunday-morning dialler?

The dry rasp of the doorbell brought Rick to his feet and he slipped the photo to the bottom of the pile. 'Just a minute!' Through the peep-hole he saw Jack, wrapped up and stamping his feet. He opened the door.

'Hey, big guy!'

'Jack. Surprise.'

'Yeah. I just came in from the Island. Thought I'd stop by.' He removed his coat, gloves. 'Brass monkey weather out there, pal.' He followed Rick into the sitting room. 'So what's doin'? Any news?'

'Nope.'

'Unbelievable. Hey.' He picked up the *Mets Yearbook*. 'This yours?'

'Adrienne's.'

Jack opened it. ' "Your partner in crime and cookies." Who's this? From that Ruby, right?' He saw the look on Rick's face. 'Birds of a feather, pal,' he said, 'birds of a feather.' Jack picked up the snaps, studying Mickey and the girl. He snorted. 'I recognize him. Who's the dog?'

'She writes advertising jingles.'

'And who's this?' He was staring at Adrienne and Adonis.

'No idea. Here,' Rick said, passing Jack the Mahler missive, which he read with a growing frown.

'Psss. How d'ya like that?' He handed it back. 'Y'know, nothin's gonna change with Adrienne or any of 'em, pal. Not till the old lady croaks. In fact, she could be waxed right now and it would still be too late for the rest o'them. What about that husband o'huz? Why doesn't he lay down the law? She should be at home makin' dinner for her old man and mindin' her own business. Joinin' the local Amateur Operatic Society and screamin' her head off in the boonies, instead of pokin' her snitch into ya personal life.' He looked at Rick. 'But none of it woulda happened, pal, if Adrienne hadn't allowed it to happen.'

'Wanna drink, Jack?' Rick brought one of two bottles from the fridge.

Jack stood as the glasses were set. 'Champagne, eh?'

'Yup.' Rick screwed the wire free.

'For the homecoming, huh, pal?'

A mini-explosion and the cork hit the ceiling. 'How well you know me.'

'Well enough to know there's somebody better out there. And I'll drink to that.'

Rick smiled. 'I'll drink to anything. Good luck and good health. The only – '

'The only two things that really matter. Yeah, I know.' The two men drank in silence, while a pale setting sun cast long shadows over Folsom.

After Jack's departure, Rick lay belly down on the big Boukhara, arms stretched in front of him, fingertips pressing the base of the champagne glass down on the thick orange pile, watching the bubbles surface. Unlike she, who lurked somewhere, submerged. *Cherchez-ma-femme. Mais comment?* At the promise of every turn, the despairing sight of the same blank wall. Like the man lost in the original maze, there seemed to Rick to be no way out.

It was mid-afternoon on Monday before Farben called. 'You were right and I was wrong,' he said. 'She just called me. She doesn't want to reconcile. At *all.* I think she's making a mistake and I told her so. But I can't get any sense out of her. Different things come out of each side of her mouth at once. She talks about the mother, the family, the children, what a mess everything is, and I say, "Yes, your family's your family, but Rick is your husband. You said yourself he was the centre of your life." She says she knows that but she can't go on because there's been a betrayal of trust.'

'What betrayal of trust?'

'She was kind of vague.'

'How the fuck can you be vague about a betrayal of trust?'

'I agree.'

'So what did she say?'

'Something about you telling Dom you two were married, but

220

that was second, there was something else. Something she told you in confidence about the mother.

The bullshit 'interfered with' story. 'What did she say exactly?'

'She didn't.'

'Then hear it from me.'

Farben snickered. 'Jesus. That's really weird.'

'It's not enough to bring down a marriage, Greg.'

'Certainly isn't. I just don't think it's over, really. I think she's going to come back to you.'

'When?'

'When Dom goes back to Patrice. I understand he's agreed to go into counselling.'

'Oh, Christ!' Rick laughed. 'So when is she supposed to return to the arms of the husband she's still in love with?'

'In about six months?'

'I'll try not to hold my breath.'

'What?'

'I thought she didn't want to reconcile at *all*? To me that means divorce, inevitably.'

'I don't think it means that, necessarily.' An awkward pause. 'And if it did come to that, it could be somewhere like Reno in a year's time. I don't think she knows *what* she wants at the moment – except she wants to go to California. You leave for Tucson tomorrow, right?'

'Yes.'

'Well, good luck. It'll be good to get away from all this for a while.'

'Sure. In the meantime, thanks for all your help.'

'A pleasure. Really. Call me.'

'I will.' Rick pushed the phone to the wall, and lay smacked out on the deck in the crucifixion logo.

> *Some priority . . .*
> *Some trust . . .*
> *Some marriage . . .*
> *Strike three!*
> *Nails, please.*

221

Waking early, he showered, shaved, and mechanically packed a garment bag with light summer clothes. Checking occasionally at the window, he at last saw the sleek grey lines of the long limo as it slid into the kerb below. Snapping up his airline ticket, he turned to leave, stumbling against her guitar. The echoing thrum brought a memory of her quavering voice, as he stopped to set the instrument straight. Catching sight of something lying behind it, he picked it up. It was her appointments diary for the past year, about the size of a small chocolate bar. He stuffed it in his pocket and ran, wishing for a hypodermic that would put him away for a year, to awaken to '*La vie en rose*'.

As the padded-cell limo pulled up at United Airlines, Rick reflected there are few things more terrible than being strapped in with your own despair.

The plane stopped to refuel in Denver. They were allowed off for a half hour, and Rick made straight for a prefabricated bar, serviced by a couple of young Coloradans. Though attractive and pleasant, as he ordered a nothing drink, they were not her. 'All those that lose their heart are one the same.'

He'd spoken it unawares, and one of the waitresses said, 'Excuse me?'

'What?' he said absently.

'I'm sorry, I thought you said something.'

'No. I'd just like another one of . . . whatever that was.'

'Red wine,' she said. 'But there isn't any more. I'm sorry.'

'OK. I'll take anything.'

She looked at him. 'You have to tell me.'

'OK. I'll, er . . .' He saw a Cuervo bottle. 'I'll take a tequila – and a beer.'

She brought them and looked at him strangely. 'That'll be six dollars.'

'You'll have to forgive me. I'm a little jet-lagged.'

She smiled. 'Been flying a lot?'

'Yes, yes,' he lied. 'I've been . . . up in the air for about two weeks now.'

Back on the plane, Rick fished out the appointments book. It hurt to look at her handwriting. And to see the host of Christian names and numbers that meant nothing to him. All her family's birthdates (even Harry, the gym instructor's) were entered – Mickey's linked with a set of stars! Her father's, he recalled was the day before his own – and there it was, marked. His own was a blank. He thumbed back to their wedding day. Blank. There wasn't a reference to him anywhere. Anyone reading it would never have known he existed. He bit his lip. In the years they had been together, he had never received a card from any of her family. Nor was he mentioned in hers at Christmas or in any of their letters to her that she'd given him to read.

He shook his head, flipped a page near the end, and stared. There, in Farben's own handwriting were the words, 'Greg's birthday', in green ink. The intercom crackled, and he slid the book back into his pocket.

The plane was sinking towards Tucson when the big silver dollar dropped. He sat forward with a jolt and froze. He'd assumed he had indeed been the centre of her life as remarked to Farben. Assumed she'd been fighting a battle with friends and family over him, while he stood back to give her breathing space. Now there was to be no reconciliation. *At all*, Farben had said. So in less than four weeks, while Rick was locked in Arizona, Adrienne would be in California, separated, uncontactable, and perhaps looking to settle there on a permanent basis. Pastures new.

Passing through the lounge area he was nearly run down by one of those sneaky, noiseless airport carts.

In the shock of the baking Tucson air, at the door to the ole West, his heart was thudding. The knuckles of the hand that gripped his bag were bone white. Rick saw a battered yellow transit van with a languid, pasty-faced young woman in cream dungarees, leaning her ass against the hood. Dark glasses up on her hair. Chewing gum. His head spun like a tumble drier, rumbling in an airless world. As he approached, she nudged herself upright. 'You Mr Neilsen?'

'Yes.'

'OK. Let's go.'

Great welcome! Things hadn't changed much out here since

Billy the Kid, then. They drove in silence for about half a mile. Boka dow. Boka dow. Boka dow. The van had an engine knock, or maybe it was a wheel, he couldn't tell. Boka dow. He gazed out at the flatland, trying to imagine tumbleweed, Jesse James, Gene Autry, the Sons of the Pioneers. Boka dow. Boka dow. Stop it now. Stop it now. His head sang in hypnotic tandem with piston or wheel as his eyes fixed with a thousand-yard stare on the flatland, arid and salmon-pink, melting into a wide blue miles-away sky at a shimmering line of mountains, snow, like bakery icing, on their peaks. Mirage. Unreal. This is winter. Go back. Boka dow. Go back now. Can't go back. No time. No room to manoeuvre. Suddenly his voice in the hellish heat of silence. 'Can you stop at a bank? I need to change some money.'

'First you have to have a medical.' The voice, look-I've-already-missed-lunch testy. And at that precise moment Rick Neilsen chucked in his hand. *Basta la commedia.*

'Turn around,' he said softly.

'What—' she began.

'I said, turn around. We're going back to the airport.' As she opened her mouth to protest, he saved her breath. 'Please don't talk, just drive.'

In the departure area, Rick checked the flights to New York. There was one in fifty minutes which made two stops then a change in Pittsburgh. No matter. He bought a ticket, then thought, as a group of very Irish faces paraded by, chattering excitedly, that he would handle it through Farben. Make Greg tell Dan who, in turn, would cope with the movie people. That would keep everything at arm's length until he was back in Gotham. Forty minutes till takeoff. He called Greg collect.

'Good to hear from you, Rick. How's Tucson?'

'Fine.' OK, sports fans, now the fast ball whacked into the bleachers. 'I'm just booking myself on a flight back to New York.' Rick brought the receiver round to the front of his face looking at all the little holes as the sounds blabbered out.

'My God! Oh my God! Why? My God what's happened? Oh my God!'

Returning it to mouth and ear Rick said. 'Nothing happened, Greg, I'm coming back to straighten everything out. That's all.'

'Whaddya mean? Fuck. I've . . . Oh my God. Whaddya gonna do?'

Rick imagined the watery blues bulging behind the gig-lamps and the spatter of diarrhoea against the fan blades. 'I'm coming back to get divorced.'

'Uh, Rick, I-I'll God-er-there's no need for that.'

'I rather think there is and that's what I've decided.'

'But . . . Y-You can get divorced anytime, Rick, anytime, like Reno in a year's time.'

'No, Greg. Now. I want divorced *now*.'

'But what about the job?'

'There is no job, as from a half-hour ago. I want you to call Dan and have him square it with the movie people.' Rick gritted his teeth. 'I can't do this job, there's just no way. I'm in no fit state. Tell Dan. That's all and that's final.'

A jittery pause at the other end. 'I-I just hope you're doing the right thing.'

'I *know* I'm doing the right thing.' He heard the Pittsburgh flight number announced over the P.A. system. 'I have to go. They're calling my flight. I'll be wanting to talk to you when I get back, Greg. Please make yourself available. It won't take long.'

'Y-you got it.'

He replaced the receiver guessing, as he did so, that Farben was already dialling her number.

On the plane, he buckled himself in next to a little old lady, hoping there would be no delay. Opening his eyes at a sudden commotion, there was the group he had seen in the hall, cramming into the row in front. The shamrock faces peppering Grandma with goodbyes as she blessed them. After a few minutes they left and, as the plane began to move, Grandma nervously fished out a set of beads and crossed herself, lips moving in silent prayer.

'You'll be all right, Grandma,' he said, gently.

'Ah, bless you,' she cooed.

He wanted to lean over her, her parish priest, and whisper, confessional-like, 'Bless me, ah. Don't ya know that I'm benighted now?' Instead he simply winked. She smiled. An old Catholic on her way back to the auld sod having checked on her brood for maybe the last time.

A fat man in a tan suit stuffed himself into the aisle seat and Rick got a deadly whiff of halitosis. Sweating, the creature fastened its seatbelt and, almost immediately, began a neurotic tapping of a metal pen against the belt hasp. With Gran, on his starboard side, doing her paternoster abacus and Arbuckle with his Morse-code belt buckle on the other, Rick felt pincered in the jaws of a gigantic click beetle, and a welter of unhappy remembrances began to turn in his head like a circulating Lazy Susan. The October Sunday she had returned from workout. In the past, they had always made love soon after these returns but, in October and November she had, uncharacteristically, protested she must shower first because, 'I'm all stinky.' On two of those October Sundays she had returned soon after leaving, protesting, 'I forgot my gym-bag.' Something she had not done since ever he had known her. It and she were inseparable. Then why mention it – except maybe from fear that he might draw the conclusion that she was not bound for where she said she was?

He imagined her making love to another at that very moment, while he sat locked in impotence twixt Gran and Dungbreath. Imagined her displaying her grand, athletic straddle. He had taught her to shag him like one of those tight-assed young fillies astride her show-jump mount – in the saddle, in control and loving it, the dewy fur-burger pounding joyously upon her buckeroo. She had learned quickly, eagerly exploring him, thoroughly excited by each carnal sip and snippet, squirrelling them away to hoard in secret for some magic spring. He had been touched, aroused, stimulated by turns and all at once by her naïve curiosity, amazed at her capacity and depth, the deep, slippery ease of total penetration, giving the full horn to sensation as she took him every time and every way, in a luxuriant smiling silence, the perfect sex receptacle, born to be ravished.

> With rush of breathy little sighs,
> With push of milky, open thighs,

226

The Giaconda smile belies
The coral secrets buried deep in mud-green eyes.
Cornucopia.

Monkey shown, monkey show how monkey like done, or monkey do.

Hands clasped round neck of lover, feet on wall,
Knees wide at ten to two.
Thighs drive the sheath down shaft as then you ball
Your love as he balls you.
Fervid, passionate devotion.
Poetry, in sexual motion.

Adrienne had never been a torrid lovemaker. Indeed, Rick's want had been the utter capitulation of her body to him, while words, thoughts, feelings, sealed themselves behind the smiling, enigmatic eyes. Yes, she had been his vessel, under his command, until she had changed course, pitching him overboard, to flounder in her wake. He sat back, tried to stretch his legs. Adrienne's physical, sexual aspects were incredible, but that, to Rick, was not what the electricity had been about. It was her extremes of cleverness and naïveté that had been the allure, the trap. The cunning, the *naif*, the monkey.

The nightmare journey brought him at last to Pittsburgh, where he boarded the New York flight. Aloft, the aircraft banking steeply, from out the black infinity Rick saw the scattered flashings of a thousand winter stars. Diamond eyes in Argus' cloak.

The night has a thousand eyes,
And the day but one;
Yet the light of the bright world dies
With the dying sun.

The mind has a thousand eyes,
And the heart but one;

Yet the light of a whole life dies
When love is done.
And that will be all for Neilsen.

At ten minutes to midnight, exactly fourteen hours after leaving Folsom, he walked through the doors of the Watering Hole fresh from his whirlwind tour of six major American cities. Ordering a drink, he was surprised to find himself not even tired. His eyes were bright in the mirror, and tomorrow he would get going. And more than he would get going.

Next morning about eleven, he ran eight laps round Folsom in his tracksuit. It took exactly twenty-eight minutes. He left messages for Frank and Jack that he was back in New York. He should really call old Leo, but he didn't want to sit before him looking as foolish as he felt. Not till he knew how he wanted the business tackled. On his last lap there was a pop-pop-popping sound behind him and Rick heard his name being called. He stopped and saw a figure at the kerbside perched on one of those funny-looking two-foot high motorbikes, unfastening his helmet.

'Hello, Rick!'

It was his landlord, Norman Martin.

'Norman, hi,' Rick panted.

'I'm on my way to a meeting, but I thought I'd stop by and touch base with you. Are you staying on at the apartment?'

'Sure. Why?'

'I got a call from Adrienne, saying she was leaving for good, and that she wanted her name taken off the lease. Is that true? Is she leaving?'

'She's left.'

'I'm really sorry to hear that.'

'These things happen.' Rick wanted to shriek with manic laughter.

'Are you feeling all right?'

'Yes, I'm fine.' Ready to be committed, he thought, but otherwise in sparkling mid-season form.

'When did she call?'

'A while back. Must've been the second or third of January. I had just got back in the office.' The hammer descended on the skull, and the brain was rattling. 'She left me a couple of numbers where she could be contacted, but I haven't called. I can have her name taken off the lease easily enough. It's a fairly simple matter.'

'Sure.'

'But *you're* planning to stay on?'

'For the time being, yes. I'll pay the rent as usual.'

'Fine. I just wanted to be sure what was happening.' Re-fastening his helmet, 'Well I won't keep you. Oh – happy New Year.'

'Yes, happy New Year.' The mini-bike stuttered off to bear its rider uptown. Happy pop-pop-pop-pop-farting New fucking Year!

Rick stood frozen to the spot. 'I had just got back in the office!' The second or third of January. Name off lease. Banks. Disappearo. Fast work. He knew the cheques had been cashed in the first days of January. Now knew she'd called to get her name off the lease before Rick had even got into New York. So what else was a consideration? Had he been seriously misled about desire for reconciliation from the start? There can't have been a thought of it. Surely Norman Martin had just handed him the proof.

Racing to the apartment, Rick snatched up the phone, dialled, and was put straight through to Leo, Doge of Detachment.

'You'd better come and see me. Eleven o'clock tomorrow morning suit?'

'Fine.'

'I'll see you then.'

Click.

That night Rick had a dreadful dream, waking ten times at least. Wishing it was true, then glad it wasn't.

Each time he faded back into a sleep, the shapeless plot would stagger on where it left off, just like a movie, where she would appear at random, asking 'Could they try again?' Then, as he put his eyes to to hers – 'Except it wouldn't work.'

'No, no!'

'I want to but can't. I wouldn't be able.'

The 'No, no' had come from another. A ten year-old girl in GAP-style pyjama suit, who slipped between them.

There were rooms within each sequence, but he seemed to have no room of his own. He wandered into one he sensed was his. The bathroom floor was flooded from leaking taps. Then he was in a courtyard, sunless with dark foliage, shadowing people who walked naked. Or were they? Suddenly, he was himself naked. In a panic. Something was there to cover him, but not enough, something like an elasticated Dyna Band exercise strap which managed to stretch about his loins like a short spartan tunic, but he could not trust it to stay in place. People laughed and taunted him. As he blazed angrily towards them they multiplied. He was in danger.

His box of small belongings and some cash now lay open on a grey street corner where she came to him again, hyper, eyes faraway, not green but lightning blue, smudged underneath, saying she needed help. Only a little money. She had to meet someone.

He woke, she went away. He slept and there she was. Inevitable but remote, with words of love, but eyes elsewhere, till he was forced to slap her to make her focus on him, freezing immediately for fear that she would flee. Then there was money in a dish. Coins that were his. Counted in towers of silver and bronze, round like medieval castle corners. The bulk of his money lay within another room. Not seeing her, he ran back to check, but first put his hand into his right jeans' pocket. Relief. A wallet and two paper-bound rolls of coins, which turned into Life Savers.

A blankfaced stranger appeared, to tell him that she had to have the hit. Didn't he know? Turning back, the money in the dish not stacked now, but scattered in a ruin. He tried to spill the remnants into a plastic bag to make sure she wouldn't have enough to buy the hit that was destroying her. She was around, but somewhere else with dealers. Then there she was back on the street, the face a decade older, the body muscle atrophied. He was terribly afraid for her, and terribly afraid when she looked at him without seeing. Again she came to tell him how she needed, and when he grabbed her to cry out, 'You must stop this!', 'We could try again,' she said, 'but it wouldn't work.' The eyes bright but in another universe. The face older but the same to him. The body slack, but the same to him.

The last dream was the most terrible. A hospital ward. White mist. Himself in a barred bed. There were baby cries. A woman who had lain with him now left his bed and snapped the bars back shut. Through the mist he could not see her face, only body, bra and panties, and her feet, long, black like patent leather, spurs upon each heel, nails of polished ebon, as she took from him a fluorescent vial, what he knew to be his sperm. Secreting it within her panties in the very moment that she metamorphosed, moving away, changing gender. Paralysed in speech and movement, he watched the bra and panties older figure take the form of the naked back and bottom that he knew so well, turning itself sideways to show him his own cock, sprung from her mound in full erection as she/he moved through the mist towards a pile of blue gym mattresses where lay a beauteous teenage girl, blonde hair fanned wide, body spread and open, in the deepest sleep. He watched his own stiff King become a rod of shining white translucency before being put into the still-as-death Rapunzel. At the moment of deepest penetration, triumphant eyes turned to regard him in his prison bed. 'I am making a child of the Devil!' The laughter brilliant, chilling. Succubus, Incubus, Rapunzel, Demon, Vortex. He awoke exhausted.

Jerome appeared on his left as he had at the prenuptial session, armed yet again with pad and pen. Once more they sat before old Leo, who asked the questions. Rick replied. Jerome scribbled. Screw Reno. Could there not be a quickie split? Something legal, binding and lasting? Rick's thoughts were not in his words as he talked, his eyes flickering about the room. Had the summer den of dreams he'd sat expectant in become this wintry place, this dry-wood parlour, despair, like dust, gathered in its corners?

Leo regarded Rick with the same dispassionate gaze he had reserved for the wedding. Well, you can't expect sympathy from a lawyer. They deal with a ton of this shit weekly. 'Just bail me out, Leo. There *has* to be a way!'

'It only takes a day in Santo Domingo. Only one of you need go.'

'And it's completely, absolutely legal?' Leo nodded. 'OK. She goes.'

'Why not you?'

'She wants it. Let her go do it.'

On his dark leather throne, Leo leaned back, his fingers interlinked. A kilo of plump sausages.

'If you can get her to sign a paper accepting the amount we've discussed, and she goes to Santo Domingo, all you have to do is sign the paper she takes with her.'

'She'll do it.'

'And you'll get this fellow, what's his name. . . ?'

'Farben.'

'. . . Farben, to call us here? He's going to handle this for her?'

'Yes.'

Leo stared at the ceiling. 'If it can be arranged this way, you'll be getting off pretty light,' he said.

'It'll be arranged.'

Jerome leaned forward. 'Right, I'll start preparing the papers for her to sign, then you can come in and add your signature and she can be on her way.'

Rick noticed Jerome's thick wedding band, something he'd never had. 'Thanks.'

'I'm sorry it had to end this way.' At least he sounded sincere.

'Thanks.'

Leo sat impassive. Rick wondered what he looked like at funerals.

Back in Folsom Rick took a deep breath before dialling Greg's number, and wasted no time getting to the point. 'How much is it going to cost me to be rid of our friend?' Farben named the figure. It was exactly half the money in the corporation! Half his US holdings. 'Accepted,' Rick said dully. 'On certain conditions. You find an independent lawyer who agrees that figure with her and submits it to my attorney.'

'I think that can be done.'

'And this figure will be minus the sum that she drew against the corporation the other day.'

'OK. I'll talk to her.'

'Hold it. Wait a minute, Greg. One more thing.'

'I'm listening.'

'She gets on a flight to Santo Domingo, stays one night, goes through the motions, and comes back with the rubber-stamped splitola.'

'Rick, she's going to California.'

'Not for at least two weeks. This only takes a day, Greg.'

'Why can't you go?'

'Because I've run my ass halfway round the world trying to paste together something that never was worth a fuck. It's over, so she takes it from here. Whatever Lola wants, let Lola go get.'

'Why not Reno in a year's ti—'

'Now. I told you, I want divorced *now*.'

Rick spent the day in a succession of Irish pubs over on Second, watching the Giants in the Superbowl playoffs. Nothing he drank affected him in the slightest. Finally, he ate half an Irish breakfast at ten o'clock at night, before cabbing on home. There was a message on the machine. 'Jerome. It's seven o'clock. She's signed the papers. They were messengered to us late this afternoon. Can you come in and add your signature tomorrow, say at eleven? Then she can be on her way to Santo Domingo.'

Beep. Click.

Rick sprawled on the sofa. 'Betrayal of trust.' Christ, that was a good one. Where did she dream them up? Well, the wheels were in motion, but even on this last lap he still couldn't believe it was over. Next morning he called Jack and arranged to meet him at noon at Lindos, a Greek restaurant over on Third. The signing shouldn't take long.

At ten thirty he was halfway out the door when the phone shrilled. It was Farben. 'Adrienne wants to pick up her things as soon as possible,' he said.

'Well, I'm going out right now.'

'How about tonight?'

'Short notice isn't it?'

'Better to get it over and done with, Rick.'

'What time?'

'How's seven o'clock?'

'I think I can manage that.'

'There's just one problem.'

'Only one?'

'She doesn't want you to be there.'

'I do *live* here, you know.'

'She said she'd just feel better if you weren't there.'

'Oh, I'll bet.'

'This is very painful for Adrienne too, Rick. You seem to forget that.'

'I don't forget anything, mister. Not one damn thing.' But he decided to stay out of her way and headed over to Madison and old Leo's office. Adrienne's signature was bold, steady and smooth. Next to it, he scrawled his own. So that was it. No more to say.

It was too early to meet with Jack. Rick walked in a daze of thought. He looked at his watch. It had stopped at five past ten. He'd forgotten to wind it. Shit and derision. He gazed round in search of a clock, locking instead on to a figure squatting in a doorway. The man was dressed in a blue-sheen raincoat, shoes just short of yesterday's shine. Not on his knees, but resembling a praying Arab, a filthy yellow burnous-style headpiece covering his head and shoulders. A silenced parrot underneath its cloth. Who was he? A failed shoe salesman? Eighty years ago, he might have been taking a photograph. The figure never moved. Not a tremor. 'Petrified within this roaring city,' Rick breathed. There were so many, and their plight was all the more disturbing to him now because of his own stress. The man across the avenue needed only the smallest shove to send him skidding down the street of broken dreams, a Bowery bum.

Rick found an empty Chinese restaurant with a small bar and ordered a Heineken. 'Wuh Hai ke cumin' hup. Fuh dorrah.' Rick drank it down and left a fin. Four bucks for a Heineken? No wonder the place was empty. The bar clock said twelve. He was late. Shit. On the street, he crossed to the unSamaritan side, away from the frozen patch of yellow remaining still in its doorway. It was twelve fifteen when he got as far as Lindos. Jack was saying goodbye to someone as Rick approached.

'OK, so long, Suds,' he heard him say. 'Ay, big guy. Thought you'd forgotten.'

'Sorry, Jack. I got held up.' Rick lied.

'No problem. Shit takes time.' There was only one table left. A double in the window. They took it as Whoopee (the waiter who looked like a Greek Eddie Cantor) arrived, and they placed their order.

'Who was that?' Rick asked, as Whoopee pattered off for some retsina.

'Suds?' said Jack. 'Oh, he's a funny guy, Rick. You'd like him.'

'That's his name?'

Jack laughed. 'Real name's Vittorio.'

'How come Suds?'

'Well, I'll tell ya. Vito loved to drink, y'know. Loved a good time, but he never drank Scotch or vodka, stuff like that. He liked amaretto, wallbangers, that kind of shit, but he was really partial to crème de menthe.' Rick wrinkled his nose. 'He used always to go to this bar run by a buddy o' his, Joe – Joe the Diver. That's another story, pal. Anyway, this day Joe's just openin' up, settin' up the bar, all that, and there's this glass of that green soap concentrate sittin' there – strong stuff, y'know, and he goes through the back leavin' Vito at the bar. So while he's waitin', Vito sees this big shot of crème de menthe sittin' all by itself. Thinks it's a freebie and throws it down. Well. There's a major gasp, and then these sounds – like a rhino havin' a fuckin' heart attack or somethin', and Joe comes runnin', man, wonderin' what 'n the world is goin' on, and stops as he sees Vito's spinnin' around like a top in the middle of the floor with his eyes about a yard out on stalks. Geezer was fuckin' *green*, Rick. Greener than what he'd just drunk. So Joe grabs him shoutin' "What's the matter, Vito, what's the matter?", while the poor bastard's fightin' for breath and pointin' at the glass. Joe sees what's happened and gets a carton o' milk from the fridge and starts forcin' it down the guy's throat. He gets him to the john and Vito's in there for an hour, moanin and goin' at both ends, and every time the toilet flushes, the suds are frothin' two feet over the bowl, and the bubbles are seepin' out from under the door. Oh, man. I'm tellin' ya.' They both laughed.

Jack caught the look in Rick's eye. 'You all right, buddy?'

'I'm all right, Jack. It's the picture in the attic that's the problem.'

235

Rick spent two hours packing her stuff. At last it was done and her trunk, boxes and suitcases were stacked in the hall outside the apartment. The only thing left was the blue dress. He put it in a leather holdall and stood it just inside the door, turning Farben's words over in his head.

'Just one thing – she doesn't want you to be there.' Oh sure. She couldn't look him in the face. She'd tipped her hand, knew he'd seen the cards. No . . . no . . . Wait. He laid his shoulders square against the front door, thinking. She didn't want him to see who was helping her move her shit. And just as quickly Rick felt certain he knew who it was. She'd told him her close friends were splitting up. Just before the 'I'm all stinky' new Sunday workouts and the beginning of the Sunday morning silent phone calls. Calls to wind him up. 'Yes,' she'd told him. 'Harry and Ettie were splitting up.' Handspring Harry, her gym coach. Rick had remembered. Seeing him watching Adrienne. The Spanish Fly eyes poached with lust. The videos he'd made of Adrienne and Ettie – except there was about ten seconds of Ettie on all of them, *hours* of Adrienne – that maybe he could jerk off over till the poached lustings looked at last into mud greens.

Well, whether it was Handspring, Apollo, or Quasimodo made no odds. You pays your money and you takes your choice. It was her choice and Rick's money. The final humiliation would be a C.O. Jones repeat with Handspring Harry. Forget it. At six thirty precisely, Farben razzed the bell. He was all smiles and charm, the sparse gooseberry 'tash doing its best to give his features some authority. The eyes behind the bins were shining. 'I'm supposed to call as soon as I arrive,' he said. 'Adrienne's at Ruby's.'

'Go ahead.'

He was dialling already, then as, 'Ruby?' he said brightly, Rick knew it wasn't Ruby on the phone but *her*.

'I'll be back by seven thirty,' Rick said. 'That should give you more than enough time.'

'Sure. Great. I've told Adrienne to be here no later than seven. I've got to be somewhere at seven thirty myself.'

'Key's there on the coffee table,' Rick said. Farben picked it up. 'Leave it with the elevator man when you're through.'

236

'You got it.'

Rick went to the door, and picked up the holdall. 'Just one thing.' He stared at Farben for longer than he needed to. 'Make sure. She's on. That plane.'

Rick headed for the Watering Hole. He would wait the time out there. The first person he saw inside was Frank, Frank who seldom drank, downing what looked suspiciously like a large Scotch. Rick took the adjoining barstool. 'What are you, the house drunk?' he said.

'I have every right to be.' Frank screwed up his face. 'There's this woman. On the floor below.'

Rick raised his eyebrows, and a finger for a large cognac. 'She's nuts.'

'So?'

'So she's found out my name and keeps hollering out in the wee small hours that I'm molesting her, that I'm responsible for doing this and that to her. Screaming out my name. Day and night. The last time, ten minutes ago. I can't sleep, can't work . . . it's driving me crazy.'

'Why don't you complain to the management?'

'I did. I went down to see them. They don't do anything.'

'Call the police.'

'I *called* the police.'

'And?'

'They told me it was a domestic affair, that they couldn't interfere. I'm going to have to get a lawyer.' Rick imagined old Leo, watching, impassive, as the babbling Frank was led away. 'This woman is certifiable.'

'Scary.'

'You bet.'

'She could be waiting on the stairs one night, in the black dress, like in *Psycho* – with the butcher knife.'

'That's not funny, Rick.'

'I'm sorry. I didn't realize you were so upset.'

Frank's face swelled maroon with indignation. 'Wouldn't you be upset living on top of a howling banshee, waking you in the dead of night, raving out your name to the whole building?'

'Probably,' said Rick.

'Probably? You bet your life you would! Since a lot of the mental institutions are closing down through lack of funds, there are thousands of these people on the loose. The city's putting them in here.'

'I know. I'm one of them.'

'But at least you live at the other end of the building. The Queen Nut is next to me!'

'And there's nothing you can do about it?'

'Nothing!' This last almost a cry.

'I'm sorry.'

'You're sorry? Imagine how I feel. Rick got a flash of the trunk standing outside his own apartment, the lid springing open to reveal the Queen of utter Nutterdom about to take a cleaver to Farben & Co. 'Rick, it's not funny, believe me.'

'I wasn't smiling at that, Frank.'

Picking up his bag, Rick made a date to meet Frank later that week at Raga, the stylish Indian restaurant. Back at Folsom, the elevator man gave him the key. It was seven forty-five. The place was silent and deserted. Well, almost silent. A tinkle from the window told she'd left the crystals. And all the photograph albums. Bye bye jetsam of Memory Lane. He put his head round the bedroom door, saw something lying on the bed. The *Sherlock Holmes* video, taken from the plastic bag at the door and chucked into the centre of the counterpane. For Rick to take back to the store. Oh, well, good luck to them. So long, Adrienne Louise Rader.

Two days later he got a call from Jerome. 'I just received the papers. With your permission I'll messenger them down to you right away. Congratulations. You're a free man.'

'That's it, then?'

'That's it. Free and clear!'

Rick looked at his reflection in the mirror. 'Congratulations,' he said. 'You're free.' He shuffled around the living room space. Free. In his little cell of memories. Inside the walls of Folsom prison.

At seven o'clock, the buzzer rasped. He gave the elevator man a buck and sat down to open the envelope. Running his eyes down

238

the typed horseshit, Rick stopped at the word 'incompatible'. He lay back on the sofa, closing his eyelids, suddenly exhausted. It had been quite a journey. From 'lover, great big wonderful man, and poet' to 'incompatible' in the space of seventeen days. The clear white paper lay where he had dropped it, as one hour later he left, his thoughts so far away, he didn't feel chill January's surly blast at the street door. At the corner, he looked down at some huddled lumps in a doorway. Ye Gods, it was people. How many? Three? Four? A hairy, filthy face leered out at him and extended a blackened begging hand, in an odd cut-off mitten. 'Spare some change?' As the man emerged into the light, Rick was amazed at the youthfulness of the face. Please God, he thought. May I never finish up like that. In winter at the alley's end or in murderous heat of summer, drawing finger doodles in the dust, sucking on an empty bottle of Old Ben rum and sitting in the middle of my own piss. Reeking of bad booze, the young man came closer still. 'Spare a quarter for a cup of coffee?' Rick gave him five dollars, and turned away. He would be warm soon. Not they. Rounding the corner, he stood in a phone booth and pretended to make a call, trembling slightly. The tatterdemalion derelict had opened the floodgates of his own anger and misery, his fear of being alone. In that moment he was as lost as they. His eyes brimmed. He would have dried his face on his sleeve, but his nose was running. He felt utterly wretched. Holding each side of the booth, the cold penetrated to his finger bones. That there were hundreds in this bitter New Year who were getting it ten times rougher was no consolation. It was simply a matter of holding on.

The subadar-major swung the restaurant door open to the exotic smells of Raga. Rick saw Frank almost at once. Opting to keep on his winter jacket, he slung it round the shoulders of the chair as they greeted one another. The place was busy, with a very Indian foursome immediately to his right. The women in glitzy saris, red bullet hole in the middle of each forehead, the men darker than most Indians Rick had ever seen. As dark as the golfer, Vijay Singh.

'What's it like to be a free man?' Frank said, with rehearsed levity.

239

'Do I look OK to you?'

'Sure.'

Rick gave him a slightly old-fashioned look.

'A trifle tired, perhaps.' A bottle appeared and Frank filled their glasses. 'I took the liberty,' he said. 'Gewürztraminer. I trust that's right?'

'As long as it's Alsatian.'

'Woof.'

Rick lifted his glass. 'Good luck and good health. The only two things that ever really matter.'

'Now my toast.' Frank looked at him earnestly. 'Here's to a long and happy association.'

Rick smiled at him. 'You might at least try to look a little pleased about it.'

Frank laughed. 'Know what you want to eat?' he asked.

'Sure.' Contemplating a turbaned waiter, Rick wondered what the reaction would be if he ordered the two things he couldn't get at home. Lobster thermidor and a blow-job.

Frank flagged at the same waiter who came over immediately. 'We're becoming popular,' he grinned. 'Took me ten minutes to get the wine.'

They ordered and the waiter took off, completely ignoring the gesticulating Indian on Rick's right. Frank reached down to his briefcase and produced a bulky manila envelope which he handed over. 'For you.' It was his new screenplay.

'Wow! Quick work.'

'And relatively painless.'

Rick turned it over. 'Thanks.'

'Don't open it now. You're leaving tomorrow, right?'

'Yes, in the evening.'

'Read it on the plane.'

'Part for me in it?'

Frank sipped. 'Begins on page one. Goes all the way through. Name of Alex. Can't miss him.'

'Stands out, huh?'

'Thinks he's tough.' He gave Rick his naïve look and they both smiled. 'I'd love to know what you think. Call me from Paris.'

'I will.'

Frank shifted. 'Speaking of calls. I gotta make one myself. The aromas have got to me.' He went quickly to the john and Rick put down the envelope, aware of a small altercation off to the right. The gesticulating Indian of moments ago was castigating a silent waiter, ending with a somewhat unfortunate choice of words.

'Look, I have been fingering you for twenty minutes and still you do not come.'

It was pure Peter Sellers. Rick wanted to lean across and whisper to him, 'You don't know how lucky you are, Veeraswamy. You should have known my second wife.' With Adrienne, Rick had always been patient and gentle, coaxing her into her climaxes, holding her, telling her softly, when she said she was sorry how long it was taking, *not* to be, that it was always a pleasure, never a task for him, and gradually he'd eased her mind, relaxing her until at last, she could deliver up her joy within the space of half an hour. Always with a swelling child-bearing push of her tummy muscles, and a little gasping sigh.

She had never been vocally demonstrative in sex, except once. Hunan Hand is a disorder produced when the volatile oils in chilli peppers, which are water soluble, come into contact with the mucous membranes. Snapping off a piece of poppadum, Rick dipped it into the chilli sauce and remembered the Hunan Lips episode. They were staying at a hotel near the Canadian Rockies, close by a hot-air balloon deployment. On this particular morning, he'd heard them lighting up and, leaving Adrienne out for the count, had got up to watch, munching on a breakfast of cheese and chillis. 'Boons,' he said, remembering his mother's happy laugh as she'd mimicked his childhood attempt at the word. Wistfully, he gazed out at the candy-striped and gaily patterned colours as off they rose at intervals, floating away south. Framed in the doorway, he studied Sleeping Beauty, where she lay naked, splayed across the bed, round breasts gently rising and falling. 'Boons,' he said again, and laughed softly, seeing the fur-burger smiling in repose. Nuzzling close, he gently opened up her knees, and as he kissed the nub within the burger, her legs clamped like a nutcracker on his skull as, with a mighty gasp and eyes on stalks, she all but levitated

241

from the bed and sprinted to the bathroom, trailing a wailing shriek worthy of *The Mummy's Tomb*. Ramming her ass on the pan. 'Jesus Christ!' she howled. 'Fuck!'

'What's wrong?' Rick called, coming quickly to the door.

'I'm burning. Oh, fuck! What's happening? I'm burning!'

As she plucked and patted at her nether lips, the nickel dropped. 'Oh, dear. I'm sorry, sweetie. It was me. I've been eating chillis.'

'Oh, my God, my cunt's on fire! Jesus!'

He watched the figure splashing at itself, and began to laugh, receiving a towering glare of disapproval as, with an oath, the door was kicked shut. 'Don't wet it,' he lilted. 'You'll only make it worse.'

'Asshole!' she shouted.

'I'm sorry.'

'Go away.'

'I forgot.'

'You forgot? Oh you asshole. I'm on fire. Oh, my God.' That had been the biggest vocal *and* physical response he'd ever gotten from her. And from then on, pre-screw chilli was off limits. Verboten.

He was laughing as Frank came back. He smiled quizzically and sat. 'Something tickle your fancy?' he asked. Rick nodded and told him of the, 'I've been fingering you for twenty minutes' episode. Frank laughed, and was still smiling as the last of the food was set before them. They made some small talk during dinner, till at last, placing knife and fork together, I've been a goddam fool,' Rick said softly.

Frank looked across at him. 'But you're your own fool. A fool of love. You're not alone in that. How about some cognac?'

Half an hour later, warmed by good hot coffee and a nightcap, they took to the street. Frank waved and a cab pulled over.

'I'm going to walk,' Rick said.

'You sure?'

'Yeah. I fancy a stroll. May be a while till I see li'l ole New York again.'

'*Hope* not.'

'I hope not too.' He smiled. 'Thanks for everything.'

They shook hands warmly. 'Take care, Viking. You're sure you don't want to share this cab?'

'No thanks. The longship's only three blocks. I mustn't keep the hornéd ones waiting. It's a long swim to Asgaard.'

'I'd love to drop you. I'd be delighted to meet them.'

'How would I explain you to them?'

'Suit yourself, Great One.'

'I'll call you tomorrow.'

Smiling Frank got in, the cab took off and Rick, one arm aloft, a Raga sentinel, watched as the shadow in the window squirmed around to wave adieu.

It was cold on the avenue, with wind promising rain. Traffic speeding by. How he loved New York. He would probably die here. Oh Gad. And be put in one of those awful funeral parlours. Casketed and lightly made up. Disney shriek of horror thrill. A crematorium in Queens. No. Rather shipped back to the Western Isles, put on a raft, towed out, soused, set alight, burned at sea. Barbecued in open air. Where did that come from – the wish to be burned, not only in the open air, but at sea? Viking race memory? Anyway. Then. Did you need a licence for that sort of thing? Was it legal? Knowing his luck, it would probably be bungled by a cadre of imbeciles who'd never put to sea, poling about for weeks with a bunch of firelighters and sodden matches trying to dispose of his blackened corpse. 'Probably,' he said softly.

A sloe-eyed hooker sidled out of late-night shadow. 'Show you a good time?' The voice light, chocolate, warm.

'No,' he said very gently – and raising his hat. 'But thank you for the compliment.' Crossing the street to the brittle echo of her laughter, he came to rest at Folsom's Watering Hole. He peered in. The barkeep dishing out prescriptions, listening to the tales of Hoffman. 'Yeah, yeah, yeah.'

Behind him a cab drew up. He turned. A woman in a hurry pushed past him, the line of a tear on her cheek, leaving the cab door open. Lacrimae mundi. Another little heartbreak. Catching his eye, the cabby shrugged as he pulled the door shut. 'Beats me, buddy.'

He watched the yellow trunk speed off down Broadway.

Oldsmobile, it said. 'Yeah. Beats me too.' He looked back to the Watering Hole. Poor tear-cheek was settling at the bar. He was seeing her in profile, her head almost sunk in a big brown bag as she groped for something to light the trembling Lucky on her lips. She was teeny. Reddish hair. Sat on a stool. Feet dangling. Raggedy Ann, he thought. The bartender turned towards the mirror, raising up a glass, as she sparked and her profile suffused in tiny flare. 'May it warm you, you poor wee thing.' Rick said, hearing himself say it, and wondering who she was and what had happened to her. It was raining, oh so slightly. You know? That small rain. That wets you through. He decided to have a drink, then changed his mind. It was time to get the hell out.

Behind him, a freezing mist shrouded the Seine. He slid his key in the heavy door and pushed inside. The moulded ceilings and marble floor of the long hall were splashed with cold, white light as he pressed the switch. Climbing the stairs, he entered the upper house. It was almost midnight. Without putting on the lights, he dropped his bag.

The big sitting room, its soft brown tones obscured in darkness, lay silent, only the streetlamps below giving shape to familiar objects. A kaleidoscope of sepia, crystal, silver and gold was reflected suddenly in the searchlight sweep of headlights from a passing vehicle. Rick moved towards the shadow of the stairs, went up another flight to the blue room. He padded in the gloaming like an old retainer in a Chekov play, turning on the table lamps, one by one. This room he'd fashioned for her, for them both. In blue. Such a cold colour in winter. Sleep was impossible. He moved restlessly about the house. On the big living-room desk he stared at his favourite photograph of her and decided it was Salvation Army time. He went to the lumber room and fetched some trash bags. In them he stuffed shoes, socks, pantyhose, knickers, leotards, the few dresses there were, a couple of hats, a beret. Downstairs, he disposed of a number of old songbooks, tapes, a comb, hairbrush, odds and ends. From every corner of every room, she stared at him, invoking Sam's observation, 'You only had to look round any room within that house to see how

244

much you loved her.' Ming would have noted that too. He took up a photograph. From their early days. Her eyes brim-full, with that immortal promise once given him at the Stone Resort and in Le Cirque. The smile dazzled him.

Gathering up the frames, he stripped each one of her, closing his eyes as he did so. He placed the photographs face down upon his desk before consigning all of them to a brown paper bag. The blue room he did last, ending almost exhausted with his big fists resting on the antique server beneath the huge glittering mirror. Shoulders bowed, he spied the hideous blind goblin head that Mickey had fashioned, the cheap coloured glass set in its brow glinting like an evil eye. Crossing smoothly to the centre window, he at once cleared the shelf before it of ornaments, pulled the french doors wide, then moved to grab the obscene head. The colour of a new horse-chestnut, so smooth it felt, it might have been covered by a fine slime; the pickled skull of a long-dead infant. With a shudder and with a hitch-kick in his stride, he drew back his arm and fast-balled it savagely into the winter night. He waited in the stillness and heard a 'clock' sound like the fall of a hollow chocolate egg, and knew it had descended upon the icy pathway at the river's edge. He pushed the doors to, quietly replaced the ornaments, and sat at the Ibach, opening the lid, slowly, gently, staring at the keys. Agonizing stillness. A deeper emptiness than he had ever known. Softly he began to play 'I'll Remember April'.

'Come on, sing it, once.'

'I can't.'

'Yes, you can. Last four lines. No tears for her, now.'

He sang with the still small voice of a child.

> *The fire will dwindle into glowing ashes*
> *For flames and love live such a little while.*
> *I won't forget, but I won't be lonely.*
> *I'll remember April and I'll smile.*

Acknowledgements

My grateful thanks to my editor, Paul Sidey, for the wisdom of his experience.

Also to Faber & Faber Ltd for the use of extracts from Philip Larkin's 'Aubade', from *Collected Poems* by Philip Larkin, edited by Anthony Thwaite.

To John Murray (Publishers) Ltd for the use of an extract from 'Norfolk' by John Betjeman from his *Collected Poems*.

And for the extract from 'I'll Remember April' (Raye/De Paul/Johnston) © 1941, 1942 Leeds Music Corp, assigned to MCA Music. Reproduced by kind permission, MCA Music Ltd.